DANVERS TOWNSHIP LIBRARY

A31300 292720

W9-BVN-512

BooK 4

Praise for Amanda Hocking

"Hocking hits all the commercial high notes. . . . She knows how to keep readers turning the pages."
—*The New York Times Book Review*

"[*Wake*] will please fans and likely win new ones . . . the well-structured story and strong characters carry readers."
—*Publishers Weekly*

"There is no denying that Amanda Hocking knows how to tell a good story and keep readers coming back for more. More is exactly what they will be looking for once they've turned the last page." —*Kirkus Reviews*

"Filled with mysteries, realistic characters, and lots of action . . . *Wake* is the next great book. A worthwhile read."
—*RT Book Reviews*

"Hocking's novel effectively melds myth and contemporary teen life. High school, family, young love, and mythology all combine to create an easy-to-read paranormal suspense story that will have fans eagerly awaiting new installments." —*Booklist*

"Amanda Hocking has a gift for storytelling that will grip readers and keep them wanting more. . . . Entrancing." —*LibraryThing*

"Explosive and interesting . . . a nice, smooth story with unique mythology and lovable characters. I thoroughly enjoyed it."
—*The Teen Bookworm*

"Pure imaginative brilliance! *Wake* is full of thrills, eerie suspense, and mystery . . . incredibly difficult to put down."
—*The Book Faery*

"Real and vibrant. The first in a brand-new series that reawakens everything we love in underwater mythology, *Wake* by Amanda Hocking will certainly leave you with the desire to pick up more of her titles." —*A Cupcake and a Latte*

"An amazing story . . . ravishing yet explosive. I am enthralled with the amazing characters and fast-paced plotline. The thrill of the water, the history that propels the reader deeper, *Wake* is awesome!" —*Books with Bite*

"Entertaining and surprisingly dark. Amanda Hocking once again had me enjoying her writing and the world she created before my eyes." —*Millie D's Words*

"Amanda Hocking is like a breath of fresh air in the young adult paranormal market." —*That Bookish Girl*

"Amanda Hocking is an author whose storytelling skills keep getting better and better." —*Bewitched Bookworms*

"Amanda Hocking surpasses all expectations." —*SmartBookWorms*

"A wonderfully adventurous and dynamic series, full of high intrigue, mythology, paranormal lore, romance, and suspense. I can't wait to be swept away in the new world of the Watersong." —*Fallen Angel Reviews*

"Amanda Hocking has such an easy and elegant way with her language—her stories just seem to flow and her words dance. This is going to be another series that I'll fall for. I absolutely cannot wait to see where she takes us with the next book." —*Into the Hall of Books*

"Great chemistry . . . plus a family history that just makes your heart ache, and you've definitely got a recipe for a fantastic new series. Get your hands on this now!" —*YA Books Central*

Also by Amanda Hocking

Elegy

Amanda Hocking

St. Martin's Griffin ❧ New York

This is a work of fiction. All of the characters, organizations, and events portrayed in this novel are either products of the author's imagination or are used fictitiously.

ELEGY. Copyright © 2013 by Amanda Hocking. All rights reserved. Printed in the United States of America. For information, address St. Martin's Press, 175 Fifth Avenue, New York, N.Y. 10010.

www.stmartins.com

Library of Congress Cataloging-in-Publication Data

Hocking, Amanda.
  Elegy / Amanda Hocking.—First St. Martin's Griffin edition.
      pages cm—(A watersong novel ; [4])
  ISBN 978-1-250-00567-0 (hardcover)
  ISBN 978-1-4299-5650-5 (e-book)
  1. Sirens (Mythology)—Fiction.   2. Supernatural—Fiction.   3. Sisters—Fiction.   4. Love—Fiction.   5. Blessing and cursing—Fiction.   6. Seaside resorts—Fiction.]   I. Title.
  PZ7.H65828EI 2013
  [Fic]—dc23

                                                                2013019387

St. Martin's Griffin books may be purchased for educational, business, or promotional use. For information on bulk purchases, please contact Macmillan Corporate and Premium Sales Department at 1-800-221-7945 extension 5442 or write specialmarkets@macmillan.com.

First Edition: August 2013

10 9 8 7 6 5 4 3 2 1

For Nanny

ACKNOWLEDGMENTS

When I started writing the Watersong series, my grandma was alive. When I finished the final book in the series, she was not. She'd been battling Alzheimer's for years, so she never read any of my books, although she'd read hundreds of my short stories and poems. And she'd saved everything I'd ever written—from Christmas cards to high school assignments. If Nanny had ever come across it, she saved it.

It would be impossible for me not to acknowledge the massive impact she had on me and my writing. Every word I've ever written should be dedicated to her.

That's not to say she was the only person supporting and encouraging me, although she may have been the most unconditional with her love. I have been very fortunate to have phenomenal family and friends.

A big thank-you to both my mom and dad, who always believed in me, and my stepdad, Duane, and stepmom, Lisa, for taking care of me, even when they didn't have to, and to my brother, Jeremy, who has always been my biggest fan.

As always, a massive thank-you to my assistant/best friend/ viceroy of my life, Eric, who makes sure that everything happens. He makes everything possible, and handles all my moods, which can range from catatonic to Faye Dunaway in *Mommie Dearest*.

Thank you to the rest of my friends—Fifi, Valerie, Greggor, Pete, Matt, Gels, and Mark—who for some reason enjoy my presence, but also tolerate my many absences when I'm off playing with my imaginary friends.

Writing may be a solitary activity, but making a book isn't. It requires a whole team of terrific people, like my editor, Rose Hilliard, who makes everything better than I can ever do on my own, and Lisa Marie Pompilio, who makes the most gorgeous covers for the books, as well as everyone else at St. Martin's Press who do all the millions of things that make the books spectacular.

My agent, Steve Axelrod, and his rights director, Lori Antonson, are amazing. Seriously. When people say that authors don't need agents anymore, I shudder, because I can't imagine navigating all of this without Steve's experience and knowledge.

I also want to give a shout-out to the Other House, who made the book trailers for the Watersong and Trylle series, just because I think they're so fantastic.

And last, but probably most important, I have to thank all of the readers. Without you guys, I would just be a crazy person talking to myself. Thank you so much.

Elegy

ONE

Threatening

Harper had been rehearsing what she wanted to say to her roommate Liv all morning, but when Liv threw her against the wall of their dorm room, Harper knew she was in trouble.

It had only been six days ago that Harper moved into Sundham University housing and even met Liv. When she'd moved in, Liv had been almost tripping over herself to help Harper unpack and assuring her that they'd be "total BFFs" by the end of the semester. She'd shown Harper around campus, talking in a never-ending stream about everything under the sun.

But then Harper had turned around and rushed back to Capri the very next day, when all hell had broken loose with her sister, her boyfriend, and the sirens.

When Harper had been hit with an intense panic last week, Liv had followed her out to the car. She kept insisting that she ride back with Harper to make sure she got there all right, and Harper practically had to push Liv out of the car.

She couldn't explain the psychic bond she shared with Gemma, let alone the monsters who awaited her back in Capri, so she couldn't let Liv go with her.

That was how Harper had left Liv—standing out in the pouring rain, desperate to be her friend. And she returned to something completely different.

Liv slept soundly all day long—missing all her classes. Then she'd stumble in and out late at night, when Harper was trying to sleep, banging things and making noise without any apology.

Harper didn't want to tell Liv what to do, but she couldn't keep missing so much sleep.

By Tuesday, she'd finally thought she'd come up with what she wanted to say, and she kept repeating it over and over in her head as she walked up to the dorm room. Taking a fortifying breath before opening the door, Harper was determined to get her point across without lecturing Liv.

It was only a little after noon, and Harper had figured that Liv would probably still be sleeping. So it was with some surprise that Harper discovered that her roommate was not only awake but entertaining a guest.

Wearing only her pajama shorts and a pink bra, Liv was straddling a guy lying on her bed. Harper averted her eyes as soon as she realized that Liv wasn't completely dressed, but she'd seen enough to realize that Liv was making out with him more ferociously than she'd ever seen before.

Both Liv and Harper had loft beds, so they were located on

top bunks with their desks below. That meant that Harper didn't have the greatest view of the guy from where she stood, but thanks to a pair of guy's jeans and a T-shirt rumpled up on the floor, she discerned that he wasn't wearing much clothing either.

"Oh, sorry," Harper said quickly, and turned around, attempting to give Liv some privacy. "I thought you were alone."

"Get out," Liv hissed, and there was an edge to her voice that Harper hadn't heard before.

The few words they'd exchanged the past couple of days contained a sweetness in them, like honey, but that had been replaced by something entirely venomous.

"Yeah, sorry, I will, but I just need to grab my chem book." Harper hurried over to the desk underneath her loft bed and searched for her textbook.

Part of the reason she'd chosen now to have the conversation with Liv was that she needed to come back to the room to switch books for her afternoon classes.

"Hurry up," Liv snapped.

"I'm trying," Harper assured her.

She dropped her backpack onto the desk chair so it'd be easier for her to look. Normally, organization was her strong suit, and everything was in its place, but now that she was trying to get out of here, her book had vanished.

"Maybe you can join us," Liv's male companion suggested.

Harper chose to ignore him, instead thinking that her time would be better spent searching for the book. She still had her back to Liv as she was throwing everything off the desk, but she heard movement behind her, then a creaking bed.

Liv groaned. "Get out."

"It'll only be a second." Harper turned around to scan the room.

"*Get out!*" Liv roared, and the anger in her voice seemed to reverberate through Harper's head. For a moment, she could only stand there—dazed and unable to remember what she was looking for.

Harper shook her head, clearing some of the confusion, and feebly said, "I'm going as fast as I can. I just . . . I need the book first."

"Not you," Liv said. "*Him.*"

Before either Harper or Liv's boyfriend could say anything, Liv pushed him out of the bed. He tumbled down, landing on the floor with a painful-sounding thud, and he groaned.

"Are you okay?" Harper crouched next to him, and he slowly sat up.

He rubbed the back of his head. "Yeah . . . I think so."

Harper looked him over just to be sure, and she was relieved that he was still wearing his boxers. His bare torso revealed several fresh scratches on his chest and shoulders. His lip was bleeding, too, but she wasn't sure if that was from the fall or something that Liv had done.

"What don't you understand about the words *get out?*" Liv asked, leaning over the edge of her bed to glare down at them.

Her eyes—which had seemed wide and innocent when Harper first met her—now appeared much darker and more calculating.

"I'm going," the guy said. He got up quickly, wincing as he did, and picked his clothes up off the floor.

That's when Harper finally discovered her missing chem book. It had been hidden underneath his jeans.

He didn't even wait to get dressed before he left, preferring to walk out into the hall in his underwear rather than spend another minute in their dorm room. Not that Harper blamed him.

"Got my book," Harper told Liv as she shoved the textbook into her backpack. "So I'll be out of your hair."

"You don't have to rush out of here now that he's gone."

Out of the corner of her eye, Harper saw Liv jump down from her bed and land on the floor in one graceful movement. The honey had returned to her voice, but Harper wasn't sure if she could trust it, so she turned around slowly. Liv's blond hair fell in waves that landed just above her shoulders, and though she wasn't as tall as Harper, her tanned legs appeared long, extending below her micro pajama shorts.

"I figured he'd want some privacy, you know?" Liv glanced back to wink at Harper, then grabbed a tank top out of her drawer.

"Yeah." Harper forced a smile and tried to sound happy for her roommate. "He seemed . . . nice. Is he your boyfriend?"

Liv scoffed. "He wishes. I woke up thirsty and hungry, so I went down to the commons to get a soda out of the machine, and I picked him up, too."

"Oh." Harper leaned back against her desk. She thought about straightening up the mess she'd made, but she didn't want to take her eyes off Liv. "Do you think you'll see him again?"

"Just because I said you could stay doesn't mean we have to talk," Liv said, pulling her shirt on over her head.

Harper sighed and considered leaving, but she knew she'd

have to talk to Liv eventually. She might as well get it out of the way now.

"Actually, um, I have been wanting to talk to you," Harper said, plunging into the conversation.

Liv narrowed her eyes. "About what?"

"Just life." Harper shrugged and tried to keep her tone casual. "I haven't really been able to talk to you much, so I thought we could check in with each other."

"Why? It's not like we need to be besties or something." Liv snickered.

"No, but you said that you wanted to be friends, and I thought we could be."

Liv tilted her head, as if she had no idea what Harper was talking about. "Did I say that?"

"Yeah." Harper nodded. "You said it a few times, actually."

"Oh." Liv sounded utterly bored with the conversation and picked at a loose thread on her pajama pants. "Was that last week? It seems like a lifetime ago."

Liv turned back around to go through her dresser again. Harper could only gape at her, astounded by the change.

"Did something happen?" Harper asked, as Liv pulled a jean skirt out of a drawer.

"Why? What do you mean?" Liv kept her back to her as she slipped out of the pajama pants and pulled on the skirt.

"I don't know. You just seem . . . different."

When Liv turned back to her, Harper noticed that same darkness in her eyes, like a shadow had been pulled down to mask a new malevolence, and Liv smirked. "So that's what this is about?"

"What?"

"I'm going out and having fun, and you're jealous?" Liv stepped toward her, and instinctively Harper tried to take a step back, but she had nowhere to go. The desk was right behind her, so she just straightened up.

"What? No." Harper shook her head. "I'm glad you're having fun with college. But I was wondering if you could keep it down when you come in at night." There was no point in making small talk anymore. "You've been waking me up, and I can't sleep."

"You don't even want to be my friend, do you?" Liv kept walking toward her, and all the silk in her voice had been replaced with an icy edge. "You just wanted to tell me to shut up."

"No, that's not what I'm saying," Harper hurried to correct herself. "I think that you're a really nice girl—"

Liv cut her off with a laugh that sent an unpleasant chill down Harper's spine. "Oh, I am not a nice girl."

She was actually shorter than Harper, but it felt like she towered over her. There was something so imposing about her presence that Harper couldn't explain, and she swallowed back her fear.

It was at that moment, with Liv staring up at her with her wide, cold eyes, that Harper realized Liv was insane. That was the only way to explain Liv's dramatic and violent mood changes.

"Whatever. I have no idea what you're talking about, and I need to get to class," Harper said. "You went from zero to crazy in like three seconds, and I don't have time for this."

"I'm not crazy!" Liv shouted in her face, spittle landing on her cheeks. "And I'm not done with you yet."

"I'll talk to you later, okay, Liv?" Harper tried to keep her words soothing and even. "I have to go, and if you were smart, you'd get ready and go to class soon. Or else it's not going to matter if we get along or not because you won't be here much longer."

"Was that a threat? Are you threatening me?" Liv demanded.

"No." Harper leaned over to get her backpack, taking her eyes off Liv for only a second. "If you don't go to class, you won't—"

Liv was a flicker of motion in Harper's peripheral vision, then Harper felt a hand tighten around her throat. Liv slammed Harper back against the wall hard enough to make a mirror fall off and shatter on the floor.

With Liv's hand clamped around her neck, Harper was pinned to the wall. Liv's fingers were surprisingly long, and her grip was inescapable. Harper could barely breathe and clawed vainly at Liv's arm.

"Liv," Harper croaked out as she continued to struggle.

"Don't ever mess with me, Harper," Liv commanded in a low growl. "If you ever threaten or talk down to me again, I will totes destroy you, you dumb bitch."

She let go of Harper then and stepped back. Harper gasped for breath and rubbed her neck. Her throat burned, and she bent over coughing.

"What the hell, Liv?" Harper asked between coughs. She was still hunched over and looked up at Liv. "I wasn't threatening you! I was saying that if you want to stay in school, you have to go to class."

A wide smile spread across Liv's face. "You're right. If I want to stay, I'd have to go to class. But I don't want to stay. And I don't care what anybody says or thinks. I'm not going to live with a shrew like you any longer than I have to. I'm out of here."

Liv slipped on her shoes, grabbed her purse, and left the room, humming a tune under her breath as she did. Harper couldn't place the song, but she was certain she'd heard it before.

TWO

Night Call

It was the same dream she'd been having every night since Lexi had been killed. Gemma was out in the ocean. The water was cold, and the waves crashed around her, crushing her.

It was the night Penn had given Gemma the potion to change her into a siren and then tossed her into the ocean wrapped in Persephone's shawl. Gemma felt like a fish in a net, trying to claw her way out of it before she drowned.

Then she felt the change happening, the siren monster taking hold somewhere deep inside her, filling her with an angry hunger. But her body didn't shift. Her legs wouldn't turn into fins, and she couldn't fight her way to the surface.

Her wings broke painfully through her back and tore through the fabric, freeing Gemma. But they flapped uselessly underwater, and just when Gemma was certain she would drown, she surfaced. The relief at being able to breathe again was short-lived, though.

The dream then shifted, and instead of the night she'd become a siren, she was now in the rainstorm from last week, treading water in the crashing waves below the cliff outside the sirens' house.

Lexi's decapitated head was flying at her, the strings of blond hair flowing out behind it. But Lexi was still alive, her eyes wide and aware of everything, and she screamed at Gemma through the razor-sharp teeth that filled her mouth.

That's when Gemma would wake up, cold sweat on her brow and gasping for breath. She sat up in her bed, hoping that she'd be able to calm herself down enough to go back to sleep again, but she never did.

It wasn't that she'd liked Lexi a lot. It was how powerless and trapped Gemma had felt. In that moment, when she had been at the bottom of the cliff while Lexi was fighting with Daniel at the top, she'd never felt so weak or afraid.

Gemma refused to let herself feel that way again. From now on, she had to be in complete control of her siren powers, and not the other way around.

A loud knocking at the front door disrupted her thoughts and made her jump. Gemma grabbed her cell phone from her bedside table, checking to see that it was after midnight, and she didn't have any missed calls or text messages.

She waited a few seconds to see if the knocking continued, and when it did, she leapt out of bed. Her dad had work in the morning, and she didn't want to wake him.

"Took you long enough," Penn said when Gemma opened the door.

"Shh. My dad will hear you." Gemma glanced back toward the stairs behind her. The lights upstairs were still off, so it was a safe bet that he hadn't heard anything.

Penn shrugged. "So?"

"So, let's go outside and talk." Gemma stepped out into the night, closing the door quietly behind her. It would be easier to just go outside than try to explain common decency and consideration for other people to Penn.

It was a new moon, so aside from the dim stars, the sky was completely black. Gemma hadn't turned on the outside light, so at first, she could only make out the dark shapes of three girls standing outside her house.

Then she felt a shift in her eyes, and her pupils expanded. The siren senses had kicked in automatically, changing her eyes into ones like an owl's, so she could see clearly in the darkness.

Penn stood directly in front of her, but Thea and another girl stood a few feet back. The new girl had blond hair and wide eyes, and there was something familiar about her, but Gemma didn't stare at her long enough to figure out what it was.

The only thing that really mattered was that there was another girl, and what the implications of that were.

"What do you want?" Gemma asked.

"I wanted to introduce you to your new best friend." Penn stepped to the side, so she could gesture back at the girl behind her.

"Hi." The girl smiled and waggled her fingers at Gemma, causing Thea to scoff and turn away in disgust.

"Who the hell is that?" Gemma asked Penn.

"Don't you remember?" The new girl stepped away from Thea and moved closer to Penn, so Gemma would be able to get a better look at her. "I'm Liv. I was your sister's roommate at college."

"Until she decided to drop out today and come live with us," Thea muttered. She stared out into the night, managing to look both bored and irritated in a way that only she could.

That's why the girl looked familiar. Gemma had only met her briefly last week while helping Harper move into her dorm. Liv had been friendly, but Gemma had had too many other things on her mind to really register her.

Besides that, Liv's appearance had changed. She hadn't been unattractive exactly, but she had been rather plain. Now her face was brighter, her hair glossier, and there was a general sultriness to her that hadn't been there before.

The changes were subtle, but they were unmistakable to Gemma. Liv still maintained some of her doe-eyed naïveté, and Gemma was a little surprised that she hadn't recognized Liv sooner because of that.

"Why? Why would she drop out?" Gemma asked Penn, without acknowledging Liv yet. "How do you even know each other?"

"Isn't it obvious?" Penn asked, smiling wide. "She's your new sister."

Gemma sighed. "Yeah, I figured that."

"Don't look so disappointed," Liv said cheerily. "I'm lots of fun, I promise."

"She sure is," Thea said, sarcasm dripping from her husky voice.

Penn cast an annoyed glare at Thea but turned back to Gemma with an overly optimistic smile. "Gemma. Must you always be a Debbie Downer? I mean, come on! This is a good thing. If we hadn't turned Liv, we'd all be dead in two weeks. Liv just saved your life! You should be thanking her."

That was true. And while Gemma hated to admit that she felt mildly relieved, she also felt tremendous guilt. Liv was now wrapped up in this horrible mess, too, and if Gemma had broken the damn curse already, nobody else would've had to get hurt.

"You never thanked me for saving your life," Gemma said.

"That's because you were a total bitch about the whole thing," Penn reminded her. "Liv *wanted* this."

"You did?" Gemma asked, speaking to Liv for the first time.

"You didn't?" Liv sounded flabbergasted. "This is amazing, Gemma! This is the greatest thing that's ever happened to me!"

Gemma held up her hand to silence Liv's exuberance and glanced back at the house, but no lights had gone on, so they were probably safe.

"Oops, sorry," Liv said. "I forgot about your dad."

"See?" Penn pointed to Liv. "That's the kind of response you should've had."

"Sorry I wasn't doing jumping jacks like Little Miss Sunshine over there." Gemma motioned to Liv.

"Apology accepted," Penn replied.

"So, why are you guys here so late?" Gemma asked.

"We were going to go for a swim, and I thought it would be a great time for you to meet Liv since she's moving here now,"

Penn explained. "Plus, you're going to have to help show her the ropes."

"The ropes?" Gemma shook her head. "I barely know them. How am I supposed to show her anything?"

"Penn just means that she wants help babysitting," Thea said dryly.

"I don't need a babysitter," Liv interjected with what Gemma thought was a bitter undercurrent. "You guys already showed me everything this past weekend. I'm good. I'm ready."

"She might be a *tad* overzealous, and she needs a little reining in sometimes," Penn said.

"I do not!" Liv shouted indignantly, which Gemma thought to be a completely out-of-place response.

Almost anytime Penn had ever spoken to Gemma, she'd done so either with a condescending sweetness or a bitchy bossiness, but here with Liv, she was speaking reasonably, even kindly. It didn't seem to warrant Liv's petulance.

"Well, that all sounds great, but I'm going to pass on the midnight swim," Gemma said.

"Really?" Penn asked. "Since when have you ever passed that up?"

"Since I'm trying this new honesty thing with my dad," Gemma said. "I told him I wouldn't sneak out or run off anymore, so I'm not going to."

"That sounds lame." Penn wrinkled her nose in disgust. "You're lame."

The outside light flicked on above her, meaning that her dad was awake, and Gemma swore under her breath. A few seconds later, he opened the front door with his new shotgun in hand. He didn't point it at them, but he wanted to make sure they knew he had it.

No matter how many times Gemma had told him that his gun wouldn't hurt the sirens, Brian insisted on getting it every chance he got.

He didn't know how else to protect his daughter from them. He couldn't have them arrested or tell their parents, he couldn't fight them because they would tear him apart, he shouldn't even talk to them because their song would hypnotize him.

So he got a shotgun and glared at them from the doorway.

"All right, well, it was nice chatting with you," Gemma said as she edged back toward the door. "But that's my cue to head back in."

"Lucky," Thea muttered.

"It was nice to meet you again, Gemma," Liv said, and leaned forward, like she meant to shake Gemma's hand.

"Yeah, have fun," Gemma said, and hastily slid back in the house without touching Liv.

"What's going on? Why were they here?" Brian demanded, and he stood so close to the front door, Gemma almost ran into him as she came back in. Then he gave her a strange look.

"What, Dad?" Gemma asked, staring nervously at his confused expression.

"Your eyes . . . are different," he told her, sounding a little pained.

That explained why the dim living room appeared so bright. Her eyes hadn't changed back yet from their bird form. She blinked several times and willed them to shift back, and finally, the living room looked dark again, with only a small lamp providing light.

"Is that better?" Gemma asked.

"Yeah," Brian said, though she could already tell by his expression that she looked normal again. "What did those girls want?"

"I don't actually know," Gemma said, and realized that wasn't the whole truth, so she added, "They wanted to introduce me to the new Lexi."

"They found a replacement for her?" Her dad raised his eyebrows in surprise. "That was fast."

"Yeah, it was," Gemma said.

She neglected to tell her dad that part of the reason it was so quick was that they already had the girl lined up. Liv had probably been meant to be Gemma's replacement, but when Penn decided to kill Lexi instead, they had to change their plans.

The fight last week, where Lexi tried to kill Gemma and Daniel actually turned out to be a good thing. It bought her a few more weeks. Based on how quickly they turned Liv after Lexi's death, it would've only been a day or two longer before Penn had killed Gemma. Liv was all primed to go.

"How long were they here for?" Brian asked.

"Only a few minutes."

"Why didn't you wake me up when they got here?"

Gemma walked past her dad and sat down on the couch in the living room. "I didn't want to disturb you. I know you have to get up in a few hours, and I wasn't going anywhere."

"You know the deal, though," Brian said firmly. "You tell me what's going on. You keep me in the loop."

"I know, and I am."

Her dad seemed to relax a little and sat down in his recliner next to her. "How are things going with the scroll?"

"They're . . . going," Gemma said, and she was tempted to lie.

Things were not going well. After Thea had given her the scroll, Gemma, Harper, and their dad had stayed up all night looking at it. It was written in an ancient language. They'd originally thought it was Greek, but upon attempting translations from the Internet, they'd found it impossible to decipher.

Last Saturday, Harper and Gemma had gone up to see Lydia and show her the scroll. She made copies of it since Gemma didn't want to leave it with anybody else, and Lydia said she would work on translating it and finding out any information she could from it.

While Lydia was busy with that, Gemma had decided to work on trying the next best thing—destroying the scroll. Harper was against it, arguing that they didn't know for sure how the scroll worked. If they destroyed it, it might kill all the sirens—including Gemma. Gemma was willing to risk it, but Harper kept insisting that they should translate it first.

But it didn't matter anyway. Gemma hadn't been able to do anything to even slightly damage it.

The scroll was made out of a thick papyrus. It almost reminded Gemma of cardboard, but it was thin enough to roll up. The paper itself was beige, and Gemma wasn't sure if it had always been so or if the color came with age. The ends were uneven and slightly yellowed, but, otherwise, it didn't look the worse for wear.

The ink was a very dark brown and iridescent. When she tilted the paper in different light, the ink would shimmer and glisten. She wondered if it was the ink itself that gave the paper its powerful properties, or if it was under some kind of spell.

It definitely had some kind of magic protecting it. Despite its thickness, the papyrus felt fragile under Gemma's fingertips, reminding her of a dried-up corn husk. It felt like she should easily be able to snap or tear it in half.

But she couldn't. Scissors wouldn't cut it. They just bent the paper without damaging it at all. She tried garden shears, and even got her father to help her with his table saw. The paper would just bend and fold. Nothing could break through. It even jammed up the shredder at the library.

Fire wouldn't burn it. Water wouldn't warp it. Gemma was running out of ways to try to destroy it. When she dipped it in water, the ink seemed to glow, but when she took it out, nothing had changed. The ink held strong, and the scroll remained intact.

If destruction was off the table, then she had to figure out how to read it. Until Lydia came back with the official translation, Gemma was doing her best to interpret it herself by searching the Internet for documents with similar writing.

Brian was trying to help out with the few clues Bernie had given him, but so far, none of them seemed all that helpful. The information Bernie had passed on to him sounded mostly like random superstition.

"Nothing new yet?" Brian asked.

Gemma pulled her knees up to her chest. "Not yet, no."

"It's only been a few days, though. Give it some time. When is that girl supposed to come back with the translation?"

"Lydia? I don't know for sure." Gemma shook her head. "She's hoping sometime this week."

"Once you get that, we'll be able to figure this all out," Brian assured her.

"Yeah, I know." Gemma forced a smile. "I'll be okay. You don't need to worry."

"I know you'll be okay, but it's my job to worry. I'm your dad."

They talked a little bit longer before Brian went back to bed. Gemma went to her room, but she knew that she'd be unable to sleep for the rest of night.

It was still so strange talking to her dad openly about everything. It was nice, since keeping everything a secret had been a huge weight on her chest. Sometimes, she felt bad about telling her dad the truth, though. She didn't want him to worry about her, not when he had so much to deal with.

That's why she still kept parts to herself. Like how Liv's turning into a siren was probably a very bad thing. It freed Penn up to look for a new replacement, which meant that Gemma's clock was once again counting down.

But more than that, a new siren was another monster to stand in her way. Penn wanted to kill her, Lexi had actually tried to kill her, and with her luck, Liv would probably feel the same as Penn and Lexi.

Liv was just another siren Gemma would have to get out of the way before she could finally be free of this curse.

THREE

Coincidental

Once Harper had calmed down after Liv attacked her yesterday, her first thought had been, *This girl's a siren.*

She'd almost immediately dismissed it though, assuming she
just had sirens on the brain. But there were some signs to back
up the claim, besides Liv's irrational rage and superstrength.
Her dirty blond hair had taken on a more golden shine, and her
brown eyes had a richness to them.

But Harper eventually decided that she couldn't be sure. She
hadn't been paying close attention, and Liv could also be on drugs
or have a serious mental disorder, which would explain the dramatic mood swings and violent strength.

After Liv had stormed out, Harper took a few minutes to catch
her breath, then she gathered her things and went to her classes.
When she came back later that afternoon, the dorm room was
completely trashed—or at least Liv's side of it was, with some of

the mess spilling onto Harper's half. The bed was dismantled and broken, her posters were torn off the wall, and random junk was strewn all over.

Harper had considered sleeping out in the commons area that night, but most of Liv's stuff appeared to be gone, so she decided to risk it. She'd been safe because Liv didn't come back at all, and Harper hoped she never would.

When her afternoon psych class was canceled because the teacher was absent, she went out to the campus lawn instead of going back to her dorm. It was a class she had with Liv, so it didn't give her a chance to find out if Liv was really gone, but it was still a good opportunity to do some homework.

Besides, the weather was gorgeous, especially after the previous week's oppressive heat. There was almost a chill to the air, and that was a nice change. She pulled out her textbook, planning to brush up on her medical terminology, and she didn't realize how much time had passed until her phone rang.

When she grabbed her phone and saw the time, she cursed under her breath. Even though she was in a hurry to make an appointment, she had to answer it. It was her dad calling from his lunch break, and he would worry if she didn't pick up.

"Hey, Dad," Harper said, struggling to shove her books into her backpack with one hand while she held the phone with the other.

"Is something wrong?" Brian asked, already tense with worry.

"No, everything's great," Harper lied as she slung her bag over her shoulder. She hadn't told anyone back in Capri about

Liv attacking her. Enough things were happening that they didn't need to worry about her roommate problems.

"You sound out of breath," he persisted.

"I'm just running late," she said as she walked briskly across the campus lawn. "I have a meeting in a little bit with Professor Pine."

"Who's that?" Brian asked.

"Remember? I told you about him before," Harper said. "He's the history teacher who used to be an archaeologist."

"Oh, yeah, Indiana Jones," Brian said.

Harper laughed. "Yeah, him."

Brian seemed to hesitate before asking, "It's about Gemma, right?"

"Yeah." Harper nodded and lowered her eyes, as if the other students hanging out on the lawn would read her expression and know what she was talking about.

"Well, if you're busy, I won't hold you up."

"Sorry. I don't mean to brush you off," Harper apologized, and she paused when she reached the doors outside the faculty building. "But I'll see you when I come home this weekend for Gemma's play."

Once she got off the phone with her dad, Harper headed inside to find Professor Pine's office. She didn't have him as a teacher, but she'd talked to her advisor, who'd referred her to him because of his archaeology experience.

When Harper had given him a call the day before to set up the appointment, she'd had to fabricate the backstory for how she'd found the scroll. He probably would've sent her to a psychologist if she started talking about monsters and curses. So she'd told him simply that her sister had found an old scroll in Bernie McAllister's house when she was cleaning it out after he'd died, and they had a few questions about it.

Pine had been kind enough to set up a time to meet her in his office, although he sounded dubious about being able to help that much. Still, Harper was willing to follow any lead to find out more about the scroll.

Harper was getting a handle on the campus quicker than she'd expected and managed to find his office with five minutes to spare. The frosted glass on the door read PROFESSOR KIPLING PINE. She thought about waiting outside, but his door was partially ajar, so she gave a slight knock.

When he didn't answer, she pushed it open wider and saw a man hunched over his desk. He appeared to be in his early thirties—a little young for all the traveling his office and reputation suggested—with blond hair combed to the side.

Earbuds ran from his ears to an iPad resting on his large oak desk, precariously close to an open can of Red Bull. In front of him he had a small box covered in symbols that reminded Harper of a cross between a cryptex puzzle and the Lament Configuration from *Hellraiser*.

The professor wore a small spyglass attached to his glasses, like the monoculars jewelers used to inspect diamonds. He had a tiny needlelike tool to poke at the box, then he typed rapidly on the iPad next to him, apparently documenting some miniscule discovery.

Since he was so immersed in his work, Harper took a moment

to look over his office, which was rather hard to do since it was filled floor to ceiling.

His office was a mash-up of ancient Egyptian, steampunk, and technomodern. Artifacts and old books were overflowing from the shelves, mixed in with all kinds of vaguely antique gadgets. An ankh, an old globe with a spyglass protruding from the side, and a flashing digital scale all occupied the same shelf. Then there was a slick computer, the tablet on his desk, and something flashing a blue laser light buried in a corner among textbooks and newspapers written in Syrian.

Professor Pine's office was like the strangest episode of *Hoarders* ever.

"Professor?" Harper asked hesitantly.

"Yes?" He lifted his head to look at her, peering out from around the monocular, and pulled out one of his earbuds.

Harper had to suppress a smile when she realized that he kinda did look like a young Indiana Jones. Unfortunately, he wasn't sporting a tweed jacket or fedora. Instead, he wore a dress shirt that was unbuttoned to reveal the Joy Division T-shirt underneath.

"We had a meeting at one fifteen." Harper gestured to one of four clocks he had in his office—the only one that told the correct time. "I'm a few minutes early, but I can come back—"

"No, come on in." Professor Pine pulled out the other earbud and clicked something on the iPad before moving it aside on his desk, along with the puzzle box. "Harper Fisher, right?"

"Yeah." She smiled at him.

He gestured to the ergonomic chair across from his desk. "Have a seat."

"Thank you again for seeing me," she said. She slipped off her backpack and dropped it by her feet as she sat down.

"On the phone, you said that your sister had found some kind of artifact?" The professor took off his glasses and set them on his desk.

"Yeah, it's, um . . . an old scroll," Harper said, struggling to find the right word for it.

"And she found it near where you live?"

"Kind of. An older family friend passed away recently, and we were cleaning out his house. She found the scroll among his things."

He leaned back in his chair and rubbed his chin. "Where are you from again?"

"Maryland," she answered. "Capri, specifically."

"It's probably not that ancient, but I could take a look at it," Pine offered.

"I don't have it with me, but I have some pictures on my phone." Harper quickly pulled her phone out of her pocket.

He held his hand out for it. "I'll have a look."

Harper scrolled through her phone until she came to the photos she'd taken of the scroll. Over the weekend, she'd easily taken two dozen pictures.

"We think it's ancient Greek," Harper said as she handed him the phone.

"Well . . ." He put on his glasses, removing the monocular first, and examined the pictures, turning the phone to the side to get a better look. "It has some of the qualities of Grecian text, but I'm not sure that's what it is."

"Do you think you could translate it?" Harper asked.

Marcy's friend Lydia was already working on the translation, thanks to the visit that Harper and Gemma had paid to Cherry Lane Books on Saturday. But the sooner they got the translation, the better, and if Professor Pine could do it now, that would save them time.

"Sorry." He shook his head. "I'm a bit rusty on ancient languages. Egyptian was always my forte." He motioned to the Eye of Horus poster he had hanging behind his desk.

"Can you make out any of the words?" Harper asked.

"I can pick out some letters." He scrolled to another picture and propped his head up on his hand, then shook his head again. "But this isn't truly Greek. Is there a way I can zoom in?"

"Yeah, sorry. Here." She leaned over the desk and enlarged the picture for him. "Is that better?"

He nodded. "Yeah, see this . . ." He let out a deep breath through his teeth. "If I had to guess, I'd say this was possibly Phoenician or maybe Aramaic. That might be a kappa or an aleph"—he pointed to a jagged figure that looked like a cross between a "k" and an "x"—"but I can't say that with any certainty."

"So there's nothing you can tell me?" Harper asked, trying not to sound deflated.

"Not without looking at it more." He handed her back the phone. "There's a good chance that it's nothing. The reason I can't decipher it is probably because it's chicken scratch and a mixture of old languages thrown together to look ancient."

"And what if it's not?" Harper pressed. "What if it's real?"

"If it's real . . ." He sighed and took his glasses off, tossing them on his desk. "Again, I'd have to see it to be sure, but it's incredibly old and amazingly well preserved. Where did you say you found it again?"

"Um, in the attic."

"Do you have any idea where it came from before then? Or how it got there?" Pine asked.

"Not really. I think Mr. McAllister had some Greek relatives," Harper lied.

He leaned back in his chair, thinking. "And you're from a town called Capri?"

"Yes, Capri, Maryland."

"You know, the real Capri is an island off the coast of Italy. But centuries ago, it was part of Magna Graecia—or Great Greece. Many Greeks still refer to it that way." He swiveled a bit in his chair, so he had to look back over his shoulder to see Harper. "When was your town founded? Do you know?"

"June 14 . . ." Harper furrowed her brow in thought. "I think like 1801? Or 1802? Something like that."

He raised both his eyebrows in surprise. "That's oddly precise."

"We have a Founder's Day Picnic every year on the fourteenth of June." She shrugged.

"So Capri—*your* Capri—is a relatively young town, at least compared to the island off Italy, which was settled nearly two thousand years ago." He paused as he stared out the window. "What are the odds of an ancient Greek scroll just happening to turn up in a fairly modern town named after an ancient Greek island?"

"I don't know," Harper said. "The town was founded by a man from Greece, and he named it after an island where he'd spent his childhood because it reminded him of Capri. Or at least that's what they told me in grade school."

"That's the thing." Pine leaned forward and rested his elbows on his desk. "According to the pictures you have on your phone, that scroll has some signs and hints at possibly being old, but that seems like *too* much of a happenstance, doesn't it?"

"I'd never really thought about it," Harper admitted.

And she hadn't. In her research of Greek mythology, she had learned that sirens were from the island of Anthemusa, and by some texts, that was believed to be an earlier name for the island of Capri.

When Harper had read that, she hadn't given it much thought. It never seemed all that relevant *why* the sirens had chosen her Capri. It seemed far more important to try to figure out how to get rid of them. At one point, Harper had just assumed that the sirens had stopped there because the name reminded them of home, and then they'd gotten caught up in turning Gemma.

But none of the sirens seemed to be particularly nostalgic, and on many occasions, both Penn and Lexi had talked about how much they hated it there and how they wanted to get out. Now, with Professor Pine pointing out the obvious correlation, Harper began to wonder what exactly had drawn the sirens to Capri in the first place.

"I just don't trust things that are coincidental. But, you know, obviously, I don't think you or your sister are trying to dupe anybody with this," Pine went on. "I don't think you made this or are attempting some kind of a hoax, although you might have one being perpetrated on you."

"I don't know about that." Harper lowered her eyes and shook her head.

"And I would be more than happy to take a look at the real thing if you could bring it in," Pine said. "In fact, you'd be doing me a favor. I'd really love to get my hands on it. Even if there's only the slightest chance that the thing is legit."

"My sister is pretty attached to it, but I'm going home this weekend. I'll see if I can get her to part with it for a few days."

That would be easier said than done. Gemma didn't like allowing the scroll out of her sight for too long, afraid that Penn would find it, or it would disappear.

"Well, if you can get it, let me know." Pine leaned back in his chair. "It'd be really interesting to see what it turns up."

Thanking him, Harper closed his office door behind her, realizing dourly that she was leaving with more questions than she'd come with. But at the top of her list was figuring out what language the scroll was written in and finding out why the sirens had come to Capri.

FOUR

Provocative

Daniel slipped on his work boots just as his phone began to vibrate in his pocket. Harper had been text messaging him on her break between classes, and he'd showered and gotten dressed while reading her lengthy explanation about her meeting with the professor at college.

Unfortunately, neither Harper nor Gemma appeared to be making much headway with the scroll. Daniel helped as much as he could, but so far, that mostly amounted to letting them bounce ideas off him and contributing when he could.

He'd hoped that they'd be closer to cracking this curse by now. Mostly, it was for the obvious reasons—he wanted Gemma safe and free, and since the sirens killed without mercy, they needed to be stopped.

But there was a selfish reason, too. He wanted a reprieve from his "date" with Penn. In order to keep Harper and Gemma safe, he'd agreed to let Penn have her way with him. They'd decided on last Friday as the official day for it, but since he'd been injured on Thursday during the fight with Lexi, Penn had postponed things until he healed.

They had yet to set a new date, and that was making him nervous. Penn wasn't the type to wait for things. He was afraid she was brewing some other mischief, something that could hurt him or Harper or Gemma even worse.

But right now, he pushed Penn from his mind. He pulled his phone out from his pocket, knowing he needed to focus on his girlfriend. He loved Harper, and if he wanted to be with her, he couldn't spend all his time worrying about Penn.

So he can't really tell me anything until I bring him the scroll, Harper texted.

Sorry the teacher couldn't help you more, Daniel texted back as he walked out of his house.

He locked the door behind him even though he lived out on Bernie's Island because he didn't trust Penn or the other sirens not to go in and rummage through his things. Locking the door wouldn't stop them if they really wanted to get in, but at least there'd be evidence of a break-in, so he'd know they'd been there.

Daniel had made it halfway down the trail to the boathouse when he got another text from Harper: *So I was thinking about coming to town for your birthday next week.*

Daniel stopped to reply to her since texting and walking had never been his strong suit. He was a few feet away from the boathouse, standing among the cypress and pines, when he typed back to her, *You don't have to do that. We can just celebrate this weekend.*

"Ooh, it's your birthday next week?" Penn asked, her voice mellifluous in his ear.

"Holy crap, Penn." He wheeled around, shoving his phone in his pocket before she could read any more of the messages, and tried to look like she hadn't scared him. "You can't sneak up on a guy like that."

Penn smiled, apparently proud of having frightened him. Her black hair was dripping wet down her back, and her dress was soaking, so it clung to her flesh. She usually flew over on her visits to the island, but maybe since it was the middle of the afternoon, she thought swimming would be less conspicuous than a giant bird flying in the sky.

"Sorry," Penn said, without the slightest hint of sincerity.

"How did you do that, anyway? You didn't make a sound." He gestured out to Anthemusa Bay behind her, which should've made some kind of noise when she climbed out. Not to mention all the pine needles and twigs on the ground that should've crunched or cracked under her feet.

She shrugged, still smiling. "It's an evil-villain trick."

"Evil villain?" Daniel arched an eyebrow, surprised that she was self-aware enough to realize that's what she was.

"What?" Penn smirked and started walking to the side, circling him, but he stayed where he was, with his eyes facing forward. "You thought I didn't know that you'd cast me as the villain in your little soap opera?"

"I'd never really thought of my life as a 'soap opera.'"

She'd made her way back around and stopped right in front of him, but she was closer this time, nearly touching him. "You didn't answer my question. It's your birthday next week?"

"Yeah, on Wednesday." He nodded. "I'll be twenty-one."

A bald cypress had broken in half during the storm last week, so the trunk was leaning down at an angle, almost blocking the trail to the boathouse. Daniel had been meaning to clear it up, but he'd been so busy with everything else that he hadn't had a chance to.

"You're still such a baby," Penn remarked, and she walked back to the fallen tree. She leaned against the rough bark, making it move slightly and the branches groan. "I'm really robbing the cradle with this one."

"You could try dating a shark," Daniel suggested. "They live a long time, and they're the closest thing to your species."

Penn did not look amused. "Charming."

"Thanks, and I hate to cut and run like this, but I really have to be going," he said, and stepped to the side, meaning to make his escape.

She was up in a flash, blocking his path before he even had a chance to react. "Not so fast, Birthday Boy."

"Listen, Penn, I'm sure you came out here so I could render *payment* on our little agreement, but I really can't right now," he insisted. "We're having one of the last rehearsals for the play, and I need to be there for last-minute tweaks and touch-ups."

"I don't think you're in a position to tell me what I can and can't do," Penn assured him with such cool certainty that it terrified him. "You're already mine. It's just a matter of collecting what I'm owed."

Daniel didn't even see her move. One second he was standing directly in front of Penn, the next he was on his back. He knew he'd fallen to the ground because he felt twigs cracking under his back and the wind being pushed from his lungs, but, otherwise, he didn't know how exactly Penn had gotten him there.

He only had a split second to ponder it before Penn was on top of him, straddling him between her legs, and he felt the cold water from her dress seeping in through his jeans.

"Trust me, Daniel." She smiled down at him as she slid her hands underneath his T-shirt. "You'll thank me for this later."

"I seriously doubt that," he muttered. She leaned forward, pushing up his shirt as she did, and she stared down at his exposed chest and abdomen. He craned his neck up, trying to see what she was getting at. "What are you doing?"

"Checking you out," Penn replied simply.

Her fingers were cold when she touched him, and he inhaled sharply. He laid his head back down, not wanting to watch her hands slide all over his torso, her tanned fingers moving over the purple-and-gray bruise that covered most of his right side.

"Yeah, I can see that, but—" He winced as she pushed painfully on his ribs.

"It's still sore?" Penn asked, and she moved her hands away, alleviating the pain.

"Yeah. Lexi wasn't messing around."

Daniel had put up as much of a fight as he could against the giant bird-monster, but Lexi had thrown him around plenty. The worst of it had been when she'd thrown him through the window, causing the massive bruise and possible cracked rib on his right side. He refused to go to the doctor, so he couldn't be certain how bad the damage was, but he could get around okay, so he knew he could recover.

The rest of his injuries were mostly scratches and bruises from broken glass and Lexi's talons. He did have one particularly nasty cut on his chest, and all the tiny holes in his right arm from Lexi's teeth when she'd bitten him. Most of the scratches were healing up fairly well, except for the bite wound, which seemed like it was going to take its sweet time to get better.

"I'm sorry I didn't rescue you sooner." Penn touched his bruise, almost tenderly, and she leaned down, first delicately kissing his ribs, then kissing the claw mark on his chest, right above his heart. "I can't believe that wench hurt you like that."

It almost sounded like there was actual concern and empathy mixed with the normally hollow velvet of Penn's voice. He'd never seen Penn show any amount of compassion before, and he had no idea how to respond.

"I am grateful that you saved my life, and I did mean it when I thanked you before," Daniel said finally, once she straightened back up. "Are you okay with it?"

"What do you mean?" She'd stopped staring morosely at his chest, and she tilted her head quizzically and narrowed her eyes.

"I'm probably a jerk for asking, and I should just let it go, but . . ." He pushed ahead anyway. "You killed your sister. You don't regret it at all?"

Penn relaxed and shrugged. "She wasn't really my sister."

"Penn . . ." He sighed.

"What's to regret, Daniel?" Penn asked, and any of the earlier warmth she'd had in her voice was replaced by venom. "She was obnoxious and mean, and I hated her. I've spent almost three hundred years with her."

"Would you have killed her? If she hadn't been about to eat me?"

"Not then, no. But soon, probably. Maybe not." She shook her head. "It doesn't matter. I made a choice."

"And what choice was that?" Daniel asked.

"That I wanted you, and I would do anything to have you." She smiled. "She was in our way."

"*Our* way?"

"Yeah." She laughed a little. "Our way to be together."

She leaned down, her hands still on his chest, and pressed her lips to his. His heart raced in his chest, and he didn't try to slow it. Penn might mistake his unease and agitation for excitement, and that would be better.

He tried not to think of Harper, and he had to restrain himself to keep from pushing Penn off. Nothing she did felt *bad,* but everything about it was wrong. All her touches, her kisses, they were all pleasure mixed with equal parts revulsion, and if he thought of Harper, it would be impossible for him to handle.

They'd kissed before, but Penn had always been more aggressive—like she thought she'd be able to devour him. This time, though, she showed the same gentleness and control that she had a few moments ago.

There was something almost tender about it, but he felt heat burning there, too. Even when Penn tried to use restraint, she couldn't completely hold back who she was. The way her body pressed against him through the thin, wet fabric, and even the way her tongue encircled his—she was a creature made almost entirely of desire.

She sat back up, a light smile playing on her full lips. Her black hair cascaded forward, shielding her face from him. Daniel reached up, brushing her hair back and tucking it behind her ears. For a moment, he let his hand linger there, and she leaned into it, pressing her cheek against the palm of his hand.

He searched her eyes, scanning them for any of the warmth or tenderness he'd felt in her kisses. In a strange way, he almost wanted to find it. Somehow, it would make him feel better if there was some humanity to her, if she had some heart left.

Her irises were nearly black, only one shade lighter than her pupils, and he stared into them. But no matter how deeply he looked into Penn's eyes, he could see only an empty darkness. She was cold and hollow inside.

"You're going to kill me, aren't you?" Daniel asked, and took his hand away from her face, letting it fall back to the ground.

"Do you want me to answer that honestly?" Penn asked. The hint of a smile had fallen away from her face, but, otherwise, her expression was the same.

He nodded.

"Probably, yes," she told him without remorse. "But not for a while."

"Will it hurt?" Daniel asked, keeping his expression and voice as calm and even as hers.

"Depends on whether you piss me off or not. But I have ways of making it painless."

She was still staring down at him, and he couldn't handle her gaze anymore. More accurately, he couldn't handle this game she was playing with him. If she wanted him, and it would keep the people he loved safe, then he'd rather just hurry up and give himself to her.

He sat up and put his hand on the small of her back, pushing her closer to him, then he kissed her. He moved more aggressively than she had been just now, but it still didn't match her ferociousness in some of their earlier encounters.

"What are you doing?" Penn asked, pulling away from him almost as soon as he'd started kissing her.

"I thought this was what you wanted," Daniel said, bewildered by her resistance.

She shook her head. "I told you that I didn't come here for that."

"What's wrong with now? We can just get it over with."

"Just get it over with?" Penn laughed and pushed his hand off her back. "How romantic." She got up and climbed off him while he just stared up in total confusion.

"Wow. It's like the *Twilight Zone* out here. Are you seriously turning down sex?" he asked.

"No, but I want the mood to be right. It's been so long since I've really had to chase someone down, and when I have you, I want to *savor* you."

"So . . ." He scratched his head, then got to his feet. "If you didn't come out today for the whole sex thing, then *why* are you here?"

"Daniel, I knew your hearing was messed up, but I didn't

know your listening skills were so bad. I already told you. I came out to see if you've healed enough to perform."

"I hurt my arm and my ribs, and I have a couple scratches. I think I'll be okay."

She bit her lip. "You only say that because you don't know what I have in store for you."

"When you say stuff like that, you think you're being flirtatious, but you're really not," Daniel said as he smoothed out his shirt and brushed off pine needles and leaves. "Given that I know what you're capable of, that comes across as more of a threat than innuendo."

She laughed. "Since you handled that roll in the grass just fine and seem to be doing so well, I think you're just about ready for our date. So we should reschedule in . . ." Penn cocked her head, as if thinking. "One week from today?"

"A week? But that's my . . ." He sighed as it dawned on him. "Birthday. You knew that. That's why you picked it."

"I want to give you the best birthday present ever. And what could be better than a night with me?"

"Oh, I'm sure I could think of a couple things," he muttered.

"Now, Daniel, you shouldn't say things like that. You wouldn't want to hurt my feelings, would you? Because if you did, then I might get angry, and I might have to take out some of my rage on your girlfriend and her sister." She smiled at him as she spoke. "I might even have to kill them."

"I'm just keeping it interesting, Penn," Daniel replied coolly, instead of throwing her to the ground and telling her that if she ever touched Harper, he'd kill her. "I know it's the thrill of the chase that gets you off, so I can't make it too easy for you."

"That's why I like you. You know exactly what I want."

She leaned into him and kissed him on the mouth. She put one hand on the back of his head, running her fingers through his hair and holding him to her. Then he felt her teeth sinking into his lip. He was about to push her off when she let go and stepped back.

"Eight o'clock on Wednesday night," Penn said as she backed away from him. "You and me."

"I won't forget," he promised her.

Penn laughed, then turned and ran down to the end of the dock. She dove off and went into the water with hardly a splash.

He could taste the blood from his lip, and he wiped it away with the back of his hand. His heart pounded in his chest, and he felt like throwing up. Every encounter he had with Penn left him feeling like he needed to shower.

He was ashamed to admit that a small part of him liked it, which made him crave the shower all the more. As much as he detested Penn, she sparked something in his anatomy that he couldn't completely control.

Penn had left his clothes wet and dirty from throwing him on the ground, and he'd have to change before he went down to the theater. He really did want to shower now, but he wasn't sure he'd have enough time to, so he pulled out his phone to check the clock.

That's when he saw he had two missed texts from Harper. In all the commotion with Penn, he hadn't noticed his phone vibrating.

But I want to do something special for you, Harper had texted when Penn interrupted.

Daniel? Are you still there? That was her newest text, the one that came when he didn't respond.

Daniel stared down at the phone, unsure of what to say, and feeling worse than he'd ever felt before. While he'd been kissing Penn, Harper had been texting him, completely oblivious to the fact that Daniel was cheating on her.

He knew he'd do whatever it took to protect Harper, but he didn't want to betray her like this. She deserved more from him.

But he knew that if he told Harper about his pact to sleep with Penn, she'd try to talk him out of it. She might even succeed. And it wouldn't be worth it. Saving their relationship would be meaningless if it meant sacrificing Harper and Gemma's lives.

I have to go to class. I'll talk to you later. Love you. Harper texted him as he stared down at his phone, trying to decide not only what to reply to her but also what he should do about the whole situation with Penn.

In some strange way, that text seemed to solidify his decision. Harper loved him, she trusted him, and she needed him now more than ever. He had to protect her the only way he knew how to, even if it meant that he'd lose her forever.

Sorry. I love you, too, Daniel replied, and hoped that she truly understood how much.

FIVE

Mistaken

"When will Penn be back?" Liv asked for the thousandth
time since Penn had left earlier that afternoon.

Thea sighed loudly and flipped a page in her script. Her back
was against the arm of the couch, so she could rest the book on
her legs. A flyaway hair had come loose from her messy bun, and
she smoothed it back and tried to ignore Liv.

"Thea?" Liv said when she didn't respond.

"I don't know," Thea replied, and made no attempt to mask
the annoyance in her voice.

"But I'm sooo bored," Liv whined like a small child on the
second day of summer vacation. "Can we go swimming, at least?"

Thea slid lower on the couch, so she was lying on her back,
and her knees would block Liv from her field of vision. "You can
go swimming with Penn when she gets back."

"But you have no idea when she'll be back?" Liv flicked the

TV off and sat sideways on the couch, so she could face Thea fully. "Do you even know where she went?"

"Nope," she said, but that wasn't entirely true. She had a good idea of where Penn had gone, but she didn't know for certain.

Penn was being unnecessarily shifty lately. An hour ago, she'd declared that she had to go somewhere and that Thea would have to stay behind with Liv. When Thea reminded her that she had a play rehearsal she needed to get to, Penn just told her that she'd done the play several times before and didn't need the practice.

And then Penn dove off the cliff behind their house, crashing into the waves and swimming off, leaving Thea alone with Liv.

Liv sighed in frustration. "Is this why Gemma doesn't live with you guys?"

"Gemma prefers to live with her family."

Liv shook her head. "I don't get that. And I thought I was supposed to be Gemma's replacement. Why is she still here instead of Lexi?"

"We already told you. Things changed. Penn's priorities shifted. Gemma stayed, Lexi's gone."

The breeze outside picked up, blowing salty air in through the broken windows on the back of the house. During the fight last week, Lexi had broken out several windows and damaged a lot of their furniture. New windows were coming in later this week, but for now, Thea taped plastic over them if it got too cold or rained, but today it was nice, and Thea enjoyed the fresh air.

As for the broken furniture, Thea and Penn hadn't replaced much of it yet, other than getting a new television. Everything else, they basically just fixed with duct tape and set it back in its place. The entertainment center was cracked, so the TV slanted to one side, and the stuffing was coming out from the cushions on the chairs.

"Can't we at least do something fun?" Liv asked.

"No, we can't. I'm already missing play rehearsal right now to babysit you. So you can watch TV or entertain yourself while I read my lines."

"Babysit?" Liv scoffed. "Why would you even say that? I don't need a babysitter. I'm eighteen."

"I said it because it's true." Thea moved her knees to the side, so she could stare directly at Liv. "You need a babysitter."

Liv's mouth dropped, and her eyes were pained. "That's so mean."

"How is it mean?" Thea sat up and set her script aside. "You've only been a siren since Friday, and you've been nothing but trouble.

"We went to all the trouble of getting campus housing to move you, so you'd room with Harper," Thea went on. "As was our plan. Before you even became a siren, Penn told you that we wanted you to keep an eye on Harper. But instead of doing that, you attacked her, then went on a spree and killed three people, including a psych teacher. Penn and I had to drop everything to come clean up your mess."

"Oh, that's no big deal." Liv waved it off with a smile. "You guys can charm your way out of anything."

"No, it *is* a big deal," Thea said, trying hard to emphasize her point. "I don't want to spend all my time disposing of your bodies and washing up your blood. You can't control yourself, Liv. End of story."

"I can control myself just fine. Right now, for example, I'm perfectly composed," Liv said in her too-sweet voice with a perfect smile plastered on her face. She actually batted her eyes, which made Thea groan.

"If you don't like this, it's your fault," Thea said. "You said you wanted this. You *asked* to be a siren. And then we trusted you and left you on your own, and you went batshit and almost ruined everything for us."

Liv's smile fell, and her eyes darkened. "I did not go batshit."

"You threw a huge tantrum because you didn't like the way Harper talked to you. Penn asked you to do one simple thing." Thea held up one finger to demonstrate. "*One* thing. She gave you the gift that you wanted, and in turn, she just wanted you to keep tabs on Harper and help find out what Gemma is up to. That's it. And you couldn't handle it."

"I could handle it," Liv insisted. "I just didn't think it was fair."

"Well, life isn't fair." Thea shrugged. "Get used to it."

"I don't know how you can give me all this power and expect me to do nothing with it. I can change form, and I can control men with my voice."

Liv had been getting louder as she spoke, and by the time she stood, she was practically shouting at Thea. Her eyes had changed from their usual dark brown to golden-eagle eyes, and Thea could see the beginnings of her fangs protruding from her mouth.

"I can kill at my discretion," Liv said, her voice booming through the living room. All of its sugariness had dissolved. "I decide the fate of everyone I come in contact with. I'm practically a god, and you want me to sit on the couch while you *read*?"

Thea said nothing for a minute, almost in shock at the maniacal glint in Liv's eyes, before finally whispering, "Penn made a terrible mistake with you."

With that, Liv dove at her. Thea leaned back, her head resting on the arm of the couch, and Liv hovered over her. She was still mostly human, aside from the many jagged rows of teeth in her mouth. Her face was mere inches above Thea's, and her eyes were filled with contempt.

"No, *you're* the one who made a mistake," Liv said, her voice mutated by the monster inside her, making her sound demonic. "I am not some little parakeet you can keep in a cage."

"Neither am I," Thea growled.

Her hand was around Liv's throat in a second, her fingers elongating and tightening around Liv's windpipe—not enough to kill her but enough that Liv could feel her power and strength.

"You think you're so powerful, little girl?" Thea asked, and leaned even closer to Liv as her eyes widened in surprise. "I've had this power a lot longer than you, and I actually know how to use it. I will not hesitate to rip off your head and spit down your throat if you do not calm the hell down."

The back door slammed shut, and Liv instantly retracted her teeth, and her eyes changed back to normal. Thea didn't let go of her throat, though, so Liv remained hovering over her, even after Thea heard Penn's wet footsteps on the floor as she walked into the living room.

"What is going on here?" Penn asked, and Thea finally let go of Liv, allowing her to sit back down on the couch. "I leave for a few hours, and come home to this? I thought I told you girls to play nice."

"We were playing nice," Liv said sunnily. "Thea and I were just getting to know each other."

"Yeah, we were having a real heart-to-heart," Thea muttered, and sat up straighter on the couch.

Penn stood to the side of the living room, eyeing the two of them, and said, "It looks like it."

"You're all wet," Liv said. "Were you out swimming?"

"I was out taking care of something," Penn replied, and sat down in a chair, seemingly not caring that her dress was soaking wet and would dampen the furniture.

"Oh, I was wondering if we could go swimming. Thea said I had to wait until you got back," Liv said.

"Maybe later." Penn smiled briefly at her, then turned her attention to Thea.

"Because I've been sitting inside all afternoon without anything to do—" Liv began, but Penn held up her hand to cut her off.

"Have you talked to Gemma today?" Penn asked Thea, completely ignoring Liv.

Thea picked up her script from where she'd set it aside on an end table and pretended to be immersed in it. "She texted me to ask why I wasn't at rehearsal."

"Do you know if she's still searching for the scroll?" Penn asked as she combed her fingers through her long hair.

Thea kept her eyes fixed on the page and her face as expressionless as possible when she said, "She hasn't said anything lately."

"What scroll?" Liv asked.

Penn glared at her. "The scroll you were supposed to be watching out for. Remember? Back when the plan was for you to stay with Harper and make sure she didn't figure out how to kill us all. You were supposed to find out what she knew about the scroll, but instead, you threw a fit, and now you're here."

"Oh." Liv paused. "*That* scroll."

"Yes, *that* one," Penn said, and rolled her eyes.

"But . . . you guys still have it, right?" Liv asked.

"I have it under lock and key," Thea lied, and avoided making eye contact with anyone.

She'd given Gemma and Harper the scroll last week, but if Penn found out, she'd kill her. Not figuratively, but literally rip off her head, tear out her heart, and murder her. Penn had put Thea in charge of the scroll because she didn't trust Lexi with that kind of responsibility, and Penn was too busy playing with Daniel to concern herself with it.

That was the one good part about Liv's leaving college. If she snooped around Harper long enough, she'd have been bound to figure out that they had the scroll, and Penn would eventually deduce that Thea had given it to them.

That didn't change the fact that Liv was psychotic and couldn't handle a simple assignment.

"Where is it?" Liv asked.

Thea cast her a look. "Like I would trust you with that information."

"What would I do with it? I don't want to hurt you guys." Liv smiled warmly at them. "You're my family."

"It's better if you don't know," Penn said. "The fewer people that know, the safer it is."

"Well, if Thea has it, then Harper or Gemma obviously don't. So we're safe. What does it matter if I'm at college or not?" Liv asked.

"Why don't you just go out and swim for a while?" Penn suggested. She kept her tone amazingly even when she talked to Liv, using more self-discipline than Thea knew she had.

"Really?" Liv asked, and practically jumped off the couch.

"Penn," Thea hissed. "She shouldn't be unsupervised."

Penn waved off Thea's concern. "She can handle it for a few minutes. I'll come out and join you, so stay close to the bay." As Liv darted off to the back door, Penn called after her, "And don't kill anyone! I mean it."

"I won't. Thank you!" Liv shouted as she ran out the door.

"It's so ridiculous." Penn shook her head. "We have one siren who refuses to feed and another one who won't stop. Maybe we should have Gemma and Liv hang out together, and they can rub off on each other. Then they'll end up somewhere in the middle. Like me."

"You think you're in the middle? You eat like once a week," Thea said.

"It's better than Liv, who thinks she should eat three times a day. And your once-a-month diet is impossible."

"It's not impossible."

"What was all that about when I came in?" Penn asked.

"Nothing much. Just that Liv is totally insane and horrible and way worse than Lexi and Gemma combined."

"She's not so bad," Penn insisted. "She's new. Give her time."

"Really?" Thea arched an eyebrow. "That's the card you're playing now? You were ready to behead Gemma for much less."

"We've got two horrible sirens, and we need to make at least one of them work."

"And your money's on Liv?" Thea was dubious.

"My money's not on anyone right now." Penn sighed and stood up. "I should probably go out and join her."

"You're really going to swim with her?" Thea asked.

Penn shrugged. "Why not?"

"You've been swimming for a while," Thea said. "I mean, I assumed you were out stalking Daniel, too, but it couldn't have taken that much time."

"I wasn't stalking him." Penn laughed and started walking toward the back door. "And I swam around for a bit after I talked to him."

Thea got up and followed Penn. "How did it go?"

"What?" Penn stopped near the kitchen island and turned back to face Thea.

"Your talk with Daniel. Based on your current good mood, I'd guess it went fairly well."

Penn smiled coyly. "Don't worry about it."

"Why are you sneaking off to see Daniel anyway? Why don't you just tell me that's where you're going?" Thea asked. "I know you are, and I don't care that you have some weird crush on him."

Penn laughed and put a hand on either side of Thea's face,

almost cradling it as she spoke to her. "Thea, my dear sister, I love you. But we've spent nearly every day of our entire lives together. This is something that I want to keep private. Just for me. Let me have it."

Then Penn leaned forward, giving Thea a quick peck on the cheek before turning around and walking away.

"Okay . . ." Thea was too dumbstruck to talk for a second. "What's going on? You're freaking me out. Did Daniel do something to you?"

"Nothing's wrong," Penn assured her as she opened the back door. "And don't worry. Everything will be fine. I'll get Liv under control, and this will all work out. I promise."

Penn laughed again, then shut the door behind her. Through the broken window, Thea watched as she jumped off the cliff.

Thea put her hands on the back of her head and let out a deep breath. Penn's attempts at calming her only made things worse. Whenever Penn assured her that everything would turn out okay, things always went to hell.

So if the past was any indication, all of this was going to end up very, very bad.

SIX

Breathless

It was still strange, waking up in a house without Harper. The laundry wasn't magically folded in the basket, and the dishes didn't miraculously do themselves. Gemma didn't mind stepping up and filling the hole her sister had left at home, but it still felt very weird.

The freedom was nice, not that Harper wasn't still texting and calling her all the time. Gemma wasn't completely sure how Harper managed to get schoolwork done, but knowing her, she was probably finishing it all, along with extra credit assignments.

The biggest thing Harper's absence had left her with was time to think. Gemma no longer had somebody across the hall to discuss things with. She had told her dad everything now, but it wasn't the same as talking to Harper.

As Gemma scrubbed the dishes from last night's supper, her mind wandered to all the things that worried her. Like if she would ever really be able to break the curse, and what was taking Lydia so long with the scroll translations.

And why had Thea skipped play practice the night before? Thea claimed she had to babysit Liv while Penn ran an errand, but she refused to explain beyond that.

Daniel had shown up late for rehearsal last night, and he'd seemed out of sorts. Gemma tried to talk to him about it, but he'd just brushed her off. She couldn't help but fear that Thea's absence and Daniel's uneasiness were tied together.

After Gemma rinsed off the last dish and put it in the drainer, she leaned against the sink. She stared out the window at Alex's house next door, and her worries were replaced by a familiar longing pulling at her heart.

It had been over a week since she'd last spoken to Alex, and that conversation had been tumultuous. He'd yelled at her until she finally explained to him that she'd gotten him to break up with her using her siren song. He was hurt and furious, but then he'd kissed her.

It was the first time she'd kissed him in over a month, and sometimes at night, she'd replay it over in her mind. He'd been angry, so his lips had pressed against hers with urgency and passion, but the tenderness hidden beneath had been unmistakable. The very thought of it made her heart ache.

Gemma decided that she wasn't going to live this way. He was right next door, and if she missed him, then she should go see him. She didn't want to waste what little time she had left on this earth missing someone who lived right next door.

She dried off her hands, smoothed out her hair, and walked

over to Alex's house. Taking a deep breath, she knocked on his front door. But all of her confidence completely disappeared when he opened the door, and she saw him standing in front of her.

His T-shirt pulled taut against his chest and arms, and Gemma'd almost forgotten how much more muscular he'd gotten since he started working at the docks. He'd gotten his chestnut hair cut since she'd seen him last, but it was still a little longer than he usually wore it, so it landed just above his eyebrows.

Alex looked older, and she hadn't gotten used to it. There was still some of his innocence, some of the boy next door hidden in his features, but he had a new maturity and strength to his face—a hardness in his jaw and brow that wasn't there before.

But it was his eyes that struck her momentarily mute. For the first time in a while, she could actually see *him* in them. Lately, his mahogany eyes had been a mask revealing nothing, but now there he was, the boy she'd fallen desperately in love with, and it was enough to take her breath away.

"Hello?" Alex asked, sounding bemused as she stared dumbly up at him.

"Hey," Gemma said with a dopey smile. "Hi. I hope you don't mind that I stopped by."

"No, of course not." He grinned, his whole face lighting up, and he stepped aside. "Come on in."

"Are you sure?" Gemma hesitated before entering, but he gestured widely to his house.

"Yeah. I've been meaning to talk to you," he said.

"You have?" Gemma asked uncertainly as she slid past him.

"Yeah." Alex walked toward the living room, so she followed

him, and he looked back over his shoulder as he talked to her. "I mean, I talked to Harper when she was still in town, and she kinda updated me on everything that's going on with you."

"Did she?" Gemma asked. "That's good. I think."

Daniel had borrowed Alex's car last week, then used it in an attempt to rescue Gemma, and he'd gotten it bogged down with mud. Harper and Daniel had returned the car to Alex and helped clean it up.

Gemma had wanted to help, but she was afraid that things would still be weird, so she'd focused on trying to translate the scroll while Harper had filled Alex in on all the goings-on with the sirens.

"So what did you want to talk to me about?" Gemma asked.

Alex motioned for her to sit down, and she sat tentatively on the couch. He remained standing for a few more seconds, then sat down at the other end.

"I didn't like the way we left things last week," he said finally. "But I didn't want to bother you with stupid drama."

"You're not bothering me," Gemma said quickly.

He smiled crookedly and stared off at the brick fireplace in the corner. His mother had decorated the living room in shabby chic, and the couch was covered in a weird, flowery pink fabric. Grade-school pictures of Alex hung in frames made of reclaimed wood.

Gemma let her eyes linger on a picture of him when he was twelve. His cowlick had been atrocious, but even then, there'd been something cute about him. He'd walked her home from school in the rain once, when Harper had been sick.

He'd been in middle school at the time, but he walked over to the grade school to get her because he had an umbrella, and he didn't think that Gemma would. That might have been the very early beginnings of her crush on him.

"I don't know exactly what I'm supposed to do, anymore." Alex ran a hand through his hair and looked over at Gemma.

"What do you mean?"

"With you. I'm not your boyfriend, and I don't even . . ." He shook his head. "I just wanted to tell you that I worry about you, and if you need me—for anything—I'll be there in a second. I want to help you."

She smiled at him. "Thank you."

"Sorry, I've been talking, and you came over here to say something. Sorry. Go ahead."

"No, it's okay," she said. "I wanted to check up on you."

"On me?" He was taken aback. "Why?"

"Because of how things went the last time we talked."

His face paled for a moment. "I'm sorry for yelling at you."

"No, you had every right to," Gemma said.

"No, I didn't." He shook his head. "I was angry, and I was hurt, but I know that whatever you did, you did it because you cared about me. You were doing what you thought was best to protect me."

"I really did, Alex." She met his eyes when she said it, hoping to convey her sincerity. "I really hope you understand that. Everything I did, I did because I—I cared about you."

"I know that. And even then, I think I knew that. I was just in such a fog of confusion and misery and just . . . bleakness. But I shouldn't have lashed out at you like that. It was uncalled for, and I'm sorry."

"It's okay. I understand," she said. "You've been going through something terrible, and it's my fault. You should be mad at me. I did something major to you without even asking."

"Gemma, it's okay. I'm okay," he reassured her.

"You do seem to be doing so much better than the last time I saw you."

It wasn't just the look in his eyes, the way he looked more like himself—although that was a big part of it. Alex just seemed relaxed and calmer. Before, he'd been so brooding and angsty, but now, there was a lightness about him again.

"I'm *feeling* so much better," Alex said with a relieved smile. "It's like this fog has been lifted, you know?"

"I'm glad to hear it," she said, and she meant it.

But what she didn't dare ask was *why*? Not because she didn't want to know but because she was afraid of what the answer might be.

When she'd used the siren song on Alex, it had been to make him stop loving her. And he had. Or at least it appeared that way, but it had also caused him to spiral into despair and anger.

Now he was better. He should still be trapped under the spell, and though she was very happy that he wasn't, Gemma didn't know how to explain it. The siren curse hadn't been broken, so the song should still have an effect on him.

Unless he didn't love her anymore. Maybe it wasn't the song itself that hurt him but the fact that it conflicted with his own feelings for her. And if he stopped loving her, the conflict would disappear.

"I'm not like *happy* happy, but I'm closer than I've been in a while," Alex went on with the same broad smile.

"I will find a way to get you all the way back to normal," she promised him, forcing back the lump in her throat. "I'm going to find a way to undo the curse, then that will set you free, too."

Or at least that was her plan. From what Lydia had told her, and from Thea's story about Asterion and the minotaurs, once the curse was broken, it was like it had never existed. With Asterion, that meant that the immortality the curse had given him along with his bullhead had been taken away, and since he was centuries old, he'd turned into dust.

Although no one had explicitly stated it, Gemma hoped that if the siren curse was broken, any enchantments of their siren song would be lifted as well. She didn't know for sure if breaking the curse would only affect the cursed themselves—so Thea and Penn would turn to dust, but all of the siren spells would still live on—but she hoped it would erase everything, including the spell she put on Alex.

Until then, she could only hope the spell would continue to weaken until any lingering enchantment eventually disappeared.

Not that it would make that much of a difference anymore, not if Alex had set himself free by falling out of love with her.

She was surprised to feel the ache in her chest growing, her heart tearing in half all over again. This is what she'd wanted. Setting Alex free and away from her to keep him safe. It was best for him, and she knew that.

But it felt like losing him all over again. After their kiss last week, she'd been rather stupidly and selfishly hoping that they would be able to be together again once this was all over—or sooner than that, if she was being completely honest.

"Is this about the scroll that Harper was telling me about?" Alex asked, pulling her from her thoughts.

He sat at the other end of the couch, his dark eyes resting on her, and the distance between them had never felt so great. All she wanted to do was reach out and touch him, to have him pull her into his arms one last time and taste his lips as they pressed against hers.

But she couldn't, so she forced a smile and nodded. "Yeah. We're still working on it, but we'll find a way."

"You do what you need to do for yourself, but you don't need to worry about me."

"How can I not worry about you? I broke you."

"That's the thing." He licked his lips. "I don't really feel *broken* anymore."

"I noticed," she said, hoping her words didn't sound as pained as they felt.

"And I think . . ." A slight blush broke out on his tanned cheeks, and he lowered his eyes. "I think it was because we kissed."

Her heart skipped a beat, and she stared at him in surprise. "Really?"

"Really." He lifted his head, evenly meeting her gaze. "Every day I've felt more and more like myself since then."

Gemma didn't know if that was true, or why kissing would alter the effect the siren song had on him, but at that moment, she didn't care. She'd been certain that she'd never be able to be with Alex again, and now she had a chance, and nothing else mattered.

"Well . . . we could try kissing again," Gemma suggested with bated breath. Her blood pounded in her ears, and her cheeks flushed.

At first he only stared at her, his expression blank and his eyes unreadable, and she was afraid she'd gone too far. It probably lasted just a few moments, but to her, it felt like an eternity, where she couldn't breathe, and her heart pounded madly in her chest.

Then, finally, he leaned in to her and kissed her gently on the mouth. There was the tenderness that she'd come to know and love, the almost innocent way he kissed her.

But that was quickly replaced by the sense of desperation. It had been so long since they'd really kissed, and that added a fervor that made her skin flutter. The way Alex was touching her whetted the appetite of the siren inside her, but she silenced it. She refused to stop kissing him.

He pushed her back down on the couch, so he was on top of her. He held himself up with his arms, but she felt the slight weight of his body against her, the firmness of his chest and stomach against the softness of hers.

As he kissed her deeply, she wrapped her arms around him, pulling him closer to her. He felt so much different than he had before. Through his shirt, she felt his muscles, warm and solid under her fingertips. His back and shoulders were broader than she'd remembered, and his kisses more demanding.

When she tried to pull him to her, Alex didn't move. She'd have to use her siren strength to get him to budge, and she didn't want to let the monster out. Alex was still kissing her. He had one hand on her side, gently squeezing her.

He seemed to want to take things slower than she did. The hunger inside was flaring up, and the flutter was running across her skin. Not to mention the heat in her belly, spreading like a flame down her legs.

Putting her hand on his chest, she pushed him up so she could catch her breath, and she felt his heart hammering against the palm of her hand.

"Is something wrong?" Alex asked, his eyes searching hers.

"No." She smiled up at him. "You're stronger than you were before."

"Sorry."

"No." Gemma laughed. "It's just . . . strange. I got used to the way you felt in my arms, and I've been kinda clinging to that memory. And now you're different."

"You're different, too." He brushed back a hair from her forehead. "You feel the same, but your eyes . . ."

"What?"

"I don't know. They look older somehow. You've been through a lot this summer."

"We both have," she said.

He took a deep breath and in a low voice, he said, "I've missed you."

"I've missed you, too."

When Alex kissed her again, Gemma decided that she didn't

care about the monster. In that moment, all she wanted was to feel Alex and be as close to him as she could be. She'd missed him so much, and she wanted to feel him, holding her, touching her, encompassing her.

With her lips still pressed to his, she reached down and started pulling up his T-shirt. Alex tried to mumble some kind of protest, but her mouth on his silenced him. They separated long enough for her to pull his shirt up over his head, then they were kissing again, his bare flesh pressed against her.

Alex had slid his hands up her shirt, preparing to do the same thing, when a loud clearing of the throat interrupted them.

They both looked up to see Alex's dad standing in the living room. His expression was unreadable behind his glasses and graying beard, but both Alex and Gemma hastily proceeded to sit up and scramble to straighten out their clothes.

"Dad, I didn't think you'd be home until later," Alex said as he pulled on his shirt, muffling some of his words. He'd moved to the other end of the couch, putting as much distance between himself and Gemma as he could. "I thought you were at the school all day."

"And I thought you got your job back, Alex," Mr. Lane said in the same emotionless voice that Gemma had heard him giving lectures in at the high school.

"Uh, yeah, I did, I don't start at the dock again until tomorrow." Alex smoothed out his hair as Gemma combed a hand through her own.

"I haven't seen you around in a while, Gemma." Mr. Lane took off his glasses and began to clean them with his shirt.

Gemma laughed nervously. "Things have been crazy lately, Mr. Lane."

"Are you looking forward to being a junior in a couple weeks?"

"Yeah, I guess." She smiled at him because she wasn't sure how else to respond.

"Alex could've been enjoying college, too, if he hadn't gotten all turned around," Mr. Lane remarked once he put his glasses back on. That was the first time his tone had taken on anything really disapproving.

"I'm getting myself back on track, Dad," Alex said with a heavy sigh.

"I should probably get going," Gemma interrupted, since the situation only seemed to be getting more awkward and tense by the minute.

"Yeah, I'll walk you out," Alex said, getting to his feet before Gemma even had a chance to.

He ushered her out to the door and held it open for her. She stepped out on the front step and turned back to face him.

"Sorry about my dad," he said.

"No problem." She chewed her lip and stared up at him, waiting for him to say something or kiss her good-bye. When he didn't, she said, "So . . . I'll see you around?"

"Yeah." He nodded. "Definitely."

Alex gave her a small wave, then shut the door. Gemma turned around and walked back to her house, wondering what had just happened.

The brief makeout session had been nice, but she had no idea what it meant. Especially with the brush-off he'd given her at the door. Admittedly, they were both flustered, but everything felt more confusing than ever.

She still cared about Alex so much, and she wanted to believe that he still cared for her. But maybe Alex was just trying to get back to normal, and he thought kissing her would help.

Which brought up another concern. Why was Alex back to normal? Was it the kissing, and if it was, why would that even work?

Or was it as she feared? When she used the siren song on him, she'd broken his heart. He didn't love her anymore, so the negative effects of the song were fading.

Maybe things were really over between them forever, and what they just shared had been nothing more than an extended goodbye kiss.

SEVEN

Translation

W hat the hell happened here?" Marcy asked as she surveyed the carnage on Liv's half of the dorm room.

Harper had been working on a paper on her laptop when Marcy texted her and said she was on campus. She hurried to finish up her thought, so she could save the document and leave. She'd told Marcy just to come on up to her room and barely even noticed when she came in.

"What?" Harper glanced over her shoulder and saw Marcy staring at the dismantled bed, the pile of Liv's clothes, and shredded books and posters. "Oh, that."

"Oh, *that*?" Marcy scoffed. "What do you mean 'oh that'? Half your room has been destroyed."

"It's my roommate's half," Harper pointed out.

"Yeah, I can tell, it's like perfectly down the middle. Did you run a piece of tape down the floor, and say, 'Here, you can wreck that half'?"

Harper shook her head. "No, she messed up her stuff when I wasn't here, so I picked up all her stuff and put it on her half."

"Of course you did," Marcy muttered. "God, you're so meticulous sometimes, it's gross."

"Thanks."

"That wasn't a compliment."

"Can you give me like three seconds?" Harper asked, glancing back at her laptop as she typed. "I'm just about done with this, then I'll be able to tell you all about my roommate from hell."

Harper went back to finishing up her homework, but it only took a few seconds for Marcy to get into trouble. She heard Marcy poking around behind her, then the sound of tumbling wood as the rest of the bed frame clattered to the floor.

"Oops, sorry."

"It's okay. I'm done now anyway." Harper clicked save, then closed her laptop and swiveled her desk chair around, so she could face her friend.

"You should really have someone take this out of here." Marcy jabbed her thumb at the mess behind her. "It's probably a fire hazard or something."

"I want to, but I don't know if I should. She still technically lives here."

"So what happened?" Marcy leaned over, inspecting the bed frame more closely. "Why'd she go all Tasmanian devil on you?"

"I don't know. I think she's on drugs or something. I tried talking to her, then she freaked out on me. She did this." Harper tilted her head to the side and pulled her hair back, so she could show Marcy the scratches.

"Wow." Marcy's eyes widened behind her black-rimmed glasses. "You really need to talk to someone. You can't let her come back here."

"I know. I just don't want to deal with it. There's way too much other crap going on, and I haven't had a chance to even look for a job here, and I'm so backed up on homework, and I don't know what to get Daniel for his birthday, and oh yeah, I still haven't cracked the code to the scroll that's trapped my sister in a horrible curse."

"How about cuff links?" Marcy asked.

Harper scrunched up her forehead in confusion. "What?"

"Daniel, for his birthday. Every guy should own a nice pair of cuff links."

"Thanks for the tip, Marce." Harper stood up. "Should we go see Lydia now? I have to meet with a study group in a couple hours."

Marcy nodded, so Harper grabbed her purse, and they walked out into the hall.

"You're taking this whole college thing way too seriously," Marcy said, as Harper locked the dorm room behind her.

"Did you go to college?" Harper asked once they'd started walking down the hall, past the other dorm rooms.

"Yeah, for a year," Marcy said. "I went to this New Age college in Arizona. They had no grades. I thought it would be awesome, but they kept making me talk about my feelings. I did learn how to play disc golf, so it wasn't a total loss."

"What did you go for?" Harper asked.

"I don't know. They didn't really have majors, but I was

working for a degree in sunshine or something. It clearly wasn't for me."

"Clearly," Harper agreed, as they reached the elevator. Ordinarily, she would've taken the stairs, but she knew that Marcy wouldn't be up for it.

When they got to the lobby, they walked onto the campus lawn. Some of the maples had already begun turning orange and yellow, but the air still held the warmth of summer instead of the crispness of fall.

They made their way over to visitors' parking and got into Marcy's aging Gremlin. The air didn't work, but she'd left the windows down, and a few leaves had made their way inside. The car sputtered and jerked as Marcy tried to start it.

"We could've taken my car, you know," Harper pointed out.

"Lucinda will do it. Give her time." Marcy turned the key again, and finally her car roared to life. "There we go."

Within a few minutes, they arrived at Cherry Lane Books. The town seemed to be bustling a lot more now that school had started. The closest parking spot Marcy could find was nearly a block down, and she had to parallel park, which Lucinda did not seem to enjoy.

The windows on the bookstore were tinted too dark for Harper to see through, and the arch above the door creaked as she pushed the door open. There was almost a spooky air about the place, which made it all the more strange that such a cheerful little pixie ran it.

"Hey, guys!" Lydia beamed at them as Harper and Marcy came inside. She was carrying a stack of Edward Gorey books to the children's section, but she walked to the front of the store. "How are you doing?"

"I got off work early, so I'm doing pretty fantastic," Marcy said, sounding about as happy as Marcy was capable of sounding.

"You guys can have a seat if you want." Lydia gestured to a children's sitting area while she placed the books on the shelves.

There was a child-sized chair shaped like a dragon across from a My Little Pony recliner. In between them was a Lego table, where kids could play. Marcy chose the dragon chair, which was much too short for her, and she began shifting around to get comfortable. Harper sat on the floor, crossing her legs underneath.

"I'm sorry I don't have much to tell you," Lydia apologized. "This translation is ridiculous."

Harper couldn't help the sinking feeling in the pit of her stomach. She didn't realize how much she'd been hoping Lydia could really help them until the hope began to fade.

"I need to explain why this process is taking so long," Lydia said, and sat down in the My Little Pony chair, which seemed to fit her petite frame almost perfectly. The bright purple flower she wore in her hair was coming loose, and she tucked it back behind her ear.

"English didn't exist back then," Lydia went on. "Even if something translates to an 'a,' it's not necessarily the same kind of way we use an 'a,' and the words are in an entirely different language, and once I figure that out, I then need to translate them again into English.

"The problem is that I don't think it's written in just *one* language, and it appears to be some kind of slang as well," Lydia elaborated. "Unfortunately, back in the day, they weren't real constant about language or grammar, so it can get pretty tricky."

"I can't say I'm not disappointed, but I guess I'm not surprised," Harper admitted. "What about Achelous and Demeter? Were you able to find out anything on them?"

"I still have feelers out, but so far, it's not looking good." Lydia shook her head. "The last anybody was in contact with Achelous seems to be about two hundred years ago, then he just fell off the map. I'm not sure if he went into hiding or what, but he hasn't been confirmed dead."

"I've been meaning to ask you. How does one become confirmed dead?" Marcy asked.

"Two or more immortals must see your remains shortly after you're dead. If they can see you die also, that's a bonus," Lydia answered.

"How come only immortals can confirm it?" Marcy asked.

"Most mortals don't know what they're looking at. Humans don't have a good grasp on the magical, so they might think they're seeing a werewolf die when it's just a crazy hairy guy. Or they might think it's a human dying, when really it's Athena."

"*I* would be able to tell the difference," Marcy said definitively.

"Maybe you would, but experts only trust testimony from other immortals," Lydia said.

"What about Demeter?" Harper asked.

"She's even trickier," Lydia said. "She's been off the grid for a very long time. Something really spooked her, and she hasn't interacted with any other immortals in centuries."

Harper raised an eyebrow. "Something spooked her?"

"I've heard that it was Achelous' daughters. I know that the sirens are his daughters, but that's not how my source referred to them. I'm assuming that they are one and the same, but I don't like passing off assumptions as fact."

"So what did Achelous' daughters have to do with Demeter?" Harper asked.

"They were trying to kill her," Lydia explained. "They hate her. Demeter doesn't have a lot of enemies because she's the goddess of earth and growth and helped people farm and raise families. She's a nice one. So she stayed above the surface for most of her existence, but then, once she had a target on her back, she went underground the way a lot of gods have. Hades has been off the grid since almost the beginning of time."

"Wait, wait, wait." Marcy waved her hands to stop Lydia. "Hades is still alive?"

Lydia nodded. "Yeah. He lives in Iceland."

Marcy put her hand to her chin and seemed to think about that. "Interesting."

"If he's off the grid, how come you know where he is?" Harper asked.

"Nobody messes with him there. He's lived there for like five hundred years. He has a quiet life now," Lydia said. "And Demeter did pop up for a while in Asia, but I'm not sure if she's still there. When I find her, I'll tell you.

"In the meantime, I do have more bad news about the muses." Lydia frowned. "I thought they were all *probably* dead, but the last two that I thought had any chance of being alive—Erato and Polyhymnia—have been confirmed dead. Sorry."

"How many muses were there?" Marcy asked.

"Nine originally," Lydia said. "The first one died fifteen hundred years ago, and they've been dropping off ever since. The last one died only fifty years ago, and she lived right in Maryland. The sirens might have been looking for her when they came to Capri."

"Why would they be looking for a muse?" Harper asked.

"Muses keep secrets. Their lovers were gods and immortals, and they would divulge all their hidden truths. A muse might know where Demeter is, or Achelous, or how to break a curse, or any of a million other things the sirens might want to know."

"You think a muse would know how to break the curse?" Harper asked.

"Possibly." Lydia wagged her head from side to side, like she was skeptical. "But we'll never know. When the last muse died, she took all her secrets with her."

"Why would the sirens come to Capri for a dead muse?" Marcy asked.

"They didn't know she was dead," Lydia said. "It takes a while for news to travel in supernatural circles. It's not like they can post things on Twitter. And Thalia was the last one, so they'd—"

"What? *Thalia?*" Harper cut her off. "The last muse's name was Thalia?"

"Yes, she was the muse of comedy," Lydia said, looking confused by Harper's reaction.

Harper had read about the muses a hundred times, but somehow, all their names had become a blur in her mind. She hadn't been focusing on the ones who weren't related to the sirens, so she'd almost completely overlooked Thalia.

But it had stayed somewhere in the back of her mind. That's why the name sounded so familiar when she was looking at pictures of Bernie's wedding. And now it all came together.

"Bernie's wife was named Thalia," Harper said, speaking rapidly. "She died in 1961 or '62. That's like fifty years ago."

"You're talking about Bernie of Bernie's Island fame?" Marcy asked. "That could just be a coincidence, Harper."

"It could be, but . . ." Harper shook her head, thinking of what Professor Pine had said yesterday about things being too coincidental. "It's not. Bernie always used to say that his wife inspired him to build that cabin for her. I think he even referred to her as his muse before, but I just didn't put it together until now."

"How did Thalia the muse die?" Marcy asked.

"I'm not completely sure," Lydia said. "She was mortal, and it was natural causes."

"That's Thalia McAllister!" Harper persisted. "She died falling off a ladder after she'd married Bernie. She probably became mortal for him."

"Muses have done that," Lydia said. "Fall in love, get married, become mortal, then die. That's part of the reason why there aren't any left."

"She might have known how to break the curse?" Harper asked, the excitement making her voice high.

"She might have, yes. But that won't really help now," Lydia told her sadly.

"Daniel found a bunch of papers and old photographs in Bernie's house. Bernie had hidden them up in the attic. He didn't want people to find them. Dad said that Bernie had told him that eventually someone would come looking for him, probably sirens. Dad just thought Bernie was being superstitious and paranoid, but he was right."

"The destruction of a curse isn't the kind of thing Thalia would've written down, and she wouldn't have had to," Lydia explained. "A muse's memory is practically eidetic."

"But this is it," Harper insisted, and got up. "This could be our chance. I have to get home to look through Bernie's stuff."

"No, you have to go to your study group." Marcy tried to stand up, but it was more of a struggle since she was wedged into the dragon chair. Harper took her hand and helped pull her to her feet. "I can go to your house, and me, Gemma, and your dad can go through Bernie's stuff. If it's in there, we'll find it."

"Fine," Harper agreed grudgingly. "I trust you. But you have to call me the second you find anything."

"Harper, I wouldn't get your hopes too high." Lydia stood up and looked at Harper gravely. "There might be something useful in her papers, but it's very unlikely that she'll have the instructions on how to break something that I'm not even sure can be broken."

"We have to try, though," Harper said. "Thank you for everything, Lydia."

She practically ran out of the shop, and Marcy struggled to keep up with her since Marcy was completely opposed to jogging. As they walked down to the car, Harper slowed enough for Marcy to keep up.

"Oh, my god," Marcy said. "It's like Christmas morning."

"It's better than Christmas!" Harper shouted, unable to stop herself. "We could be free of those psychotic witches once and for all. Wouldn't that be amazing?"

"Yeah, it certainly would," Marcy agreed.

"This might really be it, Marcy."

Marcy sighed. "It might be, but it's probably not that simple."

EIGHT

Ransack

"Well, this clearly isn't working," Marcy said, as Daniel dangled his legs through the hole in his ceiling.

He'd been crawling around in the narrow attic above his house. The only way in or out of the attic was through a square doorway in the ceiling above his closet, and he slid through it before dropping to the ground.

"Sorry, Gemma," Daniel said as he brushed dust and cobwebs off his clothes. "There's nothing up there but mouse poop and a skeleton from a bat, which was actually pretty creepy."

"Nice," Marcy said, nodding in approval.

Gemma leaned past Daniel and peered up into the darkness, as if she'd be able to spy something that he hadn't been able to see with a flashlight.

The whole time Daniel had been searching his attic, Marcy had been sitting on his queen-sized bed. While he was out of sight, she'd taken the liberty of going through his nightstand drawers. Now that he was back, she was absently leafing through the worn copy of *The Old Man and the Sea* he had on his nightstand.

"Have you even read this?" Marcy asked Daniel, and gestured to the book. "I bet you haven't even read it. I bet you put it on the nightstand so people would think you're smart. Do you think Hemingway impresses Harper?"

"No, I think that was my grandfather's book, and I have read it," Daniel said. "Twice."

"I have *101 Ways to Live Longer* on my nightstand, so if I die in my sleep, when the paramedics or mortician or whoever come in, they'll see it, and be all, 'Well, I guess that book didn't work,' and they'll have a good laugh," Marcy said. "It's important to laugh in times like that."

"Are you sure you didn't miss anything?" Gemma asked. She was standing on her tiptoes and leaning on the T-shirts Daniel had hanging in his closet.

"I looked in every nook and cranny," Daniel assured her. "There's nothing up there."

Gemma sighed. "There has to be something we missed."

"Why? Why does there have to be something we missed?" Marcy asked.

"Because." Gemma stepped out of Daniel's closet and ran a hand through her hair. "If Thalia was a muse, there just *has* to be something, and I looked through all her papers last night—"

"I know," Marcy said, without looking up from Daniel's book. "I was there. I helped, remember?"

After the visit to Cherry Lane Books, Harper had called

Gemma and instructed her to immediately start going through the box of Bernie's stuff she'd left in her bedroom. Gemma did as she was told, and when Marcy returned from Sundham, she joined Gemma.

They'd spent hours going through the box, making sure to look over and analyze every scrap of paper for any possible clue or hint to Thalia's true nature. Unfortunately, it all ended up being fairly ordinary.

It seemed to be Bernie's collection of Thalia's things, his memories of her, and not any of her actual stuff. Mostly it was photographs, wedding programs, and newspaper clippings about their marriage and about Bernie buying the island and building the cabin. He'd even pressed flowers from her bridal bouquet and a few from her funeral.

Nothing pointed to her being a muse or supernatural at all, and there was definitely nothing about how to break the curse or kill the sirens.

"My point is that there has to be something," Gemma said.

"You keep saying that, but I don't get why there *has* to be anything," Marcy reiterated.

"Marcy, can you give it a rest with the negative commentary?" Daniel asked.

"I'm not trying to be a bitch. I just really don't understand," Marcy said.

"Penn, Lexi, and Thea ransacked this house looking for something." Gemma turned to Daniel. "You remember that night back in June, when I ran off with the sirens? We came out here because *they* were out here. They killed Bernie, and they were tearing his house apart."

"You think they killed Bernie because they were trying to find Thalia's notes or whatever?" Daniel asked.

"Right. They *believed* that something was here," Gemma said. "I think that's why they came to Capri in the first place. Looking for something in this house. And I'm not saying that it will break the curse, but it's something they thought was important."

"Are you sure they haven't already found it?" Marcy asked, setting Daniel's book on the bed next to her.

"I don't think so." Gemma furrowed her brow, trying to remember that night. "When I got here, they were still going through stuff. I think Thea was digging around in the kitchen. If they'd found what they were looking for, they wouldn't have still been searching."

"But they left without it," Daniel said. "And Penn's been back to the island a few times, and she hasn't looked for anything."

"Penn's been back?" Gemma asked, and he immediately lowered his eyes and scratched the back of his head. "Like, to visit?"

Daniel shifted his weight from one foot to the other. "It's not like I can just tell her to get lost."

"Actually, you can," Gemma said.

"Not if I want to keep the peace." He looked at her then, his hazel eyes imploring her to understand. "We both do what we need to do to keep the people we care about safe. Right?"

"Yeah but . . ." Gemma trailed off. "Does Harper know about this?"

"Does Harper know about all the things you're up to?" Daniel countered.

Gemma sighed and stared up at the ceiling. Of course Harper didn't know everything. In fact, Gemma knew about Penn's interest in Daniel, and she'd specifically chosen not to tell her sister about it. She trusted him not to do anything to hurt Harper, and telling her sister would only make her worry.

But Gemma hadn't known that Penn was *visiting* him. That changed things. Gemma kept things from Harper that would only scare her—not things that could actually hurt her.

"So . . . what's going on with you and Penn?" Marcy asked.

"Nothing." Daniel shook his head. "She just has a crush on me or something, and I tolerate it because I don't want to piss her off."

"Tolerate it how?" Marcy asked. "With sex?"

"Marcy." Daniel scoffed, but he lowered his eyes again.

"Daniel," Gemma said firmly, and moved so he'd have to look at her. "We made a deal, remember? We said we'd tell each other everything, so we could have each other's backs."

"No, that wasn't the deal." He shook his head. "The deal was that *you'd* tell me everything so I could have your back. I can handle myself, but really, there's nothing to handle." He forced a smile. "Nothing's going on."

"But if something is . . ." Gemma paused, choosing her words carefully. "If something happens. You can tell Harper. She'll understand."

"I know," Daniel said. "I do, and I will, if anything does happen. But right now, I can't bother her. She's got way too much on her plate, with school and all the siren stuff."

"Yeah, and don't forget her roommate from hell," Marcy added.

Gemma turned back to Marcy, relieved by a break in the tension. "Oh, you mean Liv?"

"Yeah." Marcy tilted her head, looking confused. "I thought you said she was nice when you met her."

"She seemed nice enough," Daniel agreed. "Kinda forgettable, I guess, since I don't remember her that well."

"She's a siren now, so she's a bit more memorable," Gemma said.

"*What?*" Daniel asked.

"She's what?" Marcy asked, almost in unison with Daniel.

"How long has she been a siren?" Daniel demanded. "You let Harper live with a siren?"

"No, no." Gemma shook her head and raised her hands defensively. "Liv hasn't been a siren that long. A week, tops. But she moved out on Tuesday, and that's when I found out she was a siren. So I haven't told Harper."

"Why wouldn't you tell Harper?" Daniel asked with mystified anger.

"Because Liv was gone and out of her hair, and I didn't want to worry Harper about there being another siren," Gemma hurried to explain. "I thought I'd tell her this weekend, when she's home, so I can make sure she doesn't freak out."

"Well, you should have told her sooner," Marcy said. "Liv

was a total psycho. She like trashed the room and attacked Harper."

"What?" Gemma asked, and it was her turn to sound shocked. "When?"

"What are you talking about?" Daniel asked.

"I don't know. I think . . . Tuesday or something?" Marcy shrugged. "You guys really need to talk to each other. This whole keeping-secrets thing is bullshit."

"I'm not trying to keep secrets," Gemma said. "She's already under so much stress, I just don't want to add anything on top of it."

"Why didn't she tell me about it?" Daniel asked no one in particular.

"Probably for the same reason you haven't told her about Penn's visiting you," Gemma said.

Marcy sat up straighter, and her blank expression seemed to brighten. "I just realized that I'm the only one completely in the loop. I know everything that's going on around here."

"I'm pretty sure that's not true," Daniel said.

"Wanna bet? Try me," Marcy said.

"Okay." Daniel thought for a minute before asking, "Where are more papers from Thalia?"

"I don't know." Marcy raised one shoulder in a half shrug. "In some secret hidden space."

"Thanks for illuminating that for us," Gemma said dryly. "It's really helpful."

"No really, what if there's a secret space that's not out in the open," Marcy expounded on her earlier statement. "You bend a candlestick to the side, and a door pops open, or you move a book, and the bookcase twirls around to reveal a hidden chamber. That kinda thing."

Daniel crossed his arms over his chest. "Since this is a one-bedroom cabin, and not a mansion, and every square foot is accounted for, I don't think that's an option."

"Then try under a loose floorboard or something," Marcy suggested. "That's where I hid all my personal items when I still lived at home with my parents."

"Are there loose floorboards?" Gemma looked up at Daniel.

"I don't know." He shook his head. "I guess we'll look."

The three of them split up to search for loose floorboards or any kind of "secret" nook they might have missed in the house. Marcy attempted to take Daniel's bedroom, but he shooed her out and suggested she try the living room.

Gemma went into the bathroom and tried to peel back any loose tiles. She didn't find anything, but she did manage to break a porcelain tile in half. She was on her hands and knees, looking for any loose boards in the kitchen, when she heard Marcy swear.

"Did you find something?" Gemma asked, and she instantly got to her feet so she could look over the kitchen counter.

"No." Marcy was kneeling beside the couch and scowling at her fingers. "But I got a splinter trying to pull a board up."

"I don't think there's anything under there." Daniel sighed. He came out of his bedroom and shook his head sadly. "I haven't noticed anything loose or creaking, and I think this is a dead end. And you have to be at the theater soon for the play."

"Dammit." She'd forgotten, and she dug her cell phone out of her pocket to check the time. "I have at least another ten minutes before I need to leave here. Let's just keep looking."

Marcy stood up. "Is there anyplace we haven't looked?"

"I don't know." Daniel glanced around his living room.

"What about that?" Marcy asked. She'd started sucking on her finger, presumably in an attempt to remove the splinter, but she pointed to the fireplace with her free hand.

"What?" Gemma asked.

"In the fireplace." Marcy took her finger out of her mouth so she'd be easier to understand. "That stone's a different shade of gray."

The whole fireplace was done up in large river rocks. Most of them were varying shades of light to medium gray, smoothed and polished to look nice. But one stone near the end of the mantel was a very dark gray with a bluish tone to it.

"Did you replace that stone or something?" Gemma asked Daniel, but she could already feel her heartbeat speeding up.

"No, I didn't." He shook his head and walked over to the fireplace, with Gemma right at his heels.

Slowly, almost gingerly, Daniel touched the stone. He started to wiggle it, and at first, nothing happened. Then he started pushing and pulling at it harder until it finally began to budge. As he started to slide the stone out, Gemma held her breath.

"Here." He handed it to her, then he reached into the dark hole left in the fireplace and began to dig around. "I found something."

"What is it?" Gemma asked.

"I don't know. I think . . ." He let his sentence trail off as he pulled out a small, leather-bound book. "It's a book."

"Oh, my gosh." Gemma nearly dropped the stone trying to take it from him, but Daniel caught the rock and set it on the ground. He stood behind her, peering over her shoulder as she flipped through it.

As soon as she saw the words, she knew. The small, delicate cursive matched the handwriting on the back of some of the pictures they'd gotten from Bernie's house.

"'On June 16, 1961, I married my one true love, Bernard McAllister,'" Gemma read aloud. "This is it, you guys. This is Thalia's journal."

"I told you I know everything," Marcy said.

"Does it say anything else?" Daniel asked. "Like anything about sirens?"

"I don't know." Gemma flipped through the pages with trembling hands, scanning the faded ink on the yellowed pages. "It seems to be a lot of day-to-day stuff. Their garden. How much she loves Bernie."

Then Gemma flipped to the back, and her heart sank.

The journal had been divided up into three sections—a calendar at the front, the journal pages in the middle, and a "notes" section in the back, for important information, like birthdays and addresses.

Writing covered the last section, written over the typed words, in the margins, sideways, to the ends of the pages and off them. Thalia had completely filled it . . . and all of it was written in symbols and shapes—a language that Gemma didn't understand.

"Crap," Gemma said. "It's in Greek or something again."

"Maybe it can help Lydia with the translation she's working on," Marcy suggested.

"We could bring it out to her tonight," Gemma said. "See if she can make anything out of it."

"You can't," Daniel said. He'd been reading over her shoulder, but he took a step back now.

"What? Why not?" Gemma asked.

"*The Taming of the Shrew* opens tonight. Remember?" he asked.

She waved him off. "No, I have an understudy or something. I need to stay and read this."

"No, you need to go be in the play," Daniel said.

"That's insane." Gemma shook her head. "This could be the piece we've been looking for."

"You can't even understand all of it," Daniel said. "And if you skip the play, Thea and Penn will know something's up, and that could be bad news. You don't want them breathing down your neck while you're trying to figure out this journal."

Gemma sighed. "Good point."

"Thank you," Daniel said. "Now come on. I'll take you guys back to the mainland."

Gemma grumbled, but she did as she was told. On the boat ride back, she sat down in the sleeping quarters, safely away from the spray that might damage Thalia's journal. She sat cross-legged on the bed and decided to read the parts she could decipher, and she started from the beginning.

In big letters in blotchy dark ink, Thalia had written an important inscription on the back of the front cover:

Elegy

My dearest Bernard—if ANYTHING happens to me, you need to dispose of this. Nobody can ever find the secrets I've kept within these pages. It could be dangerous if in the wrong hands. For your safety, please destroy this.

NINE

Understudy

Behind the closed door emblazoned with a fallen starlet's name, Gemma leaned in front of the mirror, applying thick eyeliner. Outside in the hall, she could hear people scrambling around to get ready for the first show, starting in twenty minutes.

In the reflection, Gemma glanced over at Thea. Like Gemma, Thea already had her costume on, but unlike Gemma, she already had all her makeup on, too. Her crimson hair was piled up in loose curls, and her lipstick was nearly the same shade.

"Are you nervous?" Thea asked when her emerald eyes met Gemma's in the mirror.

"What?" Gemma lowered her eyes and pretended to dig around for her blush in the oversized makeup case that sat on the counter. "No. Not really."

"Good." Thea leaned forward, inspecting her reflection more closely, and tucked back a curl that had fallen loose. "You don't need to be. Even if you forget a line or botch a scene, everyone will still love you."

"How does that work?" Gemma asked. "Will the whole audience be completely enraptured with you and me?"

Thea shrugged and sat back in her chair. "If we were singing, maybe. But by now you have to understand it. We have a natural talent for attracting attention, but when you project and try, your charms are that much more charming."

"Let's say you were trying. Could you captivate the whole crowd?" Gemma asked as she applied her blush more heavily than she normally would. The lights from the stage required darker makeup to show up.

"If I wanted to, yes." Thea's eyes narrowed behind her long lashes. "What are you getting at? Are you planning on raising a small army?"

"No. I just don't completely understand how the siren song works." Gemma set aside her makeup and turned to face Thea directly, so they weren't talking to each other through the mirror.

"It's simple. You sing, you control whoever hears the song."

"But for how long?" Gemma asked, trying to keep her words from sounding as desperate and hopeful as they felt.

Ever since her heated visit with Alex yesterday, Gemma hadn't been able to stop thinking about what it meant. Why did kissing him seem to have a positive effect on him? And why wasn't he angry and filled with hate anymore?

She'd assumed that once the siren song was in place, it would be that way forever. But with Alex, something else was going on.

Unless, of course, it was just as she'd feared, and Alex had fallen out of love with her on his own.

"It depends. The more you mean it, the more you project, the longer the effects of the song will be active," Thea explained.

"But eventually they will fade?" Gemma pressed.

"Sorta." Thea shook her head, like that wasn't exactly how she would put it. "Like with Sawyer. Penn told him that he loved her, and he had to give us his house. If he hadn't died, and she'd left him, eventually he would've stopped being infatuated and obsessed with her. But he would still believe the house was hers even if he lived to be ninety."

Gemma leaned back in her seat, letting out a crestfallen breath. "I don't understand. If he was still following her orders, and she ordered him to love her, how is he able to stop?"

"The siren song is all about giving orders. Do this, don't do that, give me this, go there," Thea elaborated. "But Demeter made it precisely so it had no effect over the heart. It can't change who a person is. If you hate peach cobbler, the siren song can make you eat it, even smile as you chow it down, but you'll never actually like it."

"But what if you keep eating peach cobbler? Will you remember you hate it?" Gemma asked.

"If there's not a siren constantly whispering in your ear, telling you that you love it, then yes, you probably would." Thea paused, and when she spoke again, her voice was lower and huskier than normal. "Love and hate are very powerful emotions that sirens have no control over, no matter how much Penn likes to pretend we do."

"So when Penn commanded Sawyer to love her, he never really did," Gemma said, affirming what she'd always known. As soon as she'd been cursed, the sirens had told her that mortal men could never love them. "He just acted the way a person in love with her would act."

"And Penn does know that. She just finds that people are easier to control when they believe they're in love with her."

"Your heart doesn't change. You still love or don't love who you always have," Gemma said to herself, her words quiet and breathy, and Thea cocked her head.

Yes, the sirens told her that men would never love her, but Alex had. He'd been able to because he always had, and maybe he still did. The siren song couldn't change the way he felt about her, and when she kissed him, it helped remind him of how he really felt, of who he really was, and it dragged him out from underneath the fog of the spell.

After all of this, he might still love her, and as the realization hit Gemma, she couldn't help but smile.

A loud knocking interrupted her elation, and she turned to see her dad pushing open the *Marilyn* door to the dressing room.

"I hope we're not intruding," Harper said as she squeezed in beside their dad.

He nearly gasped when Gemma smiled up at him, and his words were barely audible when he said, "You look so much like Nathalie."

She lowered her eyes, and her cheeks flushed a little. "Aw, thanks, Dad."

Thea looked at Harper in the mirror, her green eyes flat. "Hello, Gemma's family."

"Hey, Thea." Harper smiled thinly at her.

"Hello, Thea," Brian said, nearly growling at her, and Gemma saw his hand clench into a fist at his side.

Brian knew what Thea was now, that she and Penn were sirens. His natural instinct was to yell at them and tell them to leave his daughter alone, but since their siren song could still work on him, Harper and Gemma tried to get him to interact with them as little as possible. That was hard for him sometimes, especially at times like this, when all he really wanted to do was wring Thea's neck.

"I'd invite you in, but it's so crowded." Gemma gestured over to Thea, but it was their costumes hanging along the wall that took up the most space in the cramped room. "Did Marcy talk to you?"

"Yeah, yeah," Harper said quickly, probably not wanting Thea to catch on that they were talking about finding Thalia's journal. The less Thea knew about what they were doing, the safer it would be for her if Penn were to question her. "Marcy's here, actually."

Marcy had been lingering in the hall since it was so crowded in the dressing room, but she leaned around the doorframe. "Are you gonna yak?"

"No, Marcy, I don't think I'm going to throw up, but thanks for that lovely euphemism." Gemma smirked.

"Marcy, why don't you and my dad go find our seats? I want to sneak back behind the sets and say hello to Daniel real quick," Harper said.

"Good idea. We'll let you finish getting ready." Brian turned back to Gemma. "Knock 'em dead, sweetie." He bent down and kissed her quickly on the temple before departing.

"We just wanted to wish you good luck," Harper said, and started backing out the doorway.

"Thanks, Harper." Gemma smiled gratefully up at her.

"You can wait here for one minute," Penn insisted from out in the hall. Under her usual sultry velvet tone, Gemma could hear the irritation in it, and she stood up so she could look past Harper out to the hallway.

It wasn't until Penn pushed past the assistant director and reached the doorway to the dressing room that Gemma finally understood why. Liv was trailing at her heels, her large eyes looking petulant and her mouth turned down in a tight scowl, and Gemma's heart froze in her chest.

"Oh, good, you're all here." Penn's face flushed with relief, her full lips turned up into a smile, then her dark eyes settled on Harper. "I think you two know each other, so it'd be fine if Liv waited here with you, right?"

"I . . ." Harper trailed off, too stunned to say anything, and her hand went to her throat.

"Great!" Penn clapped her hands together, then turned to Liv. "Stay here. Don't move at all. I just wanna go backstage for a minute, and I don't need you getting in my way."

Liv rolled her eyes. "Whatever." Once Penn was gone, disappearing into the crowd in the hallway, Liv turned back to Harper. Her irritation melted away, and her aw-shucks grin spread across her face.

"Liv?" Harper asked once she found her voice. "What are you doing here?"

"Just coming to see the play with Penn," Liv told her in a voice that was all peaches and cream. "How are you doing?"

"Who the hell cares how I'm doing?" Harper hissed. "What are you doing here?"

"Notice anything different about me?" Liv asked, then twirled around for her.

Harper gaped at Liv, and the color drained from her face. "You're the new siren."

"Sorry, Harper, I was gonna tell you," Gemma offered lamely.

Harper stepped into the dressing room, deliberately leaving Liv alone in the hall before slamming the door shut behind her. Harper crossed her arms over her chest and glared down at Gemma, making her feel small and guilty.

"How long has my college roommate been a siren?" Harper asked, her tone harsh.

"Former roommate," Thea corrected her. "She dropped out because she sucks."

Gemma shrugged, trying to seem calm and nonchalant. "I don't know when she became a siren. A few days ago?"

"It was on Friday," Thea supplied.

"Harper." Gemma took a deep breath and looked at her apologetically. "I'm sorry I didn't tell you about Liv being a siren sooner. But I have to be onstage in like ten minutes, so can we talk about this later?"

"Whatever. Fine." Harper sighed.

"As soon as the after-party wraps up."

"An after-party?" Harper raised an eyebrow.

Gemma waved her hands, trying to emphasize that it was no big thing. "Yeah, the mayor's putting on this whole big thing because his son is in the play, and I'm going."

"You can come, too, if you want," Thea said. "Friends and family of the cast are invited."

"Thanks, *Thea*," Harper said, giving Gemma a hard look since she hadn't bothered to extend the invitation.

Gemma looked up at her, her eyes pleading with her. "Can you please go find your seat, and we'll talk about this later?"

"Okay. Fine." Harper tried to put aside her anger and took a deep breath. "You look nice. And good luck."

"Thank you." Gemma smiled up at her, and Harper left her to finish getting ready.

TEN

Revelry

This was the last place Gemma wanted to be. She should be at home, going through Thalia's journal or trying to decipher the scroll. But even if there weren't far more pressing matters waiting for her elsewhere, she still wouldn't have wanted to come to the after-party.

"They have an ice sculpture?" Marcy asked, eyeing the frozen swan on the center of the hors d'oeuvres table. "Who has an ice sculpture at a summer event?"

"I don't know," Gemma said. "But you know the deal—we just have to stay here long enough for Penn to see us, so I look like I'm acting normal and having a good time. Then we can bail."

Once the play had finished, and Gemma had gotten changed into her regular clothes, she and Marcy walked over to the hotel while Harper stayed behind to wait for Daniel. Mayor Crawford had rented out the ballroom and had it all done up for the party.

It had been decorated with twinkling lights and bouquets of flowers on each table, along with the ice swan.

"Where is she anyway?" Marcy asked. "Or Thea or Liv, for that matter?"

"I don't know," Gemma admitted, and made her way toward the appetizer table, smiling politely at an older woman who told her she'd done a great job in the play. "With my luck, they're probably not even coming, and I showed up for no reason. Maybe we should just bail."

"No way. I just got a plateful of shrimp." She held up her plate to show Gemma. "I'm staying. Do you think the drinks are free?"

"No clue." Gemma'd picked up a plate, so she grabbed a couple crab puffs.

As she was leaving the table, a couple other people came up to congratulate her on her performance. She thanked them, but as soon as they were gone, she made a beeline for the edge of the room, where she could linger in the dim light without having to make small talk, and Marcy followed her, probably also equally happy to avoid it.

"Oh well," Marcy said through a mouthful of shrimp. "I shouldn't drink anyway. It'll probably end up just like my prom, which would be fitting since this looks exactly like my prom. It was even held here."

"You went to prom?" Gemma asked in surprise.

Marcy shrugged. "It was a different time back then."

"That was like seven years ago."

"Eight," Marcy corrected her.

"It can't be *that* different," Gemma insisted.

"Oh, look, there are your friends." Marcy pointed as they arrived.

Even though Thea was technically a guest of honor at the party, Penn led the way, striding into the room like she was a model on the runway. Thea and Liv flanked her on either side, and Thea looked as unhappy to be there as Gemma felt.

"Do you want me to pretend to laugh, so it looks like we're having fun?" Marcy asked when Penn looked over, winking at Gemma.

Gemma shook her head. "No, I think I'm okay."

In the center of the room, there was a small platform set up, sitting about a foot off the ground. When Gemma had gone to a homecoming dance here, that's where the band had played. There wasn't one playing now, though Sting was wafting out of speakers around the room.

Mayor Adam Crawford climbed onto the platform, holding a flute of champagne in one hand, and his son offered a hand to help steady him as he stepped up. The mayor wasn't particularly overweight, but he had enough of a waddle to his step that it made it hard for him to step up that high.

He clinked his glass, using his wedding band, and the music overhead fell silent.

"It seems like everyone's here, so I just wanted to say a few words before the party really gets under way," Mayor Crawford said, his booming voice carrying easily through the ballroom. "As most of you know, I'm the mayor of this fine town, and this handsome young man is my son, Aiden. You may recognize him from tonight's performance as Petruchio."

He gestured down to Aiden, who stood at the side of the platform. Aiden was actually very attractive, with sandy blond hair and a stunning smile, although his smile wasn't quite what it used to be. He'd had a nasty cut above his lip and a black eye, and while they'd healed up for the most part, there was still a small scar just above his lip.

For a brief moment, Gemma had taken a liking to Aiden, and they'd gone on a date nearly two weeks ago. Afterward, Aiden had assaulted her. Gemma had been ready to let the monster inside her out, but thankfully, before she had, Alex intervened, punching Aiden several times.

"Thanks," Aiden said, smiling his new, slightly crooked smile and waving at the audience as his father talked about him.

"It was a wonderful production, but it wasn't all thanks to my son, of course," Mayor Crawford went on. "Praise goes to the capable director, Tom Wagner, and to the rest of the cast, particularly his costar Thea Triton, who played the contrary Katherine."

He motioned to Thea, and she waved demurely when people clapped for her. She smiled, and it was one of the few genuine smiles Gemma had seen her give. Thea loved performing, and Gemma suspected that the only time she was truly happy was when she was on the stage.

Even as the applause died down, the mayor let his gaze linger on Thea, so long, in fact, that his wife loudly cleared her throat.

"And all of his costars were phenomenal." Mayor Crawford

finally pulled his eyes away from Thea and scanned the crowd. "Are you all here? Why don't you all come up?"

Thea and Aiden climbed onto the platform first since they were the closest, but the rest of the cast and even the crew started making their way up, crowding around the mayor. But Gemma stayed where she was, picking at her crab puffs.

"I think you're supposed to go up there," Marcy told her.

"I'm fine here."

"You should go up there," Marcy persisted. "You want to look normal, don't you?"

Gemma sighed and handed her plate over to Marcy. "Fine."

She slid through the crowd until she made her way to the platform. There was hardly enough room on it, so she stayed on the floor, standing next to the platform even though Thea motioned for her to join them onstage.

"Isn't this a wonderful cast we've got here?" Mayor Crawford asked, alternating between beaming at his son and staring at Thea. "I hope all of you enjoyed tonight's performance of *The Taming of the Shrew,* and if you did, you can tell your friends, because there are three more shows this weekend."

The mayor looped one arm around Aiden's shoulders and his other arm around Thea's waist as he continued, "Not to mention that At Summer's End is kicking off. Tomorrow, in addition to more performances of the play, there's a fish fry at noon at the Bayside Park Pavilion and a regatta at Anthemusa Bay at four."

He continued to list all the events going on this week, trying to get everyone pumped up for the At Summer's End Festival.

As he talked, Gemma kept her eyes on Penn and Liv. Penn was doing something on her phone, and Liv stared up at the stage with rapt interest. Her lips were pulled back in a wide smile, and as Gemma watched, her teeth lengthened and grew.

At first, Gemma thought Liv's gaze was fixed on the mayor, which seemed kinda gross to her. But as soon as the mayor had finished, and the music came back on the speakers, Liv rushed toward Aiden.

Seeing her fangs out, Gemma feared the worst—that Liv's new siren appetite had gotten the best of her, and she was about to devour Aiden right in front of everyone.

Gemma was just about to dive between them to stop that from happening, but a split second before she did, she saw that Liv's teeth were back to normal. When she smiled up at Aiden as she put her hand on his arm, she looked human.

Even with his new scars, Aiden was still gorgeous. Not to mention that he was the son of the most powerful family in Capri. And he didn't seem to mind being cornered. Liv had a siren's charms now, and he smiled radiantly at her as she laughed and batted her eyes. Maybe it was her appetite for affection and power that needed to be whetted.

At least for now. Gemma knew exactly the kind of monstrous hunger that lurked just beneath the surface, and Liv didn't seem like the type to go long without being satiated.

"This is some party, huh?" Thea asked as she climbed off the platform, and Gemma turned away from Liv and Aiden to look back at her.

"Yeah, it's something, all right." Gemma walked a few feet away to where it was less crowded, then stopped with Thea to talk. "So are you bringing Liv with you everywhere now?"

"It seems that way." Thea sighed.

"You don't trust her enough to leave her by herself?"

Thea gave her a sidelong glance. "You know how new sirens are."

"I do." Gemma turned to face Thea fully and crossed her arms over her chest. "Which is why I don't understand why she was Harper's roommate."

"That was Penn's idea."

"So Liv was supposed to be some kind of spy?" Gemma pressed.

"Not originally." Thea ran a hand through her long, scarlet hair and refused to meet Gemma's eyes. "Before Penn killed Lexi, Liv was supposed to be your replacement. But after Lexi died and you were still part of the circle, Penn thought it'd be good to have someone on the inside gathering dirt on you."

"And you didn't think that was a bad idea?" Gemma asked, then lowered her voice, trying to make it sound slightly menacing. "I mean, she could gather some dirt on you, too."

Thea finally let her eyes meet Gemma's. "What was I supposed to tell her? 'No, you can't spy on Harper because you'll find out my dirty secrets'?" She shook her head. "I just went with it and hoped the two of you weren't stupid enough to say anything in front of Liv."

"Why wouldn't you just tell me about this?" Gemma asked.

"Penn didn't want me to, and I'm already putting myself at

enough risk helping you, all right?" A flicker of fear shot through Thea's emerald eyes. "I've put my neck out for you much farther than I ever should have, and if this all goes to hell—which I'm certain it will—I need to have my back covered."

"You don't think I can break the curse?" Gemma asked.

Thea looked over to where Penn was still busy on her phone, too distracted and too far away to hear anything they were saying. "As far as I know, the curse is unbreakable."

"Then why'd you even bother to give me the scroll?" Gemma asked, her voice barely above a whisper.

"Honestly? I don't know. I think I was just sick of Penn destroying everything."

"Do you regret giving it to me?" Gemma asked.

"Not yet." Thea paused, then said, "If I live long enough, I might. But soon, it'll be a moot point."

"What do you mean?"

"If that curse isn't broken soon, Liv will destroy us all. But either way, there aren't going to be any sirens around for much longer." Her lips pursed together in a thin smile.

Marcy had been standing on the other side of the room, but she'd refilled her plate with shrimp and made her way over to where Thea and Gemma were talking.

"What are you guys talking about?" Marcy asked through a mouthful of food.

"How much fun this is!" Thea said with far too much exuberance. Then she rolled her eyes and walked away.

Marcy wiped her mouth on the back of her arm. "What was that about?"

"I don't know." Gemma shook her head and sighed. "Everything just kind of sucks right now. And Liv is horrible."

"Duh. She's an evil, murderous sea wench. If she isn't being horrible, then she isn't doing her job."

Gemma knew she was right, and that was the worst part of it.

"So anyway, who's that foxy guy?" Marcy asked and pointed vaguely to the middle of the room.

"What guy?" Gemma asked, glancing in the general direction that Marcy had pointed. "Aiden?"

Marcy scoffed. "No, that guy's a dick. That cute one with the nice butt." She pointed again, and this time it was directly at Kirby Logan. He was at the appetizer table, and he sniffed a cracker before putting it back down.

"Kirby?" Gemma asked.

Marcy nodded. "Yeah, him."

"You're into Kirby?"

"No. Maybe. Why? What's it to you?" Marcy narrowed her eyes at Gemma.

Kirby was cute, so that's not what surprised her about Marcy's liking him. It was mostly just the fact that Marcy liked *anybody* that shocked her. Plus, he was only nineteen, and Marcy was twenty-five. Not that she acted like it.

"Nothing," Gemma said. "He's just like a lot younger than you."

"So? I've always fancied myself a cougar," Marcy declared. "Is he nice?"

"Yeah, he's really sweet." She paused before adding, "He's a pretty good kisser, too."

Marcy wrinkled her nose in disgust. "Gross. You kissed him?"

"We dated for like a minute." Gemma waved it off. "It doesn't count at all. If you're into him, then by all means, have at him."

"Saliva stays in your mouth for three months after you kiss someone, so his mouth is all full of your germs," Marcy said.

"I'm pretty sure that's not true. And even if it is, I'm not all that germy. I promise."

"Whatever." Marcy handed her plate to Gemma, then wiped her hands on her jeans. "I'm going in."

Gemma picked at what little food Marcy had left on her plate and watched as Marcy went up to Kirby. She considered moving closer so she could overhear them because she couldn't imagine how Marcy flirted. But Kirby was a nice enough guy, so it hopefully wouldn't be a total disaster.

ELEVEN

Flirtations

Hey, Gemma," Harper said, and Gemma glanced over to see Harper and Daniel approaching her, hand in hand. "Sorry it took so long for us to get here. Daniel had to clean up and get the set ready for tomorrow."

That's what Harper said, but she lowered her eyes when she said it, and her dark hair looked a little mussed. Daniel's shirt was also buttoned crooked. If Gemma had to guess, she would've said they'd stayed behind a little longer to get in a quick make-out session.

Not that she blamed them. They were new to this long-distance thing, and as much as they both insisted it was fine, being away from each other had to be hard. So it was good when they could get a moment alone together.

"I understand," Gemma said, smiling to herself.

"You were great in the play tonight, by the way," Daniel said. "Or at least you looked that way from backstage."

"Thanks," Gemma said. "The set looked amazing."

"It really did," Penn chimed in, and Gemma had to fight back a groan as Penn smiled up at Daniel. "You are quite the handyman."

Daniel had been here for all of a minute before Penn found him. Gemma didn't completely understand what was going on between the two of them, but whatever it was, it couldn't be good. She trusted Daniel not to do anything to hurt Harper, but Penn's interest in him was definitely getting more intense.

"Hello, Penn," Harper said, smiling tightly at her. She'd been holding Daniel's hand, but he let go and moved away from her slightly. "I didn't know you were coming to this party."

"I wouldn't miss it for the world." Penn winked at Daniel, who shifted uncomfortably. "So how are your studies going, Harper?"

"Better, now that you've taken my roommate off my hands. It's much quieter." Harper kept smiling at her. "So thanks for the favor."

"You know me." Penn's tone got even more seductive than normal. "I love to serve."

"I think I'm gonna go get a soda," Daniel said, taking a step away. "Do you want anything, Harper?"

"A bottled water, please," she said.

"I'd like a glass of wine," Penn told him before he'd escaped.

He hesitated, glancing between Harper and Penn, then asked, "What kind?"

Penn smiled broadly. "Red. Merlot."

"I'm not sure if the bartender will serve me without ID, but

I'll see what I can come up with," Daniel said, and hurried away to the bar.

"Your boyfriend is very eager to please," Penn told Harper as she stared after Daniel.

"Liv seems eager, too," Gemma interjected, and pointed to Liv. "She's coming on pretty strong, actually."

She was mostly just trying to change the subject because the tension between Penn, Harper, and Daniel was almost painful. But Liv had gone beyond flirting. She and Aiden were all over each other, and they were still standing right in the middle of the room.

Penn glanced over at Liv. "She can handle herself."

"Aren't you supposed to be babysitting her?" Gemma asked. "If she hasn't fed yet, she's dangerous."

"Trust me, Gemma—she's plenty dangerous even when she has fed," Penn said in a way that made her blood curdle. "If you don't like what she's doing, you can stop her."

"She's not going to listen to me," Gemma countered.

"She's as much your problem now as she is mine," Penn replied coolly. "Remember that."

"How is she Gemma's problem?" Harper asked sharply. She'd probably been trying to bite her tongue, but Penn had gotten to her. "You're the one that made her. Don't you have any sense of responsibility?"

"Not really, no." Penn shook her head. "Liv can kill anyone she wants. She could turn this party into a bloodbath, and I wouldn't care. You're the one with a superiority complex. If you don't like what she's doing, deal with it." She smiled widely at

Harper's apparent shock. "Hell, if she wanted to have a feast tonight, I'd probably join in."

Daniel arrived back, just in time to keep Harper from freaking out on Penn. "Here you go, ladies." He handed the water and the wine to Harper and Penn. "The bartender wasn't going to give it to me, but when I told him it was for you, he obliged, so hopefully it's to your satisfaction."

Penn took a sip, then moaned. "Mmm. You always know how to keep me satisfied."

Daniel cleared his throat. "It was more the bartender that's trying to satisfy you, not me."

"This is getting gross, and I think Liv is going to mount Aiden, so I'm going over there," Gemma said. "Mostly so I can be not here."

She didn't think Penn would kill Harper right in the middle of the room, and she really didn't want to be a part of that ridiculous conversation. Besides that, Liv and Aiden were getting out of hand, and since Penn had no plans to intervene, Gemma knew she had to do something before Liv lost control.

"Oh, yeah?" Aiden whispered, his lips hovering just above Liv's as she pressed her body against his.

"Hey, you two," Gemma said, loudly and forcefully so they'd pay attention to her. "I don't know if you realize this, but you're standing in the middle of a crowded room, practically making out. So maybe you should cool it."

Aiden slowly turned toward her, and he had that familiar glossy look in his brown eyes. It was the same one she'd seen in Sawyer's before, and it made her stomach knot up. Sawyer had been so completely under the sirens' spell, he'd been unable to save himself. Gemma had tried, but it had been too little, too late, and Lexi had murdered him.

"Jealous, Gemma?" Aiden asked with a lazy smile. "You could always join in."

"No, she most certainly cannot," Liv hissed with an ugly venom.

"Sorry." Aiden shook his head. "I don't know why I said that. You should get lost, Gemma."

"I wouldn't have joined in anyway," Gemma said. "What I'm saying is that you're drawing a lot of attention when you should probably be keeping a low profile."

"Why? I'm the star of the play," Aiden said, and that wasn't the siren spell talking. That was the kind of thing Aiden would normally say. "Everyone should look at me, and Liv is the hottest girl in the room."

"Aw." Liv giggled.

"Liv, you had your fun," Gemma said. "Come on. You should spend some time with me, so we can get to know each other. You said you wanted to be friends, right?"

"I've already made a new friend, Gemma," Liv insisted. "And if it's bothering you so much, maybe we should just get a room."

Gemma knew what it was like to be new and ravenous—an uncontrollable hunger gnawing just beneath the surface. Romance and fear both stoked the beast within, but really, if Liv hadn't fed yet, then anything would make her hunger flare and spark the transformation.

The one and only time Gemma had allowed herself to become the monster, it had been terrifying, and it had turned into
a bloody mess. She'd actually been unable to stop it, and she
couldn't let Liv get to the point of no return. Because then it
wouldn't be just Aiden that she'd have to worry about—everyone
in the ballroom would be in danger.

"We're in a hotel, so we can just go right upstairs." Liv bit her
lip as she looked at Aiden.

"Yeah, we could have our own room in a matter of minutes."
Aiden smiled and wrapped his arm around her waist. "Then
nobody could tell us what to do."

"No, that's a horrible idea," Gemma said firmly. "You can't
do that."

"Gemma, we're doing it." Liv tried to step away, but Gemma
moved and blocked her path.

"No, Liv, I don't think you realize what you're saying or how
dangerous it is. You shouldn't be up there alone with him or any
guy."

"I don't think you realize how dangerous I am, Gemma." Liv
ran her tongue along her teeth, so Gemma would notice that her
incisors had gotten more pointed.

Her wide eyes had gone dark, and Gemma realized dourly
that Liv knew exactly what kind of monster she was. Gemma
had never learned how to transform on command because she
never wanted to risk even letting a little bit of the monster out,
but Liv already seemed to understand and embrace it.

If Liv took Aiden up to that hotel room, Gemma was certain

that he wouldn't come back alive. And if Gemma stood in her way, she wasn't completely sure that she'd stay alive, but she had to do something.

"You had your chance, and you weren't into it," Aiden said. "You don't need to be a cock block."

"Aiden may be a huge jerk, but I can't let you do this," Gemma said, her eyes fixed on Liv. "I won't let you hurt him or anybody."

Liv stepped closer to her. "You think you can stop me?"

"I think you need to get yourself under control, or I won't need to stop you," Gemma clarified. "Penn will take care of you the same way she took care of Lexi."

"Please." Liv scoffed. "She hates *you,* not me. And I can get rid of you without lifting a finger." She smiled, then commanded, "Aiden, get rid of her."

Aiden grabbed Gemma's arm, but she instantly got free and glared at him.

"Get your hands off me, Aiden," she snapped. "I am doing this for your own good, but if you touch me again, I will break your arm."

"Is everything okay here?" Daniel asked, approaching them.

"Yeah, it'd be great if Gemma could just get out of the way," Liv said.

"Well, she's not going to." Daniel stood behind Gemma and crossed his arms over his chest. "But more importantly, Penn wants to see you over there."

"She does not," Liv insisted with a whine in her voice, and Gemma glanced back to where Penn stood on the other side of the room. She had that devious smile, the one she got whenever she seemed to enjoy watching Gemma suffer.

"She does," Daniel assured her. "And she asked me to come over here to get you, and if she has to come over here herself, well . . . that wouldn't be good at all."

"Ugh." Liv groaned. "She's worse than my mother."

Aiden tried to follow as she walked away, but Daniel put a hand on his chest and stopped him.

"Dude," Aiden said, giving him a hard look.

"I think it'd be better if you stayed back and cooled off," Daniel said, and he let his arm drop when he was sure that Aiden wouldn't follow him.

Gemma glanced back, watching, as Liv pouted to Penn. For her part, Penn looked annoyed and not at all happy to see Liv, then she turned and trudged toward the door, with Liv trailing behind her.

"This is the worst party ever," Aiden muttered, and walked off in the direction of the bar.

"It totally is," Gemma agreed, and ran a hand through her hair. Then she turned to Daniel. "Penn didn't send you over to retrieve Liv, did she?"

"No, she didn't," Daniel admitted. "Actually, she told me that Liv was your problem, and she hoped that Liv ate Aiden's heart in front of everyone."

"Well, that's pleasant," Gemma muttered. "I can't believe she let you come over."

"She was too busy exchanging insults with Harper to really notice that I was even leaving until it was too late. If she had, she probably would've threatened me with dismemberment or death."

"Probably," Gemma agreed, and glanced around. "Do you think I can get out of here now? The sirens are gone, and I made an appearance, right?"

Daniel smirked. "You certainly did."

"I think I'll just grab Marcy and get out of here."

"And I'll get back to Harper." Daniel took a deep breath and headed back over to his girlfriend.

Marcy was still standing near the appetizer table, talking with Kirby. He was smiling, so it couldn't be going that bad.

"How do you feel about turtles?" Marcy was asking Kirby when Gemma walked over, and she was really sorry that she hadn't heard the beginning of the conversation.

"Like the reptile?" Kirby asked.

"You know they are reptiles." Marcy nodded her approval. "That's good. Some people think they're amphibians."

"Who thinks that?" Kirby arched his eyebrows in confusion.

"Too many people," Marcy replied wearily.

"Hey, Marce, sorry to interrupt, but I think we're heading out now if you wanted to join us," Gemma said.

"Oh, cool," Marcy said. "I guess we're heading out then."

"Okay," Kirby said, but when Marcy started to walk away, he stopped her. "Um, did you want to exchange numbers, then? So we could watch the *Finding Bigfoot* marathon together?"

"Yeah, yeah." Marcy smiled and pulled out her phone. "That'd be great." They exchanged numbers, with Kirby fumbling a bit as he tried to type it into his phone.

"Wow. I'm impressed," Gemma said as they walked away.

"Why?" Marcy asked.

"You got his number *and* made a date."

"What can I say? I've got mad game," Marcy said.

TWELVE

Musings

Brian dropped a pancake onto Harper's plate, and she mumbled an offhanded thanks. While she appreciated his making her breakfast, her attention was focused on Thalia's journal.

After they'd come home from the party last night, both Gemma and Harper had gone through it. They'd taken turns reading it aloud, with Harper lying in her bed and Gemma sitting in the old recliner in Harper's room.

Lying down had been a bad idea, but they'd made it almost halfway through before Harper had fallen asleep. She'd been so worn-out from trying to catch up on her schoolwork that she'd barely made it past midnight.

Gemma, meanwhile, appeared to have stayed up most of the night. When Harper awoke in the morning, Gemma was passed out in the chair, with Thalia's journal lying open on her chest, opened to a page very close to the end.

Harper was careful not to wake Gemma when she took the

journal from her, then covered her up with a blanket before coming downstairs for breakfast. Now Harper was rushing to read through it and catch up to where her sister had left off.

"Is there anything useful in there?" Brian asked, sitting down at the kitchen table across from Harper.

"What?" Harper lifted her head to look at him.

"Is there anything that might help you?" Brian pointed to the journal.

"I don't know." Harper leaned back in her chair. "I think so, but it's complicated."

"Was she really a muse?" Brian asked.

"Yes, she was. She was the very last one," Harper said. "She'd been living underground, in hiding, because something was coming after the muses and killing them. She doesn't say what, but based on what I know now, I think it might have been the sirens."

"The sirens want to kill everything, so that makes sense, but what do you mean? Based on what you know now?" Brian asked.

"It's how she describes them." She flipped back a few pages. It was toward the end of the book when Thalia seemed to grow more afraid, writing more about what was after her and what it meant.

"*Beware of the songs,*" Harper read aloud. "*I tell my love that nightly, reminding Bernard that he can never trust the charms of those that come from the sea. Their songs will enchant him, but he mustn't let them. If they come for me, I won't be able to protect him, not like I once did. Now that I'm mortal, I can fall for their songs as easily as he, so I must ready him for their poison.*"

"He'd say things like that. 'Beware of the songs.' I wish I'd paid more attention to Bernie's stories." Brian shook his head sadly. "But I just thought they were stories. I didn't put much stock in them."

"What did he tell you?" Harper leaned forward and rested her arms on the table.

"I've already told you as much as I can remember." Brian pushed his pancakes around in syrup, but he didn't seem to be in a hurry to take a bite. "When he had a few drinks, Bernie would tell me to watch for sirens. He said that his wife wasn't afraid of anything, but she was afraid of them."

He set down his fork and stared off. His brow furrowed as he tried to remember more about Bernie's stories.

"He said he knew they would come eventually," Brian said at length. "He told me to beware of their songs." He shook his head. "No, that wasn't it. It was . . . 'Beware the ones that sing, for their songs are poison . . .' Or something like that."

"Did he talk about it often?" Harper asked.

"No. Actually, he only mentioned it a few times when we were at the bar, and even then, it was only a sentence or two in passing. Usually just a drunken warning about being wary of the singing temptress.

"There was one time, though," Brian went on. "Me and your mom went out with Bernie, for his birthday or New Year's or something. You and Gemma were really young at the time. In fact, I think Nathalie was still breast-feeding, so she wasn't drinking.

"Bernie really got to talking about Thalia and the sirens and muses and nymphs, because your mom kept asking him about it. She was really interested in that kind of thing. But I wasn't paying that much attention, and I was drinking, and I don't remember much about it anymore." Brian lowered his eyes. "But your mom, she would know . . . if she could still remember anything."

"Did he actually call them sirens?" Harper asked, eager to pull her dad's thoughts away from her mom. Thinking about Nathalie only ever made him sad.

"Yeah, he did." Brian nodded. "Usually, he'd call them temptresses or vixens or harlots, but he did use the word 'sirens.' But the only thing I really remember him saying was that they sing, they were beautiful, and they were deadly."

"He didn't tell you how to handle them or anything?" Harper asked.

Brian chewed the inside of his cheek, thinking. "No, he just told me to avoid them."

"But you said he knew they were coming for him. Why did he think that?"

"I'm guessing it's because of that book right there." Brian pointed to the journal lying on the table. "But he didn't really specify. He implied that it had something to do with his wife."

"They didn't kill Thalia, right?" Harper asked.

She'd read in a newspaper clipping that Thalia had fallen off a ladder and died, and earlier, Lydia had confirmed that she'd died of natural causes. But Harper just wanted to be sure that Bernie didn't suspect foul play. If he had, and he was afraid of the sirens, he might have covered it up.

"No, no, I don't think so," Brian said. "Bernie talked to me in depth about her death after your mom got hurt since Thalia had an accident, too. He blamed himself for it because he wasn't there when she fell. He really loved her."

"And she really loved him." Harper stared down at the pages, covered in Thalia's delicate handwriting and lovely scrawls. "Their story would be romantic if it weren't so tragic."

"Why?"

"They met in England in 1960 and instantly fell in love. Thalia goes on for pages and pages about how much she loved him and describes every intricate detail of their first meetings." Harper flipped through the pages to demonstrate. Portions of the journal were nothing more than sonnets, all dedicated to *Bernard*. "I think some of it might help Gemma, but I'm not sure if it will help break the curse."

Her dad tilted his head. "What do you mean?"

"When Thalia met Bernie, she was a muse, but he fell in love with her, deeply and passionately, and it wasn't because of her supernatural abilities. He really loved her for her."

"How does that relate to Gemma?"

"Well, her and Alex," Harper explained, and Brian's mouth turned down in a deep scowl. "Dad, I know this is tough for you. But she really loves him, and I think he really loves her."

"Then why haven't I seen him around lately?" Brian asked.

When Harper and Gemma had told their dad about everything, Gemma had glossed over the part where she had used a siren song on Alex. It wasn't that she was trying to keep it from him, but it was still painful for her to talk about. She'd rather leave it unsaid.

"Things are complicated between the two of them," Harper said, brushing over it for Gemma's sake. "But Thalia offers a glimmer of hope." She flipped through the journal, looking for the right page. Then she found it, near the front, right after the passage where Bernie asked her to marry him.

"Perhaps it is the heart that is the most supernatural thing of all," Harper read aloud. *"Not just because of the power it wields over mortals and gods but its ability to remain unchanged even in the face of peril or temptation. No curse, no spell, no creature on earth or in heaven can reroute its true course. What the heart loves, the heart will always truly love."*

When Harper looked up from the faded pages of the journal, her dad had fallen silent. Though he tried to hide it, she could see the pain in his eyes, and she knew he must be thinking of Nathalie and how he still loved her.

"There are a few other gems in here," Harper said, trying to change the subject and ease her dad's sadness. "We may not have figured out how to break the curse yet, but there are definitely plenty of things in the journal to give Gemma hope."

"But Thalia knew they were coming for her." Brian pushed his plate aside, too interested in what his daughter was saying to eat anymore, and he rested his forearms on the table. "You said that, right? Why did they want to kill her? And how did she know they were coming for her?"

"I don't know why they wanted to kill her, exactly. They might've just been looking for information. Muses kept a lot of secrets, so maybe they were torturing and killing them to find something out.

"But it wasn't until after she came to Maryland that she began to worry about their finding her," Harper realized, staring at the cover of the journal. "When she first met Bernie, she was in England, and she mentioned nothing about the sirens. It was when she came here, she began to fear them."

"How did they end up in Maryland?"

"Didn't Bernie ever tell you?" Harper asked.

"He said he was following Thalia," Brian said. "But I never knew why *she* came here."

"Thalia wanted to become mortal," Harper explained. "Muses had all kinds of weird stipulations about love and how long they could be with someone, and she wanted to give all that up to be with Bernie. But she needed to find a god or goddess to help her."

Brian took a sip from his coffee. "And that brought her to Capri?"

"She'd heard that Achelous was here, but he wasn't."

"Okay." Brian nodded, but still looked confused. "And who is Achelous again?"

"He's the freshwater god, and he happens to be the sirens' father. Well, Penn and Thea's, anyway."

"So Thalia came here looking for the sirens' dad, and the sirens are looking for her. That can't be a coincidence."

"No, I wouldn't think so," Harper agreed, thinking about what Professor Pine had said about coincidences. "But the thing is . . . Thalia never found him."

"Found who?" Gemma yawned as she walked into the kitchen.

Harper glanced up at her sister, who had apparently just woken up. Her hair was coming loose from a sleep-disheveled bun, and she wore the same T-shirt and sweats she'd fallen asleep in last night.

"Achelous," Harper answered, as Gemma sat down in the chair between her and their dad.

"Did you get any sleep?" Brian asked, eyeing his daughter. Gemma looked a little tired, but her siren beauty masked most of the signs, so it was hard to tell exactly how tired she might be.

"I got enough," Gemma said, and she reached over and grabbed part of the pancake left on her dad's plate. While Gemma didn't strictly need human food any longer, she still had an appetite for it. Even though it no longer tasted nearly as good as when she was human, she had still managed to acquire a taste for it again. "Are you done with this?"

"Yeah, but I can make more," Brian offered, but she was already taking a bite.

"I'm fine," she said after she swallowed it down. "Achelous is dead. Lexi told me."

"Yeah, but . . . Lexi was an idiot," Harper pointed out.

"True." Gemma licked her lips. "But she seemed convinced of it. And nobody's seen Achelous in like two hundred years. So I'm inclined to think she was right."

"So how did Thalia become mortal if she never found a god?" Brian asked.

"She didn't find Achelous, but she did find a god," Harper said. "Or a goddess, actually. Diana."

Brian shook his head. "Who's Diana?"

"Thalia only devotes a sentence or two to her in the journal." Harper had reread the part about Diana at least fifty times, hoping it would provide new insight, and she quoted it verbatim for her dad: *"It is with the aid of the goddess Diana that I am able to make the transformation from muse back to mortal. About her, I can say nothing more. She guards her privacy more fiercely even than I do."*

"That's where this gets weird," Gemma said, and she'd begun to perk up. She pulled her knees up to her chest and leaned forward on the table. "Diana is a Roman goddess of hunting and the moon and werewolves or something. She's this strong feminist, and certain Wiccans worship her."

"I thought it didn't say anything more about her in the journal?" Brian asked.

"It doesn't. In my recent research of all things mythological, I've been studying up on everything," Gemma explained. "And I picked up some information about Diana. But that's my point. She's not a Greek goddess. She's *Roman.*"

"So?" Harper shrugged, not seeing the weird part. "They're similar. And Lydia mentioned Horace before, and he's Egyptian. Just because the gods have a different etymology, it doesn't mean they don't exist. And beyond that, I would assume that different cultures had different names for the same god."

"So this Diana goddess, is she still around here?" Brian asked.

"I don't know," Harper said. "I don't think they ever were around here, per se."

"Then what was Thalia doing here?" Brian asked.

"She came for Achelous. According to the journal, the last time anybody had seen him was here, and she was trying to find his trail," Harper elaborated.

"But she didn't find it because he's dead," Gemma added.

"Well, probably dead," Harper said.

"Why Achelous, though?" Brian asked. "Why not any of the other gods or goddesses? There have to be a lot of them, right?"

"I don't think there are really that many anymore, but Achelous always had a good relationship with the muses," Harper said. "He actually fathered children with two of them."

"Wait." Brian held up his hand. "The muses are Penn's and Thea's mothers?"

"Right," Harper said.

"So Thalia was their aunt?" Brian asked.

"Right. But I'm pretty sure they weren't close," Harper said. "In fact, from what I've gathered, the sirens have had no contact with any other of their family members in centuries."

"Okay." Brian thought about it for a second, and it must've satisfied him, because he said, "Just wanted to clarify. Now continue."

"So Thalia's in Capri, and she thinks that Achelous will help her because he's helped muses in the past. But she can't find him. So she goes to this soothsayer—"

"What *is* a soothsayer?" Gemma asked, cutting Harper off.

"I don't know exactly. I think it's kind of like Lydia," Harper said. "But that's how Thalia referred to her."

Then something occurred to Harper, and she flipped through the book, scanning the pages until she found the name she was looking for. "The soothsayer was named Audra Panning." She looked up at Gemma. "Do you think she's any relation to Lydia?"

"Yeah. Her last name is Panning, right? And she's from Capri because she went to high school with Marcy." Gemma nodded. "We should call Lydia right now."

"I don't have her number, and Marcy is coming over in"—Harper craned her neck to check the clock on the microwave—"like twenty minutes to get the book. She's taking the journal out to Lydia's so she can translate the back part of it, so Marcy can ask her then."

Gemma pushed back her chair. "Well, I should get dressed, so I can go with her."

"You can't go with her," Harper said. "You have the play today. Two shows."

Gemma scoffed. "That's dumb. I should be going out there instead of doing this stupid play. This is way more important."

"You're doing what you need to do right now, which is placate the sirens. That's a really huge part of making this all work," Harper told her calmly. "Because if they're pissed off or suspicious . . . it's not good for anyone."

"You need to do what keeps you safe, Gemma," Brian said, and his tone was much more firm than Harper's had been. "And right now, that's acting like everything's normal. You need to do that, so you don't draw attention to your friends, who are putting themselves at risk to solve this."

"But *I* should be the one putting myself at risk," Gemma insisted. "This is my problem, not theirs."

Brian balled his hand up in a fist and slammed it down on the table, frightening both the girls. "I hate that I can't protect you from this. It's my job. You're my little girl, and I'm supposed to . . ." He gritted his teeth and shook his head. "All I want to do is run up that hill and beat the hell out of those girls for getting you into this mess. And I know I'm not supposed to say that, because I'm your dad, and I shouldn't condone violence, especially not on girls.

"But they aren't girls," Brian growled. "They're monsters and . . . it takes all my strength not to go up there and settle this for you. Because I know I can't. No matter how badly I want to take your place, to save you from all of this, I can't."

"Dad, you're doing everything you can do. You're supporting me, and you're helping me." Gemma reached over and took his hand.

"But it doesn't feel like enough. As long as you're in danger, anything I do will never be enough," Brian insisted. "So if the safest place for you is going to that play, pretending everything is fine, while that friend of yours gathers information, then that's what you need to do. Do you understand me?"

Gemma lowered her eyes and nodded. "I do."

"We'll solve this, Gemma," Harper promised her. "And we have a clear course of action now—find Diana, the goddess who helped Bernie's Thalia become mortal. And if Lydia is related to Audra, the soothsayer who helped Thalia find Diana, then Lydia might know something."

"Do you think this Diana will know how to break the curse?" Brian asked.

"I don't know," Harper admitted. "But she knew how to free Thalia from her being a muse, so she must know something."

"So those are your leads?" Brian asked. "Trying to find Audra or Diana?"

"Yep." Gemma touched the journal sitting on the table. "And, hopefully, this book will lead us to them."

THIRTEEN

Glimmer

"We should stop there!" Nathalie pointed to a McDonald's and leaned over quickly, so the seat belt locked in place, and she glanced down at it in irritation. She tried to unbuckle it, but she didn't even have the hand coordination to push the button anymore.

That's why she only wore pants with elastic waistbands and shoes with Velcro or slip-ons. On the outside, she might have looked like an ordinary woman in her early forties, other than her penchant for fuchsia leggings and teen heartthrob T-shirts, but her brain injury had left her impaired in many ways.

"Becky said you already had lunch," Harper reminded her mother as she drove past the McDonald's.

They'd only made it five minutes outside of Briar Ridge, where Nathalie lived in a group home, and Harper was already wondering if she'd made a mistake. She glanced up in the rearview mirror to see how Daniel was doing in the backseat, but he seemed to be taking it all in stride.

Their initial meeting had actually gone really well. It was the first time that Daniel and Nathalie had met. Since Nathalie could be pretty boy crazy sometimes, Harper had been afraid that she'd throw herself at Daniel or something. But Nathalie had been so excited about leaving that she hardly made a fuss about him.

While Harper had been hoping that Nathalie would talk to him a bit more than she had, she figured it might be better this way, so Daniel didn't get too overloaded right away. He'd have plenty of chances in the future for her to hit on him.

"I haven't had a burger in *so* long," Nathalie insisted, and slumped back in her seat.

"I'm sure you've had burgers where you live, Mom," Harper told her calmly.

"But I haven't gone out for so long." Nathalie continued to pout.

"Maybe after the play," Harper suggested. If things went well, Harper had considered taking her mom out for supper, but it really depended on how she was doing. "We don't want to be late, though."

"What are we going to see again?" Nathalie asked, and her mood seemed to lighten.

"*The Taming of the Shrew*," Harper said even though she'd already told her four times today. Nathalie had a hard time with her short-term memory. "It's Gemma's play."

Nathalie cocked her head. "Isn't she too young to be in a play?"

"No." Harper paused, then looked over at her mom. "How old do you think Gemma is?"

"I don't know." Nathalie shrugged. "Seven?"

Harper swallowed. "That's how old she was before the accident."

"Oh." Nathalie stared out the window at the highway and let it sink in. "That's right. I've been getting things mixed up lately."

"It's okay, Mom." Harper gave her a reassuring smile. "Everybody gets confused sometimes."

Nathalie didn't remember much before the accident, and she hardly ever mentioned anything about the girls' being little or anything that happened before. But that seemed to be changing.

While Nathalie had been rushing around the group home looking for her purse before they left, Harper had a chance to talk to the head of staff, Becky. Becky had said that there'd been a subtle in change in Nathalie over the last two weeks.

Nathalie seemed to be having bouts where she could remember things. One afternoon, she'd said that she had to get going, so she could get home and make supper for her husband and kids. When Becky had tried to ask her more about her family, Nathalie had appeared confused and changed the subject.

Another morning, Nathalie got up early and got ready. The staff asked where she was going, and Nathalie said that she had to be at work early to do the quarterly reports. Before the accident, Nathalie had been an accountant, but she hadn't mentioned anything about that in years.

Hearing all this from Becky made Harper feel guilty for not visiting her mother last week. Harper and Gemma usually came out every Saturday, but last Saturday, they'd gone up to Sundham to show Lydia the scroll and hadn't been able to make it.

When they'd visited before, they'd brought along their dad, and Harper wondered if seeing Brian again had triggered something in Nathalie. But she had seen him other times in the past and he'd never jogged her memory before. Nathalie had even lived at home for a short time after the accident. And then, she hadn't remembered anything about him.

Becky assured Harper that she didn't need to feel bad about missing one visit. Nathalie didn't seem upset or agitated by the resurgence of memories. In fact, Becky thought she was doing better, and her headaches hadn't been flaring up either.

Usually, a couple times a week, Nathalie would suffer painful migraines, and no medication had been able to help her so far. But Nathalie hadn't complained of any head pain in two weeks.

Her mother was obviously going through some changes, and once this mess with Gemma was finally taken care of, Harper vowed to devote more time to seeing her.

"We should stop there." Nathalie pointed to an ice-cream place advertised on a billboard. "They have the best ice cream there. When Brian and I were first dating, we used to go get ice cream all the time."

Harper's grip tightened on the steering wheel, and she kept her eyes fixed on the highway in front of her, afraid that if she said something, looked the wrong way, that it would break it. She held her breath, waiting for Nathalie to say more and finish the memory.

Because in that moment, in those few seconds when her mom was talking about dating Brian, it was like she was a normal mom. Harper was just like any other girl, and Nathalie was just like any other mom, talking about her younger days.

But when Nathalie didn't say anything else, Harper knew she had to keep the conversation going if she wanted to hang on to the moment a little longer.

"You and . . . and Brian?" Harper licked her lips and gave her mom a sidelong glance. "You remember dating?"

"What?" Nathalie faced her, blinking. "Brian? Who's Brian?" She turned around and looked at Daniel in the backseat. "Oh, is that you?"

"No, I'm Daniel." He smiled at Nathalie, but his eyes flitted over to Harper, checking to see if he'd said the right thing.

"And you're Harper's boyfriend?" Nathalie asked.

Daniel nodded. "Yeah, that's right."

Nathalie sat back in her seat and shook her head. "I never dated him, Harper. What are you talking about?"

"You said Brian," Harper pressed on, hoping to help her mom recapture the memory. "You said that when you were dating Brian, you went out for ice cream."

"I don't know any Brians." Nathalie's tone had taken on a hard edge, and Harper knew that her mom was getting irritated. Nathalie had been known to fly into a rage when she was contradicted. "Are you teasing me? I don't like it when people make fun of me."

"No, Mom, I'm not teasing you," Harper said gently. "I'm sorry. I just misheard you."

"Are we there yet? This car ride is taking *forever*," Nathalie whined.

Harper sighed. "We'll be there soon."

For the first time in a very long time, Harper had seen a glimmer of her mom. She knew she was still in there, buried somewhere in damaged brain tissue and misfiring synapses. The woman who had sung to her when she was sick, who had made her school lunches just the way she liked them, and always got her just what she wanted for her birthday, that woman had to still be in there.

And it wasn't until that moment, when Harper had caught that glimmer, that she realized she'd been hanging on to the hope that her mom would come back. She thought she'd resigned herself to Nathalie as she was now, but she hadn't.

While Harper would always love Nathalie, no matter what she remembered or how she acted, there was no changing the fact that she still desperately missed her mom and wanted to talk to her again.

FOURTEEN

Taming

Gemma wiped the powder from her face and stared at her reflection underneath the bright bulbs that lined the mirror. The dressing room smelled overpoweringly of roses since Thea had gotten half a dozen bouquets after the last three performances.

They'd just finished up the evening show, so everyone was free for the night. The hallway outside was alive with noise and the excited chatter of all the cast and crew preparing to go out and celebrate. There seemed to be some kind of euphoria that they were all experiencing, a high from a production well done.

But Gemma didn't feel any of that. In the early show, she had a little bit, when she saw her mother sitting in the front of the theater with Harper, applauding every time Gemma came out onstage. She'd felt an exuberance and pride then, but it hadn't lasted long.

Now, with everyone bustling around, changing into street

clothes, cleaning up, and making plans, Gemma felt like she was moving in slow motion. The world seemed to rush around her, and all she could do was stare ahead vacantly.

She barely even recognized herself anymore, and it wasn't just the glow of her skin or glisten of her hair from the sirens' curse. There was a hardness in her expression, and a blankness in her eyes. It was that look—the emptiness that had edged its way into her golden eyes—that she saw reflected back in Thea's emerald eyes.

And Gemma realized that's what resignation must look like. And compromise. And loneliness. It was all the small things she had given up, all the little parts of herself that she'd let Penn take away from her, so she could survive, so her family and friends could survive.

If she didn't break free from this curse soon, then she never really would. If she gave enough of herself away, eventually she'd never be able to get herself back.

"So are you coming or not?" Thea asked, and Gemma became aware that she'd been talking for a while. Gemma had just tuned her out.

"What?" Gemma asked, and turned away from the mirror to look back at Thea.

She'd changed out of her Renaissance costume and slipped into a formfitting dress. Her red hair had been pulled up, and her heavy stage makeup washed off. Then Gemma noticed that it was nearly silent, meaning that most everyone had gone, and she wondered how long she'd been staring off into space.

"What is going on with you?" Thea asked in her low rasp, and narrowed her eyes.

"Nothing." Gemma glanced down at her costume, the fabric suddenly feeling heavy and stiff, and she pushed back her chair. "I need to get changed."

"I know. I asked you why you hadn't changed yet like ten minutes ago, and you never answered me," Thea said.

"Sorry." Gemma ran her hand through her tangles of hair and lowered her eyes. "My head was a million miles away, I guess."

"Yeah, I guess so," Thea agreed.

"Will you help me?" Gemma asked, and turned her back to Thea, so she could unhook the many fasteners of the gown.

"So where was your head?" Thea asked as she began to undo the costume.

"I don't know." Gemma lowered her eyes, so Thea couldn't meet her gaze in the mirror. "Just elsewhere."

"Were you thinking about the scroll?" Thea asked, her voice barely above a whisper.

"No," Gemma answered honestly.

She probably should've been thinking about it, but she'd been driving herself insane trying to analyze the scroll and now the journal.

There had been a setback with the journal, too, and that helped account for Gemma's current listlessness. She didn't want to tell Thea about that, though. Thea'd already gone out on a limb to help, and she didn't need to burden her with added worry and frustration.

Besides, it gave her plausible deniability. If Penn ever cornered Thea and demanded to know about Gemma's activities, Thea could answer honestly that she didn't know.

Since Gemma was busy with the play, and Harper was with Nathalie, Marcy had agreed to take the journal out to Lydia's so she could try to translate the back parts. When Marcy had stopped by to pick it up, Harper had asked her if she knew anything about one of their big leads on being able to find Diana—Audra Panning.

Marcy did know something about Lydia's great-grandmother Audra, but it wasn't good news. She had died years ago.

One of their biggest hopes of finding the goddess was dead. It seemed like anytime Gemma thought she'd be able to break the curse, something happened that would make it more difficult.

"Have you found out anything more?" Thea asked.

"I don't think there's anything more to find out," Gemma said, admitting her greatest fear.

"I told you that," Thea said, but she sounded apologetic.

"*Thea!*" Liv's voice wafted down the hall, her song seeming to penetrate through everything.

It should have been a lovely sound. Liv wasn't quite the enchantress that Lexi had been with her song, but her voice was on a par with Penn's, which even Gemma found seductive when Penn was really giving it her all.

But for some reason, when Liv sang, it sent chills down Gemma's spine. Her words had a beautiful velvet layer, but beneath it, there was a supernatural quality that felt like nails on a chalkboard.

"*Thea*," Liv called again, and Thea groaned, making Gemma wonder if Liv's voice had the same effect on Thea as it did on her.

"I'm in the dressing room!" Thea shouted.

"Penn sent me down to get you because you're taking forever." Liv leaned against the doorframe and tousled her blond hair. "And I want to get out of here."

"You guys have big plans for this evening?" Gemma asked.

She slid back to the corner of the dressing room, where she planned to do a kind of dressing gymnastics. There was no divider or privacy in the room, and Gemma had to attempt to pull on her T-shirt and jean shorts around the costume, so Liv didn't get a peek at more than Gemma wanted to show.

It was strange because Gemma had changed in front of Thea and the other actresses in the play several times today, not to mention all the times she'd gone swimming with the sirens, and they'd seen her in various stages of undress.

So it wasn't the being seminude part that bothered her. It was Liv, and her large, hungry eyes, and the way Gemma would be able to feel them searching her. Just thinking about it made Gemma feel violated, and she hastily pulled her shirt on over the dress.

"You didn't tell her about our plans?" Liv shook her head and made a clicking sound with her tongue. "That's not very sisterly, Thea."

Thea leaned back against the makeup counter, folded her arms over her chest, and rested her weary gaze on Gemma. "I didn't think you'd want to join us. We're going out of town."

"To a club filled with tasty boys," Liv added with an excited giggle.

Gemma knew exactly what that meant—they were going to feed.

"I think I'll pass," she said as she fumbled with her shorts, but she could already feel her stomach rumbling at the thought.

Over the past week or so, she'd been shoveling down as much human food as she possibly could. But none of that did anything to satiate the more primal appetite that was growing inside her. It had been exactly two months since she'd last eaten, as the hunger pains reminded her every day.

Soon, it would be the autumnal equinox, and Thea warned Gemma that she would need to feed by then. Her siren's charms and power grew weaker the longer she went. Her voice wasn't throaty like Thea's, but it didn't have the same silky edge that Penn's or even Liv's had.

Thea had once gone so long without feeding that she caused irreparable damage, making her sultry voice huskier and deeper for the rest of eternity. Thea refused to say much about the months she'd gone without eating other than telling Gemma that it had been excruciating, and she'd gone absolutely mad with hunger.

But Gemma didn't need any of those warnings. She could feel it in her stomach, in her bones, in her very being gnawing at her day in and day out. A constant reminder that her body would make her feed whether she wanted to or not.

The dress was sliding down as she tried to pull the shorts up under it, and she almost fell over before successfully getting them up around her waist. When she'd finished, she stepped out of her dress and exhaled deeply, blowing back the hair that had fallen in her face.

"But isn't that kinda dangerous?" Gemma asked, which was about as close as she could get to talking them out of it. She hated the idea of their feeding, of killing people, but she didn't know how to stop them.

"Why would it be dangerous? We're the most dangerous predator in the club," Liv pointed out.

"But you're new," Gemma told her. "You're still not completely in control."

"I'm always in control." A sly smile spread out across Liv's face, and her words began to sound like a veiled threat. "You think you'd know that by now, Gemma."

"So do you want to join us?" Thea asked with exaggerated enthusiasm that meant she'd rather be doing just about anything other than going out with Liv.

"It sounds like a blast, but I think I'll have to pass this time," Gemma said, denying her hunger for as long as she possibly could.

"It's your loss," Thea said, but she sounded envious that she didn't get to skip it herself.

"See you around, Gemma." Liv wagged her fingers as she departed, and Thea followed her reluctantly.

Gemma waited until after they'd left before she hung up her costume and straightened up the dressing room. Harper was home this weekend, so maybe after the last performance tomorrow, Gemma could convince her to go out for a swim with her. It wouldn't be anywhere near as good as feeding, but it might help take the edge off the pangs that jabbed into her stomach.

By the time she'd finished getting everything put away, Gemma was completely alone in the theater. The last crew member had dropped by on his way out, reminding her to turn out the lights before she left.

Daniel was usually the last one out, or at the very least, he'd wait around for Gemma. But with the set built, he didn't have much work to do except get it reset for the next day's show. Besides that, with Harper in town, he was eager to spend as much time with her as he could.

As Gemma flicked off the lights by the back door, watching the theater go black behind her, she was suddenly struck by how lonely she was. When she went home, Brian would be asleep in his recliner in the living room, with a *Saturday Night Live* rerun playing on the TV. Harper would be out with Daniel, and Gemma would go into the house by herself.

Up in her room, she'd scour the computer or texts in hopes of being able to translate the scroll until her eyes were bloodshot and aching. Only then would she lie down, hoping for a dreamless sleep.

But first it would elude her, no matter how tired she was, and she'd lie awake, thinking of Alex, replaying every moment with him until she missed him so much she thought her heart would break. And when she did finally succumb to sleep, it would be filled with the nightmares of being trapped underwater and of Lexi dying.

This was her life, and it had never felt so desolate before.

When she pushed open the back door, she'd decided that she would go against Harper's and her dad's wishes and sneak off for a night swim alone. She had to do something if she wanted to keep her sanity.

"Gemma," a voice said from behind her, and a figure stepped out from the wall.

Her eyes quickly adjusted to the darkness, but Alex emerged from the shadows into the illumination from the streetlight that lit up the parking lot behind the theater. He'd been waiting by the back door, and he'd stopped her on her way to her bike.

"Alex?" Gemma asked, and hoped she didn't appear as disarmed as she felt. She'd just been thinking about how much she missed him, and he'd materialized before her.

His broad shoulders etched a shadow on the ground. When his dark eyes landed on her, the same eyes she'd fallen in love with, she found it hard to breathe. The very nearness of him made her heart swell, and, for once, she found something that blotted out her appetite.

"I was just about to head out." A relieved smile crossed his face. "I thought I'd missed you."

"I just took a while cleaning up." She motioned back to the theater behind them.

"How was the show tonight?" Alex asked.

"It was good. Everyone clapped at the end, so it must not have been too terrible," Gemma said, and she was pleased when he laughed at her lame attempt at a joke. "Did you see it?"

"No, I wanted to." He shook his head. "I thought about it, but I was afraid you'd get mad if you saw me."

"Why would I be mad?" Gemma asked.

"I don't know. I guess . . ." He paused, gathering his thoughts, before looking down into her eyes. "I have no idea how you feel about me anymore."

"Alex. My feelings for you haven't changed. I've never stopped . . ." She wanted to say *loving you,* but it seemed too intense, too real, so she lowered her eyes, and continued, ". . . caring about you. I only ended things with you because it was dangerous, and I didn't want you getting hurt."

"I know, but I acted like an ass for a while, and I haven't been there for you like I should've been," Alex said, sounding angry with himself.

"You weren't there for me because I wouldn't let you be," Gemma said.

"But I should've . . ." He turned his gaze to the sky and took a deep breath. "It's so dumb because I've been standing out here, practicing what I wanted to say to you over and over again, then it's like every time I see you, all my words just disappear. You make rational thought so impossible."

"I'm sorry," she said softly.

"No, don't be sorry." He looked back at her, and there was something smoldering in his dark eyes that caused a heat to grow in her belly and her breath to catch in her throat. "What I want to say, what I really want to say is . . ."

He put a hand on either side of her face, then he leaned down and pressed his lips to hers. All she could do was kiss him back and relish the warmth of his mouth against hers, and the way his fingers tangled in her hair.

When he stopped kissing her, breathing roughly, as he looked at her, Gemma saw her whole world in his eyes. For a moment, he was the only thing that existed in her life, and there was an exhilarating simplicity in that. If only she could just love him, then everything else would be all right.

"I want to be with you," Alex said, his voice low as his eyes searched hers. "I don't know if that's what you want or what's best for you. And I don't care if it's dangerous or what might happen to me. I just want to be whatever you need me to be, whether it's your friend or your boyfriend or a total stranger. Whatever you need, whatever you want from me, I'll give it to you."

Gemma wanted nothing more than to accept his offer, to throw her arms around him and say that as long as they had each other, everything would be okay.

But she knew that wasn't true. The cold reality of her life, of the monsters she had allowed to take over everything she held dear, wouldn't let that be true.

Tears formed in her eyes, and she struggled to find the words. "Alex, you know I want to be with you, but—"

"Then nothing else matters, Gemma," he said firmly. "Not the sirens, not your curse, not even your sister. I'll do whatever it takes to be with you."

"Are you sure?" Gemma asked, and she felt her resistance fading.

"Gemma, I'm in love with you, and I have been for . . . *years*, probably," Alex admitted with a rueful smile. "I never stopped, not even when you put a spell on me. Nothing can ever make me stop loving you."

"I love you, too." She smiled. "And I promise never to try to make you stop loving me again."

Gemma stood on her tiptoes and wrapped her arms around his neck. He leaned down, kissing her, and she tried to let herself enjoy the moment with him instead of thinking about the hundreds of ways this could all end badly.

She loved Alex, but more than that, she needed him, and she wasn't ready to give him up again.

FIFTEEN

Rehearsing

G emma had meant to go home after the final show on Sunday. She'd made tentative plans with Harper to go for a swim later today, and she was excited to get out and do that. Besides, she'd spent enough time lingering around here last night.

But as she was leaving, she heard the clattering of boards and the sound of Daniel's grunting. She'd climbed up the back stairs of the theater, so she came up backstage. There was Daniel, in a flannel shirt and ripped jeans, taking down the set.

"Working overtime?" Gemma asked as she walked toward Daniel, her footfalls echoing through the empty theater.

"You know me. I can never get enough." He glanced back at her with a grin.

"Where's everyone else?" Gemma asked, referring to the rest of the crew who had been working on the sets and production. Daniel had been the head of it, but he hadn't done it all alone.

"I sent them home. I'm trying to salvage some of this for other plays or odd jobs, so I figured I might as well do it myself." He was working at pulling nails out of a fake awning above a plywood doorway, and he looked back at Gemma.

"Want any help?" Gemma asked, looking up at Daniel.

"Sure." He motioned to another awning.

Gemma had to use a stepladder to reach it, but she had no problem pulling the nails out from the wood. She got the other two awnings down in the time it took Daniel to get one down, and under her breath, she began to hum.

"What has you in such a fine mood this morning?" he asked, referring to the cheerful tune on her lips.

"I'm not . . ." She paused, hesitant to tell him about Alex, but then decided to go for it and hurried ahead. "I got back together with Alex last night."

"Oh yeah?" Daniel glanced back at her. "Well, that explains it."

"That's it?" she asked uncertainly.

He turned to face her. "What do you mean?"

"You're not gonna lecture me on how it's a bad idea or it's dangerous or how I should be focused on things like breaking the curse?" she asked, and Daniel laughed, surprising and confusing her.

"I assumed you were as focused on breaking the curse as anyone possibly could be," he said. "And you and Alex want to make a go out of it, then why would I try to stop you?"

Gemma shrugged. "I know Harper would."

"Yeah, well, Harper tried to convince me it was bad news getting involved with her, and look how that turned out," Daniel said, turning his attention back to the set.

"Are you glad that you're with Harper?"

"Yeah, of course I am," he answered without hesitation.

"You don't regret any of it? Not even after everything you've been through?" Gemma asked.

"No. I mean, yeah, it would be nice if monsters didn't try to kill me, but the situation is what it is." He'd pulled enough nails free from the plywood as he spoke. "I'm not gonna stop caring about Harper because things get rough and occasionally really *weird*. I can't just stop. That's not how love works."

When the wall came down, Daniel took one end, and Gemma the other. But really, she didn't even need his help, and she ended up carrying it on her own, over to the pile with other scrap wood while he went back to pulling out nails.

"For such a little thing, you're awfully strong," Daniel commented, as she walked back over to him.

Harper was on the tall side, taking after their mother that way, but Gemma was fairly short and slender. If she hadn't been endowed with supernatural strength, she probably would've struggled with lifting most of the wood on her own.

She waved it off. "It's the siren thing."

"But if I understand this right, you're not as strong as you can be." He'd stopped what he was doing, holding a hammer loosely in his hand, and faced her.

"What do you mean?" Gemma asked.

"This form, when you're human." He motioned to her. "You're stronger than the average teenage girl, stronger than the average grown man, too, apparently, but it's not your full potential. Like when Lexi was that bird thing, she was much stronger than you. Or is that just because she was older?"

"I think it's a combination of both," Gemma admitted. "Lexi knew how to use the power she had, and the monster is stronger than our human form."

"So . . . why don't you use it?" Daniel asked.

Gemma shook her head and looked away from him. "It's complicated."

"I'm sure it is, and I don't mean to rag on you, but Lexi almost killed us," he said without any accusation. "She was actually *really* close to killing me, but if you had been that monster, you would've done a hell of a lot better in a fight."

"I know, and I am so sorry that you were in that situation," she said, rushing to apologize again.

"Gemma, I'm not trying to make you feel bad." He stepped closer to her. "I'm just saying that you need to do everything you can to protect yourself and the people you care about. If Harper had been up there instead of me, Penn wouldn't have killed Lexi to protect her like she did with me. Harper would be dead now."

Gemma'd already thought of that, and she swallowed hard. "I know. But you don't know what it was like. When I was the monster, I wasn't in control of myself at all. It took me over and I couldn't think straight and . . ."

"I know that you hurt someone," he said softly. "But Lexi seemed in control of herself when she was the monster. And if Lexi could do it, and she was a reckless idiot, you can do it."

"I know that I need to practice, but I'm just afraid of what could happen when I lose control."

"You're stronger than this, Gemma," Daniel said in a confident way that made her look up at him. "You can get ahold of this, you can be in control of your powers. You just have to try."

"Like . . . right now?" Gemma asked.

"Why not? We're alone in an empty theater." He gestured widely at the stage. "If you rampage, you'll break a few seats and tear some curtains. Nothing I can't fix."

"What if I hurt you?" Gemma asked.

"You won't."

"How can you be so sure?"

"I just am."

She shook her head. "I don't even know how to."

"How did you make the wings happen before?"

"I was scared as hell." Gemma remembered the attack at the sirens' house with perfect clarity. "I thought Lexi was going to kill you, and it just happened. My fingers and teeth have changed before, too, but it's only when I feel threatened, or I'm really, really hungry."

"Okay. So recapture that emotion. I can threaten you if you want," Daniel offered.

"No," she said quickly. "That doesn't seem safe."

"How about this? Think of Penn or that horrible new siren Liv," he suggested. "And they're going after Harper or Alex. Hell, they're going after both of them. Really picture them hurting the people you care about most."

Gemma closed her eyes and tried to will herself to feel the terror she'd felt before. In her mind, she pictured Liv's wicked smile and Penn's shifting into the bird-monster. And then she imagined them going after Alex and Harper, which wasn't hard to do since she'd already imagined it a hundred times before.

Normally, she'd try to ease her panic and get the images out of her mind. She'd do something proactive, like researching the scroll or going swimming to clear her mind, but now she let it linger. She made herself feel the absolute terror and rage at the thought of losing the people she loved the most.

And then she began to feel it. The flutter across her skin, radiating all over her body. It was a subtle, pleasurable feeling. It seemed focused in her hands, as an odd, stretching sensation passed over them.

When she opened her eyes, she could visibly see it happening. Her fingers were elongating, the skin stretching unnaturally. Her nails even began to grow, changing color from white to a dark brown as they thickened and began to hook like talons.

"Oh my gosh. My fingers . . ." Gemma gasped, watching her hands transform.

She'd been afraid that if she stopped focusing her energy on transforming, that it would stop, but now, since she was terrified about losing control, the fear seemed to push it on. Her fingers continued to grow until they were nearly a foot long. The skin stretched tight on her hands and arms, making the bones stand out more sharply.

"Does it hurt?" Daniel asked, peering at her hands.

"No, it tingles . . . and it feels kinda good, actually," she admitted.

The flutter continued over her skin and all throughout her. Heat surged through her arm muscles, but even that felt oddly good. Her heart seemed to beat differently, and it felt as if it were expanding her chest, pounding more forcefully and pumping blood more rapidly through her veins.

When her wings had torn through her back during her final encounter with Lexi, that had been incredibly painful. She'd felt the skin ripping. But this was much different.

"That is so weird," Daniel said, sounding in awe of her transformation as her arms began to stretch and grow.

"My mouth itches," Gemma said, and the words came out with a lisp when her tongue hit against the sharp points of her new teeth.

The roof of her mouth was burning hot, and she could taste blood, but she wasn't sure if it was from her gums as new teeth tore through or from her tongue's hitting against them.

"Ugh." Gemma groaned. "It's hard to talk with these teeth."

Daniel stared at her with wide eyes. "Okay, that is *really* gross."

"You're not helping," Gemma said dryly.

Thankfully, she couldn't see herself, but she knew exactly how Lexi and Penn looked when they changed. They had a mouthful of hundreds of razor-sharp teeth poking jaggedly out of their mouths, so their lips were stretched around them in a thin, red line.

Gemma could feel the tightness of her lips, and her vision

changed, becoming clearer as her eyes changed into the yellow, birdlike eyes of the monster. She could even hear the bones in her face cracking as they shifted and moved to accommodate a much larger mouth.

"I'm sorry, but . . ." Daniel shook his head. "That's just . . . not pretty at all."

When the bones stopped cracking, she realized she could hear much clearer than she had before. The sound of Daniel's breath and even the sound of his heartbeat echoed in her ears.

And the transformation seemed to make her hungrier. Not ravenous like she'd been before, when she'd killed a man, but it was gnawing inside her, spreading out from her stomach with insistent electricity.

"Should I do more?" Gemma asked, and her voice had taken on that slightly demonic tone she heard when Lexi and Penn spoke in this form.

"Can you do more?" Daniel asked.

Her legs hadn't shifted at all, and her wings hadn't broken out yet, so she knew she could go further. But she wasn't sure that she should. "I don't know."

"How does it feel? Are you still in control?" Daniel asked.

"Yeah. I mean, I'm not eating you, but I do feel hungrier." She breathed in deeply, trying to calm the hunger growing inside her, but it only made things worse. "And you smell . . ."

"I smell?" Daniel asked, confused.

"Yeah, like . . ." Gemma didn't know how to explain it. Nothing on earth had ever smelled the way he did just then. "Delicious."

"Seriously?" His eyes widened. "You want to eat me right now?"

"Kinda, yeah. I can hear your heart beat, and it's like . . ." Gemma closed her eyes and sang along with the melody of his heart. "Da da dum, da da dum."

"Holy shit," Daniel said in complete awe. "Your voice was really beautiful just then."

"Really?" Gemma asked, and looked at him.

He didn't have that glassy stare in his eyes the way humans did when they were under the siren spell, but there was something not quite right about his gaze, like he was captivated by her.

"Yeah." He shook his head, trying to clear it. "I'm not under your spell, at least not the way I think normal guys would be, but yeah, you had me kinda entranced just then."

"You have no idea how hungry I am. I think I need to eat soon." She tried to lick her lips but could only run her tongue along her teeth. Her stomach growled, an audible, angry sound, and her body trembled with hunger. "Well . . . maybe I could eat now. You could get someone, right? Some horrible person?"

"Some horrible person? Where would I find some horrible person?" Daniel asked, and he'd taken a step back from her.

Her back and ribs began cracking as her torso stretched out, and she felt herself losing her sense of reason. Her thoughts were getting blocked out, and she could barely remember the name of the guy standing in front of her. She didn't know where she was, and she didn't care. The only thing that mattered was the burning hunger inside her.

"I don't know. But you should totally find them right now."

"Gemma . . . you're changing more." He stepped back again and stared up at her, now that she was towering over him. "I think you need to get yourself under control *really* fast."

"I will," she hissed. "I just need to *eat*."

"Your voice just now, it was not pretty at all. You're losing yourself, Gemma," Daniel said forcefully. "Let's bring it back."

There was a blackness coming over her thoughts, and she knew she was losing control. She knew that the monster was taking over, and soon she'd be run by some kind of primal instinct that she didn't trust or understand.

"Gemma," Daniel said, keeping his voice calm but firm. "Gemma, you need to get under control."

"Daniel," she said, mostly because she just wanted to say his name. She wanted to make him a real person who she knew and cared about and not a meal she'd have for supper.

The sound of the door opening at the front of the theater echoed, and she cocked her head, listening for the sound of a new heartbeat. Maybe this would be someone she could eat.

"Shit. Gemma. Somebody's coming." He held his hands up to her and tried to push her back behind the curtain but without really touching her. "Get back."

"Daniel . . ." She moaned but moved back, hiding behind the velvet curtain.

"Hello, Daniel," the director, Tom, said in his lilting British accent. "I thought you'd be gone by now."

The thought of devouring Tom or Daniel, or maybe both, was consuming her. The way their blood would taste warm and sweet down her throat. It took all her strength to keep herself hidden behind the curtain.

Tom sounded especially delectable. Her emotional attachment to Daniel helped keep some of her hunger at bay, but she didn't feel anywhere near as strong about Tom. He might not even be a nice guy. She'd seen him yell at Kirby before.

When she'd killed Jason, it had been in a blackout, and she thought she'd forgotten everything about it. But now, a lingering memory surfaced—the way his heart had tasted, and how warm and sweet his blood felt going down her throat.

And then she didn't even need to justify killing Tom. Reason was leaving her entirely, and all she wanted to do was *eat*.

"No, yeah, the set's just about down," Daniel said in a nervous rush. "What are you doing here? Do you need help? What's going on?"

"I just left something in the office," Tom said. "I'll be gone in a jiffy."

Instead of rushing out to rip him open, Gemma clung to the last scrap of reason still remaining and put her long arms over her head. She crouched, trying to make herself as small as possible, and wished she could disappear into the floor. The hunger and monster were still fighting to dominate her.

She heard his footsteps retreating, then she realized she couldn't hear anything anymore. Not his heartbeat or even Daniel's. The flutter of her skin had stopped, and for a horrible moment, she thought she'd given in to the monster and blacked out like she did the last time. She fully expected to open her eyes and find herself covered in blood.

But then she realized the hunger was still there. Not as strong as it had been a moment ago, but much stronger than it had been before she'd started shifting into the monster.

"Gemma?" Daniel asked. "Are you okay?"

She lifted her head to see him standing over her. She glanced down, and her hands were back to normal. When she ran her tongue along her teeth, they felt flat and ordinary.

Her tank top had ripped when her torso had stretched out, so her purple bra was showing, and Gemma quickly crossed her arms over her chest and stood up.

"Yeah, I'm back to normal," she said, hoping her voice sounded even and not as tremulous as it felt. "I ripped my shirt."

"Here." Daniel took off his flannel shirt, revealing a T-shirt, and Gemma pulled it on, covering herself up.

"So that wasn't such a good idea," Gemma said.

"No, you did good," he said, but he didn't sound that convincing. "I mean, the first time you transformed, you completely lost control. This time, you *almost* did, but you stayed true to yourself. Nobody got hurt. You just need to practice more."

"Maybe I should stick with safer things, like learning to control my wings for now," Gemma said.

"Maybe," he agreed with some reluctance. "But I think if you want to beat this curse, and you want to keep the people you care about safe, you'll have to harness who you are. You'll have to learn to fight."

"I know." She sighed. "And thanks for being so cool about everything."

"Did I seem cool? Good. Because you're a really hideous monster, like so gross."

She smirked. "Thanks, Daniel."

"Anytime."

Daniel went back to work taking down the set, and she continued to help him, but she didn't let on how unnerved she really was. The hunger was even stronger now than it had been before, and Gemma realized dismally that her body would insist on eating even sooner.

With September rapidly approaching, Gemma had only a couple more weeks until her cravings were completely out of control. And that was assuming, of course, that Penn didn't kill her first.

SIXTEEN

Slumber

Daniel hadn't commented on her overstuffed book bag, not when she got on the boat or when she carried it into his house on the island. But then again, he probably thought it was homework.

That was the kind of hot date Harper was, and yet Daniel tolerated it with such ease and patience that she was often over-whelmed by how grateful she was to have a guy like him in her life.

"So . . ." She slipped her heavy book bag off her shoulders and dropped it on the kitchen table with a thud. "Mind if I spend the night tonight?"

"I . . ." Daniel glanced down at the bag, then at her, and seemed to be at a loss for words. "I thought you were going back to Sund-ham tonight."

"That's what I told Gemma and my dad because I didn't want to explain anything to them," Harper said. "But I don't have class until ten tomorrow morning, and I haven't been able to spend much time with you lately. So I thought maybe I could spend the night, unless—"

"No. I mean, no unless. Yeah, you can spend the night here. You can always spend the night here. You're always welcome. *Mi casa, su casa.*" He laughed.

"It would just be sleeping," Harper said. "You know . . . Not any . . . you know. I haven't changed my position on anything. I still want to wait until . . ."

"Yeah, no, that's cool, I get it," he said. "Anything you want."

She covered her face in her hands and groaned. "Ugh. I'm being totally weird and awkward, and I don't know why. You know that I care about you, and I don't want to send you mixed signals, but I'm not ready, and I should probably just go."

"No, Harper." Daniel walked over to her and took her hands in his, gently pulling them away from her face. "I care about you, and I hope there will come a time when we have sex. And I'd be lying if I said I hadn't thought about it, about how much the both of us would enjoy it." He raised her hand to his lips, brushing a gentle kiss across her knuckles.

"But I don't want to do anything you don't want to do," he went on. "I know that you're not ready, and that's fine. I'm in no rush. So if you want to spend the night tonight, we can spend all night with our clothes on, spooning, and I'll be more than happy with it. Okay?"

"Are you sure you're okay with it?" Harper asked. "I mean, it wouldn't change anything if you weren't. I want to know if you're not okay."

"I am one hundred percent sure I'm okay with it." Daniel smiled. "I waited months before I even got a kiss from you, and you know what I learned from that? You're definitely worth the wait."

Harper leaned against his chest and stared up into his eyes, and he wrapped his arms around her. She didn't know whether it was the feel of his strong arms around her or the thought of sharing the most intimate part of herself with Daniel when she was ready, but heat swept through her.

"You can't keep saying perfect things like that to me," she told him.

"Why not?" Daniel asked.

"Because I can't come up with anything perfect to say back to you."

"Okay. How about this? How about I say, I love you, then you say, I love you?" Daniel asked with a playful smile. "That sounds pretty perfect to me."

"I love you," Harper said.

"I love you, too." He leaned down and kissed her gently on the mouth. "But I was supposed to say it first."

"I beat you." Harper laughed and pulled away from him. She didn't want to let him go, but the emotions swirling through her left her feeling overloaded, and she needed a moment to collect herself.

"So do you have any homework to do tonight?" Daniel asked, following her as she walked over to the couch. "Or do I have you all to myself?"

"I could do some studying," Harper said as she leaned back

on the couch. Daniel sat down next to her, and she laid her legs across his lap. "But I think I'll skip it for tonight."

"You sure? I don't want to be the reason for bad grades."

"No, I need to take a break every once in a while, or my brain will overload."

"And nobody wants that." He grinned. "Did you go swimming with Gemma today?"

"I did." Harper nodded. "She took me out in the ocean, past the island. It freaks me out a little when she does that. She's so *crazy* fast."

When Gemma turned into a mermaid, she sliced through the water like nothing else. She'd been a fast swimmer as a human, but now she was like lightning. The waves couldn't keep up with her.

Harper would cling to Gemma, her arms wrapped tightly around her as her sister pulled her through the ocean. She stayed at the surface, so Harper could breathe, and she'd feel the sun beating down on her skin as the waves splashed over her. Even Harper had to admit, there was something truly exhilarating about it.

"Did you have fun?" Daniel asked.

"I did." Her wistful smile faded to something darker when she thought about the sirens. "What do you think of Thea?"

"I don't know." He shrugged. "Why? What do you think of her?"

"I don't trust any of the sirens, but Thea seems the most trustworthy." Harper chewed her lip. "I just don't understand why she gave Gemma the scroll."

"She could be suicidal," Daniel said, and she considered it.

"Penn's pretty easy to set off. If Thea wanted to die, she could've just pissed Penn off, then"—Harper snapped her fingers—"no more Thea. I mean, Penn took Lexi out without a second thought."

"Yeah, but maybe Thea wants to get rid of Penn, too."

"Like a murder/suicide?" Harper raised an eyebrow.

"Kinda. Except Thea clearly doesn't want to stand up to Penn or kill her."

"Why not? Penn is an evil monster."

"Yeah, but she's still Thea's sister," Daniel said. "How bad would Gemma have to be before you plotted to kill her?"

"Gemma would never be like them," she replied quickly, and shook her head.

"I know, but I'm not asking you about what Gemma's capable of," he clarified. "I'm talking about what *you're* capable of. Could you ever kill your own sister?"

"I don't know." Harper swallowed hard and stared off into space. She wanted to say no, but deep down, she hoped that she'd be able to do the right thing no matter what. If Gemma ever went off the deep end, she hoped she'd be strong enough to stand up to her sister and protect innocent lives. "But I never want to find out."

"That's probably enough dark talk for one night, anyway," Daniel said. "I think it's time we institute a new rule."

She looked over at him and tried to shake off her despondency. "So what should we do now?"

"We could watch some TV," Daniel suggested. "I have a couple episodes of *Quantum Leap* on VHS."

"Daniel." Harper tried to scold him, but she couldn't help but smile. "I thought you were gonna stop getting paid in videotapes now that you have rent to pay."

"Hey, *Quantum Leap* is a viable form of payment," he insisted. "And I already paid the rent for September. I made out pretty well working on the play."

Harper laughed, and Daniel put in the tape. She curled up on the couch next to him, and they spent the rest of the night watching old television shows in grainy, warped VHS. It didn't sound fun or relaxing, but Harper enjoyed herself immensely.

Everything was going well until she started falling asleep on the couch, and Daniel suggested that they go to bed. Harper changed into her pajamas, which consisted of shorts and a tank top. While she admired herself in the bathroom mirror, she couldn't decide if she should've gone with something sexier or more matronly.

But there wasn't anything she could do about it now, so she brushed her teeth, took a deep breath, and walked into his room.

Daniel had turned on the lamp on his nightstand, and he stood next to his bed wearing only a pair of boxers. Harper had seen him shirtless before, many times actually, and she'd always enjoyed it.

He wasn't overly muscular, but there were smooth ripples of abs and indents on his hips from the muscles that started in his pelvis. Not to mention the thin trail of hair that ran from his navel down underneath his boxer shorts that Harper found oddly provocative.

But as sexy as Harper found Daniel shirtless, that's not what left her standing nervously in his bedroom doorway. It was the amount of flesh she saw and the very nearness of him. When they were in bed together, she'd be able to feel nothing but him, and the intimacy of it was overwhelming.

"Are you okay?" Daniel asked.

"Yeah." She forced a smile and nodded but didn't step into his room. "Is that how you sleep?"

"Usually." He glanced down at his boxers. "Do you want me to put my shirt back on?"

"No," she said quickly. "Not if that's how you sleep."

"It is," Daniel said, then motioned to her. "Is that how you sleep?"

She looked down at her tank top, which suddenly seemed too thin, and her shorts, which had sleeping penguins on them, felt much too juvenile for the moment. She wished she had brought more adult pajamas. Not necessarily sexier, but something a woman would wear, like satin or silk or lace . . . but that all sounded too sexy.

But maybe that wouldn't be so bad. She looked back up at the shirtless foxiness that was Daniel and thought that if things got a little hot, maybe it wouldn't be such a bad thing. He was gorgeous, and he loved her. There were far worse ways that she could spend an evening.

"Yeah," Harper said finally, and pulled at her shorts. "These are my pajamas."

"They're nice."

"Thanks."

"So . . ." He looked at where Harper stood frozen in his doorway, then back at his bed. "Do you want me to take the couch, and you have the bed?"

"No. Part of the reason I wanted to spend the night was so I can spend time with you." She walked into his room and over to his bed.

"Okay. So let's spend time together." He smiled.

Harper climbed into bed and got under the covers. Her natural instinct was to stay at the edge of the bed, but she decided she was being ridiculous. Once Daniel got in bed, she slid over to the middle to be closer to him.

He turned out the light, and the darkness actually comforted her. Something about being hidden relaxed her.

Still, she lay on her back, practically motionless, and she felt Daniel move closer to her. His arm touched hers, and his skin felt too hot. She had no idea how he could even be that warm, especially without a shirt on.

"Is it okay if I give you a good-night kiss?" Daniel asked.

"Yeah. Of course," she said, in a voice that she hoped sounded normal.

Then his hand was on her arm, strong and reassuring. She felt his stubble first, brushing against her chin and lips. And then his mouth found hers, and when he kissed her, she realized she'd been overthinking everything.

She'd been worried about how far to go and when to go and what he'd think and all of this paranoia. But when he kissed her, all that went away, and she realized it was *Daniel*. She knew him, she trusted him, she loved him. Things would happen when they were right and not a moment sooner.

When she wrapped her arms around him, she felt her body melting against him. He kissed her more deeply, and his arm went around her waist, pressing her firmly to him. She dug her fingers into his back, pressing into his tattoo and scars.

He'd been lying beside her, but she slid her leg over his hip, pulling him between her legs. His lips pulled away from her mouth as he shifted on top of her, his kisses trailing along her jaw down to the soft flesh of her neck. One of his hands slid underneath her shirt, cupping her breast, and a small moan escaped her lips.

That sound seemed to snap something awake inside Daniel because he abruptly stopped kissing her and pulled away from her. He moved his arms to either side of her, so he was holding himself up, hovering above her.

"Sorry," Daniel said between gasps of air. "I don't want to do something in the heat of the moment that we'll regret later."

"No, don't be sorry." She laughed a little, but he didn't. Instead, he rolled away from her and lay on his back on the bed next to her. "I was having fun. We . . . we didn't need to stop. At least not yet."

"No, we do," Daniel said, his voice low and husky. "It's taking all my discipline to hold back now, and I'm not sure how much longer it will last."

She rolled up on one elbow, looking down at him in the darkness. "Then maybe we shouldn't hold back. I think that no matter when I'm with you, as long as I'm with you, it will be amazing."

"Harper," Daniel said at length. "There's something I need to tell you."

She leaned down toward him, and just before her lips pressed against his, she softly asked, "What?"

What began as a soft kiss grew deeper and more heated, silencing any of his protests, and that's precisely why she'd kissed him. Harper didn't want to hear arguments about regret, not when all she really wanted to do was be with him.

His hand cradled the back of her head, and the other gripped her hip possessively, adding more flame to the fire he'd started inside her. Then, abruptly, he tensed and pulled away again.

"What?" Harper asked, and she didn't keep the hurt from her voice. "Am I doing something wrong?"

"Just the opposite," he assured her quickly. "But . . ." He looked up at her, and even in the dark, she could feel his eyes searching her.

"I think we should wait until things are . . . *better*. Until we get this stuff with Gemma and Thea and Penn"—he said the last name with disgust—"straightened out. Okay?"

"Yeah," Harper said. "Absolutely."

He wrapped an arm around her and pulled her close to him. She rested her head on his chest, and it wasn't long before she fell asleep. And though she couldn't explain, she was certain that Daniel stayed awake for a long time after she had.

SEVENTEEN

Festivities

The glass front window of the Capri Public Library was plastered with flyers. Most of them were for the various summer reading programs, and there were a few newer ones, on bright orange paper, advertising the upcoming fall programs.

Gemma had just been glancing at them as she walked up to the door, but between the papers, she saw her own eye staring back at her. She quickly peeled back the pages in front of it so she could get to her flyer, buried at the bottom and attached to the window with duct tape.

It was from when she'd run off with the sirens back in June, and Alex had made flyers and hung them up all over town. The large black-and-white picture of her face had begun to fade, but the "HAVE YOU SEEN ME?" typed in block letters across the top was clear.

She balled it up in her hand, preferring not to remember the time she'd spent away from Capri. It seemed like a lifetime ago, a dark blur, when she'd been isolated from the people she'd loved, fighting hungers she couldn't control, and two men had ended up dead.

Instead of dwelling on it, she looked back at the window and realized that many of the flyers were outdated. She found one advertising the Founder's Day Picnic, and that had been two and a half months ago. She pulled it down, along with the other older flyers, and carried them into the library.

"What did you do?" Marcy asked. She sat behind the front desk and held a hand up in front of her eyes, blocking the sun. "You're letting all the light in."

"Are you some kind of vampire now?" Gemma asked as she walked over to the desk.

Marcy scoffed. "Like I could ever drink blood. Gross."

Children laughed loudly behind her, and Gemma glanced back over her shoulder to see the librarian, Edie, reading a story to a group of toddlers. That had always been Harper's favorite part of working at the library, and seeing someone else doing her sister's job made Gemma miss her.

Not just because Harper didn't live at home anymore since Gemma had just seen her the night before. It was more like nostalgia. The life she'd had before, the one where she was just a swimmer, and her sister just worked at the library, that was over, and it was never coming back.

"I cleared off some of the older flyers for you." Gemma turned back to Marcy and set the stack of faded and wrinkled papers down in front of her.

"Yeah, that was supposed to be my job," Marcy said, and adjusted her thick-rimmed glasses.

"Really? The thing that hadn't been done in months is your responsibility? I'm shocked," Gemma replied dryly.

"Yeah, yeah, yeah, I'm lazy, it's hilarious." Marcy waved her off. "But I was doing that on purpose. The noon sun is ridiculous through that window, so I was making kind of a paper curtain."

"Maybe you could get some of the kids to color pictures or something, and post them." Gemma pointed her thumb back at the Children's Circle behind her.

"Meh." Marcy picked up the stack so she could throw it in the recycling, but then she wrinkled her nose at one of them. "God, how old *are* these? Is that one from Christmas?"

"What?" Gemma leaned over the desk so she could get a better look. "No, it's the Founder's Day Picnic one. So it's not quite that old."

The words "Founder's Day" had been written in faded brown ink along the top, but Marcy'd apparently missed that. A caricature of Thomas Thermopolis took up most of the space, drawn to be a rotund man with a large beard. Compared to the pictures of him that Gemma had seen in school, it seemed fairly accurate.

"Oh," Marcy said. She wheeled her chair back to the recycling bin, tossed the papers aside, and wheeled herself back to the desk. "Thomas Thermopolis always did remind me of Santa. I wish we got presents on Founder's Day. That would make it a better holiday."

"Presents do make everything better," Gemma agreed.

"So what're you doing here?" Marcy propped her chin on her hands and looked up at Gemma. "Want me to help rescue you from more sirens?"

Gemma smiled wanly and tried not to stare at the pink scar that ran across Marcy's neck from when Lexi had scratched her with a talon. Fortunately, early on in the fight, Marcy had been knocked unconscious, so she'd been out of the way and hadn't gotten that injured, although she had a few bruises.

"Oh, I do have good news for you." Marcy picked up her phone and scrolled through it as she spoke. "Lydia's combing through her great-grandmother's journals and trying to match dates up with Thalia's. She thinks it'll help find the immortal you're searching for. Look."

Marcy shoved her phone right in Gemma's face, so Gemma had to lean back to read it. The name "Lydia" was at the top, and the text message was below.

Audra kept important stuff coded in her notes, so that not just any Joe Schmo off the street could read it. But I should have Diana's location figured out within the next day or two. As soon as I do, I'll let you know.

"This is amazing news." Gemma smiled. "We should celebrate!"

"Like how? Like . . . wanna go to a cook-off in Bayside Park?" Marcy shut off the phone and put it back in her pocket.

"Okay," Gemma said uncertainly. She'd been thinking of something a bit more adventurous, but if that's what Marcy wanted, then why not? "Sure, that's one way to celebrate."

"I just saw Daniel across the street, going into Pearl's." Marcy pointed to the front window. "We can grab him, then we can show the people in Capri how we really like to party."

"Oh, excellent," Gemma said, pulling out her own phone. "I'll text Alex and see if he wants to meet us because he should be just getting done with work now."

"You're back together with lover-boy?" Marcy asked. She grabbed her car keys from a desk drawer and stood up.

"Why do you need your keys?" Gemma asked. "Pearl's is just across the street."

"Like I'm coming back to work later to get them." Marcy snorted. "Anyway, are you back with that kid or what?"

"Yeah, I am . . . ," Gemma replied absently as she typed the text message. Marcy started walking toward the door, so she followed her, but she paused when something occurred to her. "Aren't you supposed to like punch out or something?"

"Nah, I'm good. It's easier if I just go," she said as she pushed open the door. "Fewer questions."

"I'm not convinced you do a full day's work here," Gemma said.

"Neither is my boss."

Once they met up with Daniel at Pearl's across the street, he and Marcy led the way down to the park since Gemma was moving much slower because she was walking and texting. They'd considered driving down there, and in fact, Marcy had fought for a bit, but there wouldn't be parking anywhere near the bay anyway. Traffic was always ridiculous during At Summer's End Festival.

Bayside Park went right up to the beach next to the bay. It was a lush, grassy area with only a few trees, a small playground, a large pavilion in the center, and a band shell at the far side, near the docks. During the winter, it sat mostly deserted, but in the summer, Capri held all kinds of activities there. It's where the Founder's Day Picnic was and where people watched fireworks on the Fourth of July.

Since it was the last week of summer, Capri was busy, and the park itself was packed. Gemma, Marcy, and Daniel had to wait over five minutes across the street from the park until traffic slowed down enough that they could make it.

"You're gonna try all the chowders before you cast a vote for Pearl's, right?" Marcy asked Daniel as they made their way through the crowd toward the pavilion where the cook-off was being held, and that's when Gemma finally figured out why Marcy had suggested coming down here. She never turned down free food, especially when it was Pearl's famous clam chowder.

"Yeah, those are the rules," Daniel said. "But I already know hers is the best."

Marcy furrowed her brow. "You seem pretty biased. I'm not sure if you're qualified to make this kind of judgment."

"Oh, I am an expert on chowders," Daniel persisted. "Nobody is more qualified than me."

"We'll see about that," Marcy said.

"Do you wanna chowder off?" Daniel turned to face her, pretending to look all angry like he wanted to fight, and Marcy met his fake rage evenly.

"Oh, hells yeah, I wanna chowder off," Marcy shot back.

"What is a chowder off?" Gemma interjected.

"I have no idea, but we're going to do it, and I'm going to rule at it," Daniel said.

"We need to set up some serious ground rules then," Marcy said.

While Marcy and Daniel debated the rules of their new challenge, Gemma looked around to see what else was going on.

Somewhere nearby, she heard a band playing a weird country version of a Rihanna song. Little kids were walking by with tigers and butterflies on their cheeks, so she guessed a face painter had to be close.

Since she was right by the cook-off, the scent of food should've overpowered everything, but she could still smell the sea, like the cologne of a lover left lingering long after he's gone. She could even hear the waves, calling to her over the crowd and the music and her friends' bickering.

Gemma closed her eyes and breathed in deeply, hoping that would satiate the hunger inside her somehow. Swimming yesterday with Harper had helped, but her appetite was only growing stronger. Her transformations yesterday must've taken something out of her, and now her body was demanding to get it back.

Her only hope was that Diana would have an answer and that that answer would come quickly. She would sooner kill herself than hurt another innocent person. She might not have been able to remember clearly when she'd killed someone, but the image of Lexi's tearing out Sawyer's heart was still vivid in her mind.

And Gemma would never do that. She could never be that monster.

Then she felt a hand, strong and warm on her shoulder, startling her from her thoughts, and she turned to see Alex standing behind her.

"Hey." She smiled and tried to erase her dark thoughts. "That was fast."

"I just came from the docks." Alex motioned to the other end of the bay. He must've had a chance to change out of his work clothes because instead of oil-covered overalls, he had on a pair of jeans and a shirt with an extra button undone on the top, revealing a bit more of his tanned chest. "Sorry if I smell like fish."

"Actually, you smell like . . ." Gemma didn't even have to breathe in, and her nostrils were filled with the scent of chemicals and fake leather. "You smell like you overdosed on body spray."

"Yeah, sorry." Alex appeared sheepish and shoved his hands in the pocket of his jeans. "I borrowed some body spray from one of the guys at work. I might have gone overboard."

Gemma laughed. "It's okay. I'm just glad you came."

"Me, too." He bent down, kissing her gently and briefly on the lips, but it sent delighted butterflies swirling in her stomach.

When he slid his hand into hers, Gemma thought she might explode. It was so simple, but she didn't think she'd ever be able to do anything like this again. At least not with Alex. She'd been afraid that her chance with him was over, and now here he was, holding her hand as they walked into the cook-off pavilion.

And nothing said romantic reunions like watching Marcy and Daniel run around, taking little sample cups of soup from each entrant, and wolfing them down with lightning speed. Well, Daniel was eating rather fast, but Marcy was literally gulping it down, then racing on to the next chowder.

"What are they doing?" Kirby asked, and Gemma looked over to see that he had joined Gemma, Alex, and a handful of onlookers in standing off to the side, watching Marcy and Daniel run around.

The breeze ruffled his dark hair, and his blue eyes were fixed on Marcy. Even though he was actually a year older than Alex, he was shorter and leaner, especially now that Alex's physique had grown muscular.

Not that Kirby was bad-looking. He was cute, with an easy smile and an earnestness about him that had endeared him to Gemma earlier this summer. Despite that, he wasn't Gemma's type, and she was happy to see him getting on so well with Marcy.

"I'm not really sure what they're doing," Gemma admitted. "It's called a 'chowder off,' I guess. I wasn't paying attention to the rules, though, but it seems kinda like some type of eating contest or race or something."

Kirby's eyes widened, and he shrugged. "Makes sense."

Gemma laughed, and she was relieved to see that he didn't seem to harbor any attraction to her anymore. In all honesty, she didn't think he'd ever truly been into her because as soon as he had the chance to take a break from her and her siren charms, he'd lost interest.

But his eyes did seem fixed on Marcy, and while that sounded like a peculiar pairing to Gemma, she couldn't really think of anyone that sounded like a true "match" for Marcy anyway. She was just about to ask Kirby if he and Marcy ever had their *Finding Bigfoot* marathon, but then Marcy threw up her arms in the air and shouted.

"Done!" Marcy announced proudly, and walked to the center of the pavilion with her arms held high above her head. Then she pointed at Daniel. "I schooled you!"

Daniel shook his head and walked over to her with a half-eaten sample in hand. "Okay, there is no way you tasted all that chowder. You could not get all the nuances and subtle flavors in them."

"Whatever," Marcy insisted, and crossed her arms over her chest. "I got the nutmeg, the hints of sea salt. That one over there in the corner had cilantro in it."

Kirby walked over and joined their group, "I suppose a congratulations is in order."

"Oh, uh, hey, Kirby." Marcy wiped her mouth with the back of her arm, which was a wise decision since she had a clam-chowder smile. "I didn't know you were watching that. But . . . yes, thank you for your congratulations. I won. And, um, I'm awesome."

"Yeah, I've noticed." Kirby smiled at her.

"I think I'm going to try the food at a normal human speed," Gemma said, and looked up at Alex. "Would you care to join me?"

"I'd love to." Alex squeezed her hand, and they walked over to the first station.

"They seem to be having some kind of moment," Daniel said as he joined Gemma and Alex. She looked back over her shoulder, and saw Marcy actually smiling at something Kirby was saying to her. "Mind if I tag along with you?"

The samples they were giving out were in little plastic bowls not much bigger than a Dixie cup. The point was to be able to taste them and judge them, not get full of them, and not many people really wanted to fill up on warm chowder on a nice summer day.

Gemma had taken her first bowl, but she hadn't even gotten to try it when she heard the sound of Liv's laughter. It was light and lyrical, but it sent the same shivers down her spine that her song had. The hair on the back of Gemma's neck even stood up.

"Oh, what fresh hell is that?" Daniel asked, looking around for the source of the laughter.

In fact, everyone was looking toward it. A siren's laughter wasn't usually that powerful, but Liv was purposely manipulating it, adding a musical edge to it. And she was doing it in the middle of a crowded park, where there were people all around she could control.

"That's Liv," Gemma said. She set her sample down on the table and stepped away, craning her neck so she could see what was going on.

"Hey." Alex took her hand, and she glanced back at him. "If you're about to get into something, I'm going, too."

She smiled at him and held his hand as they walked. If they were going to be together, and he wanted to be a part of her life, then she had to let him actually be a part of it, even the dark, scary parts. She'd protect him when she could, but he was her boyfriend, and she had to trust him to be at her side.

Penn and Thea were easier to find. They were right outside the cook-off. Thea was looking bored and picking her fingernails, apparently unperturbed by Liv, who laughed again, only louder this time.

Right next to Thea was Penn, who for some reason was getting her face painted. She was sitting on the face painter's lap, of course, with her arm around his neck and her chest pressed up against him as he painted sparkly waves along her cheeks.

"I just can't believe you'd want to be with trash like that," Liv was saying, and her sweet voice had a razor edge.

Gemma stepped out of the pavilion, with Alex right beside her, and she finally spotted Liv. The crowd had made a small circle around her. People were still walking and moving, but they couldn't help but leer when they got within listening distance of Liv.

Between shoulders and heads, Gemma was able to see Liv staring down at Aiden Crawford and some poor blond girl next to him. His arm loosely encircled the girl's waist, which apparently did not please Liv at all.

"I'm not really with her," Aiden said. His words were nearly lost in the noise, and Gemma strained to hear him. Then he stepped away from his date and moved toward Liv.

"You think you can just come crawling back to me?" Liv asked. "You'll have to do better than that."

"I'll do whatever you want. Anything. I swear," Aiden pleaded, his eyes glazed over.

"Okay. You I can work with." Liv laughed again, and Gemma wanted to put her hands over her ears to block out the sound. "But something must be done about that girl."

"Me?" Aiden's former date asked, staring up at Liv with wide, confused eyes. "I didn't do anything."

Liv stepped past Aiden, pushing him aside, and stopped

directly in front of her. Liv wasn't much taller than the girl, but she seemed to tower over her.

"You think you can just take what is mine?" Liv asked, and Gemma heard the subtle change in her voice.

Humans might not be able to perceive it, but Gemma knew what to listen for. An almost inaudible growling sound, a slight demonic warp to the vowels. That was the monster inside Liv talking.

"What's going on?" Daniel asked, coming up beside Gemma to watch the show.

"I don't know exactly, but it can't be good," Gemma said.

Then Liv's lip began to twitch. Her fangs were either about to come out, or they were already starting to.

"Shit, she's gonna change," Gemma whispered.

Alex was right beside her, and stupidly, she hadn't thought to bring any earplugs, so she didn't want him anywhere near the sirens. Marcy and Kirby were standing just behind her, both of them staring ahead at Liv, Aiden, and the girl.

"Alex, cover your ears," Gemma commanded. Alex looked like he wanted to argue with her, and she shook her head. "You can't help me if Liv gets to you, so please, just cover your ears." She turned to her friends. "Marcy, Kirby, get back in the pavilion."

She glanced up at Daniel, but she didn't know what she wanted him to do. His immunity to the song might make him valuable, but he wasn't immortal. She didn't want him getting hurt again.

So, without saying a word to him, she left and jogged over to where Penn was still getting her face painted, oblivious or indifferent to the commotion that Liv was causing.

"Penn," Gemma hissed. "You need to do something about Liv."

Penn didn't even bat an eyelash. "She's just having a little—"

"She's going to rip off that girl's head in like two seconds," Gemma said, and looked imploringly at Thea. "Someone needs to get a handle on her."

Thea sighed, but she walked off in Liv's direction. Gemma stayed near Penn because she didn't think Thea would have that much of an effect on Liv. She wasn't completely sure that Liv would listen to Penn either, but Penn wouldn't tolerate insolence.

"There's nothing here to see, people," Thea said, shooing away the crowd as she walked over to take care of Liv. It seemed to be working, too, and now Penn and Gemma had a clear view.

Gemma could see clearly that Liv's face was twitching all over, and she was probably using all of the little restraint she had. And it looked like that was about to snap.

"She won't listen to me or Thea," Gemma tried to reason with Penn. "And if you don't get in there right now, someone's going to end up dead, and your cover is gonna be blown wide open. Do you really want that?"

Penn reluctantly looked away from the face painter and stared up at Gemma. Her black eyes locked on hers, and her full lips were pressed together in an irritated line.

"Liv, she's not worth it," Thea told the new siren, making her husky voice more melodic in hopes of easing the tension. "Calm down."

"Don't touch me," Liv snapped, sounding like something from

The Exorcist. Everyone had to have heard the beast inside her. "Don't you dare touch me."

"Penn," Gemma pleaded.

"Liv, stop," Daniel said, and that's when both Gemma and Penn snapped their heads around to see what Daniel had just walked into.

He had stepped between Liv and Aiden's girlfriend, turning himself into a human shield for the girl. She was trembling, and Gemma thought she might be crying.

Daniel's back was toward Gemma, but Liv was facing her. And Liv's eyes were pure bird, and pure evil. She smiled, revealing far too many sharp teeth.

"Daniel's just killed himself," Gemma whispered, and she had no idea how to save him from getting his head ripped off.

EIGHTEEN

Rendition

The door to Professor Pine's office was shut, but Harper could hear the familiar tones of the Beatles singing about Eleanor Rigby. She knocked loudly on the door to be heard over the music. When Pine didn't answer, she leaned forward, trying to see through the frosted window on his door.

The clock on the cell phone said it was one minute after five, so Harper was right on time. Cautiously, she opened the door and peered around it. A phonograph was set up in the corner, which explained the scratchy quality of the music.

Pine was sitting in his chair, his feet propped up on the large oak desk. Students' papers were spread out around him, and he was slowly flipping through a stack he had resting on his lap.

"Professor?" Harper said, nearly shouting to be heard over the music.

"Oh, Harper!" Pine exclaimed when he saw her. "Right, of course. Come in." He sat up with a start, nearly knocking over the large can of Red Bull he had on his desk, then rushed over and switched off the record.

"Sorry, I didn't mean to disturb you," Harper said, hesitating by the doorway.

"No, you're not disturbing me." He waved her in. "I just got some old vinyl from my dad's house this last weekend. I was helping him move into a smaller place, and, of course, I had to try some of them out."

Harper smiled. "I understand."

She walked over to his desk, meaning to sit down in the chair across from him, but the spot was already taken by a crate of records.

"I'll get that. Sorry." Pine hurried around the desk and picked up the crate, then set it on the floor. "Have a seat."

"Thank you," Harper said, and obliged him.

"So, you said you had something for me to look at?" Pine asked as he went back around the desk. He was gathering the papers into a stack as he spoke, and he looked at Harper over the top of his glasses.

"Yes, I was able to convince my sister to let me bring the scroll with me."

That had been a bit of a challenge. After they'd taken their swim together yesterday afternoon, Harper and Gemma had a very long discussion about it, and Gemma finally relented after an hour of Harper's promising her that it would be absolutely safe with her.

"Oh, excellent," Pine said. "You have it with you now?"

"Yeah." Harper reached into her book bag and pulled out the

rolled-up tube. Gemma had carefully tied a string around it so it wouldn't unfurl during Harper's travels.

Pine untied the string, then carefully spread the scroll out on his desk. It was roughly two feet long, so he placed a desk lamp and a heavy tape dispenser on either end to keep it from rolling back up.

"What do you think?" Harper asked, leaning forward on the edge of the seat.

Pine let out a low whistle between his teeth. "I think that I can honestly say I have no idea what I'm looking at."

Her shoulders sagged. "Really?"

"No. I mean, I have an *idea*." He rubbed his forehead. "But it doesn't make any sense."

"What do you mean?"

"This paper it feels . . ." He ran his finger along the edge. "It should be falling apart. It has that texture, it feels authentic, but if it were, this should be . . . disintegrating." He readjusted his glasses and shook his head. "I should do a carbon testing on this."

"What about the words?" Harper asked since she didn't particularly care how old the document was. She believed it was real, which meant it was thousands of years old, but that was irrelevant to her pursuit.

"This ink is like nothing I've ever seen." Pine tilted the scroll to the side. "Do you see that? The way it changes color in the light, going from black to reddish."

"It's some kind of iridescent ink," Harper said.

"Could be." Pine took off his glasses and rummaged through

a desk drawer before pulling out the monocular. He attached it to his glasses, then leaned over the paper, analyzing the ink more closely. "Could be blood."

"Blood?" Harper asked, but that shouldn't surprise her. Of course an ancient curse would be written in blood.

"Don't quote me on that, and it doesn't really have the consistency of blood, so I can't explain why I think that's what it is, but . . ." He sighed. "Call it gut instinct. But I think it might be."

"Do any of the letters or words look familiar?"

"This might be . . ." He tapped a letter. "This is one that I thought was an aleph, and I'm really leaning toward that. And this word"—he tapped a word starting with the aleph symbol—"it appears several times."

Harper had noticed that before, but she hadn't been able to glean any meaning from it. Many of the words looked similar to her.

$$\text{K Y w K}$$

He grabbed a Post-it note and started scribbling on it, drawing out variations of the symbols. "If that's an *a*, then this could be Cypriot, so that would make the next letter an *i*."

"So it's like *a i* weird *w*-thing *a*?' " Harper asked.

"Let me check something." Pine pulled his iPad from a brief-case he had sitting behind his desk. He pushed his glasses up on his forehead and kept glancing down at the scroll as he typed rapidly. "Here we go."

He turned the screen out to face Harper, so she could see. He'd zoomed it out so a single word was clearly visible on the screen: a'ima, with αίμα written below it.

"A'ima?" Harper asked uncertainly, saying it like *ah-ma*.

"A'ima," Pine repeated, but he pronounced it *e-ma* so it rhymed with edema. "It means blood. I know, I know, it sounds like I have blood on the brain. But . . . it reminds me of something."

When he trailed off, he looked back down at his tablet, typing on it. "I don't even know why I'm thinking of this. I'm not even sure what the letters are, or if that's some kind of weird gimmel, which is sorta like gamma, then it could even be . . .

"Found it. Here." He clicked on his iPad, then tilted it toward her. He'd zoomed in again, so Το αίμα νερό δε γίνεται showed clearly on the screen.

Harper shook her head. "I have no idea what any of that means."

"It's an old Greek proverb that literally translates to 'the blood can't become water,'" Pine explained. "It's similar to the phrase 'blood is thicker than water,' meaning family is more important than strangers."

"And you think that's what it says there?" She pointed down at the scroll.

"No, I don't. Not exactly." He set his iPad aside, then leaned forward on the desk, staring down at the scroll. "That might be 'nero'—the Greek word for water—or it might possibly be an alternate spelling for the word 'black.'"

ᛏᚲᚨᚲᛁ

Shaking his head, Pine sighed. "I wish I could say for certain, but I'm going on instinct and half-remembered ancient texts. I'd need a cryptographic key to decipher it, and since this appears to be almost a mutation of known languages, I'd probably need to create the key myself. And that could take a while."

"But I think you're onto something," she persisted. " 'The blood can't become water,' would definitely apply to sirens."

"What did you just say?" Pine had been staring down at his iPad, but he lifted his head and looked at her, his blue eyes wide.

Harper's cheeks flushed when she realized she'd said too much, and she quickly lowered her eyes. "Nothing."

"No, you said something about sirens." He set the iPad aside and looked back down at the scroll. "You know more about this than you're telling me, don't you?"

"Things are very . . ." Harper sat back down in the chair, buying herself a moment as she tried to think of the right word. "Complicated."

"I can't read very much of the scroll," Pine admitted, and he sat back in his own chair. He rested his elbows on the table and stared evenly across at her. "But now that you've said 'sirens,' I'm thinking I was on the right track."

"I'm not saying that I believe it," Harper said quickly, afraid he'd think her insane. "You know the ancient Greeks, they were writing about all kinds of crazy things."

Pine studied her for a minute, chewing the tip of his pen, and he went so long without saying anything that Harper began to squirm in her chair. She was just about to pack up the scroll and dash out of there before he called the school psychologist when he spoke.

"I have a friend in town I think you should go see," Pine said, and her heart sank. He *did* think she was insane, which would probably mean that he wouldn't want to help her with this anymore.

"Is this friend an expert on ancient languages?" Harper asked hopefully.

"Not exactly, but she knows more than I do about this kind of thing," Pine said, leaning back in his chair. "Her name is Lydia Panning. She runs a bookstore."

A relieved smile broke out on Harper's face. "I know Lydia. She's helping me."

"You already had her take a look at this?" Pine asked, sounding surprised.

Harper nodded. "Yeah."

"Good." He smiled in approval. "Because this is her area of expertise. I deal more in the natural history of the world. Lydia handles the paranormal."

"So . . ." Harper was unsure how to proceed. Since Professor Pine had suggested Lydia, he obviously knew about the things she dabbled in. But she wasn't sure if that meant he knew anything more than he'd already said. "You can't help with this?"

"There's not a lot I can help you with, no," he admitted sadly. "But this is a language." He tapped the scroll. "Maybe Cypriot or Minoan. *I* can't decipher it. But I have friends who are experts in dead languages. I could pass this along to them if you'd like."

She nodded excitedly. "Yes, please do."

"Do you know what it's going to translate into?" Pine paused. "I just want to make sure that if I have friends who translate it, and they read it aloud, they aren't going to bring on the apocalypse or raise an army of the dead or something."

"No," Harper said, laughing. Then she stopped. "Well. I don't *think* it will, anyway."

"I'll tell them to read it to themselves, just to be on the safe side." Pine grabbed a camera off the shelf behind him. "You don't mind if I take pictures, right?"

"No, of course not."

He moved around, taking pictures from all different angles. He even climbed up on the desk and stood over it, so he could fit the whole thing in one shot. When he went to jump down from the desk, his foot hit the Red Bull can, spilling yellowish liquid all over the scroll.

"Oh my." Pine gasped and immediately started dabbing it with his shirt. "I'm so . . ." He trailed off mid-apology, and Harper instantly saw why.

She hadn't been freaking out like he had because Gemma had told her the scroll withstood damage of any kind without any issues. But she stood up now, watching as the lettering on the scroll began to glow bright red. Everywhere the liquid touched, the wording beneath would flare up.

"What does this mean?" Harper asked. "Why is it doing that?"

"I don't know." Pine shook his head. "Maybe the ancient Greeks were big into energy drinks."

As abruptly as it had started, the letters faded back to their normal color, which now looked dull compared to the radiant crimson. Even places where the Red Bull was still pooled above it had returned to normal.

"That was weird," Pine said.

"That was very weird."

"I'll get these pictures out as soon as I can." He set the camera aside and finished wiping the scroll clean. When he'd finished, he rolled it up carefully and handed it to Harper. "You get this back home and keep it safe."

NINETEEN

Minion

The instant Daniel had stepped in front of Liv, he knew it was a bad idea. Before he'd even intervened, he knew just how much of a bad idea it was, but he didn't feel like he had a choice.

Gemma was trying to reason with Penn and get her to deal with Liv, but Penn didn't get involved in anything unless it affected her. So Daniel's plan was to make it affect her. He theorized that he wouldn't be able to stop Liv himself, but Penn would be mighty pissed off if something happened to Daniel so close to their big date.

But then again, Penn had already killed one siren for him. She might not be so eager to kill a second one.

Behind him, he heard the girl crying. She'd already had the misfortune of going on a date with Aiden Crawford, and this psychotic siren was about to devour her, so Daniel didn't blame her for the tears.

Aiden was standing uselessly to the side, not that Daniel would expect any more from him. He did an excellent job of being a dick, and that was about it.

"Liv, don't," Daniel said, and he held up his hands palm out toward her. "Liv."

As soon as he'd heard Liv's monster voice, loud and proud in a public space, he knew that the poor girl didn't stand a chance. Liv didn't care who saw what, and Daniel could see the shift in her face. He'd seen it just the day before on Gemma, and even though he trusted Gemma, it had still freaked him out a little.

Now, as he saw Liv's lips pull back and her razor-sharp fangs extend from her mouth, it was revolting and more than a little frightening.

"Do you really think this is the time or place, Liv?" Daniel asked, keeping his voice even. He kept trying to say her name, the way he'd seen a hostage negotiator do in a movie once. He wasn't sure it worked as well on sirens, but anything had to be worth a shot at this point.

"Liv!" Gemma shouted, and she suddenly grabbed Liv's arm, yanking her back.

Liv hissed like a vampire being sprayed with holy water, turning her rage on Gemma.

"Knock it off, Liv!" Penn yelled, and her voice seemed to echo through everything.

Liv covered her ears with her hands, and Gemma winced. The people who were standing closest to them shook their heads and looked around, as if they expected to see something shouting in the skies.

When Liv dropped her hands, her face had gone back to normal. Her eyes had even shifted back to dull brown. She did not look happy, though. Her frown, her slouch, even the sulk in her eyes, all reminded Daniel of a little kid who had just gotten a spanking.

"I was fine," Liv insisted, and pulled her arm away from Gemma. "I was just having some fun."

"You were not fine, that was not fun, and you are a horrible little brat who's making Gemma look like a damn saint," Penn snapped. She crossed her arms and glared down at Liv, but Liv didn't shrink back. She held her ground and stared up at Penn defiantly. "Is that what you want, Liv? Do you want me to like Gemma more than you?"

"What just happened?" Mayor Adam Crawford came out of the crowd and walked toward them.

So far, everyone had mostly looked stunned and confused, but Daniel could hear murmurs in the crowd, and someone asked, "Did you see what happened to that girl's face?" They had seen something, and the people of Capri were going to get wise to the fact that Penn and her friends were supernatural unless they did something, fast.

"Are you okay?" The mayor put his hand on his son's shoulder. "Did something happen here? Did these girls hurt someone?"

"No, they'd never hurt anyone," Aiden said, but he sounded dazed.

"Thea, you and Gemma take care of this mess." Penn waved vaguely to the two of them. "I'm taking Liv and getting out of here."

"Now wait just a minute." Mayor Crawford stepped away from his son and toward Penn, who glared at him with repugnance. "Nobody's going anywhere until I find out what's going on in my town."

"Trust me, you don't want to know what's really going on here," Penn told him.

"Mayor, let me tell you about it," Thea purred with an added melody to her voice. She put her hand on his arm, leading him away from Penn. "In fact, why doesn't everyone gather around while Gemma and I tell you all what happened?"

Gemma appeared confused at first, but then she began to follow suit. Thea was all smiles and winks, and her voice was pure seduction. Gemma did her best to mimic Thea and let her own siren charisma shine through.

Penn grabbed Liv by the arm and started leading her while a crowd gathered around Gemma and Thea. Daniel wanted to stay behind and see how they would make Liv's small transformation disappear.

"Daniel." Penn stopped and turned back to him. "Come with me."

"I'd like to see this show." He pointed to Thea and Gemma.

"They're just gonna sing a stupid song, now come on," Penn insisted. "I want to talk to you."

Groaning, Daniel decided that going with her would be easier than arguing with her. When he started walking away, he could hear the song. He wouldn't have minded staying to listen to them pacify the crowd, but it wasn't long before he couldn't hear the song anymore.

He paused, listening for it, but there was nothing. As loud as Thea and Gemma had been singing, he should be able to hear it.

"We can control how far it goes," Penn explained when she noticed he'd stopped following her. "We can make it go on for miles or for only a few feet. Whatever we need it to do. And right now, they only need to reach the people who saw Liv's little performance."

"See? Everything's fine," Liv said. "I don't know what you're getting all worked up about."

"You know *exactly* what I'm getting worked up about, and I don't want to hear another word from you," Penn growled. "Is that clear?"

Liv started to mutter something, and Penn yanked on her arm. By the way Liv grimaced, Daniel figured it had to be painful.

When they'd reached Penn's cherry red convertible across the street, Penn all but tossed Liv inside. Liv scowled as she adjusted herself in the backseat.

"Put the top up and stay here," Penn commanded.

"I don't *want* the top up," Liv whined.

Penn leaned down, putting her arms on the car door, and her face was only inches away from Liv's. "I don't give a flying fuck what you want. Do you understand me? Now put the top up and wait in the damn car."

She walked a little ways down the sidewalk, presumably far enough that Liv wouldn't overhear her. Daniel wasn't exactly sure what she wanted with him, but he knew better than to argue with her right now.

The bronze skin of her face began to subtly ripple. Blue glitter had been painted along her cheek, going up her temple to look like waves, and the restrained movement added to the effect. Liv had really set Penn off, Daniel realized, and she was fighting the urge to transition.

Daniel considered saying something, but he was afraid that he'd only make it worse. So he just waited until Penn had calmed down enough that her skin returned to its usual smooth state. She took a deep breath and ran her hand through her long, raven hair.

"I wanna kill her," she said icily. "I want to kill her. But I'm not going to." She looked up at him, her dark eyes sparkling, and she smiled thinly. "You wanted me to. I saw that. I saw the little stunt you pulled back there, trying to get me to kill her to save you. I'm not falling for that anymore. The next time someone goes after you, I'm gonna let them."

"That sounds fair," Daniel said.

"I'm not killing any more of my girls for you. Unless it's Gemma. Then say the word, and she'll be gone like that." She snapped her fingers.

He sighed. "That doesn't even make sense. Liv is way worse than Gemma. She's the one who keeps losing her shit and defying you."

"Liv might be terrible," Penn went on, and her tone became more calm and reasonable. "But she's like a child, and that's why she'll work. She'll be a whiny baby, throw her tantrums, but if I stay firm—and we all know that I'll stay firm—then she'll learn. I can mold her into what I want. She can be the sister that I'd always hoped Lexi would be but never was.

"But Gemma." She shook her head. "I chose her because she

seemed the most suited to the siren lifestyle, but as soon as she turned, I knew we'd made a mistake. She's too . . ." Penn seemed to be searching for the word before wearily deciding on "unbreakable."

"You seem to have a lot of failed minions lately," Daniel commented. "Lexi, Gemma, now Liv. Is this why you dragged me out here? So you could vent about your problems with your staff?"

"Isn't that what boyfriends are for?" Penn reached out and touched his arm in a coy gesture and bit her lip.

Daniel rolled his eyes as he threw back his head and laughed. "I am not your boyfriend, Penn."

All the good humor instantly disappeared from her expression, and she pulled her arm back. Daniel knew he'd done the wrong thing, but he couldn't help himself.

"You don't need to laugh. And you'll be singing a different song come Wednesday."

"Assuming you hold up your end of the bargain," he reminded her.

Penn narrowed her eyes. "What's that supposed to mean?"

"You have this time bomb, Liv, running around." He motioned to the car, where Liv was pouting. "And you were going to have her stay with Harper? If she'd hurt Harper, this whole deal would be off."

"You think you can back out of this?" Penn put one hand on his chest and pulled at the collar of his flannel shirt as she smiled up at him. "You think I'd just let you go?"

"Yes, I do," Daniel growled. "This is *our* deal, Penn." He gestured between himself and Penn. "You agreed to the rules. You're the one who risks breaking it."

"I don't give a shit what Liv does." She was still smiling as she spoke, but her tenor had gotten decidedly vicious, making his blood run cold. "She could kill Harper, your mom, your dad, your third cousin twice-removed. But as long as there's one person left on this earth that you care about, then you're *mine*."

"Penn—"

"So if you even *joke* about canceling, I will rip Harper's head off," she said, cutting off his protests. "And then I will place it at the end of the bed, so she can watch it when I ravage you. Because if you don't, then I'll move on to the next thing you care about, and the next thing, and the next thing. Gemma, Alex, your parents, even the stupid waitress at that diner you love so much. I will destroy *everything*."

Daniel swallowed hard, still staring down into her black eyes, and he knew she meant every word she said. "You do what you promised, Penn, and I'll do whatever I need to do."

"So, I'll see you Wednesday?" Penn asked, and her voice returned to its usual silky cheer.

"At eight o'clock," he replied without missing a beat.

"Good." She moved away from him, walking backward to her car. "I should get Liv out of here before she decides she needs a little snack."

"Penn!" Gemma called, and Daniel looked over to see her standing on the other side of the street with Thea. "Wait. I wanted to talk to you."

Gemma jogged across the street, trying to stop Penn before she took off, and Thea followed at a much slower pace.

"We need to talk about this Liv problem," Gemma said when she'd reached Penn.

"There is no Liv problem," Penn said as she opened the car door. "Now get lost."

"Penn!" Gemma yelled, but Penn just got in the car. Gemma hit the car window, trying to make her roll it down, but she refused to. "Come on, Penn."

Penn waited just long enough for Thea to get in the passenger side, then she slammed on the gas and sped away. She nearly hit another car, but Daniel doubted that Penn was the kind of girl who ever looked where she was going anyway.

"Dammit." Gemma groaned and walked down to where Daniel was standing. "Liv is out of control. Even Thea agrees." She shook her head, as if trying to clear it, and when she looked up at him, he saw a strange suspicion in her golden eyes. "What was that about, by the way?"

"What?" Daniel asked, trying to play dumb.

"You and Penn." Gemma raised her chin, inspecting him. "Why did she have you follow her? And what were you talking about?"

He rubbed the back of his neck and looked away from her. "You know. Just Penn things."

"No, I don't know." Gemma moved, so she was in his line of vision, and when he tried to look away, she moved again. She wasn't letting him off the hook this time. "She's always talking to you, but you never tell me what she says. Vague statements and shrugs are all I ever get from you. What's going on?"

Ever since Penn had begun showing an interest in him, Daniel had been dreading this conversation. People—particularly Harper and Gemma—would demand to know the nature of his relationship with Penn, and he couldn't explain it.

Well, he could, but he didn't want to. He didn't want to admit what was going on, not even to Gemma. Not just because he didn't want to deal with the fallout but because he didn't want to say it all aloud, to talk through all the dirty details while feeling shamed by Gemma's scrutinizing gaze.

"Why are you interrogating me?" Daniel asked, unable to keep the defensive tone out of his voice. "I haven't done anything wrong."

He wanted desperately to get away from the conversation, so he started walking. Of course, Gemma followed, but he hadn't really expected any different.

"Then why are you being so evasive?" she asked.

"I'm not," he lied. "I'm just doing what I need to do."

"And what's that?"

He stopped walking, growing exasperated. "Can't you just trust me?"

"Should I trust you?" Gemma countered.

Rubbing his forehead, he let out a long breath. And then he looked her in the eyes for the first time since she'd brought this all up. "You always say that you'll do whatever it takes to protect the people you care about, right? Well, so will I."

"And what exactly do you need to do?" Gemma asked, and he groaned. She really wasn't letting this go. "Daniel. I tell you everything. You need to tell me what's going on here."

He laughed darkly. "No, I don't, Gemma. There are some things in my life that you don't need to know about that don't involve you. Not everything is always about you."

"I know that! But if you do something to hurt my sister, so help me, Daniel—"

"You really think I *want* to do anything to hurt Harper?" Daniel asked, his voice tightening with pain. "Everything I do is to keep her safe and happy. Do you understand that?"

"Yeah, I do," she admitted.

"Anything that I do, I'm doing it for her."

"Daniel . . ." She had a knowing look in her eyes, and that scared him. "I think you need to talk to her. About whatever's going on here. It doesn't matter what it is. She loves you, and she'll understand."

Before, when Penn had first propositioned him, Daniel had planned on telling Harper about it. He knew she'd try to talk him out of it, but that didn't matter. Daniel would do whatever it took to protect Harper.

But after the attack with Lexi, Daniel had realized a fatal flaw in his plan. Sleeping with Penn wouldn't be enough. If it was only one night, then he'd only prolong Harper's life by a day. Once he had sex with Penn, he had no more bargaining chips to keep Harper and Gemma safe.

That meant that he'd have to begin an affair with Penn. Once he went ahead and actually got involved with her, he'd have to do everything in his power to keep her happy and satisfied. The second she got tired of him and lost interest, Harper was as good as dead.

Somewhere in the back of his mind, he'd been hoping that Harper would be able to forgive a solitary transgression, and maybe she could. If she truly believed he loved her and was repentant.

But there would be no way that she could tolerate an affair, with Daniel constantly going out behind her back and sleeping with Penn.

So once Daniel consummated his relationship with Penn, everything with Harper was gone. Forever. There's no way she'd ever be able to trust him or look at him the same way again.

And that's why he didn't tell her. If he told Harper now, it would only lead to fights as she tried to talk him out of it. But his mind couldn't be changed. He knew that he'd do whatever he had to do to protect her, even if it meant selling his soul to the devil.

He didn't want to spend his last few days with Harper arguing. He'd never ask Harper to endure his liaisons with Penn, but all he wanted was a few more days before he lost her forever.

Since his date with Penn was set for Wednesday, Daniel planned on going up to Sundham on Friday and telling Harper in person about everything that was transpiring. They'd break up then, and in the meantime, he'd have a few more days of text messages and phone calls. A few more chances to hear her laughter, to tell her he loved her.

That's why he'd shut Harper down when things had gotten heated on Sunday night. He'd wanted to be with her more than anything in the world. But that wouldn't be fair to her. He couldn't sleep with her only to break up with her a few days later.

Daniel shook his head. "Not this time. I just need you to trust me and let me handle this myself," he begged Gemma.

"Okay," she said reluctantly. "But if you need help . . . I'm here."

TWENTY

Bastian

After the incident, Penn refused to reply to any of Gemma's text messages or phone calls. Gemma considered going out to the sirens' house, and she'd even started talking to her dad about borrowing his truck to go up there.

Then Thea texted her, *Penn & Liv getting into it. Better if you stay away for the night.*

Is she getting rid of Liv? Gemma replied.

Unlikely, Thea sent back, and Gemma groaned inwardly.

I still want to talk to Penn.

She does not want to talk to you, Thea texted.

Can I talk to you? Will you call me? Gemma asked.

Liv & Penn going out to feed tomorrow. Come by in the afternoon. I'll be alone.

That left Gemma impatiently waiting until the next afternoon.

Harper texted her to tell her about the newest developments

with the scroll, and while Harper used lots of excited exclamation points, they didn't seem that big to Gemma, who had already seen the words glow a bit with water. It sounded like the ink reacted even more strongly when mixed with Red Bull, so Harper had taken the scroll back to her room and tried spilling a few different liquids on it.

So far, Red Bull seemed to have the strongest effect, but water and orange juice both seemed to make it glow a bit. Milk apparently did nothing.

But other than glowing, nothing else happened. Harper concluded that further research was needed, but she was determined to get to the bottom of it. She asked if she could keep the scroll for a few more days, but Gemma didn't like having it out of her sight for that long. It wasn't that she didn't trust Harper, but she wanted to experiment with the scroll herself. Marcy offered to go pick the scroll up for her, and Harper agreed to return it.

She hadn't told Harper of her suspicions about Daniel, mostly because she'd told him that she wouldn't. That, and she wasn't exactly sure what he was up to. She didn't want to ruin his and Harper's relationship over nothing.

Besides, Daniel was a good guy. He was Gemma's friend, too. She decided that she just had to trust him.

When Gemma went to the sirens' house the next day, she had to ride her bike. Her car was still sitting dead in the driveway, like an especially large paperweight. The trek up there wasn't pleasant. The sirens lived on the other side of town at the top of a cliff, and Gemma had to ride her bike up a long, winding road through the loblolly pines.

Even with her extra siren strength, the ride uphill wasn't exactly easy, and it probably didn't help that she needed to feed soon. By the time she reached the chic cabin, Gemma was winded.

"You're all sweaty," Thea greeted when she opened the door.

"Thanks," Gemma said dryly. "I rode my bike."

Gemma surveyed the house as she came inside, and she was surprised to see that not much had changed since the big battle nearly two weeks ago. They'd done basic cleanup, like righting the fridge and furniture, but they hadn't fixed or replaced anything. Even the windows were still broken out, with plastic taped over them.

"Don't you have a car or something?" Thea asked her.

"It needs a new starter," Gemma said, wiping the sweat from her brow. "Do you have any water or something?"

"There's bottled water in the fridge." Thea motioned to the kitchen, but she walked over to the living room. "I'd let you use my car, but Penn doesn't think I need one."

Gemma got the water and guzzled it down before going into the living room to join Thea. Thea had sprawled out, taking up most of the couch, so Gemma sat in a chair with its stuffing gone.

"What's that about?" Gemma asked as she tried to get comfortable on the uneven cushion. "How come Penn is the only one allowed to drive?"

"I don't know." Thea let out an exasperated sigh. "She

comes up with bullshit reasons, but the truth is that Penn just wants to have control all the time. She doesn't want me driving away."

"Where would a car take you that your wings and fins already couldn't?" Gemma asked.

Thea laughed a little at that. "I didn't say it was logical. It's just a power play. Everything's a power play with her."

"I don't understand how she can tolerate Liv," Gemma said, bringing up her reason for today's visit. "Liv's the most out-of-control thing I've ever seen."

"I don't completely get it. I've tried reasoning with her, but . . ." Thea shook her head. "Penn doesn't want to admit she was wrong about Liv, but more than that, I think she just can't have two 'bad' sirens."

"She's already trying to find a replacement for me," Gemma filled in what Thea hadn't said. "She can't be troubled to find one for Liv on top of that."

"Pretty much."

"I get that Penn hates me, and she's planning to kill me, but objectively, I'm a lot less trouble than Liv."

"You're a different kind of trouble than Liv," Thea said. "You undermine Penn in a *different* way. Liv may be extreme, but she's an extreme version of Penn. They have a similar moral compass. So in Penn's mind, if Liv could just tone her act down, they'd be totally simpatico."

"And I may not terrorize the village or throw tantrums all the time, but Penn and I will never be on the same page," Gemma surmised.

Thea slid back on the couch, so she was lying down. "And, secretly, I think she considers you my ally, and that pisses her off."

"Why?" Gemma asked. "She doesn't like you either?"

"No, I think Penn likes me about as much as Penn is capable of liking anyone. But she's never really been close to anyone, not even when we were young. She always resented that I was close with Aggie and Gia."

"Gia?"

"Ligea. Our other sister. The one before Lexi."

"Lexi and Penn seemed kinda close for a while." Gemma had thought that Penn and Lexi were the closest, especially when Gemma first became involved with the sirens, but obviously, they couldn't have been that tight.

"Well, Penn tore off Lexi's wing before she murdered her," Thea said. "They were allies, maybe, but they weren't close. I don't think they ever really enjoyed each other's company."

"So you're saying that Penn has never had any friends?" Gemma asked.

"Not really. Well . . ." Thea seemed to think, and it was a minute before she went on, almost hesitantly. "There was someone, once. Bastian."

"Bastian?" Gemma asked.

"Well, Orpheus was his given name."

A few months ago, that name would've meant next to nothing to Gemma, but after she'd spent so much time researching Greek mythology, she instantly knew it. He hadn't exactly been a god, but he'd been an important figure, renowned for his musical abilities and poetry.

"The musical guy?" Gemma asked. "Didn't he play like a harp or something?"

"A lyre," Thea corrected her. "You haven't heard anything until you've heard him play. It was said his songs would make the heavens weep, and it wasn't an exaggeration. The gods were so pleased with his musical abilities, they granted him eternal life."

"If he was immortal like you guys, did that mean your siren song worked on him?" Gemma asked.

"No, it didn't. Penn couldn't manipulate him. And as much as she loves control, she's always been the most drawn to the people she has no power over."

"That's bizarre," Gemma said, but it did explain Penn's infatuation with Daniel.

"Usually, I'd say yes, but there was something about Bastian that you couldn't ignore. He was gorgeous, but it was beyond that. Charismatic, intelligent, funny, and he had these eyes . . ." Thea stared off wistfully. "They were blue, but not any shade I've ever seen in nature."

"So you were into him?" Gemma asked.

"He was Penn's lover," Thea deflected the question.

"But did she actually *love* him?"

"I've thought about it a lot since then, and I can't honestly tell you. She *believed* she loved him, and maybe that's close enough."

"What happened with Bastian?" Gemma asked. "If he's immortal, why isn't she still with him?"

"Like I said, she couldn't control him. And one night, he was just . . ." Thea lowered her eyes, and there was a long pause before she finished her sentence. ". . . gone."

"I can't imagine Penn taking that well."

Thea snorted. "Hardly. This was nearly three hundred years ago now, and she's mellowed since then. But at the time, Penn went absolutely insane. I know you think she's bad now, but you have no idea."

"What do you mean?"

"She was inconsolable, and for Penn, that means she went on a rampage." Thea pushed herself up, so she was sitting. "The first hundred years after he was gone, it was a bloodbath. Penn killed anything and *everything* without remorse. In a fit of rage, she murdered our sister Gia."

"She just murdered your sister Gia? For like no reason?" Gemma asked.

Thea ran her hand through her hair and looked away from Gemma. "She had her reasons, not that they completely made sense to the rest of us."

"So why didn't you stop her?"

"The only way I could've stopped her would have been to kill her, and I just . . ." Thea shrugged. "I couldn't bring myself to do it. She's my little sister." Then she shook her head, as if that's not what she wanted to say at all. "And I felt responsible."

"Why?" Gemma asked.

"It's hard to explain. Aggie kept hoping that with enough time and encouragement, Penn would stop. Aggie believed that if we just loved Penn and tried to show her kindness, eventually Penn would come around. But nothing we said or did mattered to her. I think that was actually the beginning of the end for Aggie."

"What do you mean?"

"Aggie'd never been as cruel as Penn, or even me," Thea elaborated. "She really wasn't cut out for the siren life. But she made do with it, killing only when she needed to and making it as merciful as she could. But Penn became relentless, and Aggie couldn't live with it anymore."

"But you could?" Gemma asked her pointedly. "All that senseless murder didn't mean anything to you?"

"It's not the same. You see the world in terms of one human lifetime, and you don't understand the fragility of everything. You're all going to die. Everyone will die quickly and easily. Illness, accidents, wars. It's amazing humans live as long as they do. But *I* will be here for another millennium. I won't turn my back on my sister for something that will be gone in the blink of an eye."

"But Aggie did," Gemma said.

"She'd always cared for human life." Thea's voice softened, the way it did whenever she spoke of Aggie. "Too much really. You'll disagree, but when you've seen as much death as we have—not even from our hands, but by the hands of time—it begins to wear on you. So Aggie began looking for a way out, which Penn was angry about. It finally came to a head this summer."

"Penn started going off the rails three hundred years ago, and it just finally got to be too much this summer?" Gemma asked skeptically.

"Aggie tried to change Penn at first, and when she realized that wasn't working, she tried to look for a more peaceable solution. Like breaking the curse." Thea motioned to Gemma then. "When she couldn't do that, she finally said that's enough."

"You mean she told Penn to stop?" Gemma asked.

"Yes. She actually suggested that we all swim out to sea and starve ourselves until we died. Naturally, Penn disagreed, so Aggie threatened to run off right before a full moon, so we wouldn't have a chance to replace her, and we'd all die that way.

"But I don't think she really meant it. She was just provoking Penn, so she'd kill her. Aggie wanted her life as a siren to be over, and death was the only way she knew out of it."

"If you both hated the way Penn was running your lives, why didn't you and Aggie just stand up to her and stop her?" Gemma asked. "I mean, if it had gotten to the point where you had to choose between Aggie and Penn, why wouldn't you choose Aggie?"

"They're both my sisters," Thea reminded her. "Our parents basically abandoned us. I'm eight years older than Penn."

This admission surprised Gemma. She knew that Thea was the eldest, but she hadn't thought it was by that much, since both Thea and Penn appeared to be around eighteen or twenty years old.

But then she remembered Penn saying that she'd only been fourteen when she became a siren. The curse apparently just made them appear to be in their sexual prime, and Gemma supposed that she looked around the same age, too.

"Eight years doesn't sound like that much, but when we were young, it was a lot, especially when our mothers weren't around,"

Thea said. "So I raised them both as my own. It's like asking to choose which one of my children to save. I couldn't do it." She shook her head. "I didn't choose."

"But you did," Gemma persisted. "You turned your back on Aggie. You let Penn kill her."

Thea didn't disagree. For a moment she said nothing and just stared down at the floor. She wiped quickly at her eyes, but not fast enough to stop a solitary tear from falling down her cheek.

When she did finally speak, her voice was thick. "I never thought she'd actually go through with it. They'd been fighting for a while, but I never thought that Penn could really do it. Not to Aggie."

"When she did, when you realized what Penn was capable of, why didn't you kill her then? Penn has killed two of your sisters," Gemma said. "Three if you're counting Lexi."

"I never counted Lexi as my sister," Thea muttered.

"You know Penn will just keep killing," Gemma went on. "If I don't stop her, she's going to eventually kill me, and Liv, and . . . you."

"If she does, I would deserve it," Thea replied softly. Then she shook her head and took a deep breath, erasing the sadness from her expression. "Anyway . . . that's how we ended up here."

"You mean, with me?" Gemma asked.

"No, here in Capri." Thea gestured around her. "It's all part of Penn's scheme for revenge."

Gemma furrowed her brow. "I don't follow."

"She blamed Bastian's absence on Demeter," Thea explained.

"It was because of the curse that he couldn't love her, and that was Demeter's fault."

"Why didn't she just try going after Bastian?" Gemma asked.

"She did, at first," Thea said. "But the longer she went without finding him, the more enraged she became. And while some of that rage would splatter on the humans around her, she focused most of it on Demeter."

"She'd been a siren for what?" Gemma tried to remember what they'd told her. "Like over two thousand years, right? And Penn just suddenly decides to get revenge on the woman who cursed her?"

"No, of course not," Thea said. "Penn's always hated Demeter, from the very moment she appointed us handmaidens to her daughter Persephone. But initially, Penn and Demeter and the other gods lived in peace. It wasn't until hundreds of years later, after we'd been exiled from Greece along with the other immortals at the end of the Dark Ages, that Penn even considered killing Demeter."

"Why were you exiled?" Gemma asked.

" 'Exiled' isn't exactly the right term, but that's how it felt," Thea clarified. "Humans just started getting wise to us. They were fearful or jealous, and they began killing gods and immortals. So it was just safer for all of us to start living underground, hiding our true selves."

"And that pissed Penn off," Gemma guessed.

Thea nodded. "Penn never wants to hide or control her whims, so she hated Demeter even though it wasn't her fault the world was changing. We'd begun looking for Demeter, but we weren't that serious. Penn loved being a siren.

"When the mood struck her, she'd ask around, but she usually got distracted before we got too far into looking for Demeter. So we had a few centuries of half-assed attempts at finding the hidden goddess between long strings of debauchery." Thea paused. "And then Penn got sidetracked with Bastian."

"Until he disappeared," Gemma said.

"Exactly. But Penn was going batshit, killing everything that crossed her. Humans, gods, anyone that Penn felt like," Thea said. "That's when Penn really threw herself into finding Demeter, doing everything she could in unrelenting pursuit, but Demeter had gotten wind of Penn's rampage. So she burrowed deep underground, and she hasn't been seen in centuries."

"Are you sure she's even still alive?" Gemma asked.

Thea shrugged. "Clio told us she was."

"Clio?"

"She was a muse we found a little over fifty years ago. Our aunt, technically," Thea said. "But we'd never had a very strong familial bond with our own mothers, let alone any of their sisters. The muses wanted little to do with their children for the most part, and Clio was no exception."

"Well, then how do you even know she was telling you the truth?" Gemma asked.

"We asked her at first, but then Penn tortured her to be certain," Thea explained. "Unfortunately, she didn't know where Demeter was, so Penn killed her."

"You tortured and murdered her?" Gemma asked. "That seems pretty extreme."

"Penn was desperate to know where Demeter is," Thea said. "We would've gone to our own mothers, but they were long since dead. We've been scouring the earth since the 1700s, looking for muses who might know anything, but we've mostly only found their corpses. Clio was only the second muse we'd encountered alive in the past five hundred years."

That explained what made Thalia so spooked in the journal. When she'd first met Bernie, she'd never mentioned the sirens at all. And then, suddenly, she'd become frightened and paranoid.

Thalia had briefly mentioned something, saying that she'd lost an old friend, but she hadn't named the friend. She'd probably gotten word of her sister Clio's murder at the sirens' hands and assumed, rightly, that they were going to come after her next.

"So you came to Capri looking for Demeter," Gemma said. Thanks to Thalia's diary, she had already put most of the pieces together. But she hoped Thea would fill in the blanks.

"No, we came looking for another muse," Thea said. "The very last one, and she was said to be here in Capri."

"But she was already dead," Gemma said.

Thea nodded bitterly. "That was our last hope."

"What do you mean?" Gemma asked

"There aren't many of us left. All the big immortals are long gone—Zeus, Aries, Medusa, Athena, you name it. They're either dead or in hiding. Hades is around, but he hasn't talked to anyone since . . . right after we became sirens. He doesn't know anything."

"Since everyone's gone, you have nowhere else to look. No clues on how to find Demeter," Gemma said, hoping she didn't sound as disappointed as she felt. While she was happy that Penn had been unable to find a muse, Gemma had been hoping for some clue, some hint at anything that could help her.

"No." Thea shook her head. "That's why I told you the scroll is useless. Aggie tried everything to break the curse. And there are no more gods or goddess to help reverse it. We're alone."

"Is that why you gave me the scroll?" Gemma asked. "Because you didn't think I'd be able to do anything?"

"No. I've just come to realize that my sister Aggie was right. We've had our time on this earth, and we've had more than our fair share of death." Thea let out a deep breath and stared emptily at the wall. "But it seems my change of heart is just too little, too late."

TWENTY-ONE

Lineage

It was the first time that Harper had gone to visit Lydia without someone calling ahead, and she felt strangely intrusive as she pushed open the door to Cherry Lane Books. Of course, that didn't make sense since it was a bookstore, and people were free to come and go as long as the OPEN sign was up.

In fact, this was about the least intrusive she'd been since it was only the second time she'd come here when the store was actually open. That meant that there were customers here this time, including a girl from Harper's biology class who was perusing the bestseller section.

Harper was starting to think that this might not be the best time. The things she wanted to talk about with Lydia wouldn't be good with an audience.

Unfortunately, the bell chimed whenever anyone opened the door, and it must've alerted Lydia. She appeared around an aisle from the back of the store before Harper could back out.

"Oh, hey there." Lydia smiled and appeared genuinely happy to see her. "I'm glad you came by because I wanted to show you something."

Then Lydia turned toward the store and, speaking loudly so her small voice would carry, she said, "Attention, everyone. I need to run downstairs to my office for a few minutes. If you need anything, push the buzzer by the cash register at the front desk, and I'll be up in a jiff. Okay?"

Her customers murmured agreement and understanding, so Lydia turned back to Harper, grinning. Lydia's outfit seemed a bit more sedate today, just a pair of skinny jeans and a purple tank top, but she wore glittery pink lip gloss that sparkled when she smiled.

"Shall we?" Lydia asked, but before Harper could reply, she started escorting her to the back of the store.

They went down the most dimly lit aisle of the store, where Lydia kept tarot cards, sensing stones, and all the really old books. And it wasn't like first editions of Charles Dickens old. Harper had once discovered one that appeared to be written in ancient Sumerian, but many of them were nearly falling apart from age.

Past that, in the back corner, Lydia pushed open a door that seemed too heavy for her. The wood had a marble grain unlike anything Harper had seen before, and as she walked past it, she ran her fingers along the glossy surface. It felt smooth and cool, like glass, under her fingertips.

"It's snakewood," Lydia said when she noticed Harper admiring the door. "It helps keep intruders out."

On the other side of the door was a small landing in front of a narrow concrete staircase. Lydia seemed to be struggling with the door, so Harper helped her push it closed, and it surprised her just how heavy it truly was.

"This is where I keep all the really old books," Lydia explained as she led the way down the steps.

"As opposed to those brand-new ones we just walked by?" Harper asked.

Lydia laughed, the tinkling sound echoing in the small space of the stairwell. "Well, the really *important* old books, then."

The bottom of the stairs opened into a surprisingly warm and dry basement, filled with bookshelves. It smelled distinctly of burning leaves, so much so that Harper began to fear that something was on fire.

"What's that burning smell?" she asked.

"It's just the potions," Lydia replied, as if Harper would know what that meant. "They keep the books safe."

While the books took up the majority of the basement, there was a small room to the left of the stairs. Lydia opened the door and gestured inside. "Won't you join me in my office?"

Harper went inside, and it was what she'd expected Lydia's office to look like. Three of the walls were painted pale pink, but the one behind her desk was wallpapered with a black-and-white fleur-de-lis pattern. Posters of book covers for J. M. Barrie's *Peter Pan*, Roald Dahl's *The Witches*, and Ralph Manheim's translation of *The Neverending Story* were hung around the room.

A computer and a framed photo sat on the simple black desk, but other than that, and the two office chairs, nearly everything else in the room was books. Books stacked in piles on the floor, on the desk, on overburdened shelves that were slouching on the walls. Three boxes sat on the floor behind the desk, and Harper couldn't see their contents, but she assumed they were more books.

"Are you sure it's okay that we're down here?" Harper asked as she sat down. "I mean, because of the customers. I don't want to take you away from your job."

"This is my job, too," Lydia explained as she moved the towers of books from her desk to the floor so she'd be able to see Harper when she sat down. "As much as I love uniting readers with their new favorite books, the reason I opened the bookstore is to help people like you. Selling books is a front for my *real* work."

"What do you mean?" Harper asked.

Lydia sat down and gave her a knowing smile. "There are just some problems that you can't go to the police for. There's no one you can call to help if you're a troll or a witch. It's not like the Ghostbusters are real, and even if they were, sometimes the ghosts need help, too."

"Do I owe you anything for all of this?" Harper asked. "You're doing so much work for us, and I'm so appreciative, and I feel like I should compensate you or something."

Lydia had never made mention of any form of payment, but now that she had referred to this as a job, Harper began to worry that she was taking advantage of her.

"No, no, don't be ridiculous." Lydia waved it off. "Nana always said that if we did the things we had to do and help those that needed it, then everything else would fall into place. And she was right."

"Thank you," Harper said emphatically. "I don't know what my sister or I would do if we didn't have you helping us."

"You're very welcome." Lydia smiled. "Now on to what I wanted to show you." She reached over to pull the lid off one of the boxes, then she stopped. "But you came here. Is there something you wanted to tell me?"

"Mostly just to ask you about your progress," Harper said. "And to tell you something about the scroll."

"What about it?" Lydia let go of the box lid and sat back in her chair.

"I brought the scroll to school yesterday to show a teacher, Professor Pine. He said he knew you."

"Oh, yeah. Kipling." Lydia smirked. "We go way back. He's a good guy."

"While I was talking to him about the scroll—I had it with me, so he could look at it—he accidentally spilled Red Bull all over it," Harper explained. "It didn't damage the scroll, of course, because nothing seems to be able to. But the ink began to glow, like a real vibrant crimson wherever the liquid touched."

"Did anything else happen?" Lydia asked.

"No, it just glowed for a few seconds. Then stopped," Harper said. "When I took it back to my dorm room, I tried a few other things on it. Water seemed to have the same effect, but milk did nothing."

"Hmm." Lydia seemed to consider it for a moment. "Do you have it with you?"

Harper frowned apologetically. "No. Sorry. Gemma was worried about having it out of her sight, so Marcy came by and picked it up this morning."

"That's fine." Lydia brushed it off. "Even if I had the scroll to look at it, it probably wouldn't matter. What happened with Pine and the Red Bull is normal."

"Scrolls glow when exposed to energy drinks?" Harper asked with a raised eyebrow.

"No, the writing reacts to different things, especially if the thing is related to the curse," Lydia said, and Harper just stared at her blankly. "Take Medusa's curse. You remember her, right? The chick with all the snakes in her hair?"

"Yeah, I've heard of Medusa."

"With hers, the paper would get incredibly warm, like scalding hot, when it came in contact with snake venom. I have no idea why or how anybody would put snake venom on it, but according to my research, that's what happened," Lydia said.

"So what does that mean?" Harper asked.

"I don't actually know for sure." Lydia shook her head sadly. "In Medusa's case, I believe that venom had been used in the ink or mixed with the papyrus or something. But I highly doubt that Red Bull was used in the creation of the sirens' curse."

"Yeah, I wouldn't think so."

"But maybe something in it was," Lydia said. "What's in Red Bull anyway? Water, sugar, caffeine?"

Harper nodded. "Pine said he thought the ink might be made of blood."

"Yeah, that would be in line with what I know about the sirens," Lydia agreed. "That could be the connection. Carbon dioxide is a waste product contained in blood, and it's also abundant in carbonated beverages, too. That would explain why Red Bull affects it, but milk doesn't."

"Yeah . . ." Harper said hesitantly. "But . . . so it doesn't mean anything?"

"Like is it some clue about how to destroy the scroll, thereby breaking the curse?" Lydia let out a long breath. "I honestly can't say one way or the other."

"Well, what about Medusa?" Harper asked. "Did venom help her destroy her scroll?"

"She didn't destroy her scroll," Lydia said. "I think she tried to for a while, which is probably how the venom experimentation came into play. But then she and Perseus fell in love—he liked the snake hair or something—so she stopped fighting it."

"Are you sure we're talking about the same thing?" Harper asked. "I've been reading a lot of mythology lately, and I'm pretty sure that nobody loved Medusa. In fact, I thought Perseus killed her."

"Originally, mythology was spread by word of mouth. In the days before the printing press, that's how information got around," Lydia said. "And some of the mouths spreading the word had their own horse in the race, and things got twisted up."

"How so?" Harper asked.

"Athena hated Medusa, and Athena was a much more powerful goddess, so what Athena said became the truth," Lydia explained. "Medusa was just a beautiful young girl, and she had an affair with Poseidon. And that pissed Athena off 'cause she had a thing for him, so she turned Medusa into the gorgon. Then, later, Athena sent Perseus to kill Medusa, but he fell in love with her instead, so then Athena finished the job herself."

"How do you know all this stuff?" Harper asked. "That's not written down in any of the books I've read. Some of it sounds similar, but Medusa's always described as a monstrosity, and Perseus as a brave hero for slaying her."

"That's because Athena was a huge asshole," Lydia said. "Think about it. She twisted their love story and made it into the exact opposite, so the rest of history would condemn Medusa. It's pretty sick.

"And as for how I know it, it's because that's what my family does," Lydia went on. "For centuries, we've been collecting all the information, all the truths from the supernatural elements of the world. We're the record keepers for the things in the world that the rest of humanity doesn't—or can't—properly record."

With that, Lydia swiveled her chair and took the lid off the box. As she began to rifle through its contents, Harper noticed the scar on Lydia's shoulder, red, beveled flesh protruding from around the strap of her tank top. Lydia had told her it was a werewolf bite, and Harper wondered about the price of being the paranormal world's memory keeper.

"That's actually what I wanted to talk to you about," Lydia said. She pulled out a green file, worn around the edges with a cracked spine. "Marcy asked me about Audra."

"Yes, she told me that you were related to her. She was your great-grandmother, right?"

Lydia nodded. "She was my grandmother's mother. And my grandma never married, and my mom never married, so it made tracing the lineage a bit easier from Panning to Panning."

"She wouldn't happen to still be alive, would she?" Harper asked hopefully.

"No, unfortunately, she's not," Lydia said. "She wouldn't be that old, though. I think . . ." She tilted her head as she did the math. "Audra would be in her eighties, but she passed away about fifteen years ago, and she'd already been in a sorry shape before. Very early onset dementia."

"I'm sorry to hear that," Harper said.

"It's a side effect of the profession, I think." Lydia sighed. "I didn't know her that well, which is why it's taken me a bit longer to break her code." She pulled papers out of the file, then she looked up at Harper. "Did Marcy explain to you about the code?"

"She said that Audra kept her journals coded," Harper said, and Lydia looked back down at the pages.

From where Harper sat, she didn't have the best angle to see them, but they appeared to be old pages from notebooks, yellowed a bit, but mostly okay. The words were written in very small cursive that she couldn't read at all.

"She did. If things weren't important, she'd write them in regular English, but if she needed to keep something especially private, she'd write in a code that only she could read," Lydia elaborated.

"Nana's code was a variation of Audra's, so that helps," Lydia said. "There's no one linear code that we go by, again, to make it hard for strangers to break. My own expands on Nana's, but Audra's code has a mind of its own, just like her.

"This file right here"—Lydia rested her hand on the green folder—"this is all of Audra's notes for the summer that Thalia came looking for her. So what I wanted to show is in here, and in fact—"

Lydia cut herself off and reached into the folder, digging around for something, and she pulled out two small black-and-white photos.

"I thought you might find this interesting." Lydia reached across the desk and handed one of the photos to her.

It showed three people. A woman, probably in her early thirties, with her light hair pulled up in a tight bun. While she was attractive, there was a hardness to her smile, and an almost devious glint in her eyes. Like she was hiding something.

In front of her stood a young girl, no more than nine or ten. Her long hair was in two braids, and she wore overalls. Her smile was bright, and it actually looked just like Lydia's.

The third woman, standing with her hand on the child's shoulder, Harper recognized instantly. It was the same radiant blonde she'd seen in all the pictures she found at Bernie's house.

"That's Thalia," Harper said, tapping the photo.

"I know. The other two people are Audra and my grandma," Lydia explained.

Harper flipped it over, finding an inscription on the back that said just as much—*Audra, Delia,* and then simply the letter *T.*

She turned it back over, searching the black-and-white photo for clues.

"Where was this taken?" Harper asked.

"I'm not sure," Lydia said. "I don't recognize the background, and I haven't found anything in Audra's notes."

The picture was taken at fairly close range, so she couldn't see much behind them. There appeared to be a flowerpot beside Thalia, overflowing with large roses. A building was behind them, but Harper couldn't see anything of it, really, other than the peak of the roof.

"What's the other picture of?" Harper asked as she handed the picture back to Lydia.

"It's a nephilim that Audra helped that summer, too." Lydia held it up for her, but Harper didn't look that closely at it, only noticing that it was a black-and-white shot of a handsome young man.

"So Audra definitely helped Thalia," Harper said.

"She did. From what I understand, she initially tried to free Thalia from being a muse . . . it's not really a curse, but it wasn't exactly a blessing, either. I don't know what you'd call it." Lydia wagged her head. "Anyway, Audra tried to help her but couldn't."

"You've been able to decipher that?" Harper asked.

"No, that part she just wrote out in regular English in her notes," Lydia said. "She didn't have anything to hide about *trying* to help someone. But then Audra went on to say that she needed to help Thalia find someone who needed her privacy respected."

"And you think that's Diana?" Harper asked.

"I think so." Lydia nodded. "I don't think that either Thalia or Audra knew exactly where Diana was, but working together, they found her."

"So where is Diana?" Harper asked.

"She's in the U.S. They drove to see her."

Harper's heart skipped a beat, and she asked, "Who are they?"

"Audra, Thalia, and I think even Nana went with them." Lydia squinted down at the papers in front of her.

"But they drove. So it can't be that far?" Harper asked. "Do you have any idea where?"

Lydia inhaled through her teeth. "I can't say yet. But I'll know soon. Very soon." She rustled through the papers. "I'm sorry. I know you don't have very much time, but I had to find Audra's things and go through them all to find the right folder, and now I'm having problems because Audra's being *very* cryptic to protect this Diana's privacy.

"But that's actually part of the good news," Lydia said.

"What do you mean?" Harper asked.

"If Audra's going through all the trouble to protect Diana, she has to be important. I'm not a gambler, but I'd put my money on Diana's being a goddess," Lydia said.

"And even if she wasn't, she still knew how to set Thalia free," Harper said. "So it stands to reason that she'd know how to set Gemma free."

"I don't want you getting your hopes up too high, but yes, I do think that Diana will know *something* that can help Gemma break the curse." Lydia smiled at her. "And I'm struggling now with trying to find her, but I will find her. This is top priority for me. Which also brings me to my next question."

"What's that?"

"I've been focusing most of my attention on the journal and Audra's notes," Lydia said. "Which means I haven't been working on the scroll translations. Is that how you wanted me to do it? Or would you rather me work more on the scroll?"

"Um . . ." Harper furrowed her brow as she weighed both the options. "I guess . . . let's find Diana. Pine sent the scroll to some of his colleagues to translate, so since he's already working on that, I'd rather have you looking for Diana."

"That's what I thought. I did have some thoughts on the scroll, but I can keep in touch with Pine," Lydia said. "I'll pass my notes along to him, too."

When Harper left Cherry Lane, she felt an odd mixture of hope and trepidation. Lydia seemed to be on the right track, which meant they were closer to breaking the curse than they ever had been before.

TWENTY-TWO

Resolve

After Liv's theatrics the day before and Thea's weary accep-
tance of their fate, Gemma felt more uneasy and restless
than normal. Liv was nuts, and no one was going to do anything
to stop her.

Gemma might have to resign herself to being a siren for the
rest of her life, but that didn't mean that everyone had to suffer.
Or that anyone else had to get hurt. It was time that Gemma got
a handle on her powers—no matter how evil and frightening
they might be—and take care of Penn and Liv herself.

The other day, when she'd practiced shifting with Daniel,
things had gone well—for the most part. But since then, she'd
been having nightmares about when she'd killed Jason. When it
happened, she'd blacked out, but now the dormant memories
were resurfacing in brutal images that haunted her nightmares.

The guilt and the hunger plagued her, but Gemma couldn't
let either of those things stop her. The hunger would only grow

stronger, so she had to learn to control it, to control her impulses and the monster inside that drove them.

She wasn't the same scared girl she'd been when she ran off with the sirens in June, and it was time she stopped acting like that.

Her room felt too small to practice any of the larger transformations, so she decided to try things out in the garage.

It was mostly empty since her dad parked his truck in the driveway, behind her dead car. A couple sawhorses, a few old cinder blocks, and a tool chest sat in the middle of the room, and Gemma pushed them to the side, so she'd have more space.

One small window let the sunlight stream in. There were no blinds to cover it, but it faced Alex's house, so she didn't think there was a high risk of anybody peeping in to see her.

So with everything out of the way and ready, Gemma focused and tried to make her wings appear.

And nothing happened.

Squeezing her eyes shut, balling up her fists, and trying with all her might did nothing. She even tried holding her breath, and her face had probably begun to turn bright red when a knock at the side door interrupted her, and she started breathing again.

It wasn't the door that led into the house or the large garage door for the cars, but the door on the side, so Gemma opened it cautiously and found Alex, grinning at her. His hair was damp, and he smelled sweetly of apple shampoo.

"What are you doing here?" Gemma asked him with a confused smile.

"I just got done with work a little bit ago, so I thought I'd stop over and see if you wanted to hang out. Then I saw you through the window." He pointed to it. "What are you doing out here?"

She wiped the sweat from her brow with the back of her arm. It wasn't even that warm out, but she'd been straining so hard, she'd begun to perspire. "I was trying to practice transforming, but it hasn't been going so well."

Alex leaned on the doorframe and cocked an eyebrow. "Transforming?"

"Like how the sirens change. I can do that, and I need to learn to harness my strength so that I can fight them," she explained. "I need to be able to stop them if I need to."

"So you're gonna turn into that weird monster now?" Alex asked, and he didn't show any of the fear or revulsion she'd been expecting.

"Eventually," she admitted. "I want to work my way back up to it. I tried the other day with Daniel, and nothing bad happened, but it's at the very edge of my control. I thought I'd try with something safer today, like just the wings."

He nodded and straightened up. "So how can I help?"

Gemma had been hanging on to the door and standing in front of Alex, blocking his entry to the garage, and when he made like he meant to step inside, she didn't move. "Thanks for the offer, but it's probably better if I try it on my own."

"Why?" He shook his head, not understanding. "You practiced with Daniel the other day."

She looked up into his eyes, trying to get a read on him, and tilted her head. "You can't be jealous over that."

"No I'm not," Alex agreed. "At least not the way you mean."

"Why on earth would you be jealous? He put himself in danger, and that's nothing you should want for yourself."

"Because you rely on him more than you do me," he told her. In the last month, Alex had gotten much better at hiding his feelings, and he kept his expression even, but his dark eyes betrayed the hurt he felt. "I'm much stronger than you give me credit for, Gemma."

"This isn't about strength. This is about my not wanting to do anything that could hurt you ever again." She stared up at him, imploring him to understand.

"You don't care if Daniel gets hurt?" Alex countered.

"No, of course I do, but . . ."

She sighed and stepped back from the door. Alex stayed where he was, standing in the doorway, and she leaned back against a sawhorse.

"You think he can handle it better than I can," Alex said.

She shrugged. "He's just been around it more."

"Gemma, I've known you for over ten years. I've seen the sirens you're fighting against. I said I'd do anything to be with you, and I meant it, knowing full well who you are and what you have in your life." He'd been walking toward her as he spoke, and he stopped right in front of her, so close that her legs were brushing up against his. "I can handle you and your monsters. But you have to trust me."

"What if I hurt you?"

He reached down and took her hand in his. "I would rather get hurt fighting by your side than live forever a hundred miles away."

"So you really wanna do this? You wanna be a part of everything?" Gemma asked.

"I do."

"Okay." She smiled at him. "Close the door."

When Alex went to shut the door, Gemma got up and walked to the center of the room. She stretched her neck from side to side and rolled her shoulders.

"I haven't figured out how to force the changes yet. I'm gonna try to make this happen, but I'm not sure that anything will."

Alex leaned back against the freezer chest and crossed his arms over his chest. "How did you do it the other day?"

"I was thinking of things that scared me," she said, remembering how she'd changed in the Paramount Theater. "Terror seems to incite the transformation, like it's a defense mechanism. But I don't think it's good for me to be so afraid, to make the change happen that way."

He nodded. "That makes sense. Like in the Green Lantern comics, the yellow power harnesses fear, making it unstable and corruptible. You want something purer, like willpower or hope or love."

Gemma couldn't help but laugh a little at her boyfriend. "I like how you can bring any topic back to comics."

"But it's true, right?" Alex asked. "How many times have you fully transformed into the monster?"

"Only once fully." She lowered her eyes, and her heart tightened at the memory. "With Daniel, I was almost full, but not completely. I've been able to do my hands a few times, and my wings just the once."

"And each time you transformed, were you scared?" Alex asked.

She swallowed hard and nodded. "I was terrified. I thought I would be hurt or killed, or that someone I care about would be hurt or killed."

"You were letting fear control you and, in turn, the monster. *You* need to be the one in control."

"So I need to just *will* wings to sprout from my back?" Gemma asked.

He shrugged. "Yeah."

Gemma thought back to when she'd made her wings come out before. Lexi had just thrown her over the cliff, and Gemma was perched on a rock as the waves crashed around her while Daniel fought for his life against Lexi back up at the top. The wings had been slow to come even though Gemma was willing them to with all her might. It had only been her fear that had finally spurred the change on.

"I'm not sure I can do it. Not without channeling some of my fear," she insisted.

"If you let your fear motivate you, then you're not in control. The monster is. And that's when someone will get hurt."

"I know, but I don't know how else to do it." She ran her hand through her hair in exasperation. "Maybe there is no other way. Maybe the sirens are all just channeling their fear and hunger, and that's how they morph."

"You really think Penn is afraid that often?" Alex asked dubiously.

"Maybe not, but she's probably hungry all the time."

Alex chewed his thumbnail and stared down at the floor. His bangs fell over his forehead, and Gemma knew that expression well. She'd seen it when he'd been working on homework or struggling with a level on a video game. He wore it whenever he was trying to work something out.

"What are you most afraid of?" he asked finally, and lifted his head.

"You mean besides getting myself and the people I care about killed?" Gemma asked with an empty laugh.

"Which are you more afraid of—dying yourself or other people dying?"

"I don't want to die, but . . . It would be much worse if something happened to you or Harper or my parents or Daniel."

"Why?"

Gemma laughed again. "What do you mean, why?"

"Why would it be so terrible if I died?" Alex asked directly.

"Because." She didn't understand what he was getting at, but he was trying to figure out something, so she decided to go with it. "I love you. But that's not even the worst part of your dying. As much as it would kill me to lose you, the real tragedy of your death would have nothing to do with me.

"You are kind and smart and loyal and amazing, and you have so much that you have yet to experience and so much that you can and will give back to the world. You need a full, wonderful life, and the thought of cutting that short, even by a second, is one of the worst things I can imagine."

"Then think of that," Alex said. "If your will alone isn't

enough, then think of love. Not just me, but Harper and your mom. Anyone that means anything to you. Love is stronger than fear."

"Okay."

Gemma closed her eyes and took a deep breath. She tried to focus on Alex—not on the fear of losing him but on how much she loved him. Thinking of his kisses, the way his arms felt around her, the way he laughed, and she imagined her wings breaking through her skin.

"You can do this. Look at me," Alex said, his voice firm and confident, and she opened her eyes to meet his. "Gemma. You've got this."

And then she saw it again, the way she had when they'd kissed before. Her whole world was in his eyes. There was only love, and only him, and as she exhaled slowly, she felt it begin. Her shoulders began to itch, then she heard the bones crack and the tearing. Heat seared both of her shoulder blades, and Alex's eyes widened, and his jaw slacked.

And she could feel them. Her wings spread out behind her, and when she moved them, she felt the air moving through her feathers.

"That is amazing." Alex was in awe as he stared up at her wings, glistening like copper in the light through the garage window.

She smiled at him. "I did it."

"You did. I knew you could."

He grinned and walked over to her. Wrapping his arms around

her waist, he leaned in for a kiss, but just before their lips met, he stopped. He pulled his hand back, and his fingertips were red.

"You're bleeding," Alex said, and looked down at her with concern.

"Yeah, the wings bleed. And hurt." She grimaced even though the pain had stopped. "I don't know why because the rest of the transformation doesn't."

He wiped the blood off on his jeans and tentatively reached up to touch one of her wings. When he ran his fingers over the silky feathers, Gemma felt a shiver of pleasure run through her.

"Maybe Demeter thought the wings were too much of a blessing, so she added a little pain so you'd know they were really a curse," Alex said as he admired her wings.

"Maybe."

"So . . ." His arm was still around her waist, and he smiled down at her. "Do you wanna take these wings out for a spin?"

"I can't exactly fly out from the garage." Gemma put her arms around his neck and leaned against him. "Thea and Penn sometimes fly around town, but they're better at entrancing people, so they forget they saw them. I'd rather not risk having to hypnotize any birdwatchers and sightseers, especially since Capri is overrun with tourists this week."

"Okay," Alex said with some reluctance. "But you owe me one flight, okay?"

"You really want me to take you out?" Gemma asked.

"Yeah. Not every part of this damned siren thing is terrible, so we might as well enjoy the good parts while we can."

He put his other arm around her, pressing her to him. Her halter top had ridden up when she put her arms around his neck, and his hands felt warm and strong on the exposed flesh between her top and shorts.

Finally, Alex leaned down and kissed her. She stood on her tiptoes, trying to kiss him more deeply, but the wings put her off balance. Gemma started to fall forward, pushing Alex back, and instinctively, her wings began to flap, trying to steady her.

The garage was really too small for a wingspan of her length to be able to flap, and she only succeeded in knocking tools off the wall and tipping over a sawhorse. She moved, trying to get away from the more dangerous tools, and she only succeeded in tumbling forward. Alex landed on his back, and she fell on top of him.

"I never realized how hard it must be for Big Bird to make out," Alex said, and Gemma began to laugh.

The garage door leading inside the house suddenly opened, and Brian leaned in, probably summoned by the noise from her knocking things down.

"What's going on?" Brian demanded.

Gemma had been lying on top of Alex, so she scrambled to get up before her dad decided to go retrieve his shotgun again. Alex hurried to do the same, smoothing out his shirt as Brian glared down at them.

"I was just trying out my wings, and I fell," Gemma said sheepishly.

Brian looked at her wings, but he kept his expression hard,

then glared back at Alex. "You may think that because my daughter has wings and all kinds of strange powers that I won't kick your ass if you hurt her. But you'd be wrong."

"*Dad!*" Gemma said, but she wasn't really mad. She knew that a lot of things were out of his control now that Gemma was exposed to dangers he couldn't fight. All he could really do was try to protect her from the things he still could, like teenage boys.

"I understand, Mr. Fisher," Alex said respectfully.

"Good." Brian nodded, and when he looked at Gemma's wings again, he was a little awed. "Those are amazing. Good work." He started to head back into the house, then he stopped. "Leave this door open. Okay?"

TWENTY-THREE

Conspiring

Her afternoon classes had ended twenty minutes ago, and Harper had just finished packing her bag when her cell phone rang. As soon as she saw the number on the screen, her heart sank. This was the last thing she wanted to deal with today.

"Hello?" she answered the phone, and hoped that she didn't sound as unhappy as she felt.

"Hello, Harper, this is Becky from Briar Ridge. I'm sorry to bother you."

"No, it's okay," she said, because what else could she say? Briar Ridge only ever called if it was important, and no matter what Harper might have planned for today, her family always came first.

"We tried calling your house, since we know you're away at school, but nobody answered, and we just don't know what to do anymore," Becky said in one hurried breath.

"It's fine," Harper insisted. "Really. What's going on? Is something wrong with my mom?"

"She's been very anxious since you took her to the play on Saturday, and we've been trying to calm her down," Becky said. "We didn't want to bother you, but it's been four days, and nothing's worked."

"Anxious?" Harper sat down on the bed, next to her book bag. "Like how? What is she doing?"

"She's been repeating lines from plays on and off, and she's more confused than normal," Becky explained. "We can't get her to sit still or eat or even take her meds. And she's been talking about you and your sister a lot, too."

Harper pushed her hair back off her forehead and exhaled. "You want me to come down and see what I can do?"

"If it wouldn't be too much trouble. We're really at our wits' end here, and we need to get her to take her pills."

"No, it's no problem." She forced a smile even though there was no one there to see it. "I'll be there in about ten minutes."

One added advantage of being in Sundham is that it was only ten minutes away from Briar Ridge. She was farther from home, but it made for quicker trips to see her mom.

This wasn't the first time that Harper had to drop what she was doing and rush out to take care of her mother, but it had been a long time. Nathalie had calmed some in recent years, but lately, everything seemed to be off-kilter with her.

Maybe it was Harper's fault for taking Nathalie to the play. It had been a long time since she'd been back to Capri. But even before the play, Nathalie had been acting strangely. The visit with Brian two and a half weeks ago must've triggered something in her.

While she raced to Briar Ridge from Sundham, Harper blasted the radio and sang along with it, trying to calm herself since she'd already been nervous when Becky had called. This was definitely not the way she had envisioned her Wednesday going, but she had to do the right thing. Her mom needed her.

As soon as Becky opened the door, Harper could hear Nathalie, telling them that she needed to get going.

"You've all been very nice, but I need to get home. I have to make supper for my husband and kids," Nathalie was saying firmly.

"She thinks she has to take care of her family?" Harper asked Becky in a low voice, careful so Nathalie wouldn't hear her.

Becky smiled thinly at her. "She's been going on about it all day. Maybe you can have a go at her."

"Sure."

Harper went into the house and followed the sound of her mother's voice. She discovered her in the living room, where Nathalie was talking to another woman who worked at the group home. Her long, shapeless dress billowed out behind her as she paced.

Nathalie's hair was greasy and tangled, like it hadn't been washed or brushed, which was unusual as she was normally a very clean person. Her eyes had dark circles under them, and her lips appeared dry and chapped. This was the worst Harper had seen her in ages.

"What's going on here?" Harper asked with as much cheer as

she could muster, and the staff member quietly excused herself, leaving Harper alone to calm her mother.

"I've been visiting with these nice girls, and they've been so kind, but I have to get going." Nathalie stopped walking enough to look at Harper for help. "My husband will be expecting me soon, and my daughters will be home from school. I have to make supper."

Harper smiled and tried to keep her words soothing. "Mom, I am your daughter."

"Don't be ridiculous." Nathalie laughed, then returned to her pacing. "You're much too old to be my daughter."

"How old do you think your daughters are?" Harper asked.

"Harper turned nine this past January, and Gemma just turned seven." Nathalie smiled when she talked about them, appearing genuinely happy for a few seconds, before fear flickered in her golden eyes.

"Mom." She stepped in front of Nathalie, blocking her path and forcing her to stop and look at her. "I *am* Harper."

"No, you're not." Nathalie shook her head and smiled uneasily. "You're . . . a woman. My daughter is a child. And I'm starting to think this joke isn't very funny. Now, I need to be going." She tried to brush past her, but Harper gently put a hand on her shoulder, stopping her.

"Nathalie, you don't have anywhere to be." Harper smiled and kept her tone light. "Your husband took your kids out for supper. You're fine here. If you had fun visiting today, why don't we visit for a while?"

"I don't want to visit." Nathalie stepped away from Harper

and rubbed her arm. Her eyes darted around the room. "I want to go."

"Let's sit down." Harper sat on the couch and patted the spot next to her.

Nathalie shook her head. "I'm not sitting down."

"So what have you been doing today?" Harper asked, hoping that changing the subject might relax her mom.

"I already told you," she snapped. "I was visiting with these girls, and I have to remember."

"What?"

Nathalie had begun pacing again, and she rubbed her temple. "I have to remember to tell them to wash it away."

"Tell who to wash it away?" Harper asked. She stared up, her eyes following her mother as she frantically walked in circles.

"She'll know what it means." Nathalie waved her off. "You don't need to worry about it."

"Okay. I won't worry," Harper said.

Nathalie stopped suddenly and looked around the room like she had no idea where she was. "Where are my girls? Is Bernie watching them?"

"Bernie?" Harper asked, surprised to hear Nathalie mention him.

Before the accident, her mother had been friends with Bernie McAllister, but she'd hardly mentioned him in the near decade since. He'd even visited her many times, especially when Harper and Gemma had been younger, and it had been hard for their dad to take them.

But every time he'd come in with them, Nathalie had asked

who he was without any hint of recognition. It was as if he'd been erased from her memories. Until now.

"Is he watching them?" Nathalie paused. "I have a date tonight with my husband, so Bernie must be watching them." She nodded, as if to convince herself.

"You remember Bernie, Mom?" Harper asked.

"Of course I do." She looked down at Harper like she was a crazy person. "Why do you keep calling me Mom?"

"Sorry. It was an accident." Harper gave her a sheepish smile. "Do you remember your husband? Brian?"

Nathalie stared off and rubbed the back of her neck. "Bernie's the one who told me, you know."

"Told you what?"

"I already said!" She shot her a glare. "If you aren't gonna pay attention, then I might as well go."

"You can't go anywhere, Nathalie. You live here," Harper reminded her gently.

"I do not. Why are you lying to me?" Nathalie's voice grew louder the more agitated she got, and she was nearly shouting now. "Why do you keep lying to me?"

"I'm not lying to you," Harper said evenly. "Will you please just sit down?"

"No. I won't sit down." Nathalie shook her head and stomped her foot. "Not when all of you are lying and conspiring, and you're out to get my daughters."

"Nobody is out to get your daughters," Harper tried to reassure her.

"You are! Don't you lie to me!" Nathalie was screaming now, her pale cheeks were bright red, and her eyes were filled with tears. "He wouldn't have told me to wash it away if you weren't out to hurt my girls!"

"Mom!" Harper stood up and held her hands out in front of her. "Your girls are just fine. I am your daughter, and Gemma is safe."

"You are not my daughter," Nathalie insisted, as a tear slid down her face. "Harper is a little girl."

"Yeah, I was," Harper said. "Nine years ago. But you had an accident, and now we've grown up. Do you remember any of that, Mom?"

Nathalie had never been able to remember the accident itself, and even Harper only had sketchy memories of it. But Nathalie usually seemed to remember that there had been some kind of accident, that she hadn't always been like this, but now it seemed like she didn't even know any time had passed. She was stuck in some lost moment in the days before the accident.

"No, there was . . ." Nathalie wiped at her face, and she started shaking her head. "No." She swallowed hard, then balled her hands into fists and began hitting herself on the thighs, hard enough that Harper could hear it. "No. No!"

"Mom, stop." Harper reached for her mother's hands, trying to stop her before she hurt herself, but Nathalie yanked them free.

She ran to the entertainment center, pushing off the knick-knacks and movies stacked on top. Anything Nathalie could grab or break or throw, she did. She was sobbing and repeating the word "no" over and over as she pulled over a bookcase, ripped pictures off the wall, and tore cushions off the couch.

All the commotion had alerted Becky, and both she and Harper tried to talk Nathalie down, but it was no use. Within only a few minutes, Nathalie had destroyed the room, and now she collapsed amid the mess.

Her knees were underneath her, her head slumped against the floor. Harper knelt next to her. Cautiously, she put her hand on her mother's back and slowly began to rub it.

"It's going to be okay," Harper told her softly.

Nathalie peered up at her and brushed her hair from her eyes. "Harper?"

Harper smiled down at her and tried to blink back the tears in her own eyes. "Yeah, Mom, it's me."

"I don't feel very well. I think I should go lie down."

"That sounds like a very good idea," Harper agreed.

After Harper helped Nathalie to her room, she covered her up and made sure she was comfortable. Becky came in with pills and a glass of water, and Nathalie took them without argument. Her outburst seemed to have exhausted her.

Harper bent down, kissed her mom on the cheek, and started to leave. "I love you, Mom. I'll see you later."

"Harper." Nathalie looked back at her, and Harper paused in the doorway. "Remember to wash it away. Promise me that you'll remember."

"I will, Mom."

She closed the bedroom door behind her, then went straight

to the bathroom. Leaning against the sink, Harper began to sob. As quietly as she could, she let herself once again mourn her mother. On days like this, it felt like she'd lost Nathalie all over again.

When she'd cried long enough, Harper splashed cold water on her face, washing away the salt and smeared eyeliner. Then she dug in her purse and reapplied her makeup until she once again looked like a normal college girl and not someone whose life was falling apart.

TWENTY-FOUR

Blood & Water

The scroll lay on the kitchen table, weighted down with coffee grounds and a two-liter bottle of cola to keep from rolling up. Any fluid that Gemma could find in the fridge, she'd tried on it, before moving on to cleaning supplies. Now chicken broth and bleach sat puddled together on the papyrus, and the iridescent ink glowed dully through the liquid, taunting her.

With her arms crossed over her chest, Gemma bounced on the balls of her feet, as if that would somehow knock an idea free, and she'd realize how to break the stupid curse.

She kept thinking back to the night she had become a siren, certain that there must be some sort of clue there. Gemma had been in the bay, enjoying a night swim, and the sirens had been dancing around a fire in the cove.

This was before Gemma knew what they really were, and Lexi sang to her, calling to her. When she swam toward them, the siren song blocked out all fear and reason, and her body moved on its own.

When Gemma reached the shore, Lexi held out her hand and pulled her to her feet.

Penn had been dancing with a shawl around her. It was made of some kind of gauzy gold material, and she placed it over Gemma's shoulders. "Here. To keep you warm."

Then Lexi had put an arm around her, and at her touch the hairs on the back of Gemma's neck stood up. Instinctively, Gemma pulled away, but then Lexi began singing again, and the siren song trapped her there.

"Come join us." Penn had kept her eyes on Gemma and stepped backwards, toward the fire.

Lexi reached into the front of her dress and pulled out a small copper flask. "Let's have a drink."

"Sorry, I don't drink."

"*Gemma*," Lexi said, her voice a song again. She held out the flask, but Gemma hesitated. "*Drink*."

Then Gemma didn't seem to have a choice. She couldn't even consider refusing. Her hands moved on their own, taking the flask from Lexi, unscrewing the top, and putting it to her lips. It seemed involuntary, like breathing.

The liquid was thick, and it tasted bitter and salty on her tongue. It burned going down her throat. It felt too heavy and hot to swallow, and she gagged.

Much later, Penn would tell her what the liquid had really been made of—blood of a siren, blood of a mortal, and blood of the sea. When Gemma had found out, she'd nearly thrown up.

The cove had seemed to pitch to the side after she'd managed to swallow the mixture, and Gemma grabbed on to Lexi to keep from falling. Everything was swayed. She tried to stand up and nearly tipped forward into the fire, but Penn caught her, and then the world faded to black.

After she'd passed out, Penn had wrapped her in the shawl completely and then tossed her into the ocean. If the curse worked, Gemma would awaken as a siren the next morning. And if it didn't, she would drown.

Fortunately—or unfortunately, depending on how she looked at it—the curse had worked, and Gemma had woken up on the rocky shore a siren.

"What am I missing?" Gemma whispered to herself now in her kitchen. "There has to be something that made the curse that will also help break it." Then it hit her. *"Blood."*

The instant she said it, she was reminded of a text that Harper had sent her on Monday after she'd visited with her professor. He hadn't been able to translate much of the scroll, and he wasn't certain about what little he had. But a phrase he'd guessed at stood out.

"The blood can't become water," she recited, repeating what Harper had messaged her.

When she'd woken up this morning, Gemma had run down to the bay and filled up a jar with saltwater from the ocean. She'd tried it on the scroll, and other than glowing a little, nothing much had happened, and the mason jar sat on the kitchen table, still half full of seawater.

"It can't be that simple," she said as she eyed the jar, but she went over to the kitchen drawer and pulled out a sharp steak knife.

Biting her lip to steel herself against the pain, she sliced the blade down her finger. As soon as the blood started flowing, she held her finger over the scroll and squeezed it, dripping it down on the words.

Quickly, she picked up the jar and poured a little bit of water over the blood. The words began to glow brighter than she'd seen them before, and using her cut finger, she smeared the blood and water together, pushing it deeper into the paper.

The words continued to glow for a few more seconds, but then they just faded back to normal. Truthfully, Gemma hadn't expected anything much different. The mixture that Penn had used to turn Gemma into a siren had been the blood of a siren, the blood of a mortal, and the blood of the ocean.

She had the siren and ocean part covered. Now all she needed was a mortal, and, fortunately, she thought she knew of one who would be eager to give up her blood. Gemma pulled out her phone and quickly wrote a text.

Within ten minutes of sending Marcy the message, her friend was knocking at the front door. While she'd been waiting for her, Gemma had tried an experiment with just her blood, and although she hadn't expected it to work, she had to give it a shot.

When Gemma answered the front door, Marcy was standing on the front step, and Kirby stood on the step below her, offering her a sheepish smile when Gemma looked at him in surprise.

"Oh. I didn't realize you were bringing Kirby," Gemma said.

"We were hanging out, so I thought he'd tag along," Marcy explained. "Besides, you said it was an emergency."

"I never said it was an emergency. I asked if you could come over real quick," Gemma corrected her. "But thanks for being so speedy."

"Is it a problem that I'm here?" Kirby asked. "I can leave or go wait in Marcy's car or something."

"Normally, I wouldn't mind, but I had kind of a . . . personal favor for Marcy," Gemma tried to explain, and gave him an apologetic smile.

"Is this about feminine hygiene?" Marcy asked.

"What? *No.* Ew." Gemma shook her head. "No, this is about the . . . scroll."

"You're talking about the whole siren thing?" Kirby asked.

Gemma was taken aback. "You told him?"

Marcy shrugged. "Yeah, Kirb's cool. If he can't handle the stuff I'm into, then we couldn't hang out. So I had to tell him about it, and he passed the test."

"Are you sure you're really cool with the whole siren thing?" Gemma asked Kirby, ignoring Marcy's assurances that he could handle all things supernatural. "Because it's gonna get even weirder."

"Yeah, I think I can tough it out." He nodded eagerly, and Marcy gave him a smile of approval.

"Okay," Gemma said, since she couldn't argue with that. "Because I need some blood."

"Does it need to be a certain type? Because I'm O positive,"

Marcy said, then pointed her thumb at Kirby. "And Kirby is AB positive."

"How do you know his blood type?" Gemma asked.

"I'm very thorough when I vet the people I hang out with," Marcy said.

"Very thorough," Kirby added with wide eyes and a heavy sigh.

"No, it doesn't matter what type." Gemma stepped back from the door and motioned for them to come in. "Let's get inside. I feel strange talking about blood on the front stoop."

"Whatever makes you comfortable," Marcy said.

"The blood just has to be mortal, but I'm not even entirely sure how much I'll need," Gemma admitted, as Marcy and Kirby followed her into the kitchen. Kirby surveyed the mess in the kitchen and did his best to look unruffled, while Marcy didn't even bat an eye.

"Should we be breaking into a blood bank?" Marcy suggested.

"I thought I'd start with a drop or two from you, then take it from there," Gemma said.

"All right. Do you have a sharp knife?" Marcy asked.

"Aren't you even gonna ask what it's about?"

"I'm gonna go out on a limb, but I'm guessing it's about breaking the curse," Marcy said dryly, and gestured to the scroll on the table. "But if you wanted to elaborate, I wouldn't mind."

"Harper told me about her professor thinking the ink was made of blood," Gemma said as she went over to the kitchen drawer to grab a new steak knife. "Then Harper told me that

Lydia thought that made sense, since the curse was usually written in something that pertained to it. And then, finally, it's so obvious—the way to break the curse is the curse itself."

"Okay, right. That makes sense." Marcy nodded. "So . . . you're turning the paper into a siren?"

"I'll use the methodology for it. I became a siren by drinking a potion—blood of a mortal, blood of a siren, and blood of the sea."

"What's the blood of the sea?" Kirby asked.

Gemma lifted up the mason jar to show him. "Just water."

"So your plan is to make a mixture of your blood, my blood, and ocean water, and then just rub it all over the scroll?" Marcy asked, and Gemma nodded, so Marcy pushed up the sleeve of her hooded sweatshirt. "All right. Let's get started."

Before they began, Gemma used a paper towel to wipe the scroll completely clean. She didn't want their blood and water mixing with residue from anything else that might screw it up.

Gemma tried to cut Marcy's finger, but she felt weird about hurting her. Then Marcy tried to do it herself, also without success, so finally, Kirby had to step in and save the day. With Marcy looking the other way, Kirby sliced the knife down her finger.

Marcy held her hand over the scroll, squeezing droplets out. Gemma's finger had already healed again, so, hurriedly, she sliced open her own finger and mixed her blood with Marcy's, then added the water last.

It wasn't as much as she would've liked, but it was enough that she could smear it on the words of the scroll. The symbols began to glow beneath, shining brightly through her blood in a vibrant crimson.

At first, it seemed no different from before, when Gemma had tried out the energy drink for herself. But then they began to blaze even brighter, the dark ink shifting from red to an orange flame, like they were on fire.

She held her breath, thinking that this might finally be it . . . and then just as abruptly as it started, it stopped. The ink faded to its usual russet color. Nothing had changed.

"Well that sucks," said Marcy. "I thought the scroll was going to burst into flames, then nothing. It's never reacted that strongly before, right?"

Gemma bit her lip and shook her head, staring thoughtfully at the scroll. "That's definitely never happened before, not like that. I wish we had the translation because I don't know *why* it happened."

TWENTY-FIVE

Eternity

Daniel sat in the driver's seat of the car he'd borrowed from Alex and took another fortifying breath. His phone was in his hand, still glowing from the last text he'd received. It'd been Harper, replying to his with, "I love you, too."

He'd wanted to say something more, but he couldn't think of anything else. This might be the last thing he ever said to Harper, and if it was, "I love you" was the only thing that really mattered in the end.

Before he'd left the house, he'd gone over everything. He made sure to leave the keys on the dining room table, along with his mother's phone number and insurance info. He'd tried to write a letter as a last will and testament, but he wasn't really leaving much behind. The only things in his life that really mattered to him were his boat and Harper.

Today was his twenty-first birthday, and he was going to have sex with a woman he hated, and though he hoped she would accept his offer to become her concubine, he knew there was a very good chance she might kill him when she was done. He would die on the day he was born. At least that had some nice symmetry to it.

He was focused on the phone, on Harper's last text to him, and he didn't notice Penn until she was knocking on the car window, smiling seductively at him. Trying to force a smile back at her, he pushed the button to roll down the window.

"Are you ever planning on coming inside, or did you wanna do it in the car?" Penn asked, leaning on the door so he could see down the front of her slinky black dress. "Because I've done it in cars before, and it's not as hot as it sounds."

"I'll go in . . . unless you planned on changing your mind about today."

Penn threw back her head and laughed. "No way. Let's go."

When he rolled up the window, she stepped back. He turned off the ignition and decided to leave the keys and his phone in the car. It would be easier for people to find if Penn killed him tonight.

He followed her into the house, and he was surprised to see how everything had been decked out. No lights were on, but there had to be a thousand candles casting a warm glow over everything. Civil Twilights played softly on a stereo, but otherwise, the house was silent.

"Your sisters are gone?" Daniel asked as he glanced around.

"Yeah. I sent them away for the night, so we have the place to ourselves," Penn said over her shoulder as she walked into the kitchen.

"I suppose I would prefer this without an audience," he said under his breath.

A bottle of wine was chilling in a bucket of ice on the counter. Without asking if he wanted any, Penn poured two glasses and walked back over to him.

"Here, have some." She handed him a glass. "It'll loosen you up."

Instead of taking a sip, Daniel sniffed the glass. "You didn't drug this or anything, did you?"

Penn laughed again and tossed her silken black hair over her shoulder. "Of course not. I want you totally present for tonight."

"Thanks." He took a long swallow, almost gulping it down.

"Why don't I show you to the bedroom?" Penn suggested.

"So soon? Shouldn't we warm up first? Get to know each other?"

When she smiled, there was a devilish sparkle in her dark eyes, one that Daniel found unsettling. "I think I know everything about you I need to know."

Taking his hand, Penn led him through the living room and up the staircase to the loft above. There was only one bed in the center of the room, covered in black satin sheets. The bed had a heavy-looking iron headboard, with a gold wrap draped across it, apparently to set the mood, and Daniel wondered dimly where Thea's and Liv's beds were.

She took his wineglass from him, now nearly empty, and set it on the nightstand next to a black candle with an oddly purple flame. Then she came back to him, standing so close that when he breathed in deeply, his chest pressed against hers. The smile playing on her lips was wicked, and she gently bit her lip with teeth that were too sharp to be human.

Her tanned skin seemed to glow in the flickering candles, and he tried to think about how beautiful she was. If he could focus on the lovely parts of her exterior instead of the vile creature that lurked beneath, he might be able to get through this.

Penn seemed to be waiting for him to make the first move, so he knew he needed to do something. He put his hand on the small of her back, pressing her body against him, and he could feel the warmth of her skin through the thin fabric.

That was all Penn needed, and a small, purring sound escaped her lips. She reached up and ran her fingers through his disheveled hair until her hand rested on the back of his neck. Her grip was strong, too strong, and her fingers felt like fire, sending hot electricity through him.

Penn kissed him slow at first, reminding him of the way she'd kissed him out on Bernie's Island. Her mouth worked gently against his for a moment, but she couldn't keep up the restraint for very long.

She put her arms around him, almost clinging to him. As she fell back on the bed, she was pulling him down with her, and he let her. He lay on top of her, and her legs wrapped around him, holding him to her. When she pushed up against him, he felt his body responding.

He needed the physical reaction to get him through this, to be able to perform and keep Harper safe, but he'd never before felt more betrayed by his own skin. Penn was repulsive and monstrous, and no part of him should find any pleasure in this.

Breathing heavily, he pulled away from her, which was rather difficult when she clung to him so tightly. He held himself up with his arms above her, and her lips were pressed into a tight pout.

"Penn, can I ask you something?"

She rolled her eyes and groaned. "Haven't we talked enough?"

"No, I need to know something."

"Daniel." She ran her hands through his hair, so her fingers went over the scar that ran along the back of his head. "Come on. You can't back out of this now."

"I'm not. I swear, I'm not," he told her honestly. "I would if I could, but I know I can't."

Penn sighed and let go of him, allowing Daniel to sit up on the bed next to her. "So what? What do you need to know that's important?"

"When this is over, are you gonna kill me?"

"I'm not a praying mantis." She still lay back on the bed, staring up at the skylight and the darkening sky above them. When he'd arrived, the sun had been setting, but now the stars were starting to come out.

"You kinda are, actually," Daniel countered.

She sat up so she could look at him directly. "Why are you even asking me this?"

"Because I want to know. Wouldn't you want to know if you only had a few hours left to live?"

"A few hours?" Penn smirked. "You're being generous."

"You told me you were gonna 'rock my world,' so I'm making assumptions here."

Her smiled changed, and Penn climbed onto his lap. She tried to straddle him, but Daniel pushed her legs to the side, so she had to settle for having her arms around his neck.

"Penn," Daniel said firmly, keeping his hand on her thigh to stop her in case she tried to wrap it around him again. "No. I'm not doing anything until you answer the question."

"What if I am?" Penn asked, the same sultry smile and glint in her dark eyes.

"What?"

She lowered her eyes, staring down at his mouth. "What if I plan to kill you when we're done? What then?"

"Then . . . I guess I'd better get busy dying."

Her eyes widened, either in disbelief or surprise. "Really? You wouldn't try to talk me out of it?"

"I don't know what choice I have," he admitted. "If I put you off anymore, you'll take it out on Harper or Gemma. And if I do it tonight, you'll probably kill me. I'm choosing the lesser of two evils."

"What if . . ." She chewed her lip, as if debating on whether or not to say more. "What if I told you there was a third option?"

"A third option?"

"Yeah." The velvet in her words grew more excited. "I've been thinking about it. I cringe at the word 'love' and all its frivolities, but I feel something for you that I haven't felt for anyone in centuries. And I'm not about to let you go."

"So you're not planning on killing me?" Daniel asked.

Penn shook her head. "Not exactly. I want you to join me."

He waited a beat before speaking, almost too afraid to find out what she meant by that. "Join you how?"

Penn slid off his lap and knelt on the bed next to him as she explained. "I mean, this is all assuming that you perform up to my expectations, and when I wake up tomorrow, I'm still as infatuated with you as I am today."

"So whatever you're plotting hangs on your ever-changing whims?"

"Exactly."

"What are you plotting?"

"You remember earlier this summer when we realized that you were immune to our song, and Gemma's stupid boyfriend was in love with her?"

He nodded. "I'm familiar with this."

"We didn't understand why this was happening, and Thea in particular was obsessed with reevaluating the curse. So we pulled out the old scroll and were going over it when I noticed some particular wording." Penn tucked her hair behind her ear as she spoke.

"It went on and on about the curse, we have to eat boys' hearts, we sing, there must always be four, blah blah blah. But there was one thing that really stood out."

"And that is?" Daniel pressed.

She smiled widely before delivering her big discovery. "It never said the sirens had to be girls."

It was a second before he managed to ask, "What?"

"We'd always assumed, and I'd never thought much about it," Penn said, speaking more rapidly in her fervor. "The four of us were the original sirens until the 1700s, when Ligea died, so we haven't used the replacement clause that much. And I'd never really wanted anyone other than a girl, another sidekick, but you've got me thinking."

Inwardly, Daniel groaned. He always seemed to get her thinking when all he was really trying to do was to get her to forget him.

"How did I get you thinking?" he asked.

"The other day, at the park. You told me I was doing a terrible job of picking minions, and you were right. That's when it hit me. I don't want a minion—I need a partner."

"A partner? And you think I'm that partner?"

He wanted to laugh, but he knew Penn would freak out if he did. He looked away from her and got up, deciding that standing would somehow make this feel better. Putting some distance between her and him had to help him think more clearly.

"Daniel, it will be perfect," Penn continued, and in her excitement, her voice had almost turned into a song. "I've gotten so bored with life, and I've done everything there is to do. I'm so sick of the world. I've seen it all before, and everything has become redundant. But with you, it could all be new again. I could show you the world."

He glanced back at her, kneeling at the end of the bed and staring expectantly at him. "Did you just quote Disney at me?"

"Maybe, but it doesn't make my point any less valid."

"I can't be your eyes, Penn. I can't give you a heart again or make you happy." He shook his head. "I know I should be trying to convince you that I'm everything you're looking for, but I'm not. It wouldn't be long before you would get bored with me; and then what? You'd have all of eternity to drag me around."

"Obviously I would get rid of you if I got bored with you," Penn said, like she was talking about tossing out expired milk.

He laughed darkly. "You're really making this appealing."

"I want you, Daniel, and I'm being as kind as I can be."

"Strangely, I believe that."

"You may not believe that you're my last chance at happiness, but I do, and I'm willing to do whatever it takes to get it," Penn said. "You need to accept my offer."

"Accept your offer? I don't even really understand what it is."

"If you say no, I will have no choice but to kill you, and Harper, and Gemma, and every last person in this shit hole little town. I'll slaughter them one by one, and I'll make you watch. You'll be the very last to die." There was no menace in her voice. She was merely stating the facts to him, and that somehow made it more chilling.

"How romantic," he muttered under his breath. Swallowing hard, he looked up at her. "And what if I say yes?"

She smiled. "If you say yes, you'll get far more than your safety and your life and eternity. I'll love you, I'll serve you, I'll feed your every desire. My life's ambition will be to make you happy, as yours will be to me. We'll live forever with incredible power and unlimited freedom. Together."

"And what about everyone else?"

"We'll leave them behind," she told him simply. "We'll go far, far away, and we'll never return to Capri. You'll never see

Harper or your family again, but that means neither will I. I'll never hurt any of them, and they'll live long, happy, little human lives. I will spare everyone, for you."

As horrible as the offer was, it still sounded too good to be true. He would have to spend the rest of eternity in emotional, physical, and sexual servitude to Penn, but he could save everyone. Everything he'd been trying for would come true. He might not be able to break the curse—at least not right away—but he'd be there with Gemma, to help her and watch out for her.

His mind raced, trying to find the flaw in Penn's plan or what other devious thing she might be scheming at.

"With me, there would be five sirens," he realized. "I thought you could only have four."

"We can only have four," Penn confirmed.

And that would be the flaw. "So who are you getting rid of?"

Penn tilted her head, like she was considering, but she considered rather quickly. "I was thinking Thea."

"Thea?" Daniel asked, startled by her choice.

She laughed. "You look surprised."

"I thought you'd say Gemma."

"I'm not stupid, Daniel. If I killed her, you wouldn't go along. I know that."

"But Thea is your sister, and she's not totally insane and out of control like Liv," Daniel countered.

He wasn't entirely sure what Thea's deal was or if he could trust her, but from what he knew of the sirens, she seemed to be the most sane and reasonable. If he had to a pick a siren to have on his side, other than Gemma, Thea was his top choice.

"She's annoying and bossy, though." Penn wrinkled her nose in irritation when she talked about Thea.

"I don't think I can spend the next hundred years or so dealing with Liv," he admitted, though he failed to add that he didn't think he could spend that long dealing with Penn, either. "If you want me to do this, then she's the one."

"You want me to kill Liv?" Penn nearly squealed in her delight, and she licked her full lips. "You're so deliciously wicked, Daniel. I thought for sure you'd have some kind of moral argument about it."

"I'm fairly certain that Liv has already killed a lot of people, and if she hasn't yet, then she will soon," he reasoned. "She's much more of a monster than Gemma or Thea, and maybe even you. I don't have any qualms with getting rid of evil."

Penn had been sitting on her knees, but she moved so she was leaning back on the bed, propping herself up with her elbows. One of her long legs dangled over the edge, but her other foot was still on the bed, so when she moved her knee, Daniel would get a peek up her dress if he was looking.

"I've never seen this side of you before, and I like it," she purred. "So as your reward, I'll do it. I'll kill Liv because you asked me to. And you can replace her."

"When?"

"Assuming all goes well tonight, then tomorrow. The next full moon is on Monday, so we should get started with the process, just in case you don't take."

"Tomorrow? Like, in twenty-four hours?" Daniel asked. The

thought of becoming an immortal monster in a day didn't seem like enough time to prepare.

"Yes. I'll kill Liv in the afternoon, you come over, drink some blood, and by the next morning, we should be all set to go," Penn said.

"Unless I die, of course," he reminded her. "You're not even sure this will work on me, since I'm a guy, and I know that it nearly killed Gemma."

"Well, yes, that is a possibility."

"What then?"

"What if you die?" Penn shrugged. "You'll be dead."

"And you're fine with that? You're so obsessed with me, but you're cool with my being dead and gone in a day or two?" he asked.

"I'm not 'cool' with it, but it's the price I have to pay. And if you say no, I'll kill you anyway."

"You know that doesn't make any sense, right? You are a socio-path," he told her as reasonably as he could. "You cannot love something and then just kill it. That's not love."

"I never said it was love, Daniel," Penn corrected him. "It's *something,* and I'm being very generous with you, so take it for what it is. I'm giving you the most I can give, and this is it."

It was true, and he knew it. This was the best he would get from her, and this would be his best chance at protecting Harper and Gemma and everyone else in Capri. He'd have to become a monster and kill strangers to survive, but that had to be better than letting everyone he loved die.

And if he was one of them, it would be easier to try to figure out the curse or at least how to stop the sirens. He'd have their superstrength, so he'd be evenly matched in a fight against Penn. This could be the way out.

"So this is it then?" he asked finally.

"What?"

"I sleep with you now, and tomorrow I become a siren." He swallowed the lump in his throat and hoped he didn't look as nauseated as he felt. "And then I'll leave this life forever and run away with you."

"You make it sound like a bad thing," Penn said, pretending to be hurt.

"No, it's not," he agreed, and forced a smile at her. "This is the best option I have."

"It is. So maybe you ought to come thank me for being so nice."

He walked over to her, almost hurrying to get to her and get this over with. He kissed her, and they seemed to be picking up right where they left off. Only Penn was more insistent now. She began unbuttoning his shirt, but it must've been taking too long, because she ripped at it, sending buttons flying across the room.

"Much better," she said as she ran her fingers over the smooth skin of his abdomen.

His skin trembled under her touch, and that must've pleased her, because she laughed. She kissed him again, then, in an inhumanly fast move, she flipped him over. Daniel was lying on his back, and she sat on top of him.

Her dress was hiked up to her waist, exposing the thin straps of her lace thong. He put his hands on her waist, letting his hands slide up under her dress. She smiled, but she grabbed his hands and pinned his arms on either side of him.

"You're mine now," she purred.

"I know."

When she kissed him again, her mouth was hungry and eager. He could feel her teeth scraping against his lips, but there was something pleasurable in it, too. She rocked against him, and when she leaned forward, he could feel the soft flesh of her stomach press against his.

His mind instantly flashed to Harper. When they'd been making out in his bed, her tank top had slid up, and he'd felt her skin against his. It had excited him, and not just because things were so heated. The thought of being with Harper like that, as close as two people could be . . .

But he had to push her from his thoughts because as soon as he thought of her, he felt sick to his stomach. He'd thought that if he couldn't get going with Penn, he could try pretending that Harper was Penn, but that would only make it worse.

To keep her safe, Daniel had to forget about Harper and focus on the way it felt when Penn ran her fingers down his chest.

Penn sat up suddenly, and for a second, Daniel was afraid that she somehow knew he'd been thinking of Harper. But then she smiled and slid farther down his legs. Penn leaned down, letting her lips travel down the treasure trail on his stomach, while her hands undid his pants.

Daniel closed his eyes and wished for the moment to be over.

A phone started ringing, a loud, plaintive sound, and Penn growled.

"That's not mine," Daniel said, in case she planned on punishing him for it.

Penn glared at the phone on the nightstand. "It's my damn sister." She leaned over and grabbed the phone, then threw it so hard against the wall it shattered. "That's better."

"You could've just turned it off," Daniel pointed out.

"That was more fun." She climbed back on top of him. "Now where were we?"

"About here." He sat up a little so he could kiss her. If they were kissing, then she wasn't unbuttoning his jeans, and he wasn't quite ready for that yet.

She pushed him back down, but he tried to hold her to him. He slid one hand up her dress, pressing against her back, and the other one wandered below the string of her panties.

"Penn!" Thea shouted from downstairs, and the front door slammed shut. It hadn't even been a minute or two since Penn had destroyed her phone, and Daniel had no idea how Thea had gotten there so fast.

"Dammit, Thea!" Penn sat up and shouted back over her shoulder, her voice filled with a rage that seemed to echo inside Daniel's head. "I will come down there, and rip your—"

"Save it, Penn," Thea said. She'd reached the top of the stairs, so she was standing at the end of the loft and staring right at Penn straddling Daniel. "I know that I'm only supposed to interrupt if there's an emergency—"

"No, I said don't interrupt *even* if there is an emergency," Penn corrected her.

"It doesn't matter." Thea was totally unruffled by the venom in Penn's tone, and Daniel sat up so he could see around Penn better. That's when he noticed that blood was splattered all over Thea's shirt and face. "All hell is about to break loose downtown. I can't deal with this myself. You need to come take care of it."

TWENTY-SIX

Carnage

Anthemusa Bay was far too crowded for a swim, but the watersong was calling to her, so Gemma settled for sitting on the beach. Night was falling, and she'd hoped that some of the people would clear out, but At Summer's End had brought in far too many tourists for that.

Earlier, there had been a classic car show at Bayside Park, but that had been replaced by a local band playing covers of hits from the fifties. The sound of their crooning an old Elvis song wafted over the beach.

Gemma dug her feet into the sand, not daring to go any closer. The water lapped at the edge of her toes, enough where she could feel the slightest hint of a flutter but not enough to bring on a shift.

Stars shone brightly in the indigo sky, and Gemma lay back so she could stare up at them. Searching for the constellations that

Alex had shown her, she almost wished she'd invited him down here with her.

But she'd wanted some time alone. Her head was buzzing from the watersong, and she needed to ease it. Her failed attempts at breaking the curse had left her crestfallen, and her hunger pangs were only growing stronger.

She needed to do something if she wanted to keep from going mad, but it appeared that it would be very late before she'd be able to sneak off for a night swim without the risk of being spotted.

Her eyes automatically shifted in the fading light, and she could see clearly in the night sky. The ocean breeze went over her, soothing her headache some, and she watched as bats took flight from the nearby cypress trees.

As she was staring up, she saw a huge bird taking flight. She turned her head, watching as it flew toward the cliff at the other side of the bay, and quickly realized that it wasn't a bird. The crimson wings were far too large for any bird in Maryland, and, more telling, she saw human legs.

Thea had taken off from Bayside Park.

Gemma sat up and looked over toward the park to see if anyone was reacting, but she couldn't hear anything other than "Heartbreak Hotel." People might not have noticed Thea— either because she'd somehow been discreet since humans didn't have the night vision that Gemma had, or she'd used her siren song as camouflage—but that was still a big risk for her to take.

Penn and Liv might not care as much about attracting attention, but Thea always did her best to avoid it.

Her heart thudded in her chest, and Gemma began to fear that something was wrong. Thea had flown toward the cliff, but once she'd reached the heavily wooded area around the sirens' house, Gemma had lost sight of her.

It was only a few minutes longer that she had to worry, because then her phone started belting out an old Heart song—Thea's ringtone.

Gemma answered the phone. "Is something going on?"

Thea waited a beat before speaking. "Yeah. How did you know?"

"I saw you flying overhead," she replied as she got to her feet. "What's wrong?"

"Meet me behind the band shell at Bayside Park."

"Why? What happened?"

"Just do it, okay?" Thea said, then hung up without waiting for a reply.

Gemma shoved her phone back in her pocket and jogged toward the park. It wasn't that far away, but she kept glancing up to see if Thea or Penn was flying above her, which slowed her down.

The closer she got to the park, the denser the crowd became, and Gemma soon found it impossible to jog because she had to weave through the people. They normally parted for her, thanks to her siren beauty, but everyone seemed too entranced by the band onstage to notice her, and she actually had to push people out of the way.

Gemma wondered if that's how Thea had flown away without being spotted—she used her siren song to get the crowd to focus completely on the band; so they wouldn't notice Thea's transition or any of the trouble going on around them.

The band shell was a concrete bandstand shaped like a seashell, so the music would project better. It was on the other side of the park from where Gemma had been, closer to where her father worked and Daniel used to dock his boat.

Behind the band shell was a thick cluster of cypress and maples, and it went down a rather steep hill before becoming the smooth trail that led to the docks.

Once she reached it, Gemma looked around, spinning in a slow circle to be sure she hadn't missed anything, but she couldn't see the sirens anywhere. She wasn't even sure if Thea could get here so fast, but Gemma headed behind the stage, like she was told.

Large speakers were set up at the sides of the band shell, and Gemma ducked around them. She pushed through a prickly bush and was beginning to think that Thea had been tricking her for some reason when she finally rounded the back of the stage.

The problem was immediately obvious. There was so much blood. Splattered against the smooth, white concrete of the back of the shell and soaking the grass all around. The leaves on the trees were even stained dark red, and parts of human intestines dangled from a branch.

Worse than walking into a bloodbath like this was Gemma's reaction to it. Instead of wanting to throw up the way she should have, her stomach growled impatiently, and she had to fight to keep her fangs in check.

It only got messier the closer she stepped toward the victim. He'd been completely eviscerated, torn open from his throat down to his groin. Most of his organs had been ripped out, and while some had certainly been eaten, parts of his liver and lungs had been left in chunks that littered the ground.

"*Finally,* you got here," Liv groaned, and Gemma realized she had become so entranced by the fresh blood and warm organs, she hadn't even noticed the siren standing beside the body.

Blood dotted Liv's cheeks and forehead in a light spray, almost like she had freckles, but her lips were completely covered. Her golden hair was soaked red from her ears down, and it dripped heavy droplets onto her shoulders. From the waist up, Liv looked like she had gotten hit by blood sprayed from a fire hose.

"Finally?" Gemma asked, trying to comprehend the situation.

"Yeah. I've been waiting forever." Liv was completely human, except for a long talon at the end of her pinky, and she used it to pick at something between her teeth. "I don't know how to get rid of this stupid body."

"I have no idea what to do with it." Gemma motioned to the band shell, rumbling doo-wop beside them. "A ton of people are here. There's no way you can get a mangled corpse past them."

"Ugh." Liv groaned and stared up at the sky. "This is all stupid. We should just kill them all."

"Kill them *all*? The thousands of men, women, and children in Capri right now?" Gemma asked dubiously.

"Yeah." Liv glared at her. "They're weak. We can take them out, and we should. Anything that stands in our way, we should get rid of. We're the top of the food chain."

"This isn't a food chain, Liv! Those are human lives!" Gemma shouted at her, not caring if anyone heard. "You can't just go around massacring people!"

"Oh, honey." Liv's irritation had given way to her innocent act. She batted her eyelashes, which were coated in blood. "Don't you even realize? Tonight, I just proved that I can. I can kill whoever I want, whenever I want."

"What are you talking about? Who did you kill?"

Before Liv could answer, Gemma crouched next to the body. His face was almost too drenched with blood to recognize, and maybe she wouldn't have . . . if she hadn't made out with him once.

"Aiden Crawford," Gemma gasped, and jumped back.

"Oh my." Liv laughed, almost sweetly, at Gemma's surprise. "Aren't you the prude?"

Gemma pressed her hand to her stomach, trying to ease the wave of nausea that hit her. "I thought you liked him."

"I did," Liv said. "But I killed one of the most prominent, eligible young men in town not twenty feet from this huge celebration, not to mention from his own father, the mayor." Liv plucked at a bit skin of stuck to her hair. "I wanted to do it right in front of everyone, on the stage, but Thea wouldn't stand for that, so I had to sneak back here and pretend I was gonna have sex with the handsome idiot."

"You killed him . . ." Gemma trailed off, trying to get a handle on what Liv was saying. "Why? To prove that you could?"

"No, no, of course not." Her mouth curved up in a smile. "I killed him because I wanted to. I was hungry, and I wanted to taste his blood."

"Liv, you're gonna . . ." Gemma was at a loss for words. She didn't know how she could possibly reason with someone so cold.

"Now I'm stronger." Liv stepped over the body, coming toward Gemma. "Much stronger than you. I'm almost stronger than Penn, and I'm certainly stronger than Thea. I eat every day, and it won't be long until I'm unstoppable."

"Unless the police or the FBI catch you first," Gemma said. "I'm sure they'd love to have you. Lock you up, cut you open, see what makes you tick."

"Gemma, I will kill them *all*," Liv told her emphatically. "I will kill everyone on this whole fucking planet if I want to."

"At first, I thought you were just a little power hungry," Gemma said. "You were having a hard time adjusting, and this was all going to your head. But now I realize that you're just insane. Totally and completely insane."

Liv narrowed her dark brown eyes, and the wide-eyed innocence instantly evaporated, changing into pure evil. Penn was cruel, but empty. Liv was full, but with darkness, and Gemma felt a chill run down her spine.

The brush beside them rustled, but Gemma didn't look away

until Liv did. She didn't want to take her eyes off her, not when Liv was looking at her like that.

"This is bullshit, Thea, and you know it," Penn grumbled, and within seconds, she appeared, pushing her through the trees.

"Tell that to Liv," Thea replied, following at her heels. She had a duffel bag slung over her shoulder, and Gemma could see a blue tarp poking out through the top.

When they emerged from the trees, there was still someone coming up behind them, and Gemma tensed up even more, fearing that a stranger had stumbled on them. Instead, it was Daniel, with his shirt unbuttoned almost all the way down to his navel. As soon as he saw her, he froze.

"What are you doing?" Gemma asked, but he just shook his head.

"Oh, this is ridiculous, Thea," Penn snapped as she surveyed the mess around her. "You could've handled this."

"Maybe, but I'm not doing it anymore," Thea said, and tossed the duffel bag down on the ground. "You think Liv is so great, then you take care of her. She's your problem now. I'm done."

"Thea, this isn't so bad," Liv tried as sweetly as she could. "I just don't know how to get rid of a body."

"You've done it enough times, you should be a goddamn expert," Thea told her.

"I can't get rid of a body in this crowd without being spotted. And I'm fine with that, but you told me—" Liv started the same spiel she'd given Gemma when she got there.

"Liv!" Penn shouted in frustration. "You need to stop making a mess and provoking the humans. Just calm down. We have eternity. You don't need to get all your killing done in one day."

Liv suggested that they leave the mess and let the animals and the rain take care of it, which immediately resulted in a squabble between Penn, Thea, and Liv about how best to deal with this, with each of them shirking the responsibility.

With the sirens otherwise occupied, Gemma edged back to where Daniel was standing. He stared down at the body lying a few feet in front of him, and she wasn't sure how much of the carnage he was really able to take in thanks to his weaker human sight.

"Was that human?" he asked.

"Yeah." Gemma nodded. "It was Aiden Crawford."

"Aiden? Holy shit."

Daniel wheeled around just in time to dry heave into the bushes. It sounded more like he was coughing than actually throwing up, but the reality of it had obviously hit him hard. When he'd finished, he wiped his mouth on the back of his arm and mumbled an apology.

"It's a lot of blood to take in," Gemma said when he turned back around.

"I didn't know there was that much blood in one human body," he admitted. "That looks like it should be five or six people. At least."

"I think Liv was making a point of splattering him around." Gemma kept her voice low, so the sirens would be less likely to notice her, but they were so busy arguing among themselves that she could shout their names, and they wouldn't look.

Daniel exhaled sharply. "Dammit. He was a dick, but . . . He was my older brother's best friend for years before John died. Aiden wasn't a good guy, but he deserved better than this."

No, Aiden probably didn't deserve this, but it hadn't been that long ago that she'd been about ready to do the same to him when he wouldn't take no for an answer. Saying he wasn't a good guy was a massive understatement.

"I know," Gemma said anyway. "I'm sorry."

"It's not your fault."

Gemma tilted her head. "Maybe it is. I brought the sirens back to Capri. The reason they're here is—"

"Don't do that." Daniel was quick to cut her off, and since he obviously wasn't in the mood to argue, she didn't push it.

"On the subject of why people are here . . ." Gemma began after a pregnant pause. "Why are you here?"

He stared straight ahead, his eyes fixed on the ground, and she could see the muscles in his jaw tense. "Don't ask me about that. Please."

Daniel had arrived late at night with Penn, and the buttons were ripped off the front of his shirt. There was only one conclusion Gemma could draw, especially after seeing Penn fawning over him so much.

She knew why he would do it, the only reason Daniel would do something like this was to protect Harper or her. That made her heart ache, like it was being torn in two, and her stomach twist in knots. Knowing that Daniel would resort to prostituting himself because of her, and how much it would kill Harper when she found out.

"Daniel. You have to tell Harper."

He sighed and just kept staring at the ground. "We all do what we need to do."

"No, Daniel," Gemma said firmly, hating that she had to do this. "If you don't tell her, I will."

"Fine!" Penn threw her hands up in the air, and turned her attention back toward Gemma and Daniel. "We'll wrap him up, then Daniel can dump his body off his boat."

"What? Why can't you guys take him out there?" Daniel asked.

"Because they'll be busy cleaning up this bloodbath." Penn pointed to Thea and Liv. "And it will look less suspicious if you take a tarp on a boat than if a girl drags a tarp into the ocean."

"Fine." Daniel shrugged, like he really didn't care what he got dragged into anymore. "I'll do it. As long as I don't have to touch the body."

"Great." Penn smiled at him. "You all can wrap up the body, then Daniel takes it out to sea, and Thea and Liv clean up all this blood."

"No, Penn. I'm not kidding. I'm not doing this." Thea smacked her hands together and rubbed them, gesturing that she was washing her hands of all this. "This is your problem now."

Penn rolled her eyes, then looked to Daniel. "See? I told you she's bossy and obnoxious."

"But Thea's not the reason you're in this mess," he said reasonably, then nodded to Liv. "*She* is."

Liv smiled at him, and in her sweetest, silkiest voice, she said, "One day, Penn is gonna get tired of you. And when she does, she's gonna tear you apart, and I'll be there to watch."

"I'm out of here," Thea said, and started heading back toward the trees to make her escape. "Sorry, guys. Best of luck."

With Penn overseeing, Gemma and Liv broke up Aiden's body so it would be easier to transfer. Daniel had edged closer to the side of the band shell, keeping a lookout, but it also kept him from having to witness their dismembering a guy he'd known most of his life.

When they were finished, the tarps containing Aiden's body fit neatly inside the duffel bag. It would still be too heavy for Daniel to carry comfortably, so Gemma offered to carry it down to his boat for him.

Penn wanted to take that job for herself, but Gemma had no idea how to get the blood out of the trees. She wiped the blood off herself as best she could, using one of the towels that Thea had tucked in the duffel bag, then she and Daniel headed down to the trail to his boat.

"I got it from here," Daniel said when they'd stopped on the docks in front of *The Dirty Gull*.

"You sure? I can help you get rid of it," Gemma offered.

"No. I got it." He took the bag from her and gave it a swing so he could throw it up over the railing and onto his boat. "I just wanna take a nice, long boat ride out past the island, then go home and take the longest shower of my life."

Some blood had gotten on his hands and arms, and he even had a few droplets on his bare chest, which had probably dripped down from the branches. But by the way he avoided looking Gemma in the eyes, she had a feeling that wasn't the only reason he felt so dirty.

"What happened between you and Penn—" Gemma began carefully, but Daniel held up his hand, stopping her.

"I know that you mean well, and I know that you think you understand, but . . ." He trailed off. "I can't talk about this with you." He swallowed. "And Harper will know what she needs to know soon enough."

"I know that whatever you've done or will do, you've done it to protect Harper and me."

He chewed the inside of his cheek and stared out at the ocean. Impulsively, Gemma threw her arms around Daniel and hugged him tightly, pressing her face against his chest. Tears stung her eyes, and she barely held them back.

"I just wanted to say thank you," she said, her words muffled against his chest. "For everything you've done and everything you've given up."

He put his hand on her head, stroking her hair for a moment and letting her hug him. Then, abruptly, he pushed her away.

"I gotta go," he said thickly. Daniel turned and got on his boat, without looking back at her.

TWENTY-SEVEN

Devastation

The clock above the fireplace said it was after eleven o'clock, but Harper assumed that Daniel had gone out with his friends. After all, he was twenty-one, so hitting a few bars would seem logical, especially since he had no idea that she was coming down to surprise him.

Several times throughout the evening, as she'd been waiting for him, she had considered texting or calling to find out where he was or when he might be home. But that would ruin the surprise.

It had already been weeks in the planning. When she arrived at college, she'd gone down to the campus clinic and gotten herself birth control. At the time, she didn't know it was for tonight, but she knew that things were getting serious, so she thought it wouldn't hurt to be on it.

The little blue number she was wearing, that was for tonight. In between trying to break ancient curses and cramming for school, Harper had snuck off to a small lingerie boutique in Sundham. She'd gotten the cute matching bra and lace panties for a birthday surprise.

She hadn't decided for sure that tonight would be the night until Sunday, when they'd gotten close to taking their relationship farther. Daniel said he'd wanted to wait until the moment was perfect, but Harper had realized that she didn't know when there ever would be a "perfect" moment.

All the troubles with Gemma and the sirens might never end. More and more, she feared that might be the case, and even when or if it ever did end, it might not be for a very long time.

And right now, Harper knew that she loved Daniel more than she'd ever loved anyone, and she wanted to be with him. Not just for today but for the rest of her life. She'd thought about it, she'd talked about it with him, and she was ready.

It would've been nice if Daniel had come home sooner, but she'd actually needed the time. After the visit with her mom earlier today, Harper needed a break to decompress. She parked her car away from the docks so Daniel wouldn't see it, and she took Bernie's old speedboat out to the island in hopes of getting there first to surprise him.

But now she'd had plenty of time to get ready, reapply her makeup, and change her pose on the couch fifty times. She didn't want Daniel to know she was here, so she'd only left one lamp on in the corner, leaving her in near darkness.

To make the house seem less creepy, she'd hooked her iPod up to the stereo and put it on shuffle, so her music played softly in the room.

When she finally heard the door handle, her stomach flipped. Harper hurriedly paused the music, so he'd see her before he heard anything, and then posed in the most seductive way possible. She didn't really know what that meant, so she ended up kind of leaning back, with her long, dark hair falling around her.

Daniel came inside the house, but he didn't notice her until after he'd turned on the kitchen light. Then he froze and stared at her with a look that could only be described as abject horror.

That was the first chance for Harper to get a really good look at him, and he looked like hell. Droplets of blood were on his chest, and he had dried blood on his hands and smeared across his forehead. His flannel shirt appeared to have been torn since it hung open haphazardly. He had his usual facial scruff, but his face appeared even more ragged. And his hazel eyes had a bleak emptiness in them, something Harper had never seen there before.

"Daniel. Oh, my god." She got up and hurried over to him. "What happened to you?"

"You've gotta be kidding me," he said flatly. "This is one of the worst days of my entire life, and now this."

"Now this?" Harper took a step back, but she tried to smile and play it off as a joke. "I'm sorry I didn't realize seeing me would make your day worse."

"No, it doesn't. Not normally, but . . ." He trailed off and lowered his eyes.

"Daniel. What's going on?" She reached out, touching his arm gently. "You're scaring me."

He rubbed his temple. "I just want to take a shower, but this can't wait, can it?"

"What can't? We can do whatever you want to do."

"Just give me one second."

Without looking at her, he slid by and went to the bathroom. As she listened to the sound of running water, Harper rubbed her hands on her bare arms and sat down on the couch. In an attempt to ease her anxiety, she turned the music back on, and "Landfill" by Daughter came softly out of the speakers.

A few minutes later, Daniel came back out. He was shirtless, and with all the blood washed off, she couldn't see any obvious wounds. Other than the scars from his previous battles with the sirens and the black branches of his tattoo stretching down his shoulder.

He had a different flannel shirt in his hand, and he held it out to Harper. "Here. Put this on. It's clean."

Her cheeks flushed as she slid the shirt on, but she left it unbuttoned. "I'm sorry if I did something wrong coming here tonight. I just wanted to surprise you."

"No, you didn't do anything wrong." He went into the kitchen and opened the fridge. "Do you want a beer or anything?"

"No. I just want you to tell me what's going on," she said. Daniel opened his beer, flipping the top in the sink, and he lingered in the kitchen as he took several long drinks. "Come here. Talk to me."

He exhaled heavily and trudged into the living room. The coffee table was right across from Harper, and he pulled it closer to her and sat on the edge of it. With a beer still in his hand, he bowed his head and let his elbows rest on his knees.

His head rested against Harper's chest, so she leaned forward and put her arms around him. She kissed the back of his head and rubbed his back, feeling the bumps of his scars under her hand.

"Daniel," she said softly, almost speaking into his hair. "What happened?"

Finally, he lifted his head and looked at her. He just stared at her for a moment, a sad smile on his lips.

"You do look really beautiful tonight."

"Thank you," Harper said, but her heart hadn't stopped racing since he'd gotten home, and she didn't want compliments. "Why were you covered in blood? Were you hurt?"

He lowered his eyes again and stared down at the bottle in his hand. "No. I wasn't hurt. That wasn't my blood. It was Aiden Crawford's."

"*Aiden?* What happened? Is he okay?"

"No." He took a long drink of his beer before speaking again. "I just dumped his body off my boat—in parts—all over the ocean because Liv tore him up. She killed him."

Harper shook her head in confusion. "Why?"

"I don't know." He laughed, a hollow sound. "Because she's a demon from hell? I don't know."

"Why did you help get rid of his body? Did Gemma call you?" Harper glanced at the table, where her cell phone was sitting. She'd left it on, so if Gemma needed her, she would've gotten a call. "Is she okay?"

"Gemma's fine. She's good," he assured her quickly. "No, she didn't call me." He paused, and it felt like a long time before he said, "I was with Penn."

"You were . . . with Penn?" Harper leaned back, pulling away from him and trying to understand what he was saying to her.

"I went out to her house tonight." He kept staring down, his words low and thick. "To have sex with her."

"To . . ." Her breath caught in her throat, and for a moment, it was impossible for her speak. "To what?"

"She told me that if I had sex with her, then she wouldn't kill you or Gemma. And if I said no, then she would kill you and Gemma. So I, uh . . . I said yes."

It was like the floor had been pulled out from beneath her. She'd been on solid ground, and all of a sudden it was replaced by empty blackness below her, threatening to swallow her up. Her mind swirled with too many thoughts, making her dizzy, and she had to keep swallowing to stop from crying or throwing up.

"So you had sex with Penn?" Harper asked, hoping she kept the quaver out of her voice. "The horrible monster who is ruining my life and my sister's life, who murders and takes whatever she wants? *That* Penn?"

"I didn't have sex with her tonight."

"But you did another night?" she asked, and if he said yes, she was certain she'd throw up.

"No," he said quickly. "*No.* I've never had sex with her."

"Why not?"

"We were supposed to tonight, but Liv killed Aiden, and that interrupted us."

Harper brushed the hair back from her forehead, and she

realized her hands were trembling. "If she hadn't interrupted, you would've had sex with her?"

He nodded. "Yes."

"So . . . did you do anything with her?" Harper asked, but he said nothing. "Daniel. Answer me."

"Yes."

"Did you kiss her? Did you take off your clothes?" she asked, and when he didn't reply, she went on, "Did she get further with you than I have?"

He breathed deeply, then so softly she barely heard him, he said, "Yes."

And then she couldn't contain herself. Without even thinking, she reached out and smacked him across the face. It was hard enough to make a loud, cracking sound, and the palm of her hand tingled. Tear welled her eyes.

"I am so sorry, Harper," Daniel said, and he finally looked up at her.

"How long has this been going on?" she asked, ignoring his apology. "When did she proposition you?"

"I don't know." He shook his head. "Maybe . . . two and a half weeks ago."

"Two and a half *weeks*?" She looked up at the ceiling to keep the tears from spilling over and laughed cynically. "Holy shit, Daniel."

"I didn't know what else to do," he said.

"You didn't?" She smiled bitterly and wiped at her eyes. "You were kissing me and holding me and telling me you loved me, and I was telling you all my secrets and you were planning to sleep with someone else? I was here, on your birthday, planning to share myself with you fully, and you're lying and sneaking around . . ."

"I know it's wrong," he insisted. "Sex with Penn is gross and horrible, but I had to protect you."

A tear slid down her cheek, and she let it. "No, Daniel. I'm not mad because you planned to sleep with her." She shook her head. "I mean, I am hurt, and I don't know if I'd ever really be okay with that. Even knowing that you did it for me, and for my sister.

"But what I'm really mad about is that you didn't tell me." She looked him right in the eyes. "I trusted you, Daniel, with *everything*, with all of me, and you . . . You didn't do the same."

"No, Harper, it wasn't about trust. I knew that if I told you, you'd try to talk me out of it, and I couldn't . . ." He paused, sighing. "I knew that when you found out, this would be over. But I didn't know how else to keep you safe."

"That is bullshit, Daniel!" She got up and walked away from him, too angry even to be near him. Pulling the flannel shirt more tightly around her, Harper glared down at him. "You weren't gonna tell me until *after*! Were you ever even gonna tell me?"

"I don't know," he admitted.

"I can't believe you." Harper buried her fingers in her hair, holding her head as she tried to process what he'd just told her. Then she took a deep breath and lowered her arms. "I sat on your couch today, texting you I love you, and you were about to go screw my mortal enemy. And I don't give a shit how noble or valid your reasons are, you should've told me, and you know it."

Daniel stood up, and she could see the tears in his eyes. "I am so very sorry, Harper."

"What were you thinking?" she asked, restraining herself from screaming it at him. She wanted to hit him and yell at him and demand to know how he could do this, how he could ruin something that was so amazing and destroy the one thing in her life that was nearly perfect.

"I just had to protect you," he said simply.

"And how did you protect me? By hurting me in the worst possible way?"

"No, I didn't . . ." He shook his head. "I didn't mean for any of this."

"All this time, you've been pushing to get close to me, and I tried to keep you at arm's length. But you clawed your way into my life, and you made me fall in love with you, and you promised never to hurt me, and you fought so hard to earn my trust." She let out a small sob when she realized the horrible truth of what he'd just done. "And now I don't think I can ever trust you again."

"You would've talked me out of it!" Daniel shouted, as if that would convince her somehow. "What else was I supposed to do?"

"You were supposed to talk to me!" Harper yelled back. "And if it would've been so easy for me to talk you out of, then it wasn't the right thing to do, Daniel! Because if it was the right thing, I would've let you do it, even if it hurt."

With a stricken expression on his face, he said, "I'm sorry."

"No. Stop. I can't hear that anymore. I think I'm gonna be sick." She ran over and grabbed her iPod and book bag from where they sat next to the fireplace. "I have to get out of here."

"No, Harper, wait." He moved toward her, like he meant to touch her, and she pulled back away from him.

"I can't. I can't talk to you right now. I can't even look at you."

"I don't want to leave things like this."

She started toward the door, pushing by him. "I don't care what you want."

"Harper. I love you," he said, and she stopped to look back at him.

"I don't believe you," she said with tears in her eyes, then she turned away and left.

TWENTY-EIGHT

Impact

Harper arrived at her house just before midnight, and she'd somehow managed not to cry the whole way home. It was completely dark, so she crept up the stairs to her old room, hoping not to disturb anyone. She'd just reached the top of the stairs when Gemma emerged from the bathroom with a towel wrapped around her hair.

"Harper. What are you doing here?" Gemma asked.

"Um, I just . . ." She ran a hand through her hair and took a deep breath.

"What happened? Are you okay?"

Harper was still only wearing Daniel's flannel shirt and her new lingerie. Fortunately, she'd buttoned up the shirt, and it was too big for her, so it covered up a lot. She'd been in such a hurry to leave the island that she hadn't bothered to put anything else on.

"I think I may have just broken up with Daniel," Harper said finally, and she started to cry.

"Oh, Harper. Come on." Gemma put her arm around her and ushered her into Harper's bedroom. She made sure to close the door behind them so they wouldn't awaken Brian, and Harper sat down on the bed.

"Did you know that he was sleeping with Penn?" Harper asked her.

Gemma had been standing in front of her, and she sighed before sitting down on the bed next to her.

"No," Gemma said at length. "I mean, I thought something might be going on, but Daniel insisted he had it under control. Then tonight, he kinda confirmed my worst suspicions, and I told him he that he needed to tell you what was going on."

Harper laughed to keep from crying. "Well, he did."

"So did he . . . actually have sex with her?" Gemma asked carefully.

"He says he didn't, but I don't know if I believe him." She shrugged. "I don't know if I can believe anything he says."

"Did he say why he was doing it?"

"For you and me. He didn't elaborate too much on it, but I guess Penn told him he either sleeps with her, or she kills us." Harper chewed the inside of her cheek. "So he was doing it to protect me."

"He loves you, Harper." Gemma put her hand on her back, rubbing it. "And I'm not saying that you should forgive him or that he was right. But anything he's done, he's done for you."

"He may have done the wrong thing for the right reason, but

that doesn't make it okay. It's still the *wrong* thing," Harper said. "As soon as Penn came to him and gave him the ultimatum, he should've come to me, and said, 'This is what's going on. This is what I need to do.'"

"I know. He should've talked to you," Gemma agreed.

"That's what hurts me the most. I don't know if I could ever be okay with his sleeping with another woman, especially one as vile and twisted as Penn. But I understand *why* he wanted to go through with it, and if it was for you, too, not just my own life, and maybe . . ."

"You don't need to sacrifice your relationship for me, Harper," Gemma told her resolutely. "I can take care of myself."

"If he'd talked to me about it, I honestly don't know what I would've said," Harper indicated. "If I could really agree to it. Because I love him so much, and I would never want him to be with someone else or whore himself out like that. And I know that sounds selfish, like my sister's life versus sharing him, so maybe I would've said yes."

Harper shook her head. "But that's not even the point."

"What do you mean?" Gemma asked.

"It doesn't matter if I would've agreed with his choices or not," she explained. "It's that he made such a drastic choice, one that really affected him and me and our relationship, and he didn't consult me at all. He snuck around."

"I think he just didn't want to worry you," Gemma said.

Harper scoffed. "You do that, and he does that, and it's ridiculous. I am eighteen years old. I am your *older* sister, and his girlfriend. You don't need to treat me like a little kid and keep hiding things from me. Stop trying to spare my feelings. I'm with you in all of this."

"I know. And I'm trying to include you in everything," Gemma said, allowing a defensive note in her tone. "I just don't want to interfere with your life more than I have to."

"You're not interfering!" Harper was nearly shouting, and she hurried to lower her voice so as not to wake her dad. "*You* are my life. You and Mom and Dad. And Daniel. You're the most important things in my life."

Gemma smiled at her. "I'm sorry, and I'll do better. I promise."

"Thank you." Harper ran a hand through her hair and tried to shake off her feelings. "And I'm sorry for being all teen angst right now."

When there was so much going on, so many things that were vastly more important than her and her relationships, Harper felt selfish and ridiculous getting so upset over them. Losing Daniel felt immense to her, but there were bigger problems at hand. Like the fact that the sirens had killed someone tonight.

"Liv killed Aiden Crawford," Harper said, and her sister lowered her eyes.

"I know." Gemma sounded so weary just then, but when she spoke again, her voice was stronger, more confident. "That's why it's so important that I work even harder. I've been practicing more, trying to harness the siren powers, and if Penn doesn't get Liv under control, I think I might have to take care of her myself."

"You're planning to kill Liv?" Harper asked, forcing herself to keep her words even.

Gemma nodded. "If I need to, yeah. If we don't break the

curse soon, I can't let her keep running around like she is now. She'll kill everybody if she has the chance."

"But are you ready for something like that?" Harper asked.

"I don't know. But I'm getting myself ready. I'm not gonna go after her right now. But . . . soon."

Naturally, Harper wanted to yell at Gemma and tell her she couldn't do any of that. It was way too dangerous going up against another siren like that, especially one as crazed as Liv.

But deep down, Harper knew that Gemma was right. Liv couldn't be left to run loose, terrorizing everyone in Capri like some kind of sexy Godzilla. Gemma was much stronger than Harper, and if she got a handle on her siren strength, then she would be able to take Liv out much better than anybody else could.

For the first time, Harper truly realized that she couldn't fight Gemma's battles. She would help her every chance she got, and she'd always have her back. But some things, Gemma would have to take care of herself.

"Don't do anything that will get you hurt," Harper said. "I don't know what I'd do without you."

Gemma leaned over and hugged Harper. It had been a long time since Gemma had initiated a hug with her, and for a moment, Harper just let herself linger in the moment, letting her little sister comfort her.

"Anyway, I've had a very long night, and it seems like you have, too. We can talk about all of this in the morning." Gemma stopped and looked over at Harper. "Will you still be here in the morning?"

"For a little bit. I'll be up kinda early to get back to school."

"I'll be up."

Just before Gemma left the room, Harper asked, "Gemma, you don't . . . Do you think Daniel *wanted* to have sex with Penn? And that's why he didn't tell me?"

And it wasn't until she said it aloud that she realized that she'd been afraid it was true. Some small part of her believed that Daniel lied to her because he secretly found her lacking and wanted to spend the night with someone far more experienced and beautiful than her.

"No." Gemma shook her head emphatically. "He seemed genuinely upset about it, and when I've talked to him about Penn, he's never expressed anything but disgust for her. Sleeping with her would have been as terrible for him as it would have been for you."

After Gemma left, Harper climbed under the covers and curled up in her bed. She was still wearing Daniel's shirt, and it smelled sweetly of him. As she cried softly into her pillow, Harper had no idea if she'd done the right thing with Daniel. The one thing she did know was that she still loved him desperately.

TWENTY-NINE

Divergence

I t was still dark out when the doorbell rang. Gemma trudged down the stairs, cursing under her breath as she went to answer the door.

"Who's here?" Brian asked as he stumbled out of his bedroom, still half-asleep.

"Not sure. I'm getting it now," Gemma called up to him.

Whoever it was had stopped ringing the bell and resorted to pounding incessantly on the front door. Gemma opened the door midpound and found Marcy in a weird, owl pajama jumper and acid-wash jean jacket combo.

"Marcy. What the he—"

"Lydia found her," Marcy said, sounding more excited than Gemma had ever heard her sound before. "She's found Diana."

"Marcy's here?" Brian asked. "Is everything okay?"

"Yeah, everything's fine," Gemma shouted, and somehow managed to keep from jumping up and down in excitement.

"Hasn't she ever heard of a phone?" her dad muttered, and she heard the upstairs bathroom door squeak shut as he went inside.

"So Lydia really found *the* Diana?" Gemma asked Marcy.

"Diana?" Harper echoed from the top of the stairs, and she raced down the stairs to join Gemma in the open doorway.

"When? How?" Gemma asked.

"Just now. Lydia's been crawling through Audra's notes and Thalia's diary, and she knew she was close, so she was staying up all night, and she finally did it." Marcy broke out in an uncharacteristically broad smile.

"Where is Diana?" Harper asked, sounding out of breath. "She's alive, right? When can we see her?"

"Yes, she's alive," Marcy said, and Harper let out a sigh of relief. "She lives just outside Charleston, West Virginia, and we can see her as soon as we get ready and go."

"West Virginia?" Gemma wrinkled her nose. "That seems like a strange place for a goddess in hiding to live."

"Yeah, well it's strange that jellyfish don't have eyes, girls have to pee sitting down, and that you're a mythical creature," Marcy said. "So let's not start splitting hairs now about what's strange."

"What's going on?" Brian asked. He came down the stairs and flicked on the overhead light. "You found somebody?"

Gemma turned back to see her dad walking down the stairs. A five o'clock shadow colored his face, and he ran a hand through his sandy hair. He was only wearing a T-shirt and boxers, but he seemed too sleepy to really care that company was seeing him that way.

"Yeah, you remember Diana?" Gemma asked him. "She's the goddess that helped Thalia out of the muse thing."

His blue eyes widened as he became more alert. "And she'll be able to help you?"

Gemma nodded. "We hope so."

"How far away is Charleston?" Harper asked, then she turned around, scanning the room. "Where's my laptop?" Then she stopped. "Shit. I think I left it in my car last night."

As she brushed past Marcy and dashed out into the chilly night, Brian stared after her in confusion.

The jagged scar on Harper's thigh from the car accident extended long past the hem of Daniel's shirt, but she didn't seem to notice even though she was normally very self-conscious about anyone's seeing it, even Gemma or their dad. But she ran outside to grab her laptop from her car without a second thought.

Harper's eyes were red and puffy, like she'd been crying all night, and her makeup-smeared raccoon eyes only added to that effect. But what had happened with Daniel last night seemed to be replaced by her new focus on getting to Diana as quickly as possible.

"Wait a second," Brian said. "Harper's supposed to be at college. What is she doing here?"

"She came in to see Daniel last night for his birthday, and she's going back to school in the morning," Gemma said, since she wasn't sure how much—if anything—her sister wanted their dad to know about the big fight with Daniel last night. "Well, she was. I'm not sure if she will now."

Brian scowled, deep lines marring his tanned face. "I told her that she shouldn't come to town for that. She's already missing so much school already."

"Are you talking about me?" Harper asked as she came back inside. "I'll get my homework. I'll e-mail teachers, it'll be fine. But this is too important."

Harper sat down in the living room chair and opened her computer on her lap. Brian might have lectured her about the importance of actually going to school, but by the intense expression in her eyes, he must've known she wasn't listening right now.

"So where's Lydia?" Gemma asked, turning her attention back to Marcy. "Is she coming with us?"

"She's in Sundham still, but yeah, she insisted on coming along. She wants to help ensure that everything goes okay."

"Are you coming, too?" Gemma asked.

Marcy snorted. "Duh. I'm not missing a chance to meet a goddess. This is pretty much what I've been waiting for my whole life."

"Okay, I got it. Charleston, West Virginia, from Capri." Harper looked up from the computer screen and tucked her dark hair behind her ears. "It looks like it's almost a nine-hour drive."

Gemma grimaced. "That sounds too long."

"What do you mean?" Harper asked.

"That's so far away from water. When I go to Sundham, I get really bad headaches, and Sundham's not even that far from the ocean. The watersong has a crazy pull," Gemma explained. "Driving for sixteen hours round-trip, we'd be gone for over a day. I'd rather not be that far inland for so long."

"Are you sure you'll be able to handle it all?" Harper asked.

"I'll make myself handle what I need to, but we have to keep this trip as short as possible," Gemma said. "Besides that, if I'm gone too long, the sirens will notice I'm missing, and we really don't want that."

"Are you telling the sirens you're leaving?" Brian asked her.

"Um . . ." Gemma thought for a second. "I'll tell Thea I'm gonna go visit Harper in Sundham. That way, if they see that I'm gone or something, it will seem less suspicious."

"Is it safe for you to go? With the watersong and the sirens, maybe you should stay behind," Brian said with a mixture of vulnerability and worry in his expression that tore at Gemma's heart.

Her dad wanted to tell her not to go, to forbid her, but to do that would only make things worse. As dangerous as he might fear this would be, he understood that this might be Gemma's last hope at breaking free.

"Dad, I have to go." She smiled at him and shrugged help-lessly. "Diana might be the one who can break the curse. I have to be there."

"I should come with you," he said firmly.

"No, you don't need to. I'll have Harper, and Lydia is an ex-pert at these things," Gemma assured him.

"I'll also be there," Marcy added.

"See? I'll be totally fine," Gemma said, but Brian didn't look completely convinced.

Truth was, she wasn't completely convinced either. She really had no idea for sure who Diana was or what they'd be walking into. Gemma was willing to try just about anything by now, but she didn't want to get her dad more mixed up in all this mess than he absolutely needed to be.

"There's a flight leaving from Salisbury airport at 6:52," Harper said. "That's in . . . just over two hours, and the airport is a half hour away. We can make it, but only if we hurry." Without waiting to see if anyone agreed with it, she got up and grabbed the house phone off the cradle. "I'll call and see if I can get tickets. Dad, let me have your credit card."

"What?" Brian asked, startled by her abruptness.

"Sorry, Dad." Harper smiled sheepishly at him and held out her hand. "I'll pay you back, but any money I have right now is in my savings account, and we kinda need these tickets now."

"No, don't worry about it. You do what you need to do."

While Harper dialed the number for the airport, Brian left to get his wallet.

"I should go get dressed," Gemma said. "Do I need to bring anything?"

"The scroll, probably," Marcy suggested, looking down at herself. "I'll run home and change, 'cause I can't exactly meet a deity in my PJs, and I'll be back in like twenty minutes to pick you guys up. I'll text Lydia and have her meet us at the airport, since that'll be quicker than going up to Sundham to get her."

"Sounds good," Gemma said, just as her dad returned with the credit card for Harper.

"All right. See you all later." Marcy pushed open the screen door, then looked at Brian and winked. "Nice undies, Mr. Fisher."

THIRTY

Inland

The farther they got from the ocean, the more intense Gemma's headache became. Harper sat in the window seat, flipping through the book on Roman mythology Gemma had brought, because Gemma's head hurt too much to concentrate. She'd had to read the same sentence over and over, and she still didn't even really understand what it was about.

The morning sun only made her migraine worse, so Gemma reached over and closed the shade.

"Your head's really bothering you?" Harper asked quietly.

"Not too bad," Gemma lied, and forced a smile.

And then, as if to somehow prove she wasn't in agonizing pain or maybe to distract herself, she decided to make conversation. Marcy and Lydia were sitting across the aisle of the plane from her, so she looked over at them.

For most of the flight, none of them had spoken much. Harper was reading the book, Gemma was trying futilely to sleep, Lydia had some of Audra's notes laid out on the tray and was going through them, and Marcy was typing feverishly on her phone.

"Are you texting someone?" Gemma asked.

"No, I'm using Twitter."

"You paid, like, twenty dollars for in-flight Internet so you could *tweet?*" Gemma asked, and for a second, she was too stunned to notice that it felt like a swarm of mosquitoes was trapped inside her brain.

"Wait." Harper looked up from her book. "You have Twitter?"

Marcy shook her head. "There's so much you don't know about me."

"What's so important that you have to tweet en route to Charleston?" Gemma asked.

"I'm just talking to Kirby," Marcy replied noncommittally.

"Kirby Logan?" Harper closed the book and leaned forward in her seat, so it was easier for her to see Marcy. "Are you guys like dating now?"

"What are you doing?" Marcy looked over at them, narrowing her eyes behind her glasses. "Why are you interrogating me about my love life? I never do that to you."

Harper scoffed. "You ask me about my love life all the time!"

"Yeah, but I just do that to be polite," Marcy said. "I don't actually care."

"That makes it so much better." Harper rolled her eyes.

"Doesn't it?" Marcy asked.

"Have you ever had a boyfriend, Marcy?" Gemma asked, since keeping this conversation going really did seem to take her mind off the pain. At least a little bit. "I've never heard you even talk about going on dates."

"Ladies don't kiss and tell." Marcy turned her attention back to her phone. "And I'm a lady in the streets and a freak with the beats."

"It's a 'freak in the sheets,'" Gemma corrected her.

"What?" Marcy shook her head. "No. I play the steel drums. I don't do anything with sheets."

"Marcy has had boyfriends," Lydia said. She rubbed her neck and looked up from the notes. "She was really serious with this guy in high school. Keith."

Lydia and Marcy were both nine years older than Gemma, so neither she nor Harper had known them in school. But Lydia had graduated with Marcy and had been really good friends with her, and Gemma just realized that Lydia might have all kinds of fun dirt on her.

"*Keith?*" Harper sounded dubious. "That's such a normal name."

"Yeah, I thought you would only date guys named Bram or Xavier or Frodo," Gemma agreed.

Marcy rested her head against the seat and sighed. "Okay, first of all, I'm not gonna date a hobbit. And secondly, obviously those names would be way cooler, but I don't get to pick my boyfriends' names." She paused, thinking. "Actually, I wonder how committed Kirby is to his name. He's always looked like a Stanley to me."

"How is Stanley better than Kirby?" Gemma asked.

Lydia leaned forward, resting her arms on the tray table, and gave Gemma and Harper an impish smirk. "Oh, and Keith was a football player."

"He was third-string and benched the whole season," Marcy said in an exasperated way, like she'd explained this a hundred times before. "He was also on the math league and a founding member of the paranormal society. It's that last fact that attracted me to him, and I was willing to overlook the whole 'jock' thing to be with him."

"Wow." Gemma shook her head. "I just can't picture you like going on dates or kissing or anything."

"You shouldn't picture me kissing. That's gross and weird," Marcy said.

"They even went to prom together," Lydia added.

Marcy groaned. "Oh, my god. This is the longest flight of my entire life. When are we getting there?"

"Marcy went to prom? Seriously?" Harper snickered.

"I know!" Gemma agreed. "I couldn't believe it when Marcy told me last week."

"Right?" Lydia sounded as shocked as they were. "For a little bit, I was afraid that it might be some trick, and the football team was gonna go all *Carrie* on her. But nope. She didn't win prom queen, and Keith really liked her."

"That prom was horrible, though. Pig's blood would've been an improvement," Marcy muttered, and began typing on her phone again.

"There really is so much I don't know about you, Marcy," Harper said.

"What are you tweeting now?" Gemma leaned into the aisle, trying to read it.

"I'm not tweeting anything. I'm Googling to see if anyone has developed teleportation technology so that I never have to go through this again."

The flight did feel long, like Marcy had said, but landing didn't make things much better. In fact, being on solid ground only seemed to make the headache intensify. Gemma bought overpriced aspirin and a bottle of water at the airport and guzzled it down before they even went to the car rental.

Since Harper and Gemma were under twenty-five, Marcy rented the car in her name, and that meant they had to put it on her credit card.

"Thank you," Gemma told Marcy for the twentieth time as they walked out to pick up their rented sedan.

"As long as I get to see some kind of all-knowing, all-powerful, magical being on this trip, then we'll call it even," Marcy said.

"This trip is really racking up," Gemma said, and she felt guilty just thinking about it. "As soon as this is all over, I'm gonna spend the rest of my life paying people back and trying to make up for the hell that everyone is going through."

"Getting back is the only repayment we need," Harper assured her.

Marcy drove, while Harper navigated in the passenger seat using the GPS and the directions that Lydia had conjured up from Audra's notes. Gemma was in too much pain to be as much help as she'd like, and she rested her forehead against the cool glass of the window and closed her eyes.

"So when we get there, I think you should let me do the talking first," Lydia said, as they got closer.

"How will we know it's Diana?" Harper glanced back in the backseat at Lydia. "Do you know what she looks like?"

Lydia shook her head. "No, Audra was careful not to have pictures or to describe her. But I usually just know."

"How? Do you have like a divining rod for supernatural elements or something?" Harper asked.

"No. Audra and my gramma were really great about being able to sense things, but with me, it comes from experience." Lydia shrugged. "When you're around something enough, you eventually pick it up."

"Do you know what kind of goddess she is? Is she gonna hurt us or be violent?" Marcy asked.

"She helped Audra and Thalia," Lydia said. "But I can't make any guarantees on how she'll react."

"She might kill us," Marcy said.

Lydia sighed. "She probably won't."

"But she might," Marcy persisted, but strangely, she didn't sound that upset about the prospect.

"How are you holding up, Gemma?" Harper turned around fully so she could really get a look at her.

"Okay. But those aspirin I took are doing nothing for my headache," she admitted.

"Because it's not real pain. It's supernatural," Lydia explained. "Pills won't do anything for it."

"Then hopefully this won't take too long," Gemma said.

"And . . . here we are," Marcy said, and Gemma looked out at the window.

Marcy had pulled up in front of a sage green building that would've looked like a warehouse if it weren't for all the plants. A large faded sign across the front read *Floral Essence,* written in a lovely scroll. Skylights on the pitched roof gave it more of a greenhouse feel, and nearly every inch of surrounding land was covered in flowers or bushes.

"This is a flower shop," Harper said as she gazed up at it.

"Yeah. That's how Audra found her." Lydia pointed to it. "At this flower shop."

Harper turned back to Lydia, and so far, nobody had made any move to get out of the car. "But she doesn't live here."

"She might." Marcy leaned forward, trying to get a better look at it. "It looks like a big place. There could be an apartment in the back."

"So, according to Audra, Diana worked at this place fifty years ago. *Fifty.*" Harper was sounding increasingly irritated. "She can't possibly still work here, not if she's trying to be incognito and not set off alarms as some weird, ageless lady living in a store."

"She's a god," Lydia reminded her patiently. "She can change her appearance. If she wants to age, she can. If she wants to be a tall, blond, twenty-year-old woman or a short, elderly, black man or a goat, she can be."

"She can be a goat?" Marcy was intrigued.

"Yeah. Didn't you ever read mythology?" Lydia asked. "Gods

were always turning into animals. Zeus was pretending to be a bull or something when he impregnated Hercules' mom."

"Why did he pretend to be a bull?" Marcy asked. "How does being a bull make it easier for him to get laid instead of being a friggin' *god*?"

Harper turned away from them and stared back out at the flower shop. "So you're sure this is the place?"

"Yeah," Lydia said decisively. "If Diana is still alive, then this is where we'll find her."

"Harper. Look at that bush," Gemma said, and got out of the car to inspect it.

It was a huge bush growing up alongside the building and nearly as tall. Each of the blossoms were bright, vibrant purple, and they had to be twice the size of Gemma's fist. As soon as she stepped out of the car, she'd been able to smell it—the strong fragrance overpowering the other plants and the city around them.

"This is just like the one behind Bernie's house," Gemma said when she heard Harper come up behind her. "Thalia planted it in the yard."

"Do you think she got it from here?" Marcy asked, as she and Lydia joined them.

"She must've," Harper said. "I've never seen roses like this anywhere else."

"Look at this one." Lydia had moved a few feet away and pointed to a fern with large pink flowers in the shape of a corkscrew. Then she looked around, gesturing to the cornucopia of vivid, exotic plant life. "The flowers and plants here all seem really beautiful and unique. She might be the goddess of nature."

"I thought Diana was the goddess of hunting," Harper said.

"The Roman goddess. But Demeter was the goddess of nature." Gemma couldn't breathe for a moment. "You don't think . . ."

Lydia shrugged. "Audra only ever referred to her as Diana."

"It could be her, though," Gemma insisted.

They were all standing outside, and a mixture of terror and hope left Gemma frozen in place. Marcy had apparently grown impatient, because she went inside, and the door chimed loudly as she entered.

"Marcy," Harper hissed, and hurried after her. "Wait for us."

Inside, the store somehow felt even more vast than it had on the outside. It was like stepping into a jungle. Vines and flowers hung from the ceiling, cucumber and zucchini were growing over crates into the aisles. It had been warm outside, but the heat and humidity were so strong indoors that Marcy's glasses fogged up, and she wiped them on her shirt.

"I'll be right out!" A woman shouted from the far end of the store. "Look around while you wait."

Gemma and Harper exchanged a look, and Gemma shrugged. The four of them started wandering toward the other end of the store, where the woman had shouted from, but it was impossible not to get sidetracked by the plants.

Gemma stepped away from the main aisle and investigated a wall of vines, strange tangles that completely covered an old, wired fence. The flowers were small, like violets, and a deep, rich blue. But it was the scent that called her in. It was intoxicating, and for a second, her head even stopped hurting.

"Hello there," the woman said again, sounding closer this time. Gemma heard the jangle of her jewelry as she walked over to the other girls. "What can I help you all with today?"

"Are you Diana?" Lydia asked, and Gemma tried to peer in through the vines to get a peek at her, but all she could see was drapey beige fabric.

"Yes, I am," the woman said cheerily.

Gemma finally came out from behind the vines where she saw a woman in her late fifties standing with Harper, Lydia, and Marcy. She looked exactly the way Gemma imagined an art history teacher or the leader of a co-op whole-foods store would look.

She wore a long dress with billowy sleeves and some kind of Indian pattern that went down to her feet. Beaded necklaces and bracelets adorned her, though none of them appeared to be that fancy or expensive. Her blond hair was a bit frizzy and pulled away from her face. When she saw Gemma, she adjusted her small, tortoiseshell glasses, then she exhaled deeply.

"Oh," Diana said, looking past the other girls and staring right at Gemma. "So you've come to kill me then?"

THIRTY-ONE

Culpable

I t's a great night for this," Alex said as he surveyed the beer tent at Bayside Park.

"Yep. Just us two guys and a bunch of drunks." Daniel took a swig of his beer. "Perfect."

Just outside the tent, he could hear the sounds of the emcee announcing the Miss Capri Pageant, and the crowd's applauding and cheering. But in here, it seemed much quieter.

The thick green fabric of the tent kept out the sunlight and the festivities of At Summer's End. Sure, there were tourists inside, and a few frat boys getting wasted at the other end of the tent, but something about the beer tent gave it an illusion of privacy that Daniel found comforting.

That's not what Alex meant by a great night, though. The weather was warm, the sky was blue, birds were singing. Even though it was officially September, this was still the perfect summer day.

Alex had come right from his shift at the dock, and he'd changed into jeans and a T-shirt, but he still smelled vaguely of grease and seawater. Still, he seemed happy to be here, and had a boyish grin on his face.

It was that grin that wouldn't let him pass for twenty-one although he had matured and looked much older than when Daniel had first met him earlier this summer. But the bartender had slapped a bright orange wristband on Alex, meaning that he'd only be served soda in the tent.

That was fine by Daniel. He'd flashed his ID, gotten a cold beer, and sat down at a picnic table in the corner. Alex sat next to him, sipping his Mountain Dew.

"I was kinda surprised when you texted me today," Alex admitted. "We don't usually hang out."

"Well, I'm always borrowing your car, so I figured that we ought to get to know each other," Daniel said, but that wasn't the whole reason.

He hadn't slept much since his fight with Harper last night. After she'd left, he'd kicked a dining-room chair in anger, snapping one of the legs. He spent most of today mending it, but eventually he'd grown tired of sitting in the house and feeling trapped on the island.

He hadn't even properly celebrated his birthday yet, not that he really deserved to celebrate. Harper was right, and he knew it. He'd blown it with her because he hadn't thought, and now he didn't want to think. Not about her. Not about last night.

So he'd asked Alex to join him for a beer. He'd like to believe that it was just because he thought Alex was a nice guy, but the truth was that his life had become so entangled with the Fisher girls that he couldn't even hang out with someone who wasn't somehow connected to them.

Gemma had texted him earlier, letting him know that she and Harper had left town to meet Diana in Charleston, so that he wouldn't worry if he came looking for Harper. But he did still worry.

And maybe that's why he'd invited Alex out, too. In case something happened to either Harper or Gemma, Daniel wanted to know. Even if Harper never wanted to see him again, he couldn't go on without knowing she was okay. Without being there to help if she needed him.

"It'll be good for us to get along," Alex said. "Since the ladies in our lives are sisters, it'll be easier if we can all hang out and have some laughs."

Daniel scratched the back of his head. "I suppose Gemma didn't get a chance to tell you."

"What?"

"I'm not sure that Harper is in my life anymore." He twisted the bottle on the table, staring down at the condensation that dripped down the glass. "We might've broken up last night."

"Really?" Alex sounded surprised. "Did she pull the same crap that Gemma did with me? Like how it's for your own good?"

"No." Daniel shook his head. "I did something bad, very, very bad, and she rightfully got pissed off. So . . ."

"Oh, man. That sucks."

"It does," he agreed. "So I got sick of sitting around the house, thinking about what a jackass I am, and I thought, what the hell? Why not see what Alex is up to?"

"Thanks." Alex smiled.

"So you're working down at the docks now?" Daniel asked when they lapsed into a silence.

"Yeah." Alex nodded. "Just until I go to college. I'm trying to enroll for the spring semester. I'm going for astronomy or meteorology. Anything about what happens in the sky, and I'm into it."

"Yeah? That's pretty cool," Daniel said, then he tried to remember if astronomy was studying the stars or horoscopes. If he figured knowing Alex, it probably had to be following stars and comets and not the zodiac.

"What about you?" Alex asked him. "Any college in your future?"

"Nah. I was never that into school. I did okay, but I'd always rather be working with my hands than reading books." Daniel held his hands out, showing the rough calluses and faded scars from years of fixing anything he found broken. "And I like what I'm doing now."

He'd worked on some pieces, like the chair he'd broken today and the coffee table in his living room. But he didn't have as much time as he'd like. He'd been hoping that with the island, he'd be able to really get working on his carpentry projects, but it seemed like the sirens took up any free time he might have.

And then the silence fell over them, growing more awkward the longer they went without saying anything. There was no TV to distract them, and they couldn't actually see the parade of girls entered in the Miss Capri Pageant.

"Look at you two," Penn's silky voice came from behind them. Daniel's hand tightened on his beer bottle, and he groaned inwardly. "Boys just wanna have fun, huh?"

"We're just two wild-and-crazy guys," he said dryly.

He felt her hand on his shoulder, her skin hot through his T-shirt. He leaned away from it, and Penn dropped her hand but sat down next to him anyway.

"What is that?" Penn leaned over Daniel to get a better look at Alex's glass, and she smirked. "Soda? Oh, Alex, I'll never understand what Gemma sees in you."

"And I'm more than okay with that," Alex said.

Daniel wasn't completely sure how the sirens' charms affected Alex. He'd fallen under them before, and Daniel suspected that if Penn really tried, she could hold him captive to her song.

But she didn't actually seem that interested in him, and Alex held his own pretty well. He wasn't falling all over himself to please her, and there was a glint of disgust in his eyes whenever he looked at her.

"So what are you doing in here in the tent?" Daniel asked, doing his best not to look over at her. "There's a Miss Capri Pageant going on out there. Don't you wanna go trick the judges into giving you a crown?"

"Please." She sneered. "Getting awarded the prettiest girl in this town is like winning cleanest hog in the pen. You have to hang out with a buncha dirty pigs to prove something that everybody already knows."

"That's quite the imagery there, Penn," Alex said.

"Since we got interrupted last night," Penn said, dropping her voice to sultry, soft words in his ear, "it seems like you're free today—"

"Speaking of last night." Daniel cut her off, clearing his throat. "Where is Liv?"

Penn groaned. She sat with her back against the table, so she was facing in the opposite direction from Daniel and Alex, and her black hair cascaded over the wood. It also made it easier for her to stick her chest out, but Daniel wasn't about to look over and catch a glimpse.

"She's on lockdown," Penn said. "I'm not letting her out of the house until . . ."

"Until what?" Daniel asked.

"I don't know." She sighed. "Maybe never again. I'm getting so sick of her attitude."

He smirked. "I told you."

"Really, Daniel?" She cast him a look. "I'm already getting enough of that crap from Thea and Gemma. I don't need it from you, too."

"That's him," Mayor Adam Crawford said, his words booming through the tent. "You, you there."

Daniel glanced back over his shoulder to see what the mayor was freaking out about. Since it was seventy degrees, he'd ditched the suit jacket, but he still wore the slacks and a dress shirt, with the sleeves rolled up. His hair was normally slicked back, but a strand had fallen forward, dipping down over his forehead.

With a severe glare, the mayor was pointing directly at

Daniel, and his petite blond wife hid behind him, looking sad and shaken. Daniel glanced around to be sure, but it was obvious that Mayor Crawford's accusation was directed at him.

He marched over to Daniel. An aide tried to stop him, but he just pushed him away. Then the aide gently guided the mayor's wife out of the tent, apparently not wanting her to witness her husband's outburst.

The mayor stood directly in front of Daniel, and he turned around on the bench, so he could face him fully.

"You." Then his eyes bounced over to Alex. "Actually, both of you were there."

"Where?" Alex asked, baffled about being brought into this. "What are we talking about?"

"During the cook-off on Monday, you had an altercation with my son," the mayor explained, and Penn snickered from beside Daniel.

"What are you talking about?" Daniel asked. "I didn't even say anything to Aiden. I was defending his date from Liv."

The mayor shook his head with a comical ferocity. "No, you got in a fight with my son over his girlfriend."

"What?" Daniel was entirely perplexed now. "No, I didn't. I—"

Penn leaned over and spoke low in his ear, "Honey, they don't remember any of it."

"What?" He looked over at her, then it hit him. "The song."

During the fight at the park, Liv had bared her teeth and almost transformed in front of everyone. To make the incident go away before the X-Files division of the FBI descended on Capri,

Thea and Gemma had used the siren song to make everyone forget what they'd seen.

Apparently, it didn't make them forget everything, though. It must've twisted things up somehow, so the mayor thought he'd seen Daniel assaulting Aiden though he'd done nothing of the sort.

Still, sitting in front of Aiden's father brought up a surge of memories. Gruesome images of Aiden's body, and the final moments when Daniel had dropped the dismembered remains into the ocean. In the back of his mind, he could still hear the splash of the body hitting the water. A wave of nausea rushed over him, and he quickly swallowed it down.

"I'm sorry you're upset about your son," Daniel said, his voice almost inaudible over the din of the beer tent. "If there was anything I could do to help, believe me, I would."

Mayor Crawford didn't seem to hear a word Daniel had said. He'd been staring down at him, his small eyes fixated on him, as perspiration slid down his forehead, and he began wagging his finger in Daniel's face.

"I know you, don't I? You're John Morgan's little brother."

Daniel nodded slowly. "Yeah, I am."

"He was always trouble." The mayor glowered down at him. "I always told Aiden to stay away from him. Aiden didn't need to get mixed up with trash like that."

"*Trash?*" Daniel got up, and it was only the realization of what the mayor was going through that kept his anger under control. John had his problems, but he was a far kinder guy than Aiden had ever been.

Alex stood up then, flanking Daniel on his side. Things wouldn't come to blows, at least not on Daniel's account. But it was still nice to know that Alex had his back, especially since Alex had toughened up so much working at the docks. He looked like he could handle himself in a fight.

"I have no idea what your problem is, but you need to shut up and get out of here," Alex said.

But the mayor ignored Alex, keeping his glare focused on Daniel, and for some reason, that kept making Penn giggle.

"You were always jealous of Aiden," the mayor said. "I saw it in your eyes, and it was still there when you fought with him. What did you do to him?"

"What are you talking about?" Alex asked. Daniel swallowed hard, but he managed to keep his gaze from wavering. "We didn't do anything to him."

"Then where is he?" Mayor Crawford demanded.

Daniel closed his eyes and shook his head. "I have no idea where he is."

"You're lying." The mayor looked like he was about to deck Daniel, and honestly, Daniel would've welcomed it. "I didn't get where I am without knowing when people are bullshitting me, and you are full of shit. Aiden disappeared last night, and you were the last person seen fighting with him."

"That can't possibly be true," Daniel said wearily.

"You've had it in for him for a long time, and I'm going straight to the police right now to tell them that," the mayor threatened.

"I had nothing to do with Aiden's disappearance," Daniel lied, because he couldn't tell him about the sirens and what they had done to Aiden.

But just then, Daniel would have given anything to tell the mayor the truth. As angry as Mayor Crawford was, he was just a scared father looking for his son, and if Daniel could give him any peace, he would've.

"I wouldn't say *nothing*," Penn said, giggling, and Daniel glared back at her.

She smiled and stood up, adjusting the hem of her short dress as she did. She stepped over to the mayor, squeezing into the space between him and Daniel. Putting her hand on his chest, she stared up at him with her charcoal eyes, and he melted as soon as he looked in them.

"Mayor Crawford, I think you're mistaken," she purred.

"What is she doing?" Alex asked quietly, leaning toward Daniel. "Is she helping you?"

Daniel shook his head because there was no easy way to answer. If he took the fall for Aiden's murder, it would be much more work for Penn to get him out of jail, so she could have her way with him.

"What?" The mayor sounded like a man waking from a dream.

"Daniel would never hurt your son." Penn reached up, slicking back the strand that had come loose from the mayor's hair. "And he was with me all night. So there's no way he could've done anything to Aiden."

"But then . . ." The mayor's face scrunched up, like he knew he should be worried about something else, but he just couldn't seem to make himself think of anything but Penn and her voice. "Where's Aiden?"

"I heard he ran off with a girl. Some hot model," Penn lied in the convincing way that only a siren could, the melody in her voice making the mayor believe anything she wanted him to. "He went to a tropical beach to live it up, and he can't use his cell phone. He'll be gone for a while, but you don't need to worry or look for him. Aiden is fine, and you won't ever try to find out what happened to him again."

"He's fine." A relieved smile spread out on the mayor's face, and something about that made Daniel feel sick to his stomach. "I don't even know why I was worried. Hmm. Are you busy tonight? You could join me for dinner."

"I have other plans, but thanks for the offer," Penn said. "Why don't you go hit on the future Miss Capri instead?"

"Maybe I will. Thank you." He smiled and was reluctant to look away from her, but when he did, he was back to his usual smooth political face. "Sorry for bothering you all, and I hope you enjoy the rest of the At Summer's End Festival."

Mayor Crawford walked away, presumably to hit on Miss Capri, and Daniel shook his head. He sat back down at the table and took a long swallow of his beer.

"What was all that about?" Alex asked, sitting back down next to him. "Do you know what happened to Aiden?"

"You'll have to ask Liv about that," Daniel said. He glanced over and saw a look of saddened understanding flash across Alex's face.

"Well, that was fun." Penn sat down, and Daniel glared at her.

"I've never really liked the mayor, and Aiden and I definitely had our differences, but that was sick, Penn. He just lost his son, and you convinced him that instead of looking for him, he should go cheat on his wife."

She shrugged. "He cheats on his wife all the time, and he wanted to run off with me right now. That was his idea, not mine."

Daniel shook his head. "That was one of the more twisted things I've seen you do."

"Would you rather have let him keep searching for his son?" Penn asked. "They'd eventually trace it back to you, and I bet they could find Aiden's blood on your boat."

"That man has a right to mourn his son," Daniel persisted.

"So you're not even gonna thank me for taking the heat off you?" Penn pretended to pout and stared up at him.

"Are you kidding me?" Daniel was nearly shouting. He hadn't been so close to smacking Penn in a very long time. "You're the reason the heat is on me. You're the one that got Aiden killed and dragged me in to help clean up the mess."

"I didn't kill him. Liv did."

"Liv is your fault," he told her. "You made her. Everything she does is because of you."

"Whatever." She gave a half shrug and tossed her hair. "The sooner we go through with our plan, the sooner I'll get rid of Liv. Just like you wanted." She leaned forward, her smile growing hungrier. "Why don't we go out to your place right now?"

"Not tonight," he said firmly.

"Why the hell not?" Penn snapped, and her smile instantly dropped. "Like you have anything better going on?"

"I need to get some things in order first."

"Like what?" Penn demanded to know.

It would have been nice if he had a few more days to get what was left in his life sorted out, but that wasn't the real reason he was stalling. According to her text message, Gemma thought she was really close to breaking the curse, and this would all be over. If Daniel could get out of this without sleeping with Penn, that would be amazing.

"They're my things, Penn. All right? Don't worry about it."

"Then when?" she asked.

"A few more days." He had to give her some kind of answer, and that ought to buy him enough time. Hopefully.

She scoffed. "That'll almost be the full moon."

"Why don't we wait until after the full moon then?" Daniel suggested. "It'll be easier for everyone."

"I don't think I can wait that long," Penn whined.

He looked over at her. "I'm giving you forever. That's what you've asked me for, and I'll do it. Just give me a few more days."

"Whatever. You need to hurry up and go through with this before I change my mind. You saw what Liv is capable of, but what she can do is nothing compared to what I have in store for you if you betray me." With that, Penn got up and sauntered off, leaving him alone with Alex, who was giving him the strangest look.

"What was all that about?" Alex asked.

Daniel had finished his beer, so he stood up to get another one. "It's way too much to get into right now."

"Are you like . . . with Penn or something?"

"No, no, hell no." He shook his head. "I love Harper. And I'll do anything for her, even if it means losing her."

THIRTY-TWO

Disavowal

The room smelled of violet—not the flower, but the color. That didn't make any sense, not even to Gemma, who'd come to accept oddities more readily, but there really wasn't anyway else to describe it. It was a rich, almost velvety scent, and when she closed her eyes, all she could see was amethyst.

Since the gods and goddesses had slowly been picked off the last several centuries, Diana assumed that every supernatural being who tracked her down planned to torture and kill her, and she'd instantly pegged Gemma as something more than human.

Once Lydia had convinced Diana that none of them meant her any harm, the older woman had led them to a small sitting room at the back of the flower shop, so they could talk. Lydia had instantly gone to the shelves, excitedly but carefully admiring all of Diana's collection.

It was filled with so many antiquities—books, statues, art, tools, musical instruments. The collection appeared to have begun with the dawn of time. Despite the number of things in such a small space, the room didn't feel cluttered. Everything had its own spot, carefully displayed on the shelves that lined the walls.

Gemma sat on a lush velvet settee next to Harper, while Diana poured them tea. Gemma had tried to decline, but Diana insisted that she needed some. While there was plenty of room to sit next to Harper, Marcy had chosen to sit cross-legged on the floor by the window, where a fat, fluffy Siamese cat basked in the sun.

When Diana returned carrying a tea tray, Harper stood up to help her, but Diana shooed her away, insisting she had it herself, and set the tray down on an elegant coffee table in front of the settee.

Gemma would've offered to help, but the watersong was reaching a level of unbearable pain. It buzzed in her left ear—the side facing the East Coast—and the vision in her left eye had begun to blur.

"I see you've made friends with Thallo," Diana said to Marcy as she made herself comfortable in her high-backed chair across from the settee. "She's always been a lover. Her sister, Carpo, is much happier watching us than making friends, I'm afraid."

A thin Siamese cat posted at the top of a bookshelf meowed at the sound of her name, and Gemma glanced back up at her.

"She's a nice cat," Marcy said noncommittally as she ran her hand through Thallo's fur.

Diana had poured five cups of tea, but only she and Harper had taken theirs. Lydia was too immersed in a book she'd found, and Gemma felt too sick to even think about drinking anything.

"I'm not sure if I'm naïve for letting you in here." Diana settled back in her chair and sipped her tea. "You have only brought three mortals with you, so I suspect that you haven't come here to battle."

"No, I don't mean you any harm," Gemma tried to reassure her again.

Before Diana had led them here, Lydia had used her extensive knowledge of paranormal elements and powers of persuasion to convince Diana that they weren't there to hurt her. But now that Diana seemed comfortable with them, and Lydia had the distraction of ancient artifacts, she was content to let Gemma do her own talking.

"You are a siren, aren't you?" Diana asked, eyeing her above her glasses.

"Yes. I am." She waited a beat before asking, "Are you Demeter?"

"Demeter." Diana smiled, as if being surprised by a forgotten memory. "I haven't been called that in a very long time, but yes, I was once Demeter."

"But you're not now?" Marcy looked up from the cat. "Aren't you still a goddess?"

Diana laughed warmly. "Goddess. You say that as if it means something."

"Doesn't it?" Marcy asked.

"Not what it used to." Diana took another drink of her tea, then set the cup on a nearby end table. "All my friends, my family, anyone who really knew me, is long since gone. I am alone, with no one to worship me, and why would they? What little magic I still have I only use on my flowers and plants. I'm an old woman now."

"But don't you choose this form? Can't you be young again if you wanted?" Gemma asked.

"I chose this form because it suits me. This face, this shop, this life, it's what I am now." She gestured to the room around her. "The goddess within me is all but extinguished."

"Why? I've read the stories about you. You were so powerful," Marcy said, as if trying to give Diana a pep talk. She'd been so set on seeing something amazing that she didn't seem ready to let the idea go. "You helped the earth. You saved people. Why give all that up?"

"Immortality is not what you think it is. Neither is power. It's not the answer to anything. It's just a different way of being, a much *longer* way," Diana tried to explain. "Anyway, if you're not here to kill me, then what have you come for?"

"I want to break the curse," Gemma said.

Diana looked down at her lap, smoothing out nonexistent wrinkles in the fabric of her dress. "Oh, well, I can't do that."

"You can't?" Gemma took a deep breath and tried not to let that get her down. Maybe she'd misunderstood. "But . . . you're a goddess."

"I already told you. That doesn't mean much anymore," Diana reiterated.

"Didn't you help my great-grandma, Audra?" With a book still in her hand, Lydia came over and perched on the arm of the settee next to Harper. "She came to you with a muse around fifty years ago, looking for a way to become mortal. She said you helped her."

"That's how you found me then," Diana said. "Are you a soothsayer?"

Lydia smiled demurely. "No, I'm not. But I followed in Audra's footsteps, trying to help those who need me."

Diana appeared bemused by her answer. "And you think helping a siren is worth your time?"

"I'm not a siren." Gemma shook her head. "Not like the others. I don't want to be a monster. I want to end this."

"I'm sorry, but I've already explained," Diana said, though Gemma didn't think she sounded even slightly apologetic. "I can't help you."

"There's nothing you can try?" Gemma persisted. "You created the curse. There has to be something that you can do. *Something* you know."

"I'm afraid not." Diana was beginning to sound weary of the conversation.

"Can't? Or won't?" Marcy asked, echoing the same thought running through Gemma's mind.

"Perhaps it's both," Diana admitted with a slow shrug of her shoulders.

"I have the scroll," Gemma said. They'd left it out in the car, but she could get it in a flash if she needed to. "I know that if I can destroy the scroll, the curse can be undone, like with Asterion and the other minotaurs."

"If you have the scroll, then you've tried destroying it, and you've failed," Diana said.

Gemma exchanged a look with Harper, wondering if she should admit the truth, but decided there was no point in lying to Diana. Not about this. "I've tried everything I can think of, and nothing even makes a mark."

"Of course it doesn't. The paper wouldn't be worth anything if it did," Diana replied.

"Is the paper cursed? Is there a way to destroy it?" Gemma asked.

"No. The paper is absolutely and completely indestructible," Diana confirmed their worst fears. "The curse is in the ink."

"The ink?" Harper asked, trying not to appear too eager, most likely remembering her own experiments with it. "So what happens with the ink?"

"I've already told you that I'm not going to help you, so if you've come all the way for this, then I'm sorry that we're going to have to cut this visit short." Any niceties evaporated from Diana's voice. "There's no reason to continue if you'll only keep asking the same question over and over."

"Why wouldn't you want to help me?" Gemma asked. "Penn has been running around doing whatever she wants for a couple millennia. This is supposed to be a curse, but she acts like it's the greatest gift ever. With all due respect, if you want to really punish her, then you should end this."

"Penn?" Diana sounded intrigued. "Is that what Peisinoe is going by now?"

"Yeah. Penn is one of only two original sirens left," Gemma said.

Diana nodded. "I always suspected that she would outlive the rest of them."

"She's going to live on, happily ever after, if we don't do something." Gemma leaned forward, resting her elbows on her knees, and tried to convey more confidence than she actually felt.

Diana cocked her head. "How old are you?"

"I'm sixteen."

"Is that your human age, or how long you've been a siren?"

"Human," Gemma said. "I've only been a siren for a few months."

"Sixteen years is your entire life. It's all of time to you, but it's a blink of the eye to me. You can't even fathom time as I do," Diana said with a condescending tone that Gemma did not care for.

"I don't understand what this has to do with punishing Penn," Gemma said.

"Because *time* has everything to do with it," Diana said. "I am very, very old. Not quite as old as the earth, but close. In the beginning, there was only us. No mortals. Just gods. But time kept moving, and we stayed the same. We squabbled and bickered among ourselves, but it soon became meaningless. It wasn't until the humans came around that life truly began.

"I waited a very long time before I bore any children," Diana went on. "I knew what life was like to be alone, to live forever, and when Persephone was born, that changed everything.

"When Penn and her sisters were supposed to be caring for

my daughter, my beloved Persephone, they were out swimming and singing, trying to impress suitors. They were supposed to protect Persephone. Instead, they were having the time of their lives while someone raped and *murdered* Persephone," Diana spat. Her lips were pulled back in an angry grimace, and her eyes blazed. "I found her bloody body discarded in a field, wrapped in the shawl that had been meant for her wedding."

But then she took a deep breath, and her whole body slacked as the anger was replaced by sadness. "Persephone was the sun to my earth, and without her . . ."

She paused and stared out at the window. Tears welled up in her eyes, and other than the sound of Thallo purring next to Marcy, the room was silent as Diana composed herself.

"It's been thousands of years since my daughter died," Diana said at length. "And yet, there is not a day that goes by that I don't think of her. Not a day when my heart doesn't ache for her. This pain that I feel, the one that I endure every day, *this* is what I wanted to give to Penn and her sisters. Death is easy compared to this."

"The siren curse sounds like a fair punishment, except that Penn has never and will never feel that kind of pain," Gemma said. "She's never loved anything enough to feel like that."

"She hadn't, no, not when I turned her into a siren. Which is why I did it." Diana turned away from the window and looked back at Gemma. "She was a selfish girl who cared nothing for anyone, and her negligence killed my only child. How could I hurt her as badly as she'd hurt me when she'd never loved, when she wasn't even capable of loving the way that I had?

"The curse itself—the swimming, the singing, the men—that's only part of it," Diana explained. "Those were the only things in her life that mattered to her, and her sisters, and I wanted her to do them again and again and again. Hell is repetition. I learned that in the years I walked the earth before humans, before Persephone. I wanted the only things in life that gave her pleasure to eventually mean nothing. Her only joys would eventually make her numb.

"The second part of the curse, the worst part, she didn't even understand." Diana smiled bitterly. "Not for centuries. In fact, it became so long, I thought it might never happen."

"What happened?" Gemma asked.

"She fell in love," Diana said simply.

THIRTY-THREE

Anathema

W ith who?" Harper asked, and by the tone of her voice, Gemma knew she feared that it was Daniel.

The truth was that Gemma herself wasn't sure if Penn really loved him or what exactly she wanted with him. She knew that whatever it was, it couldn't be good, but she didn't think that was what Diana was referring to now.

"Bastian," Gemma said, remembering the story that Thea had told her. Penn had apparently been deeply infatuated with him, and Gemma suspected that Thea had had feelings for him, too, though she denied it.

"Bastian was the name he was going by at the time, but Orpheus was his given name, the one I knew him by," Diana said. "I sent him to her."

"What? Why?" Harper asked.

"To break her heart, of course," Diana said, and smiled like this delighted her. "He was immortal, immune to her song, and that novelty intrigued her. I'd known him for some time, and he was a very attractive man, renowned for making the ladies swoon. With a little flirtation on his part, I thought he might finally be the one to make Penn feel something."

"And he did," Gemma said.

"And then he left her. Just as I asked him to." Her smile faded a bit as she thought. "Though I'm not sure what became of him since I've never heard from him again. Once he left, he disappeared, presumably going into hiding before Penn found him and wreaked her vengeance on him."

"But Penn didn't really love him," Gemma reminded Diana. "She's not even capable of it."

"She's not, at least not the way most living creatures are," Diana admitted. "But what she felt for him was more than she'd felt before. He never loved her, it was just a trick. I'd sent him on the mission to fool the selfish girl. She would never feel his love in return, no matter what she did or how she lusted after him. And then he left, and she was devastated."

"Why? If she didn't really love him?" Marcy asked.

"This was as close to love as she could feel," Diana clarified. "For her, this was *everything*. And she was a girl who'd gotten everything she wanted for so long. When she finally lost something, something that really mattered to her, she had no idea what to do."

"So you've won then. She hurt the way you hurt," Gemma said.

"*No.*" Diana was appalled by the idea. "It's not enough to lose someone, to hurt. It's the pain, day in and day out. It's the constant reminder. This is why I gave her immortality. I wanted her to feel this way forever."

"But she doesn't seem that devastated anymore. She seems fine," Harper said. "She even has her sights set on another guy."

"Oh?" Diana raised an eyebrow but didn't seem that ruffled. "Is he mortal?"

"Yes, he's my boyfriend." Harper shook her head and lowered her eyes. "Or ex-boyfriend, maybe."

"Good," Diana said. "He'll be dead soon, and she'll feel the pain anew."

"No, not good." Harper glared at her. "I don't want him to be dead soon."

"I don't mean to say that she'll kill him, or that I hope she does, although she probably will," Diana expounded on her earlier statement without any hint of apology or sympathy for Harper's pain. "Human life is very short compared to ours, and too soon, you'll all be gone."

"She's happy. She's with someone again," Gemma persisted. "How do you even know she was devastated? Penn still gets everything she wants and does anything she pleases. It's not a curse you've given her."

"For centuries, the sirens lived rather quietly and inconspicuously among people," Diana said. "Then, after her love left, she went on a mad rampage. Thousands of people were killed at the sirens' hands, with Penn leading the wave, of course."

"That's your proof that she was devastated?" Marcy asked. "Penn strikes me as the kind of girl who enjoys killing people, so that sounds like it was a big, ol', happy, fun-time party for her."

"This was different," Diana insisted. "And she killed her father."

"She killed Achelous?" Gemma asked, but that didn't come as much of a shock to her. She'd suspected he was dead, and Penn killed her sisters without hesitation.

"So many had died, both mortal and immortal, and finally, Achelous had enough," Diana said. "He knew something must be done about his daughter, but she wanted nothing to do with him. No matter how hard he tried to reach out to her, his invitations went unanswered.

"Finally, to summon her, he built her a town," she went on. "He named it after her favorite place, the island she'd grown up on. He wanted to create a paradise for her and his other daughters. The girls were right to be angry with him. He had been a very neglectful father, but he'd decided to change his ways, mend fences, and stop the bloodshed."

"Wait, wait." Marcy held her hands up in the shape of a T for timeout. "You're talking about Capri, Maryland, aren't you? Achelous was Thomas Thermopolis?"

And as soon as Marcy said it, it all made sense. Capri, Anthemusa Bay, Achelous River—these were all named after the places the sirens had lived according to Greek historians. It did seem a bit too coincidental that they would just happen onto a place that fit perfectly into their own mythology.

Diana nodded. "Yes. He told me of his plans, and I tried to talk him out of it, but he was insistent. He told me I was jealous and blinded by the loss of my own daughter, and maybe there was truth to that. But Penn had always been evil and always would be. So when she finally did come, it came as no surprise to me that within a few weeks, the sirens had killed him."

"They killed their own father?" Harper asked. "Why? After all this time?"

"Because for the first time, Penn hurt, *truly* hurt, and she blamed him for it, for not protecting her," Diana said. "She blamed me, too, and maybe he wouldn't tell them where I was hiding. He never truly believed they would kill him. He wasn't afraid of them, and that was his undoing."

"Nope." Marcy shook her head. "I can't move past that. He built Capri for Penn and her sisters?"

"He wanted to set things right, but I knew that could never be," Diana said. "Penn will never be anything but evil."

"So you granted her immortality and horrific powers," Gemma said. "That seems reasonable and really fair to every other creature living on the earth."

"I don't care if she destroys the entire planet, as long as she's miserable," Diana said.

"But you lost your daughter!" Harper shouted, unable to hide her anger and frustration any longer. "You know how badly that hurts! And how many other people will have to lose their daughters because of something you created? I will have to lose my sister, my father his daughter, because of a vendetta that's thousands of years old? Hasn't there been enough bloodshed? Haven't enough people hurt and died for Persephone yet?"

"I understand your pain, but the horrible truth is that it will never be enough. No matter what hell Penn goes through, it will never bring my daughter back. So no, she hasn't suffered enough." A harsh acrimony stung Diana's words. "She will *never* suffer enough."

"Why are you so focused on Penn?" Lydia asked. She'd been mostly content to let the others steer the conversation, but this, apparently, had been bothering her. "There were four girls who left Persephone alone that day, four girls you cursed."

"The other two are dead, and they were little more than collateral damage. Just as you are now." Diana motioned to Gemma then. "In order for Penn and Thelxiepia to be truly punished, I had to take the others down with them."

"Thelkispediplipa?" Marcy asked, stumbling over the name. "That's Thea, right?"

"Thea?" Diana said, then nodded. "Unlike Penn, Thea did actually love. She cared deeply for her sisters, and seeing them suffer was her punishment. In truth, the worst of my wrath was saved for Thea."

"Why? She's nowhere near as evil as Penn," Gemma pointed out.

"That is precisely why," Diana said. "She knew that what she was doing was wrong. She even cared for Persephone, but not enough to keep her safe. Not enough to deny Penn her pleasures to protect my daughter. If Penn was rotten fruit, Thea was the one who watered the tree."

"All that it takes for evil to triumph is for good men to do nothing," Lydia said softly, and Diana nodded again.

"That's why I sent Bastian to seduce Thea, too. But I told

him to favor Penn, so that it would break Thea's heart worst of all. I was hoping maybe she would stand up to her sister, fight for something she loved, but she never did."

"She never will," Gemma whispered.

After all she'd seen Penn do, Thea had done little more than step aside and watch it happen. Even when the sisters she claimed to love were murdered, Thea never acted to help them. She'd done nothing but obey until very recently.

Thea had begun to help Gemma, and that was a tremendous act of betrayal against Penn and showed a change growing within her. By giving Gemma the scroll, Thea had proven that she was willing to die to stop Penn, and yet her only attempts at undermining Penn had involved sneaking around behind her back.

It seemed that while Thea was on Gemma's side, the only thing she truly feared in life wasn't death but confronting Penn. She would do nearly whatever it took to help Gemma and break the curse, except for standing up to her sister.

"So it seems," Diana agreed.

"Not to belabor the point, but Achelous really made our town for the sirens?" Marcy asked. "Then why don't they spend all their time there? Why don't they love it if it's supposed to be some kind of siren paradise?"

"Because they hate their father," Gemma said.

Marcy shook her head. "Then why did they come back?"

"For me," Diana said. "They were looking for the muse Thalia, hoping she would lead them to me."

"She's going to kill you, you know," Harper said pointedly, and she was so irritated and enraged, Gemma was afraid she might get up soon and slap Diana. "If we could find you, eventually Penn and Thea will, too. And they'll kill you. You do understand that."

"I do. And I've made peace with it." Diana looked out the window again. "Maybe I even welcome death. That's why I've made my home so close to Capri. It's far enough inland that Penn won't readily travel here, but close enough that it really won't make it that hard to find." She breathed in deeply. "Forever is too long for anyone to live."

"If she kills you, you won't even see your revenge exacted," Gemma said. "If you won't even be here to watch them suffer, then why not end this? Why not let it go?"

"Or just let my sister go," Harper interjected. "She's not like them. She didn't do anything to you or your daughter. Isn't there a way that she can break free?"

Diana shook her head. "No. The curse binds them all together. I've already told you that I won't help you break the curse."

"But that's only because you want to see Penn suffer." An idea occurred to Gemma, and she licked her lips. "What if I killed Penn? Then would you tell me how to break it?"

Still staring out the window, Diana said, "If you tried to kill Penn, then you wouldn't need to break the curse."

"Why?" Gemma asked, and her heart pounded so loudly in her chest, she was afraid she wouldn't be able to hear Diana's reply over the sound of it. "What do you mean?"

Diana didn't say anything right away, then the bell above the front door of the store chimed loudly.

"I think this visit has gone on quite long enough, and I now have customers to attend to." Diana stood up. "If you'll excuse me, you can show yourselves out."

Gemma jumped to her feet. "No, Diana, please. If I kill Penn, is the curse broken?"

"I've already given you my answer," Diana said as she continued toward the door.

"Diana!" Harper shouted, and chased after her. "You can't just leave it like this. You can't just walk away!"

"Harper." Lydia grabbed Harper's arm, stopping her from running out of the sitting room. "That's enough. She's helped as much as she's going to."

"We could hold her hostage and make her tell us," Marcy suggested from where she sat on the floor, still petting Thallo.

"There's nothing we have that could hold her if she didn't want to be held, and that's not how we do things," Lydia said. "If she doesn't want to help us, we can't make her."

Diana had gone back into the store, but Gemma couldn't just let it go. Not like that. She chased after her, and when Diana wouldn't stop, she grabbed the billowy sleeve of her dress, forcing Diana to turn back to her.

"No. It can't end like this," Gemma begged her, and she was near tears. "Demeter, please."

They were nearly hidden underneath the dangling flowers and vines from the potted plants above them, but from the corner of her eye, Gemma could see the new customers. They were still far enough away that they wouldn't hear them, but they were coming closer.

Diana stared down at her, her green eyes tired, but there was a new anger that flickered behind them. But Gemma refused to look away or let go of her, not until she got an answer.

"One of the other girls, Aglaope, she came sniffing around. It must've been . . . five years back," Diana said finally, apparently seeing that Gemma wouldn't leave without something. "She never found me, but she got close enough when I heard that she'd been looking.

"I'd always liked her," she went on. "She was kind and loving, but in order for Thea to be punished, Aglaope had to be punished even worse. It pained me to hurt her like that, but her anguish was a means to an end, and oh, how she'd anguished under Penn's cruel rule for thousands of years.

"But when she came looking for me, looking for a way out, I ignored her. I liked her, pitied her, and she'd been tortured plenty, but her cries went unheeded. And if I wouldn't help *her*, what makes you think I would help someone as insignificant as you?"

THIRTY-FOUR

Renunciation

All Gemma could think about was getting out to the water. Their flight home had been delayed for hours. It was well after five in the morning by the time they got home, and she had barely made it. Her migraine had gotten so bad, she'd thrown up twice on the way back.

When they got back to Capri, instead of taking them home, she had Marcy drop her off at the bay. If she didn't get into the water soon, Gemma was certain she would die. She felt even worse than when she'd been at Sawyer's beach house and refused to eat, and her hair was falling out in clumps.

Fortunately, it was still dark out, but the sky was beginning to lighten. To be safe, she steered clear of the beaches, which would be filling up with tourists much too soon. Instead, she went down to the rocky shore along the cypress trees, where the bay began to curve toward the cove.

The jagged edges of the rocks jabbed through the thin bottoms of her flip-flops, but Gemma barely noticed. The watersong blotted out everything else. Stripping off her shorts, panties, and shirt, she stepped out into the water wearing only her bra.

As soon as the saltwater hit her skin, splashing over her feet and ankles as she waded out into the depths of the bay, sweet relief rushed over her. The pain that had been so agonizing drifted away as her skin began to flutter, her flesh shifting into the smooth, iridescent scales of a fish.

She dove out into the waves, swimming as fast as she could, pushing herself away from the land and deeper into the water, which had finally, mercifully, stopped calling for her.

It was then, with her body feeling fresh and rejuvenated and without the song clogging up her thoughts, that Gemma was able to feel the full ramifications of her visit with Diana and how truly defeated she was.

All the way back from Charleston, as a barely conscious Gemma had struggled not to throw up or sob, she'd heard Harper rambling on excitedly about all the things this could mean. They could kill Penn, and that would set Gemma free.

Or they could figure out what to do with the ink. Harper was certain there must be a way to erase it or something, even though both she and Gemma had tried exposing it to every liquid imaginable without any success. Even through her sick haze, Gemma suspected that Harper was fooling herself. But her sister seemed so excited and happy, Gemma couldn't bear to take it away.

While Gemma had been curled up on the hard chairs of the airport, Lydia had been sitting next to her, typing on her tablet.

Harper and Marcy had gone to get something to eat, but Gemma felt too nauseated to eat anything.

"Dammit," Lydia muttered. "I think she was lying."

Gemma turned a bit so she could look up at her. "Who was lying?"

"Diana."

"What do you mean?" Gemma pushed herself up so she was sitting even though that made the room spin and tip to the side.

"I've been messaging my friend, Kipling Pine. He's the professor at Sundham that Harper talked to about the scroll," Lydia explained. "He's visiting a friend of his who's a linguistics expert, and he's superknowledgeable about dead languages."

"And that means Diana is lying?" Gemma asked.

"Okay, before I tell you that, I need to explain how we translate the scroll." Lydia turned in her seat to face her fully. "We *think* it's ancient Cypriot, but it seems to be a more informal type and takes some liberties, and we need to try to translate that back into English, and that's if we can even get it into Cypriot in the first place."

"You already told me some of this when I showed you the scroll the first time," Gemma reminded her.

"I know, but I really need to reiterate." Her large eyes were gravely serious. "Even with me, Pine, and this other expert working on it, we will never have a one-hundred-percent-concrete translation. I mean, scholars still debate some of the translations in the Bible, and they've been working on that for hundreds of years."

"But you guys have translated some of the scroll, right?" Gemma asked. "That's what this is about."

"They've come up with a partial cryptographic key—which is basically saying what symbol means what letter, and with that, they're kind of guessing and going on intuition and their knowledge of Greek words to fill in the blanks. Pine's finished a passage, and he just sent it to me, and . . ." Lydia sighed and looked back down at her tablet. "I'll just read it to you."

"It starts with, 'Four of them there must always be.' And then, we think the next four words are names, but the translation is a bit rough. So what we think it says is, 'Peisinoe, Thelxiepia, Aglaope, and Ligea/Begin the curse but do not need to be at the end/One can replace one by any mortal who is . . .'"

Lydia frowned and shook her head before continuing. "Pine's saying 'granted' here, but I'm not sure if that's right. But 'cursed' doesn't seem to fit either. But it ends with something about having 'the power of the siren.'"

"Let me see it." Gemma leaned over the tablet, and she had to squint to read, since her vision had blurred so badly.

Four of them there must always be
Peisinoe, Thelxiepia, Aglaope, and Ligea
Begin the curse but do not need to be at the end
One can replace one by any mortal
Granted with the power of the siren

Gemma read it three times, but the watersong blocked out rational thought, and she couldn't seem to process it.

"What does all that mean?" she asked, looking up at Lydia.

"That as long as there are four of them, it doesn't matter who they are. Any of them can be replaced." Lydia shook her head sadly. "Even Penn."

"So why would Diana say that?" Gemma rubbed her forehead and slouched in the seat. "She said if I killed Penn, the curse would be broken. Why would she lie about that? We were about to leave anyway."

"Maybe she didn't lie," Lydia said.

"But with the scroll—"

"No, I mean Diana said, 'If you *tried* to kill Penn, then *you* wouldn't need to break the curse,'" Lydia recited carefully. "Maybe she just meant that if you tried to kill Penn, you'd lose."

"Diana knows I'm young, I probably appeared weak, and she rightfully assumed that if I was capable of killing Penn, I already would have." Gemma lay back down on the seats and squeezed her eyes shut. "So if I went up against Penn, she would kill me, and when I'm dead, I'm free of the curse."

"But that could be wrong," Lydia said, trying to sound hopeful. "I mean, Pine's still working on these translations. We're not finished, and like I said, we could've misread them."

Now, as Gemma swam the cold depths of the ocean, the futility of it hit her hard. Diana/Demeter had been their last big hope, and she had been a bust. The big clue she'd given them had been nothing more than a taunt.

The joy of being in the water had given way to a familiar desperation and an ever-growing hunger. Her practice transformations had the unfortunate side effect of making her hunger stronger, and the day away from Capri, battling the watersong, hadn't helped either.

It was September now, and the autumnal equinox was only weeks away. Gemma would have to feed soon, or she really risked losing control, especially if she wanted to keep practicing her transformations.

She'd begun to suspect that part of the reason she'd been so crazed when she'd killed Jason Way was because she'd been starving. That's why she had a better handle on the monster now, and probably why Liv seemed to have a better grasp of morphing. Liv ate constantly, so she was never really hungry, and that probably made her better at control when she shifted in and out of the monster.

As Gemma was swimming, plunging down in the darkness at the bottom of the ocean floor, frightening the fish and crabs lingering at the bottom, she felt something following her. A shadow stayed behind her, and Gemma sped up. The last thing she needed was to get in a fight with a shark this morning.

But no matter how fast she went, the dark shape in the water stayed behind her. Gemma had swum out past the bay, but now she circled back, heading toward land. She didn't glance back, but she felt it gaining on her. An electricity in the current, the subtle shifts of the approaching predator, spurred her on.

The land was too far, but a large rock jutted out of the bay. Gemma raced toward it, and she pushed herself out of the water and gripped crevices in the stone. Her torso was completely above water, but her fish tail was submerged. It would be slippery, deadweight if she tried to haul herself out, and she finally looked back before beginning the climb up the rock.

Penn surfaced from the water, laughing in a way that sounded like the cackling of a crow. "Oh, Gemma, you're so funny when you're scared."

Gemma relaxed, but she still hung on to the rock. "I thought you were a shark."

"You're lucky I'm not," Penn said as she floated next to her. "Or I'd be devouring you right now."

"Why were you following me?"

"I wanted to find out how things went yesterday." Her full lips were pressed into a blood-red thin smile. "How was your little adventure?"

Gemma looked toward the shore and pushed her wet hair out of her face. The sky above them had really started to lighten, turning purple and pink in anticipation of the sunrise.

"What are you talking about?" Gemma asked at last.

"You went somewhere yesterday, somewhere away from the water."

"How do you know?"

"We can feel it. We know whenever anyone gets *too* far away," Penn said. "You could die, and I'll have to come up with another replacement."

Gemma rolled her eyes. "And I know how you'd hate to replace me."

"Where were you?" Penn asked, but it sounded more like a demand.

"I told Thea. I went to Sundham to visit Harper."

"Sundham's not that far inland." Penn narrowed her eyes as her black hair pooled in the water around her. The water was at her chin, and Penn had never looked more like a sea monster.

Gemma shrugged. "Well, that's where I was, so I don't know what to tell you."

"I don't know what you're playing at, Gemma, but it's a very dangerous game. You don't want to mess with me."

"I'm not," she insisted.

"So then tell me where you went?"

Meeting Penn's gaze defiantly, she said, "No."

Penn pushed herself above the waves, balancing on her tail so her entire torso was showing and she could stare imposingly down at Gemma. "I am so sick of this. I have enough going on with Liv, and this whole rebellious act of yours is getting old. You need to learn your place."

Gemma's fangs were itching in her mouth, and she decided not to try to contain them. She might not be strong enough to kill Penn, but there was only one way she'd know for sure. And she was sick of dealing with Penn, sick of being a siren, sick of dreading the next time she'd have to feed, so even if she couldn't stop Penn, at least Penn would stop her.

One of them would die today. It almost didn't even matter to Gemma anymore which one it was, as long as this was over.

Gemma smiled as she spoke, revealing her jagged fangs. "Maybe it's time for you to learn *your* place."

"You little bitch," Penn said, smiling wider. "Bring it."

THIRTY-FIVE

Hostile

Gemma lunged at Penn, who didn't move or even try to block her. As she wrapped her fingers around Penn's throat, she felt them lengthening, the bones crackling as they grew. As Gemma tightened her grip around Penn's neck, they both plummeted underwater, falling toward the bottom of the ocean.

Penn's lips pulled back, stretching around her fangs, and her face began to change shape. Her cheekbones grew more pronounced, her eyes receded farther back, and her charcoal hair thinned. Her face had shifted into the full monster, reflecting the same changes that were happening to Gemma's.

Within a few seconds of their going underwater, Penn decided she'd had enough of Gemma's talons around her throat. She bared her teeth, letting out a low, guttural laugh, and gripped Gemma's arms.

Gemma's arms had lengthened, stretching the skin tight around the bone, so when Penn grabbed her, digging her sharp talons through her flesh, they actually pierced the bone. Gemma cried out in pain, and Penn pushed back, sending her crashing into the stone wall of the bottom of the rock Gemma had been clinging to.

Penn's mermaid tail had been pumping with such ferocity that when she slammed Gemma into the rock behind her, Gemma was surprised that the massive stone didn't give way behind her. Reflexively, she let go of Penn's neck, then, quickly, Penn pulled her back and slammed her into the rock again, cracking Gemma's skull against the stone.

Pain shot through Gemma's head, and for a second, she saw white. But when that cleared, Penn's cackling face hovered in the water in front of her, her wispy black hair floating around her like a dark halo.

That evil Cheshire grin was all the motivation Gemma needed. She'd always wanted to smack that hideous smile right off Penn's face, so she finally did.

Before Penn could slam her into the rock again, Gemma slapped her hard, letting her claws rake across her face as she did. When one of her talons pierced Penn's eye, she cried out in pain as blood reddened the saltwater around her.

Penn let go of Gemma so she could cradle her own face in her hands, and Gemma dove at her again. Balling her long fingers into oversized fists, Gemma began pummeling her. Since her bones were like marble, it was like punching with brass knuckles.

Penn's arms were shielding her face, so Gemma focused her attention on the soft, exposed flesh of her stomach, and she slammed her fists into it over and over, hitting her abdomen and her sides. Penn swam backward as Gemma hit her, and it wasn't until Gemma punched her chest, hitting her in the ribs directly over her heart, that Penn reacted.

She lunged to the side and tried to swim around Gemma. Gemma turned with her, thinking Penn was trying to get away, but then she felt a long arm around her neck, coming from behind her, as Penn put her in a headlock.

"Don't even think about going after my heart," Penn growled, her demonic voice right in Gemma's ear, and she tightened her arm on her throat, suffocating Gemma.

Gemma craned her neck and gnashed her teeth, biting at anything she could. Her jagged fangs tore into Penn's shoulder, ripping off the flesh and scraping against the bone. Penn moved her arm to get it out of the bite zone, and Gemma wriggled free.

As she swam away, she used the considerable strength of her fish's tail to smack Penn in the face. Penn roared and began to swim upward, so Gemma gave chase. Penn wasn't that far ahead of her, and Gemma reached out, trying to grab her.

Her talons dug into Penn's hip, and Penn sprinted ahead. Gemma refused to let go, though, so her claws raked down Penn's side, ripping scales off as they tore through her tail.

Penn reached the surface first, and Gemma heard her cursing through the water. When Gemma came up a few feet away, Penn was tilting her neck to the side, cracking it. She was surprised to see that Penn looked almost human now, other than the sharp teeth protruding from her mouth.

The scratches on her face had mostly healed, and other than a dark line across her eye, there wasn't much left of the injury. That's why Penn had shifted back to human—the transformation sped up the healing process.

Gemma had her own healing to contend with, and she allowed her face to slowly shift back. But, like Penn, she kept her fangs out.

"So you really wanna go for it, Gemma?" Penn asked, and her usual wicked smile returned. "I thought I'd let you get a few slaps out, burn off a little steam, but you really wanna do this?"

"I want this over with," Gemma said, and she was surprised at the inhuman growl in her voice. The monster was out, but she was still in control.

"You really wanna die today?"

"I won't be the one dying," Gemma said, and she dove at Penn and punched her right in the mouth.

With blood dripping from her lip, Penn snarled and reached out, grabbing a clump of Gemma's hair. She knotted her fist right at the base, with her claws scraping the skin, so if Gemma were to pull free, Penn would rip her scalp off her head.

She whipped Gemma around, so her back was pressed to Penn's chest, and as Gemma trod water, she felt her tail brushing up against Penn's. Penn yanked her head backward, and she pressed a talon into Gemma's jugular.

Gemma grabbed Penn's arm and tried to pull free, but it was like trying to move concrete. When they had been fighting earlier, Penn had to have been holding back, but right now, it had never been more clear how much stronger Penn was than her.

"You stupid, weak girl," Penn sneered, as Gemma took shallow breaths, trying not to press the talon any deeper into her skin. "You never eat. You never change form. You're starving and useless. Did you really think you stood a chance against a powerful, well-fed siren like me?"

"I thought it'd be worth a shot," Gemma admitted.

"Did you know that this is exactly how I tore off Ligea's head?" Penn asked. "I gripped her hair just like this"—she tugged on Gemma's hair to show her—"and her head just popped right off. And I can do the same to you right now. So I'll ask you again—do you really want to die today?"

Even though, a few minutes before, Gemma had thought she didn't care if she lived or died, with her death feeling increasingly imminent and her heart pounding desperately to live, she knew she had to do something.

Instead of pulling against Penn, she decided to give in to her. She stopped moving her tail, going limp in Penn's arms, and leaned back against her. Confused, Penn started to go under before pushing herself upward.

With her hand still buried in Gemma's hair, she tried to pull Gemma up with her. But Gemma slipped beneath, so Penn's talon sliced sharply across her neck and chest as she jerked away.

Gemma twisted around, yanking Penn's arm into an unnatural position. Clumps of her hair and scalp were tearing way, but she'd finally put enough distance between Penn and herself that she could turn and bite Penn's forearm, sinking her razor teeth in the sensitive part just above the wrist, tearing through the tendons and cracking into bone.

Penn howled and finally released her, and Gemma took off, swimming as fast as she could toward the shore. She didn't really have a plan for when she got there. She just knew she had to get away from Penn if she wanted to live to see another day.

She could feel Penn chasing after, but she didn't look back. She pushed herself onward, letting her arms change back into their human form. The smaller hands worked better to paddle, to help her swim faster, than the long, sticklike fingers.

The water was getting shallower. She could see the first rays of light breaking the surface and shining bright blue to the bottom. The beach wasn't far off.

And then she felt Penn's teeth tearing through the flipper of her tail. She glanced back long enough to see that Penn had torn it right off, and a thick stream of blood poured out from the gaping wound where her flippers should be.

Gemma pushed, though much more slowly without the tail; and then she was so close, it was barely deep enough to swim anyway. The rocks at the bottom scraped against her belly, and she pulled herself forward.

As she came out of the water, she was actually crawling up, pulling herself onto land with hands and elbows digging into the sand. Realizing how slowly she was going, she knew she couldn't outrun Penn, and she was wasting her strength.

Gemma rolled over onto her back, the cold sand sticking to her, and tried to catch her breath. Then Penn's head appeared over her, the sunrise backlighting her face so it was impossible to read her expression, even when Gemma squinted at her.

Then Penn laughed and rolled away. Gemma pushed herself

up, so she could see what was going on. Penn just lay on the beach next to her, with her face fully healed and an odd smile on her face.

The waves were lapping up to their belly buttons, so both of their tails were still in place, submerged in the shallows. Gemma could feel hers tingling and fluttering, but she wasn't sure if that was because her tail was trying to shift back into a leg or because it was hurrying to regrow its fin.

"Too easy," Penn said, as Gemma stared down at her in confusion.

"Too easy?"

"You fought harder than I thought you would, I'll admit that," Penn said with a sigh. "But that's not saying much."

"Why didn't you kill me?" Gemma asked.

Penn looked up at her. "Did you want me to?"

"I just don't understand why you wouldn't." Gemma shook her head in disbelief. "You hate me, and you killed your sisters Aglaope and Ligea, not to mention Lexi. You even killed your own father."

Penn narrowed her eyes. "How did you know about Achelous?"

"Lexi told me," Gemma lied.

There would be no way for Penn to fact-check that, and Lexi had told her that Achelous was dead. She couldn't tell Penn about Diana, not so much because she didn't want Penn to kill the goddess, but because in a rage, Penn might take out Lydia and Marcy, too. Her vengeance didn't always make sense.

"My father was a selfish, narcissistic man whore." Penn closed her eyes, apparently satisfied with Gemma's answer, and she folded her arms behind her head. Her tail flapped languidly through the water. "He deserved what he got."

"That still doesn't explain why you didn't kill me," Gemma said.

Penn waited a minute before quietly saying, "I promised Daniel I wouldn't."

Gemma knew that was true, but she was surprised that Penn was actually holding up her end of the bargain. Especially after Gemma had antagonized her.

"Are you in love with him?" Gemma asked.

"Love is a bullshit human emotion."

"He doesn't love you," Gemma said, and she wasn't even sure why she did. Maybe in defense of her sister Harper, whom Daniel really did love, or maybe just so Penn would know that she hadn't won.

"He can't love me," Penn corrected her. "But there might be a way around it. If that stupid Alex kid loves you, there has to be a way for me."

"You can command someone to do anything except love you, Penn. Alex's love is real, just like Daniel's love for Harper. How could he ever love something as awful as you?"

Penn went on, undeterred. "I have my ideas."

"Has anyone ever loved you in your whole entire life?"

"You've got me all figured out now, don't you, Gemma? Mommy didn't love me. Daddy didn't hug me enough. If only you could just understand me, then I'd give up my life of evil and save the world." Penn glared at her and scooted back onto the beach, pulling her tail out of the water.

"It's all a load of crap, Gemma. Do you know why I'm going after Daniel, why I'm going to have sex with him, and why I'll eventually tear out his heart?"

"Because you can?" Gemma asked, as Penn's tail shifted back into her long legs.

She'd been wearing what appeared to be a tight tank top, but when Penn stood up, pulling the wet fabric down past her hips, Gemma realized it was a minidress.

"That's right." Penn flashed a dazzling smile and bent over, so her face was level with the still-sitting Gemma. "And I *love* it. The one thing in life I still enjoy is the hunt. Chasing down what I want at any cost and getting it. And then just throwing it away once I've had my fill."

"That's an empty way to live, Penn."

"Oh, fuck off, Gemma." Penn rolled her eyes and stood up. "Like I care what you think. You think *Alex* is a catch. And I don't care where you went today. It was probably a quilting bee, knowing you and your stupid friends."

"You know me, and how much I love quilting," Gemma muttered.

"Right now, I want Daniel, and he wants me to keep you safe. So I will. But how much longer do you really think I'll be interested him? Hmm?" Penn waggled her eyebrows. "And then your human shield will be all gone, all chewed up. And I'll really show you how to behave."

Penn turned and walked up the beach, away from the rising sun, and left Gemma alone in the sand to nurse her wounds.

THIRTY-SIX

Accession

After the visit with Diana, Harper was in surprisingly good spirits. It would've been much easier and better if she'd just come out and told them how to break the curse, but she'd given them a couple of big clues that hinted to things Harper already suspected.

1. The curse is in the ink.
2. If they killed Penn, then they wouldn't need to break the curse.

She knew something was up with the ink. She just didn't know exactly what that meant or how to use it to her advantage. But she was certain that if she studied it more, maybe with the help of Professor Pine and Lydia, they'd be able to come up with something.

Killing Penn would be easier said than done, but still Harper felt rejuvenated. They were closer to breaking the curse than they had been before, and that was something, at least.

After they'd finally gotten home, Gemma had gone out for a much-needed swim, and Harper had gone to bed. When she woke up, she'd e-mailed teachers and classmates to try to get her homework and notes from the two days of classes she'd missed.

Gemma woke up much later in the day, and when Harper tried to talk to her about ways to kill Penn or destroy the ink, Gemma didn't seem interested in the conversation at all.

"Don't you have homework or something?" Gemma asked, after Harper had been grilling her for a while about why she wasn't more excited about their latest findings. Gemma had been rooting through the fridge, looking for something to eat, and Harper leaned against the counter, watching her.

"I do, but it's Labor Day on Monday, so I have a three-day weekend to get everything done."

"Then we have three more days to try to figure this all out." Gemma settled on a packet of the deli-sliced roast beef that her dad used for his lunches, eating it plain. "Why don't you relax or study or something right now?"

With that, Gemma turned and walked away, saying she was going over to Alex's as she went out to the front door.

Harper shook her head and decided to check in with outside help. Lydia had mentioned that Professor Pine was consulting an expert about the scroll. She had his number in her phone, but she'd gotten it from Lydia, not Pine personally, so she felt a bit weird about calling him.

But she quickly got over it. She was stumped, and he might know something.

It seemed to ring forever, but then he finally picked up, his voice sounding tinny and oddly far away.

"Hi, this is Harper Fisher," she said. "Sorry to call you. I know it's a bit unorthodox, but I just—"

Pine cut her off with an easy laugh. "No, don't worry about it. I planned on calling you soon. I'm actually working your, uh, case right now."

"Yeah, Lydia Panning told me you were consulting someone."

"I'm visiting someone, actually. I'm in Macedonia right now, with the copies you gave me."

"What? *Macedonia?*" Harper asked, which explained the strange sound in their connection.

"Yeah, I have a friend out here who is really great at translating dead languages, and we're definitely making some headway," Pine explained.

"Really? That's fantastic."

"I'm flying back on Monday, and I was hoping to have some real concrete answers for you then," Pine said. "Do you want to come and see me Tuesday?"

Harper glanced over at the calendar hanging next to the fridge, as if seeing it would make Tuesday feel any closer. "There's no way we could talk sooner?"

"Lydia and I have been going back and forth about some of the translations, and although it doesn't seem like much, I need the extra few days to hammer out as much as I can," he said.

"No, I understand," Harper said, but she decided to press her luck anyway. "Can I ask what you and Lydia are disagreeing about?"

"Just phrasing here and there, like whether the word is 'cursed' or 'granted,'" Pine said, then something occurred to him, because he asked, "Do you know if the sirens are connected to Jason or the Argonauts?"

"Not really." She tried to think quickly. "According to mythology, I think the Argonauts sailed past the sirens on their journey, but they put wax in their ears and withstood the song. But Gemma's never said anything about them, or Thea and Penn talking about them. Why?"

"I knew that Jason and the Argonauts went on a quest for the golden fleece and sailed by the sirens, and like you, I didn't think they had any real interaction with them," he said.

"Do you think that Jason and the Argonauts had something to do with the curse?" Harper asked, and she was already scrambling to remember if Lydia had mentioned anything about their being alive or not.

"Not exactly." He let out breath through his teeth. "Not at all, actually. I think there might be a mention of 'golden fleece' in the scroll, and the most famous connection to the golden fleece is the Argonauts.

"But that's what Lydia and I are disagreeing on," Pine said. "She thinks the word might actually be 'skin,' and not 'fleece,' since back in the day, people sometimes referred to the wool on a ram as his skin. And if it's 'golden skin,' that could just be a reference to the sirens' beauty."

"Are you sure?" Harper asked.

Pine laughed. "No. I'm not sure about any of this. But on this thing, since there's no other mention of the Argonauts, I think Lydia is probably right. We are making progress, and honestly, in a perfect world, we'd have longer than a weekend to go over this."

"Yeah, of course. Sorry." Harper pushed her hair off her forehead and nodded. "If you want to wait until Tuesday to talk, that'd be fine."

"Great. I should be a bit more sure of things by then," he said. "So I'll see—"

"Is there anything about the ink?" Harper asked, interrupting him before he got off the phone.

"What do you mean?" he asked.

"Does the scroll say anything about the ink it's written in?"

"Um, not really," Pine answered slowly. "I'll be on the lookout for it, though."

"I think the ink might be important," Harper said, not wanting to explain to him about Diana or what she'd said. She didn't know how much Pine knew about what was happening, but she didn't want to drag him deeper into the mess than he needed to be.

"If I find anything about the ink before Tuesday, I'll give you a call, okay?" Pine offered.

"Yeah. That sounds great," Harper said. "And thanks again."

"Are you kidding me?" He laughed. "I *live* for this stuff."

Harper hung up her phone and stared down at the unchanging scroll in front of her. She knew she could sit staring at it for hours, and nothing would come of it. Soon, she found her thoughts wandering back to the one place she'd been trying to keep them from the last two days—Daniel.

Since she'd left his place on Wednesday night, she hadn't spoken to him. It wasn't just that she didn't know what to say. She didn't even know how she really felt. It hurt, and she was definitely still mad at him . . . but deep down, she still loved him, and it didn't feel right leaving things like she had.

She didn't know if he'd already slept with Penn or if there was still time to talk him out of it. She didn't even know if he was still alive, and it was that thought that sent her into motion.

Talking on the phone wouldn't be enough. She needed to see him, so she took the little speedboat out to his island. The whole time, as the sun shone down on her, and the seawater sprayed over her, Harper tried to practice what she wanted to say, and she kept insisting that she wouldn't forgive and forget so easily.

But when she knocked on his door, and Daniel finally opened it, all her words and convictions fell away. She was still mad at him, but she missed him so much, it took all her willpower to keep from throwing her arms around him.

He wore his old Led Zeppelin T-shirt with Icarus on it, and the thick lines of his tattoo stretched out past the sleeve as he held the door open. His stubble seemed a bit longer than normal, and the flecks of blue in his hazel eyes stood out like sapphires.

"Hey. I wasn't expecting you," Daniel said after the two of them had stood mute, staring at each other for a full minute.

"I know. I thought about calling first but . . . I didn't."

"Yeah, I can see that. Come on in." He stepped back from the door and motioned for her to enter.

When she walked by, she made a deliberate choice to put as much space between the two of them as she could. She walked into the kitchen but stopped before going into the living room. The couch looked comfortable, too easy to sit on, and it would be so easy fall into his arms again, the way she had a hundred times before.

He stayed a step behind her, giving her room, and when she turned around to face him, he had his hands in his back pockets.

"I just want to say that my being here right now doesn't mean anything," Harper said.

"Okay?"

"We're not back together, and I'm still mad at you." She said that, but she couldn't look at him when she did.

"I thought you still would be." He paused. "You *should* be."

"I know. And I am."

"So . . ." He shifted his weight between his feet. "We are broken up then?"

She chewed her lip, unsure of how to answer that. "I don't know. Maybe."

"Okay."

"I don't want you to have sex with Penn," she blurted out. "The very thought of it makes me physically ill." Even saying it made her stomach lurch, and she pressed her hand to it in the hope that would ease the nausea.

"I know. Me, too," he said, and by the pallor of his skin and the hurt in his eyes, she believed him.

"I know why you're doing it, and I understand and respect that. And I love it about you that you would be willing to do anything to protect me and my sister." She stepped closer to him but stopped short before she got too close. "It means a lot to me, honestly."

"I just don't want to let anything bad happen to you." He shrugged helplessly. "I can't."

"The fact that you didn't tell me or even discuss this with me beforehand . . ." Tears threatened again, and she blinked them back and pressed on. "That is unforgivable, Daniel. You did something to *us*, and you didn't consult me."

He lowered his eyes. "I know. I screwed up, Harper. I really did, and I know it."

"Are you still planning to sleep with her?" And then, around the thick lump in her throat, she asked, "*Have* you slept with her?"

"No, I haven't," he replied quickly, and shook his head. "Not yet. But the deal's still in place."

"If this was like a one-time thing, and then we'd be free of her forever, I would understand." Harper chose her words carefully. "If you could just pay her off by having sex with her once, it might be worth it. But you know as soon as you do, she's either going to kill you or me or Gemma or make you have sex with her again, or all of the above."

He let out a long breath, then lifted his eyes to meet Harper's. "She's extended the agreement."

And she actually felt her heart drop, like it slipped free from her chest and plummeted into some deep, dark cavern below.

"What do you mean?" Harper asked.

Daniel rubbed the back of his neck and took a moment to

answer. "After we have sex—if she likes it—she wants to turn me into a siren."

"But . . ." She shook her head. "You're a guy."

"That's what I said. But Penn seems to think it'll be possible."

"Is she sure?"

"She thinks she is." He nodded. "I don't know if she's delusional or insane or what, but she believes that it'll work. That I could become a siren and join her for the rest of eternity."

Harper clasped her hands together, pushing them hard against her stomach, to keep from them trembling. "And you've agreed to that?"

"The deal is that she would kill Liv, and I would replace her," Daniel explained. "We'd leave as soon as I became a siren, and I'd go with Gemma. I'd be able to stay with her and protect her, and we'd be far away from you and everyone in Capri. I would be alive, and everyone I care about would live."

"But you'd be a weird sex slave to a monster for . . . *forever*. You'd give up your entire life, your soul. And that's if it works. If it doesn't work, then you're just dead, which is almost the better option."

"I know. But it might not be forever." Daniel stepped toward her like he meant to offer her comfort, but he stopped himself. "We still might be able to break the curse, and this will just give us more time."

"Just because you're a siren doesn't mean that Penn won't kill you. Or Gemma. She's killed sirens plenty of times before," she reminded him.

"But I'll be stronger. I'll have the siren power. I can help

Gemma, and we could kill Penn together. Even if we can't break the curse or it takes another thousand years to do it, it'll be better for everyone on the entire planet if Penn is gone."

It was all too much for her. She sat back on a kitchen chair out of fear that her legs would give out beneath her. If killing Penn would break the curse, and Daniel would survive becoming a siren, then he was right. He needed to do this, but the thought of it was more than she could bear.

"When is this supposed to take place?" Harper asked finally.

"After the next full moon." Daniel stood next to her, his hand on the table beside her. "Monday."

"So in like three days, you'll be with Penn, then you'll be gone?" She looked up at him.

"That's the plan."

"Does Gemma know?"

"No. I haven't told her. I hadn't told anyone yet."

She exhaled shakily. "Are you gonna do it?"

"I don't have much of a choice."

"Of course you have a choice, Daniel!" she shouted, and stood up. He was right in front of her, and she'd never been so tempted to slap someone and kiss them at the same time. "You always have a choice!"

"Then I've made my choice," he said. "I chose the thing that keeps you safe and alive. I chose the thing that can help me stop the evil that's destroying all our lives. I chose the only thing I can do to protect the people I love."

"So on Tuesday, you'll either be dead, or a siren?" Harper asked, since she didn't know how to argue with that.

"Yes," he said, and she let out a small sob.

"What if you die, Daniel? What then? You can't help Gemma or me or anyone. You'll just be dead."

"I know, but at least I died trying."

"No. That's not okay." She shook her head as tears streamed down her cheeks. "I love you."

He wiped a tear from her face. "And I love you."

"Daniel. I can't let you do this."

He dropped his hand and shook his head resolutely. "Harper, you can't stop me. And if I don't do this, she will kill you. She will kill me, and she will kill Gemma. Is that what you want?"

"No. Of course I don't want that, but . . ."

"Then I have to do this."

"What am I supposed to do? Just let you go? Stand by and do nothing?"

"Just this once."

"No, I can't do that. I can't just . . . I have to do *something*." She stepped away from him, wiping her eyes. "I should call Lydia and Pine." As she dug in her pocket for her phone, Daniel sighed.

"You don't need to call them this second."

"The hell I don't," she snapped, but she decided to text Pine instead since she'd already bothered him once today.

Does the scroll say anything about males? Harper sent him.

It says some things about men. Can you be more specific? Pine replied a few seconds later.

Can men be sirens? Harper elaborated.

I don't know. Is that important?

VERY, Harper replied in all caps.

I'll check. Give me some time, Pine texted back.

Her eyes were nearly dry now, but Harper wiped at them again and shoved her phone back in her pocket.

"Good news?" Daniel asked.

"More like no news. Not right now."

She looked over at him, and for a moment all her anger and hurt were forgotten. All she knew—all that mattered—was that she loved him so much, she wasn't sure how she'd exist without him.

He wasn't her whole life, but he'd completed it in such a way— he'd completed *her*—that without him, it would feel like half of everything was missing.

Harper walked over to him and put her hands on his chest. "Daniel, I don't want to lose you."

"You're not losing me." He put his arms around her, holding her to him as she stared up at him. "I'm right here, with you, right now."

"But for how much longer?"

He smiled crookedly at her. "It doesn't matter. 'Cause right now we're together."

Then he leaned down, kissing her more deeply than he'd ever kissed her before. There was a new desperation to it, and insistence and immediacy that made her cling to him.

Harper's phone vibrated in her pocket, and for a second, she considered ignoring it. But she knew it could be important, so she untangled herself from Daniel and pulled out her phone.

All the language appears gender neutral, Pine had texted her.

Meaning? she replied.

Meaning I think that men can be sirens. They still have to cannibalize other men to survive, though, Pine responded.

"Pine thinks you could be a siren," she told Daniel reluctantly.

"Good." He pulled her back into his arms, and she tilted her head to look up at him. "In a few days, I'll be stronger than ever, and Gemma and I will kill Penn. Then we'll have all the time in the world to break the curse."

"And I'm just supposed to be okay with that?" Harper asked as she struggled not to cry again.

"No." He shook his head. "You don't have to be okay with it. But whether you are or not, it won't change what I'm going to do. What I *need* to do."

"So what do I do?"

"Stay with me," Daniel said. "Just be with me, until I have to go."

THIRTY-SEVEN

Ardor

As Gemma followed her boyfriend into the kitchen of his house, she pushed away her earlier anxiety and unease. She'd come here to be with Alex today because she needed to just be with him, to love and feel love without worrying about all the other things that were tormenting her.

Her fight with Penn early this morning had proven not only that she was not ready to take Penn on but that she probably never would be. Penn and Liv would always be far more powerful than her because they frequently dined on human flesh.

Some of the siren power was derived from the water, but most of it—the strongest, more monstrous parts—came from feeding on the hearts of mortal men. And unless Gemma was willing to do that, she'd never be able to match them. Not unless she started eating more, and Gemma would sooner die than take another human life.

With each passing day, her hopes of breaking the curse and

ever being free of Penn were fading, at least not before she'd have to feed again, and she couldn't do that. Gemma would never kill another human again, even if that meant she wouldn't survive.

Her moments on this earth were growing shorter. So as she lay in bed trying to fall asleep when she got back from the fight, she'd asked herself—if she were to die today or tomorrow, how would she want to spend her last hours?

And at least that answer was simple. The only place she really wanted to be was with Alex. She loved her mom and dad, and Harper, and even Daniel. But there was nowhere else in the world that she felt more content or safe or happy than in Alex's arms, and that's how she'd want to spend the rest of her life.

"I just got done with work, and I'm kinda starving," Alex said as he opened his fridge. "Do you want anything?"

"Uh, I'm okay," Gemma lied.

The early-morning battle with Penn and the subsequent healing—like growing back her entire fin—had been very taxing. She'd woken with a slight ache in her bones, but a warm shower had helped that.

Her cravings were growing more intense, though. It had gotten so bad that she wanted to eat anything that was meat. A rare steak sounded amazing, but all she'd been able to settle for was her dad's lunch meat, and that hadn't sated her hunger as much as she'd hoped.

But her willpower was growing stronger. Alex was right, and thinking of love did a much better job of keeping her in control than fear or anger ever did. So when her hunger flared up, Gemma just pushed it back down and refused to acknowledge it.

"Or did you want to go out?" Alex turned back to face her, holding a Tupperware container full of spaghetti in his hand. "We could go someplace."

Gemma shook her head. "No, here's okay."

"Cool." He grinned and popped the food in the microwave, then grabbed a Mountain Dew out of the fridge and set it on the counter. "My parents are gone for the night. They went down to the carnival at Bayside Park."

"That's probably for the best." Gemma hopped on a stool and leaned on the kitchen counter. "Your parents don't like me much."

"It's just that since you and I started seeing each other, I've been acting so strange." The microwave beeped, and Alex got his food out. "And that's not your fault."

"It kinda is," Gemma corrected him. "I think they wished you'd ended up with Harper instead."

"Maybe," he admitted. "But I didn't." He shrugged and pulled up a stool next to her, so he could dig into his leftovers.

"How come you and Harper never did hook up or anything?"

"I don't know. Neither of us ever wanted to," he said between bites of food.

"I kinda always thought you guys would end up together, too."

He raised an eyebrow and looked over at her. *"Always?"*

"Well, until I started crushing on you," Gemma clarified. "But then I was kinda afraid you might."

"Hmm, and when did this alleged crushing on me begin?" Alex asked.

She'd known Alex for so long that it was hard for her to say when she stopped thinking of him as just the boy next door. But when she thought about it, it was hard to remember her life without him at all. He'd always been there, whenever she or Harper needed him.

He'd walked her home from school dozens of times, and he'd once gotten a bat out of their house while their dad was at work. When Gemma had been babysitting and thought she saw someone outside, Alex had come over to make sure it was safe. He'd gone to her swim meets, always cheering her on from the sidelines, even when Harper or her dad couldn't make it.

After the car accident, when both her mom and Harper had still been in the hospital, her dad had fallen to pieces. Gemma had gone out to the backyard to cry, and Alex had come over to her. He put his arm around her and promised that everything would be okay, and in that moment, she'd believed him.

No matter what, he'd always been there for her. Other than the ocean and her family, Alex had been the one good constant in her life, and when the sirens threatened to take everything away from her, he was still here.

"Was it when you gave me that steamy Valentine?" Alex asked, drawing her from her thoughts.

She propped her chin on her hand and looked over at him. "What are you talking about?"

He pushed the spaghetti away, apparently done with it, and wiped his mouth with a paper towel, then took a long drink of his soda before telling his story.

"You must've been like twelve, 'cause you were too old to be handing them out to just anybody. And you gave me one that had a green dinosaur on it, and it said something like 'Don't take a bite out of my heart. Be my Valentine.' And then you signed it 'xoxo, Gemma,' which I thought was awfully forward."

"What? I don't remember that." Gemma laughed. "You're making it up."

"I most certainly am not," he insisted. "I still have the card upstairs."

"You still have it?" she asked in disbelief.

"Yeah. Want me to prove it?" He pushed back his stool and got up. "Let's go."

"Fine. Let's go. But there's no way you still have this thing," Gemma said. "I'm not even sure it really exists."

She followed him to his room, and it wasn't until then she realized how long it had been since she'd last been up here. The walls were the same shade of blue they'd always been, but everything else was different.

His old twin mattress had been replaced with a full-sized bed. A chic black dresser and desk matched his new bed set. The *Teenage Mutant Ninja Turtle* and *Blade Runner* posters were both gone though his astronomy ones were still up. A sharp-looking computer sat on the desk, and a flat screen was mounted on the wall above his dresser, on which an X-Box and a stack of games sat.

"Whoa," Gemma said as she looked around. "You redecorated."

"Bought new furniture with money from my job. My parents were pissed 'cause they thought I should be saving for school, but it was time I got out of those Transformers sheets, you know?" Alex said.

He opened a drawer in his desk and started rummaging through it.

"I don't know. I liked the Transformers sheets," Gemma said, but she understood. Alex had grown up a lot this summer. She admired the strong line of his jaw and the way his T-shirt pulled taut over his arms as he opened the desk drawer and rummaged through it.

"That's how I know I still have this card. I just moved it from the old desk to the new one, and yep! Here it is!" He held up a card half the size of a postcard with battered edges and faded ink.

"Oh my gosh." Gemma laughed as she took it from him, and it appeared exactly as he'd described it. "I remember this now. You and Harper had just gone on some brainy decathlon, and you'd lost."

"It was the Knowledge Bowl," Alex corrected her. "And that was the only year we lost when I was on the team."

"You were superbummed, and I felt bad, so I got this for you. You always looked so cute when you were sad."

"I don't think 'cute' is the usual way that people describe sadness."

"But you are. Your eyes get all big, and you're like an adorable little puppy." He pretended to look offended, so she tried to save it by adding, "Like a sexy puppy."

"That's a little creepy actually."

"No, it's not," she insisted, and handed him the card. "You know what I mean."

He put the card back in the drawer and leaned against the desk. "Yeah, I do. I am pretty adorable."

"I can't believe you kept that all these years," Gemma said, and she was kind of amazed. "I don't even think I have any of my birthday cards still, and that was only in April. You kept that for *four* years."

"It was really sweet. And I may have already had a crush on you." He reached out, putting his fingers in the belt loops of her shorts so he could pull her closer.

"Really? How long have you liked me for?" She looked up at him as he wrapped his arms loosely around her waist.

"I don't know." He shrugged. "Remember the day I moved in?"

It had been ten years ago, and she'd only been six at the time. She and Harper had been watching from Harper's bedroom window as the new family unloaded the moving truck all day long. They'd seen Alex running around, but when Harper went down to say hi, Gemma suddenly had a bout of shyness and hid behind her mom's legs when her family introduced themselves to the Lanes.

Harper had started teasing her, calling Gemma a baby, which she'd denied vehemently. Then to prove that she wasn't a baby, Harper had dared Gemma to run over and kiss Alex. And even then, and despite her bashfulness, Gemma would never back down from a dare.

So she'd run over, planted a big wet kiss on his lips for exactly one-half of a second, then dashed back to her own house, giggling like a madwoman.

"You were my first kiss," Gemma remembered, and she was ashamed that she'd forgotten it. It had hardly even counted as a kiss, so she'd let the memory slide, until now, when it carried so much more weight.

"You were mine, too," Alex said.

"So you've had a crush on me since the day we met?"

He shook his head. "Not exactly. I don't think it really started in earnest until we were older."

"You told me you'd been in love with me for years," Gemma said, referring to what he'd said a few days before, when they got back together outside the Paramount Theater. "Is that true?"

"Why are you asking me all this stuff?"

"I don't know. Just curious I guess," she said, but she knew why.

She wanted to get lost in their memories, to immerse herself completely in him, so she didn't have to think of all the darkness that went on outside him.

Gemma pulled away and sat down on his bed. The new comforter was satiny and dark purple, a much more mature choice than his previous bedding. And she wondered, not for the first time, why it had taken her so long to realize how much she cared about him.

"The homecoming dance my junior year," Alex said, still leaning against the desk. "So you were a freshman."

"The homecoming dance?" She shook her head in confusion. "I went, but you didn't go with me."

"No. I didn't even go at all," he said. "But I was outside when you came home."

"You were in the front yard with Luke Benfield, doing something with a telescope, which I thought was really weird because the sun was still up," Gemma remembered.

Her dad had insisted that she be home by nine. It was still light out then, so she thought the whole thing was ridiculous.

"A comet was supposed to be passing near the sun. But that's not the point." His mahogany eyes were wistful. "You had on this dress, and it was the first time that I'd seen you where you really took my breath away. You were *so* beautiful."

A wonderful, warm feeling fluttered through her belly as she listened to him. Overwhelming love and appreciation for him filled her so much, she thought she might explode.

"And this guy was with you," Alex said.

"Derek something," Gemma filled in the blank. "His breath smelled like garlic, and he spent the whole night talking to his friends and ignoring me."

"I tried to pretend like I wasn't watching, but I saw him walk you to the steps, and he tried to kiss you, and you told him to get lost. And he walked away all defeated, and you caught me staring at you, and you blew me a kiss."

"Oh my gosh." Her cheeks burned with embarrassment, and she laughed. "I can't believe I did that. I'd forgotten, and now I'm so mortified. I was just being sassy or something, 'cause I thought Derek was still watching."

"So you only did that to spite someone else? Wow." Alex pretended to be upset. "Our whole relationship is a lie. I kinda feel like I need to question everything."

"Oh, come on." Gemma got up and walked over to him. She wrapped her arms around his neck, pressing her body against his. "It might have taken me a bit longer than it took you, but I love you now, and I'll love you forever. And that's all that matters."

"How much longer did it take you?" Alex asked as he wrapped his arms around her.

"To fall in love with you?"

"Yeah. When did you actually know that you loved me?"

"I'd liked you for a while, but I think I knew I loved you the first time we really kissed, when we were in the backyard under the stars."

"Wow. It did take you a *lot* longer," he said, and Gemma wished it hadn't taken her so long. She'd missed out on so much time with him, and so many kisses.

"Yeah, but I'm here now."

She stood on her tiptoes and kissed him, pulling herself close to him. But just kissing him wasn't enough, and maybe she'd known that when she came over here. She loved him completely, and she wanted to be with him completely.

Still holding on to him, she took a step backward, and he followed, unwilling to stop kissing her, even for a second. Then she turned him around and pushed him back to the bed. Before he fell back, she grabbed the bottom of his shirt and peeled it off.

His skin felt warm, and his muscles were firm and smooth underneath her. His hands roamed all over her, and he had her halter top up over her head in seconds. She'd had the foresight to skip putting on a bra today, and he took a moment to appreciate that.

Then they were kissing again, only this time her bare skin was pressed to his, and it was amazing how intimate that felt, how close she felt to him, and yet she still wanted to be closer.

The monster inside her threatened to surface, but she wouldn't let it. She wasn't doing this to feed her cravings or satiate her hunger, and she refused to let the siren in her have any part of this. This was about her and Alex, and how much they loved each other.

After she'd undone his pants, he rolled her over, and with surprising dexterity, he slid off her panties and shorts. For a moment, nothing more happened. The two of them lay naked together, kissing, and he took of one her hands, pressing it to the pillow above her head. His heart was pounding so hard, she could feel the rapid beat of his pulse in their entwined fingers.

Then he stopped. Her free arm was around him, holding him to her, and he stared down into her eyes.

"What?" she asked, afraid he might not want to continue.

"I just want to remember this moment," he said softly. "I want to remember everything about being here with you now and how utterly in love with you I am."

"I love you, too," she said because she was afraid to say more.

Then his lips found hers again, kissing her desperately, and when he slid inside her, it hurt, but there was a strange beauty in the pain. In knowing that it was *with* him, that they were together in a way they'd never been with anyone else, and when he let go of her hand so he could wrap his arms around her, crushing her to him, she couldn't imagine being able to feel this close to anyone.

Afterward, she lay in his arms. He kissed the top of her head and rubbed the bare skin of her back, sending pleasurable shivers down her spine. He lay on his side, and her head was pressed against his chest, listening to the sound of his heart, and their legs were tangled together.

For a moment, she wasn't entirely sure where she ended, and he began, and there was something wholly perfect in that. She clung to him, savoring the moment and wishing that it would last forever.

THIRTY-EIGHT

Disillusion

Gemma and Brian were talking beside her at the kitchen table, and Harper heard them. She was even nodding along and saying "mmm-hmm" in all the right spots. But she wasn't really listening. Her head and her heart were a million miles away, wondering what she was going to do about Daniel.

After he'd told her about his plans to become a siren and join Penn last night, she had spent a very long time trying to talk him out of it and debating with him. But his mind was made up, and in the end, she wasn't sure that she actually disagreed with him.

She didn't want him to do it because she didn't want him getting hurt, but in all honesty, if she were in his position, she'd probably do the exact same thing. To protect the people she loved, she'd be willing to sacrifice anything.

But Harper was going to make damn sure that they'd tried every other option first. If there was a way to break the curse before Daniel got trapped into a life with Penn, then Harper was determined to find it.

As soon as she'd gotten home last night, she'd pulled out the scroll. Diana had told her the curse was in the ink, and Pine had thought that the ink might consist of blood. It had reacted to water, Red Bull, and a number of other liquids that she'd exposed it to. But according to Gemma, it reacted strongest to a combination of the same liquids that made Gemma a siren.

Gemma had told her about her failed attempt with Marcy to combine their blood and ocean water to erase the scroll. It hadn't worked, but the scroll had a particularly strong reaction to these elements. It wasn't until last night, when everyone was in bed, and Harper was struggling to sleep, that something occurred to her: They'd never tried just human blood on its own. It could be that simple.

She hid in the bathroom and locked the door behind her. Using a sharp knife, she sliced along her finger deep enough to bleed. It wasn't as much as she would've liked, but it was enough. The symbols began to glow beneath, shining brightly through her blood in a vibrant crimson.

With her arms hugging herself tightly, she began to pray under her breath, hoping against all the odds that this might finally be it . . . and then the ink changed back to its usual color.

"No, no, please. That can't be it," she murmured in a frantic whisper. "Dammit. This has to work. *Please*."

Her attempts at squeezing out more blood failed miserably, and she only succeeded in rubbing off the dried blood instead of adding more. The ink didn't glow again or disappear. The curse hadn't been broken. She'd failed.

In frustration, she threw it across the room. Then she sat back on the floor, leaning against the bath and sobbing quietly into her arms.

So now, as her dad and a surprisingly cheerful Gemma talked, Harper found it impossible to concentrate or follow anything they were saying. All she could think about was that she'd failed her sister, her boyfriend, and, in a few days, everything would be gone.

"Well, that all sounds fantastic then," Brian said, responding to Gemma's telling him about Pine's translation of the scroll. "When you go see him, you can take the scroll with you again, and with his translations and what you know about the ink, you'll be able to figure out what to do. Right?"

"Yeah." Harper forced a smile and tried to sound convincing. "Right."

"Yep," Gemma agreed, but she stared down at the table.

"How come neither of you sound excited about this?" Brian eyed the two of them. "Is there something you're not telling me?"

"No, I'm excited." Gemma smiled at him. "I'm just tired. Going away really took a lot out of me."

It was hard to tell exactly how much things affected Gemma. Even when she claimed to be feeling terrible, her skin never paled, her eyes always twinkled, even her smile never lost its luster. The siren kept herself constantly camouflaged behind a mask of beauty.

"What about you, Harper?" Brian asked.

"Yeah. Everything's great." Her voice cracked a little when she said that, and she hoped that they didn't notice.

"It's getting late." Brian glanced up at the clock. "Are you girls going to visit your mom today?"

It was Saturday, which meant it was time for their weekly visit to Briar Ridge, and somehow it had completely slipped Harper's mind. She'd been making that same trek almost every week for the past eight years Nathalie had lived out there, and this was the first time she'd completely forgotten.

"I don't think so," Harper said. "I have so much going on, and I saw her on Wednesday."

"You saw her this week?" Brian asked. "You didn't tell me that."

"Yeah, she's been kinda anxious lately, so I just stopped in." Harper tried to play it down since she didn't want to worry them. "She calmed down some, but Becky says the doctors might have to reevaluate her meds if she doesn't relax."

Gemma's eyes widened, and she sat up straighter. "Oh my gosh, Harper. Is she okay?"

"Yeah, she'll be fine," Harper tried to reassure her sister before she panicked. "She just needs some quiet and rest, so it's actually probably better if we don't visit today."

"You will let me know if they have a team meeting, right?" Gemma asked sarcastically. "Or will you forget about that, too?"

"What were you gonna do today then?" Brian asked.

"There's some dance down at the park for the At Summer's End stuff," Gemma said. "I was thinking of going down there with Alex and kinda do something normal for a change."

"Daniel asked me to go to that tonight, too," Harper said.

She hadn't really wanted to go, and he'd all but insisted. If they didn't have much time left together, he wanted to spend it with her doing something nice.

"Oh yeah? Well, that sounds good." Brian clapped his hands together and grinned. "You've both been working so hard lately, and it'll be good for you to have a break from it. I promise I will spend the night scouring the scroll. You take the night off. I'll take over. I'm the dad. You're the kids. Act like it for a change."

Reluctantly, Harper went up to her room to get changed. She'd opened up her closet to start looking for something suitable to wear, but that was as far as she'd gotten before Gemma came into her room.

"Did you need something?" Harper asked.

Gemma shut the door and walked over to her. Her golden eyes were serious, and she folded her arms over her chest. "What's going on with you?"

"What do you mean?"

"You are barely here today. Did something happen?" She lowered her voice. "How are things really going with Daniel?"

"Great." Harper looked away from her sister and started flipping through the outfits hanging in her closet. "Good thing I didn't bring that many clothes with me to college. I think I left all my dresses here."

"Is Daniel still . . ." Gemma trailed off.

Harper swallowed hard as she pulled out a flowered dress. "We've come to an understanding." She held up the dress. "What do you think of this?"

"He is," Gemma surmised. "Harper, he doesn't need to do that. Tell him not to."

She sighed and hung the dress back, and finally turned to face her sister. "Gemma. It's between me and Daniel, and we've got it all figured out."

"Harper."

"Everything is fine, okay?" Harper reached out and squeezed Gemma's arm reassuringly. "Now just go get ready."

Gemma wanted to argue more, but Harper wouldn't hear of it. She shooed her sister out of her room and closed the door behind her. Leaning forward, she rested her forehead against the door and took deep breaths until the urge to cry finally passed.

To help her mood, she put Metric on the stereo and turned it up loud. She picked out a light summer dress that landed right at the knee, so her scar would be well hidden. Then, as she sang along with the music, she used the curling iron to add loose curls to her hair and carefully applied her makeup.

When she was done, she stood in front of the mirror for a few minutes. Not so much admiring herself or even making sure that she looked good. Just trying to convince herself that everything would be okay and that she could make it through the night.

"You will not worry. You will not cry," Harper told her reflection. "You will forget anything that makes you sad, just for tonight. You will enjoy the time you have with Daniel, and you will laugh and have fun."

There was nothing to be said, and nothing more to do. She turned off the music, then headed downstairs.

Alex had already arrived, and he was sitting on the couch

next to Gemma. Her sister looked radiant, and it wasn't just because of how lovely she looked in her halter dress. Or the way her hair was pulled up, with a pink carnation pinned above the loose curls.

There was a glow about her, and it wasn't the one that came from being a siren. She and Alex kept looking into each other's eyes, their expressions soft and doey. Their hands were intertwined, and when she laughed, Gemma would lean into him. Like they were sharing some private secret between the two of them.

Even though they were just sitting in the living room, and they weren't really doing anything, Harper felt like she was intruding. She tried to duck by on her way to the kitchen without interrupting, but Gemma caught sight of her.

"You look really pretty, Harper," Gemma said, and Harper stopped her escape to the kitchen and turned back to smile at them.

"I didn't see you sneak down the stairs." Alex stood up, so Gemma did, too, her hand still entangled with his. "You do look really nice. I don't see you in a dress very often."

"Thanks. You guys look great, too." She self-consciously smoothed out her dress. "Are you waiting for something?"

"Yeah, we're waiting for you, actually," Alex said, then glanced back at Gemma, as if to confirm that he'd said the right thing.

"We thought it might be fun to all go to the dance together," Gemma said.

"Oh yeah." Harper smiled. "That would be fun."

It might be fun with all four of them, but currently, Harper felt like a third wheel. Alex leaned over and whispered something in Gemma's ear, which made her cheeks flush as she smiled widely.

When the doorbell rang a minute later, Harper practically ran to answer it. She wanted to see Daniel anyway, but now she was looking for a reprieve from awkwardly watching the two lovebirds.

"Wow," Daniel said when she opened the door, and his eyes widened in awe. "You look really beautiful."

"And you look very handsome."

Wearing a crisp white dress shirt with the sleeves rolled up to the elbows and a skinny blue tie that made the flecks in his eyes pop, she'd never seen him look quite as sharp. He still wore jeans and his old Converse sneakers, but they somehow made him look even sexier.

"I should've gotten you a corsage," he said.

She laughed. "This isn't prom."

"Still." He shrugged. "You deserve a flower."

"So, we're all ready then." She stepped away from the door, so she could call to her dad, who was in the kitchen. "Dad, Daniel's here, so we're heading out."

"Hold on." Brian hurried in to stop them before they took off. Alex and Gemma had edged closer to the door, and when Brian came in, his stern gaze moved between Alex and Daniel. "You guys know the deal, right? Be home by midnight, both my daughters safe and sound and intact. You think Penn is bad, but she's got nothing on an angry father."

Gemma groaned. *"Dad."*

"We'll have them home by midnight, Mr. Fisher," Alex promised.

"You better," he warned them.

Gemma shook her head, but she stood on her tiptoes to kiss Brian on the cheek before heading out the door. " 'Night, Dad."

" 'Bye, Dad," Harper said, and started following her sister, but she felt like she was shirking her duty. She'd had one foot out the door, but she turned around to come back in. "I should stay and—"

"No. Go." Her dad put his hand on her arm and gently pushed her toward Daniel. "I'm just as capable of dumping soda and water on something as you. Now go. Get out of here. Have fun."

THIRTY-NINE

Summer's End

The lush grass of Bayside Park had been covered in smooth corkboard for easier dancing. Paper lanterns on fairy lights were strung above even though it was still light out. The sun had begun to dip below the horizon, and the sky was lavender and orange, with the first twinkling of stars breaking through.

Just off the dance floor, Harper sat in a folding chair next to Daniel, sipping the punch he'd brought over. An older David Bowie song played from speakers surrounding the park, and Harper watched the people dance.

It was a beautiful night, and one of the last true nights of summer, so the park was packed. It was hard for her to see Gemma and Alex through the crowded dance floor, but she spotted them, dancing pressed together even though the song was up tempo.

Her gaze didn't stay on them for long, since Marcy and her date, Kirby, had stolen the show. She'd worn black boardshorts and a polka-dot top, but it was clear that the shorts had been chosen because they allowed more freedom of movement.

Marcy was darting and spinning and doing all kinds of moves like she had secretly spent the past ten years as a classically trained dancer. Kirby hurried to keep up with her, but, fortunately, Marcy was such a crazy good dancer that she made him look good.

"Wow," Daniel said as he watched her spin. "Marcy is intense. Did you have any idea she could do this?"

"No, I had no clue." Harper shook her head. "I'm starting to realize that I literally know nothing about her."

"It's so strange seeing her engage in normal human activities." Daniel tilted his head, as if trying to get a better look at Marcy. "And she's dating that guy, too. What do you suppose they talk about?"

"My guess? *El chupacabra*."

He nodded. "That would make sense."

With David Bowie still crooning about monsters, Gemma and Alex broke through the crowd and walked toward where Harper and Daniel sat. Gemma was grinning so wide, it almost looked painful.

"What are you two doing? Are you just gonna sit here all night?" Gemma asked as she reached them.

"I danced. We danced." She motioned between herself and Daniel. "I'm just not very good at it."

They had danced, for about half a song, but the truth was that Harper didn't feel much like dancing. It was taking most of her energy to smile, and she didn't have much left to pretend to know how to move to the music.

"You can't sit out all night," Gemma persisted.

"We're not," Harper told her.

"Oh my gosh!" Gemma exclaimed when the song changed to "All Alright" by Fun. "This song. You have to dance *this*."

"I don't know." Harper was perplexed by Gemma's excitement. "It doesn't even really seem like a dance song."

Gemma had apparently given up on persuading Harper to dance and turned her attention elsewhere. "Daniel. Come on." She extended her hand to him. "Dance with me."

"Sure." He took her hand and stood up, letting her lead him out to the dance floor.

Alex had his hands in his pockets when he looked down at Harper. "So that leaves me and you."

"We don't have to dance."

"Are you kidding me? We totally do." He took his hands out of his pockets and held his arm out for her.

With little choice left, Harper smiled and took his arm. Once they found a clear spot, he stretched out his arm, then put his hand on her waist, pulling her closer to him. He took her hand in his, and she put her hand on his shoulder.

"You seem to be in an awfully good mood today," Harper commented. "You and Gemma can't seem to stop smiling today."

"I am in a very good mood," Alex admitted with his easy grin.

Daniel and Gemma spun by, doing some kind of exaggerated waltz that had Gemma laughing.

"Everything going good with Gemma?" Harper asked once Gemma and Daniel had danced far enough away that they couldn't hear them again.

"Couldn't be better," Alex said, then corrected himself. "Well, it'd be nicer if there wasn't that whole siren thing . . . but considering, it's actually pretty amazing."

"I'm glad. You guys seem really good together."

"Thank you." Alex looked genuinely pleased with the compliment, and Harper realized that this was probably the happiest she'd ever seen him. "Now that you're getting more used to the idea, we can start hanging out again."

It wasn't until now, with things feeling easy and simple and like old times again, that Harper realized she'd missed him. She loved Daniel and Gemma, and even Marcy, but it would be good to have Alex in her life again.

Then, unexpectedly, Alex took her hand and spun her, causing her to twirl as she laughed in surprise, then he pulled her back to him.

"It seems like you've picked up some dance moves," Harper said, as they started to speed around the dance floor. She thought he was doing a version of the Charleston, but her feet didn't cooperate as much as she'd liked.

"I've picked up a lot of things. It's been a long time," Alex said, and when she tripped on her foot, they both laughed. "Maybe we should try something slower."

"It's probably for the best since I don't really want to break my leg," she agreed, and grinned up at him. Once they began to move slowly again, she brushed a hair back from her forehead, and he smiled down at her.

"I've kinda missed you actually."

"Me, too," she admitted.

"I should be going to Sundham for the spring semester, so maybe we can be study buddies again," Alex suggested.

"That would be fantastic. I'm not doing so well in school so far." Harper frowned, knowing that was an understatement.

"Well, I'm sure once all this stuff with Gemma is solved, you'll do much better."

She smiled, trying to look as confident as Alex sounded. "Yeah. Me, too."

The song ended, switching over to Agnes Obel's "Riverside," which felt much slower than the previous one. She glanced around, looking for Daniel, or barring that, an excuse to sit back down.

While she'd been looking left, Daniel and Gemma appeared at her right, and she turned to see Daniel asking Alex, "Mind if I cut in?"

"Nope." Alex stepped back, offering her hand to Daniel. "She's all yours."

Harper slid gratefully into Daniel's arms, and out of the corner of her eye, she saw Gemma and Alex disappearing onto the dance floor again. She looped her arms around Daniel's neck, and he held her much closer to him than Alex had.

"Did you have a nice time with Alex?"

She nodded as she swayed with him. "Yeah. How about you?"

"Pretty good. Your sister's a rather enthusiastic dancer, though."

"Oh yeah?"

"Yeah. And she stepped on my foot."

"Is it okay?" She tried to step back, so she could see his foot, but he held her close to him, refusing to let her go. "Do you want to sit down?"

"No." He smiled and shook his head. "I never wanna sit. I just wanna dance with you for the rest of the night. Just like this."

Staring up into his eyes, it was hard for her not to cry. So she rested her chin on his shoulder and held on tighter to him. His arm felt strong around her waist, but his other hand was up higher, pressing warmly against her skin in the open back of her dress. The stubble on his cheek rubbed against hers, but she didn't mind.

In fact, she relished it. She wanted to savor every moment of this. The way his arms felt safe around her, the way he smelled of sandalwood, the scrape of his cheek, even the feel of his shirt underneath her hands as she hung on to him.

"I don't want this song to end," she whispered.

"I can go talk to the DJ," Daniel suggested, trying to make a joke. "Bribe him to keep playing it all night long."

Harper didn't say anything, but she didn't let go of him, either. He exhaled deeply, and she felt his breath warm on her neck. He moved his head, so that he could kiss her cheek, then she looked up at him.

He brushed her hair back, burying his fingers in the thickness of it, and his thumb lingered on her cheek. She tried to meet his gaze, but she couldn't do it. She didn't want him to see the tears in her eyes, so she closed them.

And then she felt his mouth on hers. His fingers knotted in her hair, and his hand on the small of her back pressed her harder to him. She kissed him back, hungrily, greedily, and wrapped her arms tightly around his neck, pulling herself to him.

She didn't care who was watching. She didn't care how this looked. At that moment, all that mattered to her was Daniel, and hanging on to him for as long as she could. She wanted to consume him, to swallow every bit of him, so that she'd never be without him again, so no one could ever hurt him or take him away from her.

The song finished, switching to something that sounded far too peppy, and they stopped kissing. Breathing heavily, she buried her face in the crook of his neck. His hand moved to the back of her head, stroking her hair.

"Well, this looks like fun," Penn said, her words carrying through the music and the sound of the crowd.

"No. Not tonight. Please," Harper begged into his shoulder. "Not tonight."

"I'm sorry," Daniel murmured, his words nearly lost in her hair.

"Can I have this dance?" Penn asked, sounding more like a demand than a question, and then she was right next to them.

Harper looked up and pulled away from Daniel a little bit, so it would be easier to see Penn. But he kept his arms around her, unwilling to let Harper get too far away.

"I'm dancing with my girlfriend right now, so no," he told Penn firmly. "You can't have this dance. And before you ask, you can't have the next one, either. Harper has reserved me for the entire night. She's actually reserved me all the way until Monday, so . . ."

"All right, all right." Marcy came out of nowhere to save the day and moved in between Daniel and Penn. "If you're really desperate for a dance, Penn, I'll dance with you. As long as you promise not to try any hanky-panky."

Penn crossed her arms over her chest and looked past Marcy, her dark gaze locked directly on Daniel. "I've changed my mind, Daniel. I want you tonight."

"Didn't you hear the man?" Marcy asked. "He's booked up. Take a number."

Liv's familiar laugh came from behind her, and Harper glanced back to see her former roommate hanging on to Kirby. Thea stood a few feet away, looking bored as usual, while she poured herself a glass of punch at the refreshment table.

"Marcy, thank you, but why don't you go with Kirby before Liv eats him?" Harper pointed over to where Liv was flirting. She appreciated Marcy's help, but if things were going to go down with Penn, she'd rather have her out of harm's way anyhow.

"Dammit. He's like catnip to these witches," Marcy muttered as she walked off to deal with the situation.

"That's not what we agreed to, Penn." Daniel had moved away from Harper so he could reason with Penn, but he kept one arm around her waist.

Penn shrugged. "Well, I'm changing the agreement."

"You can't just change things whenever you want," Daniel argued. "We have a deal."

"Daniel." Penn took a deep breath, and her eyes blazed. "If you're gonna do this, we're doing it *now*. Or the whole deal's off.

And you know what that means for Gemma and your little girl-friend?"

He looked away from Penn, staring off at the horizon. His jaw tensed as he clenched his teeth.

"You don't have to do this," Harper said when she saw how conflicted he appeared. "We can figure something else out."

"What's it gonna be? Do you want to end the night with her dead, or alive?" Penn asked, and based on the way her lips were curving up into a wicked smile, she already knew what his answer would be.

"Harper." He shook his head, then looked down at her. "I'm sorry. I have to go."

"No, Daniel, you don't," she insisted. "You don't have to do this."

He put his hands on her cheeks, cradling her face. "We talked about this, okay? I love you."

"Daniel." Harper was pleading with him as tears welled in her eyes.

"I have to do this, so just kiss me and let me go," he said.

She kissed him, and she could taste the salt from her tears on his lips. "I love you. Please come back to me."

Daniel didn't say anything to that. He didn't even look at her again. He just turned and walked away, moving through the crowd and disappearing off the dance floor, but Penn didn't follow right away.

"Liv, Thea!" Penn shouted, and they turned to look at her. "Make sure nobody follows or interferes. You hear me?" Then she smiled and did a small wave. "Bye-bye, Harper."

As Penn left, the crowd parted for her like the Red Sea, and she could see Daniel again. Penn's convertible was at the edge of the park, and he was standing beside it, waiting for Penn to come and take him away, and the only thing Harper could do was watch.

FORTY

Sacrifice

G emma had been dancing with Alex when she saw Penn talking to Daniel and Harper. Initially, she didn't want to intervene since Harper had insisted that whatever was going on with them was between her and Daniel.

But when she saw Daniel go, leaving her sister crying in the middle of the dance floor, Gemma ran over to her, with Alex hurrying after her.

"What's going on? Why did he just leave with Penn?" Gemma asked.

Harper was hugging herself. "He did what he had to do."

"What the hell is going on?" Gemma asked, just as Thea walked over to her, apparently deciding to follow Penn's orders to keep an eye on them. "Thea?"

"Ask your sister." Thea held up her hands. "I'm trying to stay out of this one."

Gemma glared at her, then turned back to Harper. "Is Daniel going to sleep with Penn?"

"He's doing *what?*" Alex asked, sounding appalled.

"Yes." Harper took a deep breath and stared straight ahead, at the spot where Penn's car had been parked even though she'd already sped off. "And then she's gonna turn him into a siren."

"What?" Now it was Thea's turn to look appalled, her green eyes widening in surprise. "I knew she was up to something, but *that's* her plan?"

"She can't." Gemma shook her head, thinking that Harper must've misunderstood. "He's a guy, and there are already four sirens."

"She says she's killing Liv to make him, and apparently guys can be sirens," Harper explained. A tear slid down her cheek, but her voice was flat, like she'd gone numb.

"You are so *annoying!*" Marcy shouted behind them.

Gemma looked over her shoulder to see her yelling at Liv. She stood between her and Kirby, trying to defend him from Liv's attempts at seduction. Gemma wanted to help Marcy, but she had much bigger issues to deal with first.

"You can't let him do that," Gemma told Harper.

"I don't want to. But it's his choice, and I don't know if it's the right thing or not." She pursed her lips. "If he doesn't do it, she'll kill you and me and probably Alex and Dad."

"Not if I kill her first," Gemma growled.

Her gums began to itch, as her fangs wanted to grow, and she balled up her fists to keep her fingers from extending. There had been so much she'd been willing to tolerate in Penn, but she could never stand for that.

Not only was this hurting her sister, but this would destroy Daniel. He'd been nothing but a good friend to her, and he'd already sacrificed far too much. She couldn't let him do this even if it meant that she would die stopping him.

Being a siren took away bits of her soul, eating away at it every day. She was clinging to it, fighting for her humanity, but eventually, if she lived long enough, she would lose it all. And that fate sounded worse than anything she could ever imagine, and she wouldn't let Daniel endure it.

Harper finally turned to look at her. "Gemma, you're not strong enough."

"I don't care," Gemma said, and she meant it. After her fight with Penn yesterday, she knew she probably couldn't win, but if she was dead and gone, it didn't really matter to her just then. It was her fault everyone was in this mess, and she couldn't let it go on anymore. "I'm not gonna stand by and let this happen. Give me the keys to your car."

"No." Her keys were in the small clutch purse around her wrist, and Harper held it to her chest. "I won't let you go in there alone."

"Harper."

"He's my boyfriend. If you go, I go," she insisted.

Gemma didn't want Harper getting more involved in this than she already was, but maybe if Harper went with her, she could get Daniel out of there while Gemma distracted Penn. Besides,

Harper had driven here, and it would take her far too long to get to the sirens' house without it.

She didn't feel comfortable flying. Gemma had been practicing her wings, but she didn't have quite the same skill at using the siren song. She couldn't risk taking off in front of a crowd, and she wasn't about to attempt the siren song to scramble their perception on her own.

"Then let's go," Gemma said.

"Gemma." Alex grabbed her hand. "You can't go up there to get yourself killed."

"I have to stop Penn. This can't go on any longer." Gemma squeezed his hand and looked him in the eyes, begging him to understand. "*I* can't live like this anymore. I can't let anybody else get hurt. Not when I'm strong enough to do *something*."

"I'm supposed to stop you from going up there, but I don't care. But Liv, she might care." Thea interrupted the moment to motion to where Liv and Marcy were exchanging obscenities. "Not because she listens to Penn but because she hates you and really likes killing things."

"Alex, I need you to stay here and help Marcy keep Liv from following us," Gemma said. "You know I've been practicing. I can fight Penn, but I don't think I could handle Liv, too."

He glanced back at Liv, then turned back to her. "Gemma."

"I can do this, okay? But you have to help me."

Reluctantly, he nodded and let go of her hand. "Okay."

"I love you." She kissed him, and she'd wanted it to last longer because she knew this might be the last time she ever kissed him, but she didn't have time to linger. "Be safe."

"I love you, too," Alex said. "Now go kill that bitch and come back safe."

Gemma looked to her sister. Harper looked as pale and nervous as Gemma felt, but her gray eyes had a steely determination.

They turned and pushed their way off the dance floor, nearly running under the twilight sky as they left. Behind them, Gemma heard Liv shouting at them, telling them to stop, and she hoped that Alex would be okay against her.

FORTY-ONE

Onus

Alex watched his girlfriend leave, but when he heard Liv swearing at her, he looked back. She'd been standing a few feet away, arguing with Marcy, but her brown eyes shifted into an odd green that reminded him of some kind of bird or maybe a lizard.

Since Gemma hadn't listened, Liv must've decided that she'd better catch her, so she started sprinting ahead, gliding easily on her high heels.

"Where you going, Teenage Mutant Ninja Mermaid?" Marcy shouted, and took a few steps after her. "Too chicken to fight me?"

In the few interactions that Alex had had with Liv, pride had seemed to be a sticky subject for her, so as soon as Marcy had called her out on it, she stopped. She turned around and walked back toward Marcy.

Alex didn't stop her, but he trailed behind her like a shadow.

Liv stopped right in front of Marcy, smiling down at her, and Marcy readjusted her glasses but met her gaze evenly.

"Oh, Marcy," Liv said with that syrupy voice she used too often.

Since she was a siren, it should've been hypnotic to Alex, but it had always rubbed him the wrong way, and it made the hair on the back of his neck stand up.

"If there weren't a crowd of people around, I already would've ripped out your liver and swallowed it whole," Liv went on cheerily. "But I've got better things to deal with."

She turned around, preparing to stalk away again, but Alex blocked her path, and she almost ran right into him.

"Where are you going?" Alex asked.

"Move," Liv commanded. Her voice lilted to a singsong, and he felt the fog creeping in around the edge of his thoughts.

But he'd felt that before, and he'd fought against it when Gemma used her song against him. That month when he'd been under her spell had been the hardest of his life, but at least now he knew how to keep it at bay. Not completely, and not if Liv really gave it her all, but he could keep himself together long enough to put up a fight.

He shook his head. "I can't let you do that."

"If you don't get out of my way, I will sing a song that makes you want to kill Gemma, then you can help me finally get rid of her." She smiled sweetly at him. "How's that sound?"

"That sounds great. Except for one thing." He held up a finger with one hand, telling her to wait, and with the other he dug in his pocket. When he retrieved two wax earplugs, he held them out to show her for a second, then popped them in his ears. "I never go anywhere without them."

Liv rolled her eyes. Then, without warning, she pushed him. But it wasn't the way a normal person would shove someone. It was a lot more like getting hit by a bus.

He went flying back, and he could feel himself pushing people out of the way, like a wrecking ball. When he crashed into the refreshment table, sending punch flying everywhere, he finally came to a stop.

The spot where she'd pushed him on his chest throbbed, and his back didn't feel so hot either, but he was mostly fine, and he got up quickly. He was just in time to see Liv, who had apparently decided she didn't have any more time to waste, run off the dance floor like she was the Flash.

"Are you okay?" Marcy asked as she rushed over to him.

Or at least that's what he thought she said, since he couldn't hear her that well. He pulled out his earplugs and shoved them back in his pocket, then he took Marcy's hand and let her help him to his feet.

"Yeah, I'm fine, but we have to go stop her," Alex said.

"Did you see how fast she was?" Kirby asked, since he'd followed Marcy over to check on Alex. "She's probably halfway to Memphis by now."

"She's not going to Memphis." Alex stepped over strewn-about glasses and finger sandwiches as they walked away from the overturned table. "They're going up to the house on the cliff. Did you have a car?"

"Yeah," Marcy said. "Lucinda's parked like two blocks away, though."

"Lucinda?" Alex asked.

"Yeah. My car."

"Run and get it. I'm gonna see if we can get backup."

"Okay." Marcy nodded, then turned to Kirby. "You can stay here."

"No." Kirby shook his head. "You're my date. I go where you go."

"But it's dangerous," Marcy protested.

He smiled. "Danger is my middle name."

"God, you're hot," Marcy said, then rather abruptly, she kissed Kirby on the mouth.

When she'd finished, she took his hand and ran off in the direction of the street, presumably to retrieve her car.

Alex scanned the crowd for Thea, which was easier since the dance floor had started clearing out. When Liv had pushed him into everyone, it kinda put a damper on things. The music hadn't stopped, though, and he discovered Thea standing by the DJ.

"Thea," Alex said. "Aren't you gonna do anything? I know you hate Liv way more than you hate Gemma."

Thea hesitated, looking toward the cliff, but then she shook her head, her red hair swaying on her shoulders. "I'm just trying to stay out of these things."

"Staying out of it still puts you in it," he insisted. "You know that Gemma can't fight Penn *and* Liv, so if you just stay here, you let them win. You're killing her."

Thea wouldn't meet his eyes, and her words sounded weak when she said, "She's not my problem."

Alex moved, stepping into her line of sight so she'd have to look at him, and he looked her right in the eyes. "You are worse than Penn. You act like you're so above this and that you're all moral and superior, but you're not. You're cold, and you have just as much blood on your hands as Penn does."

"I never said that I was better than her," Thea replied coolly. "And I never pretended to be good. If I somehow gave you or Gemma that impression, then I'm sorry."

He shook his head in disgust, and a car horn honked loudly.

"Alex! Let's go!" Marcy shouted.

He had nothing left to say to Thea since she'd made her position crystal clear, so he left. There was no parking on the street right in front of Bayside Park, where the dance was being held, so Marcy had pulled right up over the curb and sidewalk onto the lawn.

The passenger-side door of her tiny little Gremlin was open, and Kirby was in the backseat. Alex ran over to it and hopped into the car since he didn't have time to question the fact that they were trying to catch up with a supernaturally fast siren and using a car that had been discontinued over thirty years ago.

Before he'd even shut the door, Marcy threw the car into drive. Instead of going forward, it lurched backward, making an awful chugging sound, before finally moving in the right direction.

"Is this thing even gonna make it?" Alex asked, as it bounced down off the curb, and he heard an awful scraping sound of metal against concrete.

"You gotta have faith in Lucinda," Marcy said. "When she has to get up and go, she frickin' gets up and *goes*."

Alex remained dubious, but not for long. Marcy had her foot pressed all the way down, and though it took the car a little longer to get up to speed, once it did, it hauled. It also helped that Marcy didn't stop for anything, not even stop signs or traffic lights.

As she ran a red light, they were nearly sideswiped by a Jeep, but Marcy jerked the wheel in the nick of time, and the car squealed and got out of the way. Then she floored it again, driving the wrong way into oncoming traffic for a few seconds before she moved back over to the right side.

In the backseat, Kirby was flying all over, and Alex heard him banging around as he flew from side to side.

"Kirby, honey, you gotta buckle up back there," Marcy said. "I don't want you getting too concussed to make out later."

Though Marcy had nearly gotten them in about fifty accidents, they made it to the edge of town in record time. The sirens' house was located at the top of a cliff, and the winding road through the cypress and pine trees was steep.

Marcy took the turns much sharper than Alex would've liked, but they were only about a third of the way up when he saw the icy blue color of Harper's Sable through the trees.

"That's Harper's car!" Alex shouted, and when they rounded another bend, they were right behind her. "How'd we catch up to them?"

"Because Harper's driving. Even in a life-or-death situation, do you think she disobeyed a single traffic law?" Marcy asked.

"Probably not," Alex said. Being in a car accident when she was a kid made Harper kinda OCD about driving. "But where's Liv? She flew out of the dance like a bat out of hell."

"She's probably already at the house, trying to lay some kind of trap for Gemma."

Alex was just about to agree with Marcy, when the roof of the car came crushing in on top of them, sending the windows shattering outward.

FORTY-TWO

Ensnared

The convertible was still running when Daniel got out and
walked into the house. No candles were lit this time, and it
was rather dark inside, but he could see well enough to walk into
the kitchen.

Penn came in a few seconds later and flicked on the overhead
light while Daniel opened the cabinets near the fridge until he
found the one containing alcohol. He grabbed a bottle of brandy
and a large glass tumbler and proceeded to fill it.

"Sure, make yourself at home," Penn said dryly. She pulled
off the black stilettos she'd been wearing and tossed them absently on the couch before walking into the kitchen.

Daniel didn't respond to her. He just downed the glass in one
long gulp and slammed it down on the counter. Grimacing at
the taste, he shook his head. Beer was usually his choice of alcohol, and he'd never been that much of a drinker.

Growing up with an alcoholic father and older brother had

made him leery of substances, but since he was about to throw his life away to be a siren, he figured why the hell not get a little smashed first? It would probably make the whole experience go a lot easier if he didn't know what he was doing or couldn't remember having sex with Penn.

"Why tonight, Penn? We had a deal. Everything was all set."

"You changed the date twice." She put her hands on the counter and leaned forward. "It was my turn to change it."

"The first time I changed it was because Lexi tried to kill me, and the second time was because Liv did kill someone. So these things sound like *your* fault," Daniel pointed out as he poured himself another drink. "You're the one who delayed the proceedings."

"I'm sensing some hostility, Daniel."

"No shit." He drank this glass much slower, sipping it more than chugging it. "It was because I was happy, wasn't it? You saw me with Harper and couldn't stand it."

"Well, obviously, that pissed me off." She switched her tone from angry to sultry and kittenish. "You're supposed to belong to me now."

"I don't belong to anybody. All right?" He'd finished the drink, so he set it down on the table and walked around the island, meaning to confront Penn more directly. "Not to Harper, not to you. Not now, not *ever*."

She smiled, undeterred by his anger. "You're really gonna have to change that attitude if you want me to sleep with you."

Penn put her hands on his chest, and, gently, she pushed him back against the island. Then she slid her hands down, running them across his abdomen. He turned his head, looking away from her, so she put her arms around his neck, and she leaned in, pressing her lips against his neck.

Either the alcohol hadn't hit him yet, or it wasn't working. As soon as she touched him, he cringed. The thought of being with her only made him livid and sick.

"No. I can't do this." Pushing her off him took some strength, but he managed. He stepped away from her and wiped his neck, trying to get her saliva off him. "I'm giving you my *life*, Penn. Do you really understand what that means? And all I asked for in return is a few more days."

"No. That's not all you asked for." She followed him, unrelenting. "You want me to keep your girlfriend safe and Gemma safe and these people safe and blah blah blah. All you do is make demands, Daniel! And you have yet to give me the one thing I want from you!"

"Fine. You wanna have sex? Let's do it." He started loosening his tie, but then decided that wasn't good enough. He turned around and swept his arm across the island, knocking off the glass, the brandy, and the few small appliances and dishes that sat on it, and they all clattered loudly to the floor. "Right here, right now."

"Not sex, you idiot!" Penn shouted. "I want you to love me!"

He sighed in exasperation. "You can't bully me into loving you, Penn."

"I'm not. I will give you anything you want, everything you've imagined. Immortality, power, money." She tried to sound softer, imploring him, nearly begging him, as she put her hands on his chest and stared up into his eyes. "Any earthly pleasure you could ever possibly desire, I will give to you. I will make your life heaven on earth, and all I ask is that you love me for all of eternity."

"I will do what you say. I will be as obedient as I can," Daniel contended. "But I can't love you."

"You don't know that. You haven't even tried."

She kissed him, and it was hungrier than it had been before. Her patience was wearing thin, and there was an overt desperation in the way her lips moved against his. He let her kiss him, though, and he even tried to kiss her back.

She was unbuttoning his shirt, and he put his hands on her arms, trying to be romantic in even the slightest way. When he felt her fingers, warm and smooth but with sharp nails, running along his bare skin, he instinctively pulled away.

"You're thinking of *her*, aren't you?" Penn asked, growling.

"No. This isn't about anyone else. It's just . . ." He moved away from her and shook his head. "This is abrupt, and I need to get my head in it."

"It's not your head that I'm interested in right now."

When she went to him, he let her kiss him, and again, he tried to go along with it. But she was too aggressive, and her hand sliding down his pants bordered on painful.

"Penn."

He grabbed her wrist, preventing her from going any farther. When she tried to pull it away, he gripped it tighter, and she laughed. He grabbed her other wrist, holding them as tightly as he could, and he knew that if he'd gripped Harper this way, she'd have bruises. But with Penn, it probably barely even hurt.

"You want it rough then, Daniel?" She smiled wider. "I'll show you rough."

Still smiling up at him, he heard a strange cracking sound. He had no idea what it was until he saw her wings spreading out from her back. Pure black, they stretched out to the length of the room when she fully extended them.

"That might be a little too rough," Daniel said, and that just made her laugh again.

He let go of her wrists, so she grabbed him, wrapping her arms around his waist. Then she flapped her wings, and, with startling speed, she flew up, carrying him out of the kitchen and over the railing into the loft bedroom.

She hovered above the floor for a few seconds, and then half dropped, half threw him down. Daniel hit the bedroom floor rather painfully, then she landed, much more gracefully, on her feet.

With her wings still out, she climbed on top of him and tore off his shirt.

"You know, I never could decide which would be more fun: fucking you or eating your heart." Then she kissed him fervently, and he felt her fangs scrape against his lips and her claws dig into the bare skin of his back.

FORTY-THREE

Collide

Harper drove up the winding roads toward the top of the cliff, and she was going well above the speed limit. That surprised Gemma, who normally had to goad her sister to go faster, but now she braced herself against the dashboard.

A flash of headlights behind them caused Gemma to turn around and look behind them. She hadn't expected to see anyone she knew, but she'd recognized Marcy's old Gremlin instantly.

"Marcy is chasing us." Gemma focused, making her eyes shift from human to their more advanced bird form. "And Alex and Kirby are with her."

"What? Why?" Harper looked back, trying to see what was going on, and she almost missed the curve and drove them into a tree.

"Harper! Watch the road!" Gemma yelled, and Harper jerked the wheel back just in time.

"Sorry." Harper glanced in the rearview mirror. "I thought you told them to stay—"

Gemma was turned around fully in her seat, watching Marcy follow them, so she saw everything. The moon was nearly full above them, with just a sliver missing, and so Liv cast a shadow as she got closer.

But it all happened too fast for her to say anything. A split second after she saw the shadow, Liv was crashing down on top of Marcy's car, her golden wings spread out wide behind her. She did a three-point landing, slamming her bare feet and fist into the roof of the Gremlin with all her might.

It was enough to crush the roof of the car inward, and the windows all shattered, glass flying outward.

"*Stop!*" Gemma screamed, as Marcy's car skidded and jerked to a halt behind them.

"What?" Harper asked, but she slammed on the brakes. Then she looked behind them. "Holy crap. Oh, no."

Gemma jumped out of the car and ran toward the Gremlin to see if her friends were okay. Then Liv stood up, and Gemma realized it might not be such a good idea to rush, so she stopped.

Other than the wings, Liv appeared entirely human. Her wide eyes and bright smile still gave her that unnerving innocent look that Gemma had noticed when she'd first met her. When she stepped down from the roof of the car, her foot crunched on the hood.

"If any of them are hurt at all—" Gemma said, as Liv drifted delicately down to the ground, thanks to her wings working like a parachute behind her.

"You'll what?" Liv asked with a laugh. "Bore me to death?"

The passenger side opened first, and Alex rolled out onto the ground. It took him a few seconds, but he staggered to his feet and shook his head, shaking bits of glass out of his hair. He appeared to have a few scratches, and a thin line of blood came from his temple, but he didn't look that bad off.

"I'm okay," Alex said. "I think Kirby and Marcy are okay, too."

While Liv stared down Gemma, Harper snuck around them to help Marcy get out, but Marcy moved much more slowly than Alex had. Her glasses were crooked but unbroken, and there was a nasty gash down Marcy's shin that seemed to be making it harder for her to walk.

"Enough is enough, Liv," Gemma said, and using the focus she'd learned from practicing with Alex, she made her wings spread out behind her. Each time she used them, it got a little less painful, but she still heard her flesh tearing as the feathers broke through.

"Ooo." Liv pretended to be impressed. "Look who finally came out to play."

Kirby had gotten out of the car, and he helped Marcy off to the side of the road, where Alex was standing. Harper stood closer and seemed to be debating what to do.

"Harper, go," Gemma told her. "Stop Daniel before it's too late. I'll be up there in a few minutes."

"Cocky, aren't you?" Liv asked.

"I'm a fast eater," Gemma replied. "It should only take me a few seconds to swallow your heart."

Harper still appeared unsure, so Alex told her, "Go. I've got her back."

Alex had brushed the glass off himself, and he moved closer to Gemma, so he could defend her if he needed to. Daniel was alone with Penn, but Gemma had her siren strength and her boyfriend to help. So Harper nodded and ran to her car.

"Look at you," Liv said after Harper sped off up the hill. "You have a posse of invalids to defend you."

"It's not them you have to worry about," Gemma said.

She opened her mouth, letting her jagged fangs show in the moonlight, then she jumped at Liv. Liv was slammed back against Marcy's car, crushing the metal in, and shards of glass stabbed into her skin and wings.

Liv let out an angry squawk and punched Gemma in the face. Gemma flew back, but used her wings to catch herself before she hit the ground. Liv jumped up, flying in the air to meet the other siren, and Gemma rocked forward, then back, propelling her legs so she could kick Liv in the face with all her strength.

As Liv sailed backward, Gemma glanced down at the ground below them. Marcy had popped the hatchback of her car. It didn't open all the way, but that didn't stop Alex and Kirby from looking through it.

Gemma didn't have time to see what they were searching for because Liv had come back at her. When Liv hit her, she grabbed Gemma's dress and slammed her back into the top of a cypress tree. The branches smacked her and tore at her wings.

Liv was right. Feeding all the time had made her incredibly

strong, probably even stronger than Penn. But Gemma had a lot of anger in her, and she was ready to let it all out on Liv.

"Not so tough, are ya?" Liv asked, smiling to reveal her fangs.

In response, Gemma thrust her forehead forward and head-butted her. Liv didn't fall, but she let go of Gemma and flew back a bit, her wings flapping haphazardly for a second. Unfortunately, the head butt also left Gemma a little dazed, so she didn't recover as quickly as she'd hoped.

Her wings were tattered from the branches clawing at them, and that made it harder for her to pick up speed when she charged Liv. She grabbed Liv to throw her to the ground, but Liv only laughed, then got the best of the situation.

She gripped Gemma and pushed her downward, slamming her into the hard pavement of the road. Her wings crunched underneath, and agony shot through her back. But she gritted her teeth and refused to cry out.

Instead, she punched Liv in the face again, and again, until Liv grabbed her wrists and pinned them to the ground. All her jagged teeth were out, and a bit of saliva dripped down onto Gemma's cheek.

"I bet you're tasty," Liv said, her saccharine voice mixed with the demonic monster's.

Then she heard a bang. A flash of orange light cut through the air, then it sliced straight through Liv. It landed on the road, only inches away from Gemma's head, burning brightly. It had gone through the middle of Liv, right above her navel at an odd angle, and since it had been on fire, it left a nice singed ring that Gemma could see through.

And through the hole, she could see Kirby, looking rather dumbfounded as he held a flare gun in his hand.

"Great shot!" Marcy shouted.

Liv looked back at him and growled. "You stupid son of a bitch."

"Kirby! *Run!*" Gemma shouted as she tried to push Liv off her.

But when Liv did get up, she moved much faster than Gemma, much faster than Kirby. She raced over to him, and before Gemma had even gotten up on her feet again, Liv had ripped out his throat, and Kirby fell back to the ground, holding his hands futilely against the surge of blood.

FORTY-FOUR

Termination

The car skidded to a stop, nearly driving right into the front of the house, and Harper leapt out. The engine was running, the door was open, but she didn't care. She didn't have time to waste.

She wasn't sure if she did the right thing, leaving Gemma alone with Liv, or if coming here was even the right thing to do. But for the first time in her life, she didn't care what was right or wrong. She couldn't let this happen, and she'd do anything to stop it.

"Daniel!" Harper shouted as she ran into the house.

"What is that bitch doing here?" Penn growled from the upstairs loft.

"Harper, get out of here!" Daniel yelled.

She'd started running toward the stairs, ignoring him, but then Penn appeared, leaning against the railings and looking down from the bedroom. She'd slipped out of her dress into a black negligee, and Harper hoped that she hadn't made it too late.

But even if she had, it wouldn't be the end of the world. She did not want Daniel to have sex with Penn, but the main thing she needed to prevent, the thing she'd risk her life to stop, was his becoming a siren. And that couldn't have happened yet, not if Liv was still alive.

"I'm not letting you do this, and I'm not leaving without Daniel," Harper told Penn.

Penn smiled. "It's cute that you think you have control over anything that's happening."

Daniel appeared at the railing next to Penn. His shirt was off, and a line of red scratches ran down his chest. Jagged dots on his arm looked like bite marks.

"Oh my god, Daniel." Harper gasped. "What is she doing to you?"

"Just get out of here. Please," he begged her.

She shook her head. "No. It was stupid for me to agree to this, and I take it back. Leave with me, now, before it's too late."

Daniel made a move toward the steps, but lightning quick, Penn was around him and standing in front of him, blocking his path.

"Where do you think you're going?" Penn asked.

"To get rid of her," he said, then he slid around Penn.

Harper raced up the stairs, and he met her in the middle. She wanted to throw her arms around him, but when she tried to touch him, he grabbed her arms and stopped her.

"There has to be another way," Harper said. "A better way."

"The only other way is death, and pretty soon, I won't care, and I'll just kill all of you," Penn said. "This is starting to prove to be far more work than it's worth."

"I would rather die than spend the rest of my life as a siren or see you spend the rest of your life as a siren," Harper said, her eyes fixed on his. "And I know that you feel the same way. I know this isn't what you want. We can fight her."

"The hell you can," Penn growled, and walked toward the steps.

Daniel turned around to face her and stood in front of Harper, shielding her. "Penn, I've got this."

"You do not." Penn glared down at him from where she stood at the top landing. "You don't have anything. You are weak, and you are a waste of my time. I don't care what you say or what you want. I'm killing her, and I'm doing it now."

Without waiting to see if she would act on her words, Daniel ran up the stairs. He knocked her back down on the ground and climbed on top of her. He'd straddled her and pinned her hands to the ground, and even though Harper had never fought Penn, she knew that had to be too easy. Penn had let him do it.

"Now this is *hot*." Penn smiled up at him. "This is what I was looking for from you."

Then she lifted her legs, pushing him upward, and did a backward somersault, rolling him so that he landed on his back with her on top of him, pinning him on the ground. He grunted as he tried to push her off, and Harper raced up the stairs to defend him.

She jumped onto Penn's back, hitting her as hard as she could.

But a second later, Penn hit her hard enough to send her flying back into the railing. The wind was knocked out of her, and for a moment, she was too dazed and in too much pain to do anything except lie there.

"I should've killed you a long time ago," Penn said, and she got up to take care of Harper.

She didn't make it very far before Daniel was up. He grabbed her arm, meaning to stop her, but Penn had had enough. She grabbed him around the throat, so tight that he struggled for breath, and she lifted him off the ground that way, carrying him to the bathroom off the bedroom.

Penn threw Daniel into it, then slammed the door shut. A small fireplace was in the corner, and Penn grabbed a poker from it. With her superior siren strength, she easily twisted it around the door handle and the frame, making it impossible for Daniel to pull the door open.

Harper got to her feet, leaning back against the railing, and she could hear Daniel pounding on the door as he tried in vain to open it.

"*Harper!*" Daniel shouted as he beat on the door. "Run, Harper! Get out of here!"

"Now that he's out of the way, us girls can finally have the heart-to-heart we've been needing for so long." Penn walked slowly toward her, and as she smiled, her smooth teeth gave way to rows of jagged fangs.

FORTY-FIVE

Mêlée

Gemma had her hand around Liv's throat, squeezing it hard. She wanted to be able to pop her head off, the way that Penn had done to Lexi, but she couldn't seem to do it. It might have been because Liv was staring up at her.

Or it could've been because Liv had her claws out, and instead of tearing Gemma's hand away from her throat, Liv was trying to break through her chest and get to her heart. She could feel the talons piercing her skin and scraping her ribs.

She should let go and jump off, before Liv succeeded in breaking through and ripping out her heart, but Gemma didn't want to let her go. Not after what she'd just done to Kirby.

Then she felt a hand tugging on her wing, pulling it so hard that Gemma let go of Liv's neck and stood up. She whirled around, preparing to fight whoever was pulling at her, but it was Thea, with her own crimson wings stretched out.

"Always guard your heart," Thea said, as Liv got to her feet. "That's a siren tip."

"What the hell, Thea? You're helping her?" Liv asked with an incredulous whine.

"You really thought I would help you? After the hell you've put me through?" Thea asked.

"Whatever." Liv cracked her neck, stretching it out after Gemma had been choking her. "It's better this way. Now I can kill two birds with one stone."

Thea shook her head. "Unlikely."

Liv growled and charged at her. Thea spread her wings wide and put her hands out in front of her. When Liv hit her, Thea sent her flying back, crashing through several yards of trees.

"You saved my life," Gemma said, looking at Thea in a bit of awe.

"Don't get used to it," Thea said in her usual husky, nonchalant way.

"I hadn't planned to."

"I got this, if you want to go help your sister deal with Penn," Thea said. "I'm assuming that's where she went."

Gemma eyed Thea uncertainly. "You aren't gonna try to stop me from hurting Penn?"

"Honestly? I'm not convinced that you'll be able to, but I wish you the best of luck," Thea said, and the trees and underbrush were crackling as Liv made her way back toward them. "And I've got my hands full down here."

Liv came charging through the trees, and Thea jumped at

her. They both crashed into a pine tree so hard, they knocked it down. The trunk made a splitting sound, and when it thudded to the ground, sending up a billow of dirt and pine needles, the ground around them trembled.

With Thea handling Liv, Gemma joined Marcy and Alex. Marcy knelt on the ground next to Kirby's body, and Alex had covered him with a blanket from Marcy's car, giving him some privacy.

"Marcy, I am so sorry," Gemma said. She'd never wanted anybody to get hurt over this, especially not someone as nice and innocent as Kirby. He never should've gotten mixed up in any of this.

But she didn't have time to mourn his passing or feel guilt about it. She could spend the rest of her life regretting this moment, but right now, she needed to help Harper and Daniel unless she wanted to spend the rest of her life mourning them, too.

Marcy wiped at her eyes and nodded but said nothing.

"Are you okay?" Alex had been standing beside Marcy, and he reached out to touch Gemma's cracked wing. It hurt like hell, but it still moved, so she didn't think it was completely broken.

"Yeah, I'm fine." She brushed off his concern. "I'm gonna go to help Harper. You two should go back to town."

"Are you kidding me? After what that asshole did to Kirby and Lucinda?" Marcy asked indignantly. "I'm gonna help Thea kill her."

"Stay safe, and stay out of the way," Gemma said, since she didn't have time to argue with her. Nor did she really have any right to. If Liv had hurt Alex like that, she wouldn't have left until she'd finished her off.

"I'll make sure Marcy doesn't get herself killed," Alex said. "And you stay safe, too."

"Promise you won't follow me again." She put her hand on his chest and looked up at him. "I couldn't stand if something happened to you like that."

Gemma kissed him, and he wrapped his arms around her, mindful of her wings. The crunch of the trees, and Liv's squawking in anger broke the moment, and she stepped away from Alex.

She gave him one last longing look, then she ran up the hill, pumping her damaged wings until they finally got enough air to take flight. It hurt, but since flying would be much faster than running all the way to the top, she'd grit her teeth and make them work.

FORTY-SIX

Monstrosity

Harper stood taller and stepped away from the railing, refusing to let Penn know how scared she felt. When Penn stopped in front of her, smiling her toothy grin, Harper dropped down. She leaned back, using the railing as support, and kicked Penn's legs out from under her.

As Penn fell backward, Harper grabbed her hair, and, yanking with all her might, she pulled her toward the railing. Penn grabbed the edge, stopping herself just before she went over, so Harper grabbed her legs and flipped her upward.

Penn yelled as she fell over the balcony, but Harper didn't stay to see her land. She knew she'd be up in a matter of seconds, so she bolted across the room to the bathroom door.

"Harper? What's happening?" Daniel asked.

"I'm gonna get you out of here, Daniel," she promised, but when she pulled at the twisted fire poker, it wouldn't budge. Not even slightly.

"Don't worry about me. Just get out of here!"

"You should've listened to your boyfriend," Penn said, and her voice came from right behind Harper.

Before Harper even had a chance to turn around, she felt Penn's hand in her hair, yanking her backward, and, reflexively, she yelped.

"Penn! Don't hurt her! Dammit, Penn! Leave her alone!"

Penn didn't listen, though. She picked Harper up by her hair and threw her over the balcony. Harper screamed as she fell, but she didn't remember landing. For a moment, she blacked out, and the next thing she knew, she was lying on top of a smashed wooden coffee table, and pain was shooting through her entire body.

When she opened her eyes, Penn was floating down from the balcony, her black wings flapping slowly. Harper tried to move, but everything hurt so badly. Even just stretching out hurt her arm, but then her fingertips brushed up against the sharp, spiked end of a broken table leg.

"You have been one awful thorn in my side. I have dealt with you and your sister's crap for far too long. But the one thing that kept me going is that I knew when the day came, when I could finally get rid of you, I would make you suffer." Penn dropped to the ground next to her and crouched over her. "And today is that day."

"You first," Harper said.

With Penn's focus on taunting Harper, she didn't notice when Harper grabbed the table leg. She didn't even see it at all, not until Harper stabbed it right in her stomach, staking her all the way through.

Penn squawked in pain, and her wings flapped wildly as she staggered backward. Harper scrambled to her feet, the adrenaline pushing her through the pain, and she ran to the adjoining kitchen.

"Oh, you bitch," Penn growled, ripping the wood from her stomach and tossing it aside.

Harper pulled open the drawers and cabinets, frantically looking for anything to defend herself with. They had a hundred wineglasses, but she wasn't finding a single knife. She pulled a drawer completely out, sending spoons and forks flying all over the floor, but found nothing sharper than a butter knife.

"I normally don't eat girls' hearts," Penn began, her voice shifting from its usual silken tone to something positively monstrous. "But I am so excited to make an exception with you."

Harper looked up from her search to see that Penn had totally transformed into the monster. She was at least a foot taller, standing on long, gray bird legs. Her arms extended several feet, with hooked talons at the ends of her extended fingers.

The negligee pulled grotesquely over her elongated corpse, taut against her protruding ribs and spine. Her cranium had grown to accommodate her larger bird eyes and rows of teeth, so her black hair had thinned into wisps.

As Penn walked closer, Harper finally found a shiny butcher knife, and she grabbed it, holding it up just as Penn reached her. She wanted to stab her, but before she even had a chance, Penn knocked the knife from her hand, and it clattered to the floor.

Then Penn leaned forward, her serpentine tongue flitting through her teeth. *"Run."*

So Harper did. She didn't know how to fight her, not like that, so she ran as fast as she could, her bare feet slipping on the tile.

She'd been going toward the back door, though she didn't know what she would do if she made it through, but then she felt Penn's claws tearing against the tender flesh of her back.

As Penn lifted her, Harper heard the fabric of her dress tearing and hoped that it gave way soon. Penn turned her around, so Harper was facing her. She flicked her tongue out again, almost as if she was trying to taste her, so Harper kicked her in the face, her toes scraping painfully against Penn's teeth.

"Get away from my sister, you bitch!" Gemma shouted.

Penn craned her almost ostrichlike neck around to look toward the front of the house, and Harper peered around Penn's massive wings to see Gemma standing in the doorway.

Her copper wings were spread wide, but they looked tattered. But then as Gemma began to shift from girl to monster right in front of Harper's eyes, the wings began to fix themselves, the torn feathers replaced with glossy new ones.

Gemma's arms began to change first, growing longer, and her fingers stretched out, ending in black talons. The skin on her legs shifted from smooth flesh to gray and scaly, ending in the sharp-clawed feet of an emu.

As her torso lengthened and thinned out, her dress tore and split in two. It became a short skirt at the bottom and a small halter top above, where her collarbones and skeletal ribs jutted out.

Her eyes had already shifted into the odd yellow of a bird, but they grew larger, taking up more of her face. Her mouth lengthened and stretched out, so her lips were pulled back around row after row of sharp, jagged fangs. Her skull had expanded, and her lustrous brown hair thinned into wisps.

Gemma was no longer there. She had become the monster.

FORTY-SEVEN

Heartless

The tops of the trees were swaying and the branches crunched. Above them, Alex could hear the sounds of Thea and Liv yelling and screaming, but it sounded completely inhuman. He felt like he'd suddenly slid into Jurassic Park, and any second a *Tyrannosaurus rex* and a pack of velociraptors would come running out.

Marcy was still crouched by Kirby's body, and though she seemed reluctant to leave him, their position felt too exposed to Alex. They should be getting weapons or hiding, but he didn't want to just leave her like that.

Then Liv and Thea came flying out of the trees, and Liv slammed Thea into the pavement only a couple feet in front of Marcy.

"Come on." Alex grabbed Marcy's arm and pulled her to her feet. "We have to get out of here."

They scrambled out of the way mere seconds before Liv threw

Thea into the tree that Alex had been standing in front of. And she'd done it hard enough to make the thick trunk crack loudly, though the tree didn't fall over.

Alex and Marcy hurried around to the back of the Gremlin, but with Marcy hobbling so badly, he didn't dare go farther. She leaned against the back of the car, and he crouched beside her. He peered through the smashed windows to watch Liv walking toward where Thea leaned up against the tree, catching her breath.

"You're old, Thea," Liv said. "You think that makes you stronger, better, but it doesn't. You're weak and slow."

And Alex realized that Liv had a point. Thea had started out strong, but she'd very quickly lost her stamina. Liv clearly had the upper hand, and he wasn't sure that Thea would be able to take her on unless she got help soon.

"You're just so damn cocky, Liv. I can't wait to smack that smug grin off your face."

"I'd like to see you try."

Thea stood up and smacked Liv, hard enough that Alex could hear it from many feet away. Then they both moved so suddenly, he couldn't see much other than a flurry of feathers as they took flight.

"Let's go." Alex took Marcy's arm and started leading her around the car. When they reached the driver's side, he said, "Get in the car."

Marcy shook her head. "We can't just leave her."

"We won't," he assured her. "Just get in the car."

The door didn't open all the way, so Marcy had to slide in through the small gap and carefully sit down on a seat covered in broken glass. She tried to pull the door shut, but it creaked loudly, so she stopped.

"Do you think she can still drive?" Alex asked through the broken-out window.

"You kidding me? Lucinda can always go," Marcy said. "But where am I going?"

Thea suddenly fell from the sky, landing on the side of the road with a sickening crunch. She groaned, which was the only evidence that she was still alive, and Liv floated down, landing on top of her.

"You had a nice, long reign, but your time is up," Liv said as she wrapped her hand around Thea's throat, making her gurgle and moan as she struggled to pry Liv's fingers off.

Throughout the fight, Thea and Liv had been knocking down trees and branches all over the place. There was a thick, sturdy-looking branch only a few feet away from him, so Alex ran over and grabbed it.

He'd just picked it up when Thea spit in Liv's face. Liv cackled loudly, and as Alex ran toward her, Liv tore into Thea's chest and ripped out her heart. Two seconds too late, Alex swung the branch with all his might and struck Liv across the back.

"Not smart, little boy." Liv glared at him. "I was almost gonna let you get away."

She stood up and tossed Thea's heart aside, so it landed in dirt and pine needles. She walked slowly toward Alex, but he didn't run. He held his ground, and when he heard the car's engine clunk and rev, Liv didn't look away. She just kept walking toward him.

And then, suddenly, the car flew into life and slammed into Liv. Marcy drove the car right into a tree, and she kept pressing on the gas, pinning a screaming Liv between the car and the tree. The engine smoked and made all kinds of noises that no car should ever make, but Marcy didn't let up.

Thea rolled over and stood up, as blood dripped out from the gaping wound in her chest. One of her wings had completely snapped, and it dragged on the ground as she walked over to Alex. He couldn't help but gape at her, because he was pretty sure that she was a zombie siren at this point.

"Gimme the stick," Thea said wearily, and held out her hand, so he handed it to her. Then she walked over to the car. "Shut it off. She's not going anywhere."

Marcy did as she was told, which made it easier to hear the sound of Liv's laughter.

"You're half-dead, Thea. You really think you can do anything?"

Thea climbed onto the hood of the car, the dented metal groaning under her feet.

"You won't hurt me," Liv said. "Penn will kill you if you hurt me. That's why you never stood up for your other sisters. You can't touch—"

"*Shut up,*" Thea said.

Using the stick like a baseball bat, she swung. The wood connected hard with Liv's face, and it shattered, splinters flying everywhere as the stick broke in half. But along with it, there was a terrible crunching and ripping sound, and Liv's head flew off, landing a few feet away in the road.

Her mouth was open wide, like she was trying to scream, but only raspy breath came out. The lack of a head didn't seem to slow her body down, and her arms clawed blindly at Thea, scraping down her legs and sides.

Thea didn't seem to notice, though. She bent over Liv's bloody, gaping neck and reached down into it. Alex grimaced, but he couldn't look away. The moonlight made it harder to fully appreciate the gore since the blood didn't show up quite as red, but when Thea ripped the heart out from Liv's chest, her arm covered in dripping, dark liquid, he definitely got the picture.

Liv's body stopped moving, and it slumped forward onto Marcy's car. Thea stared down at the heart in her hands, then she shrugged and tossed it back into the trees behind her. Covered in blood and dirt, Thea jumped down from the car.

"Holy shit." Marcy pushed open the car door as wide as it would go and eased herself out. "But your heart is missing."

Thea shrugged. "It'll grow back." She was still holding the stick, and seemed to just now realize it, so she dropped it on the ground. "That's why you have to cut off the head and tear out the heart."

"If I cut off your head, it'll grow back?" Marcy asked.

"Eventually." Thea shot her a look. "But it's painful, and it really pisses me off, so don't even think about trying it."

Since Liv was gone, and both Thea and Marcy looked like they would survive, Alex turned to start jogging up the hill. He'd helped Thea take care of Liv, so he could help Gemma get rid of Penn.

"Alex!" Marcy called after him, so he stopped and looked back at her. "Where are you going?"

"I have to see if Gemma needs help."

"Wait for me." Marcy started hobbling up the hill, but she could barely put any weight on her injured leg, so she went very slowly. "No. Don't wait for me. I'm too slow. Go, but I'll catch up."

"What about you, Thea?" Alex asked.

Thea sighed and shook her head. "I won't stop Gemma from killing Penn, but I can't help her, either. I'll stay back here."

Alex nodded, and he turned and raced up the hill.

FORTY-EIGHT

Rancor

Her blood felt like hot, liquid energy surging through her veins, like she was alive for the very first time. Gemma had been the monster before, but it had never felt quite like this. The strength, the speed, the hunger, it was all there, but this time it was completely under her control. The monster would do Gemma's bidding.

Penn stood at the other side of the house, and she tossed Harper aside, like she was a scrap of meat. And that was all it took to set Gemma off. She'd been playing Penn's games for far too long.

She charged across the room, her long legs moving in strong, fast strides, and Penn bent down, letting out an animalistic roar. Just as Gemma reached her, Penn turned around and kicked her right in the stomach. Her claws tore into the soft flesh, then Gemma flew backward, crashing into the kitchen.

As Penn stomped over to her, she laughed, but it sounded more like an evil raven than anything human. Gemma had gotten to her feet instantly, but the floor was littered with silverware and broken glass, making it hard for her clawed feet to get traction.

Gemma backed up around the island, letting Penn come toward her and think she had the upper hand. Gemma hissed at her, but neither of them spoke. They could, but something about being in this form made growling and crowing feel much more natural. Words required more thought, and her brain was giving in to much more primal instincts.

Penn lowered her head and spread her wings slightly, like she was getting ready to pounce. The way she moved was predatory and almost prehistoric, but she was too focused on her prey to notice her surroundings.

One more step back, then Gemma stopped. She waited until Penn jumped at her, and then in one swift move, Gemma reached up and pulled the stainless-steel refrigerator down on Penn.

It wouldn't kill her, but it did slow her down for a second, and Gemma ran away from the kitchen, looking around for her sister. She found Harper near the back door, tearing through a broom closet.

"Get out of here," Gemma said in her demonic-monster voice.

"I'm looking for something to cut off her head with," Harper said as she pushed a vacuum cleaner out of her way. "I won't leave you."

The sound of crashing metal in the living room made Gemma turn around. Penn had pushed the fridge off herself and thrown it into the other room. Not before tearing a door off, though. Penn growled at her, and, with her long hands, she snapped the fridge door in half.

It now had a sharp, serrated edge, and Penn threw it at Gemma's head, like it was a guillotine Frisbee.

Gemma ducked, but she felt the edge knick the top of one of her wings. Penn howled in dismay, and Gemma charged her again. She bent her head low, so when Penn tried to kick her, she opened her mouth and clamped her razor teeth straight through Penn's leg.

Penn squawked and fell backward, so Gemma pounced on her. Penn was still stronger than her, and any chance she had to get at Penn's heart, she'd have to take it. Her claws had barely pierced the skin on Penn's chest when she felt herself being pushed backward.

The ground seemed to float away from beneath them, and Gemma didn't even completely understand what was happening until she felt the wind from Penn's wings. Penn was flying up and taking Gemma with her.

Gemma flapped her wings, trying to push back to the ground, but then she felt her back slamming into the peaked ceiling. But Penn kept pushing, using Gemma like a wrecking ball, and wood and shingles poured down around her.

They broke through the roof, and Penn kept going. If Penn wanted a battle in the sky, then she had one coming. With one hand, Gemma clawed her face, and with the other, she grabbed one of Penn's wings. If she ripped it off now, Penn would tumble back to the ground.

Penn must've sensed her plan, because she smiled and lunged forward. Gemma tried to cry out, but she couldn't because Penn had clamped her jaws around her neck. She was trying to bite her head off.

FORTY-NINE

Demonic

After Alex had left, Marcy ripped off the sleeve of a sweater she'd left in the backseat of her car. She tied it around the gash in her shin and tied it tight. Now she couldn't see the bone, and that was kind of a bummer, but at least she could walk better.

Thea had taken the rest of the sweater and tied it around her chest, covering up the gaping hole in her chest where a small, beating, pink blob was apparently growing into a new heart.

While she did that, Marcy had gone over and laid a few of the smaller broken branches over Kirby. He was hidden under a blanket, but she wanted to add an extra layer of protection.

"I'm sorry, Kirby." Marcy wiped at the tears in her eyes, smearing dirt and dried blood across her cheeks. "I didn't know you for that long, but you were supernice, and this never should've happened to you."

She took a deep breath and went on, "I'm also sorry that I

can't cry about you a lot right now, and I want you to know that it's not because I don't care. It's because I want to go help kill the bitches that did this to you."

"What are you doing?" Thea asked. She came up behind her and kept rolling her shoulder, making her broken wing crack.

"Saying a few words. I mean, I know he'll have a funeral later, but it never hurts to say something like that when they're freshly dead," Marcy said. "His spirit's probably close by, and I just wanted him to know that I'm sorry."

"Why'd you cover him with branches?" Thea asked.

"So the animals don't get him." Marcy turned around. "All right. Let's go."

"Where?" Thea shook her head. "I'm not going anywhere."

"What? You don't need to just sit here and lick your wounds. My friends are in trouble, and I'm not just gonna wait around back here to see if they need help."

"Who died and made you king?" Thea asked.

"You did, when I saved your life like two minutes ago." Marcy limped over to her and held out her arm. "Now help me get up to the top of the hill. You owe me one."

Thea stared at her and didn't move to help. "And this is how you're using the one?"

"Yep. This is it."

"But you're hurt." Thea pointed to her leg. "You can barely walk. How are you gonna help them?"

Marcy shrugged. "Maybe I can be bait or a distraction, or maybe Penn will just eat me instead, and she'll be too full to eat anyone else. I don't know what I can do, but I know for damn sure that if I stay down here, I can't help anybody. And I won't do that. I'm not *you*."

Thea ignored the dig and eyed her. "You're gonna get yourself killed."

"You should like that. Then I'd be out of your hair. Now let's go. Once we get up there, you can go back to not-helping Gemma or Penn."

A crashing and squawking sound interrupted the relative quiet that had fallen over the hill. Once Thea and Liv had started tearing through the trees, all the birds and other animals had scattered, making it almost eerily quiet.

But now Marcy looked up to the sky. The moon was clear and bright, and she easily saw the forms of two giant birds clawing at each other over the tops of the trees.

Thea sighed. "That can't be good."

She put her arm around Marcy's waist, so Marcy could lean on her, and the two of them started making the steep trek up the road. It was a nice gesture, but every time they took a step, Thea's broken wing would swing forward and hit Marcy in the back.

"This would be easier if you put that wing away," Marcy said as she brushed a bloody feather out of her face.

"I can't. It's broken. It's healing, and it won't go back until it's done."

"Well, hurry up then," Marcy said, and picked up her pace. Gemma was clearly in trouble, and she probably needed all the help she could get. "Maybe a car will drive by and stop for us."

"Penn chased away the neighbors because she likes privacy, so we're the only ones who live up here now," Thea explained. "And I'm also pretty sure that nobody would stop for the two of us."

"What? You have wings. You could be an angel," Marcy said. "Who wouldn't stop to help an angel?"

"You realize I'm actually more of a demon, right?"

"Yeah, I do, but a car driving by wouldn't."

FIFTY

Ordnance

Alex was almost to the top of the cliff when he heard the crash. He'd been running up through the trees, trying to go a shorter route than on the road, and he'd had to stare up through the branches. But he'd seen it just the same. Two large birds crashing into each other.

They were in the sky, so Alex couldn't really help much, but if he got to the house now, it would probably be a good time to try to get Harper and Daniel out of there.

When he made it to the house, the front door was still open, and Harper's car was parked and running right next to it. Before he even made it in, he could see that it was a disaster. Pieces of wood, food, appliances, furniture—everything was broken and strewn all over the house.

"Harper?" Alex shouted as he stepped over the debris.

"Alex!" Harper shouted from the back of the house. "I'm back here."

He ran back to see the sitting room near the windows that faced the bay mostly intact, and Harper was sitting in a pile of fragmented wood and random knives. He was about to ask her what was going on when he heard a banging sound.

"What's that?" Alex asked, looking toward the ceiling and the bedroom directly above them.

"Daniel. He's fine." Harper shook her head and stared at the mess around her. "I need to find something to help Gemma."

Alex crouched to look at what she had. "Like a weapon?"

"Yeah, anything that can help when they come back down."

He turned back and looked up through the hole in the ceiling. A solitary black feather had fallen through and was slowly floating to the ground.

"What if they don't?" Alex asked thickly, and he hated to even think it.

"Daniel is trapped here. Penn will come back eventually, and when she does, we have to be ready for her."

But she'd failed to say that Gemma would come back, and that's when Alex knew the situation had to be dire. He knew that Gemma had been practicing to control the monster, so she could fight Penn, but he had no idea how strong she was. She might be drastically outmatched.

If she was, that just meant that he and Harper would have to step up their game.

"Okay, so what have you found?" Alex asked, looking back at her.

"It's mostly stuff like this." She held up a broom that had been snapped in half so the end came to a sharp point. "I can stab her, but she's not a vampire. Staking her won't do much good."

"What does kill them? The head and the heart, right?" Alex asked, and Harper nodded. "So let's find something . . ." He'd been looking around the room, but he stopped when his eyes landed on the sharp, jagged edges of the broken fridge door. "What about that?"

"I thought about it, but I can't really lift the thing. Gemma might be able to, but . . ." She trailed off. If Gemma were incapacitated, it wouldn't do them much good if they couldn't easily maneuver it.

"The steel is just a façade. It's like glued on, sorta." Alex walked over to it and pulled at the metal to confirm this. "We can rip it off."

Harper got up and rushed over to help him. They carefully grabbed the edge and tried to tear it off, but the sharp edges made it harder for them to grasp it. The metal was slick and glued down tightly, but Alex had just started tearing up one of the corners when the remaining windows behind them shattered.

He leaned over, shielding Harper with his body since his back was to the windows, as glass, feathers, and wood rained in around them. Penn was screaming in an odd, birdlike way, as she and Gemma crashed back into the house and rolled across the floor.

FIFTY-ONE

Slaughter

G emma got up and shook the glass from her hair. She could feel the blood soaking the front of her shirt. Her entire body ached, and Penn had bitten into her left arm so hard that it had snapped the bone, and the arm hung at an odd angle.

Penn stood across from her, circling her slowly, and at least it was nice to see that Penn didn't look that great, either. Bites and claw marks had left her a bloody mess. Two of her fangs had broken in half, and she had a limp.

It was good to know she'd inflicted some damage, but her energy was waning. She wasn't sure if it was because she'd lost so much blood from the throat wounds or simply because she hadn't eaten in so long. But the fight was going out of her.

This was her last chance to get Penn, so she had to make it count.

She waited until Penn charged at her, then stepped to the side at the last minute. As Penn ran past her, Gemma grabbed onto her wing and spun her around. Then she leapt on her back and knocked her down.

Penn's wings flapped hard, beating against Gemma, but her teeth and claws couldn't reach her. Gemma pushed her down, stepping on the small of her back with all her weight. And then with the last of her strength, Gemma tore her talons into Penn's back, between her wings.

Penn shrieked and tried to buck Gemma off, but Gemma just tore in deep, breaking through her bones until she could feel the beating of her black heart. She wrapped her hand around it and ripped it out.

And then Penn pushed back, finally knocking Gemma off her. She fell back and tried to get to her feet, but her legs kept slipping underneath. They were weak, and the floor was slick with blood.

Penn came at her with full force. Gemma held her arms up to shield herself, but Penn was like a rabid animal, just biting and clawing without reason.

"Gemma!" Harper shouted, and Gemma saw her sister running toward them holding a long sheet of metal in her hands.

Penn was too focused on getting her anger out on Gemma to see Harper. Not even when Harper ran at her. With the steel in one hand, she swung to the side, like she meant to slice through Penn's neck.

Unfortunately, breaking the siren's bones required more strength than Harper had, so the metal only made it through her windpipe and throat before stopping against the bone. She tried to push it in deeper, but Harper only succeeded in slicing her hand open. As the blood began to flow, her grip began to slip. When Penn staggered back as blood flowed from the wound, the sheet of metal sliced all down Harper's forearm.

Blood began to pour from Penn's throat, and she made an angry, guttural sound.

Still lying on her back, Gemma reared up and kicked the steel. The sharp edge cut the bottom of her foot, but she pushed it through Penn's neck.

With her mouth still open in an angry smile, Penn's head slid off her torso and fell to the floor with a disturbing splat. A few seconds later, her body collapsed next to it.

FIFTY-TWO

Bloodied

Harper! *Harper!*" Daniel shouted, and he slammed into the door again. His shoulder would be bruised after this, but he didn't give a damn.

Trapped in the bathroom, he'd been unable to see anything or help in any way. The only thing he'd relied on had been listening to the sounds of things breaking and people shouting at each other.

But a few minutes ago, everything had gone silent.

"Just a second, Daniel," Gemma said, and he heard metal groaning.

When the door finally opened, he'd never been so relieved in his life. Gemma was standing in front of him, looking fully human. She was covered in blood, her clothes were ripped, but he couldn't see any wounds.

He put his hands on her shoulders, just touching her to make sure that she was real and safe. "You're okay?"

"Yeah." She nodded. "Penn's dead. And Harper's fine. Mostly."

"*Mostly?*" Daniel asked, and his eyes quickly darted past Gemma and saw that Harper had just reached the top of the landing, with Alex's help. Her right arm was covered in blood, but she was alive, and she smiled at him with tears in her eyes.

He ran over to her and pulled her into his arms, probably hugging her more tightly than he should've, but she didn't complain. She hugged him back, and he lifted her off the ground.

Then he set her down to get a better look at her. He brushed the hair back from her face and looked her in the eyes. "Are you okay?"

"Yeah." She smiled. "What about you?"

He grinned. "Never better." Then he looked at the gash running down her arm from her inner elbow to her palm. "Your arm. You need stitches."

"No, it looks worse than it is," Harper assured him. "It's not that deep. I don't think it hit any of the major veins."

His eyes darted around the bedroom, looking for something to wrap Harper's arm with. Penn had torn his shirt to bits, so it was little more than fabric and confetti; and he doubted that Harper would want to use the silk sheets Penn had just tried to bed Daniel on, even in an emergency.

Penn had draped a shawl across her headboard, and it was still there, so Daniel ran over and pulled it off. The fabric felt like gauzy satin, so it didn't feel superabsorbent, but it would help slow the blood flow at least.

"Here." He wrapped it around Harper's arm, tying it tighter

just below her elbow, so it would work like a tourniquet. "That'll tide you over."

"What's going on? Is the party over?" Marcy asked.

Daniel glanced over the railing just as Marcy and Thea came into the house. Marcy looked a little rough, but Thea looked like she'd really been through hell. She was fully human, no wings or claws, but she was completely covered in blood.

As soon as Gemma saw Thea, she took off downstairs and ran over to her.

"Every time I come to this house, there's a decapitated body in the living room," Marcy said. But she didn't seem to mind it. She crouched to inspect Penn's headless, winged body.

Gemma and Thea stood in the doorway, talking in hushed murmurs to one another. Daniel put his arm around Harper and watched them with his brow furrowed.

"Is everyone here?" Daniel asked, and looked around. "Is everyone okay?"

"Liv and Penn are dead," Alex said, and Daniel looked over at him for the first time. Then Alex's expression darkened. "But Kirby didn't make it."

"Oh, no," Harper whispered.

"How are you holding up?" Daniel asked. "You look pretty banged up."

Alex glanced down at his shirt, which was stained red with blood. "Most of this isn't mine. I've been hugging Gemma a lot. So I'm okay."

"So is this curse broken then?" Daniel asked.

"I don't know," Harper admitted. "Diana said that if we killed

Penn, we wouldn't need to break the curse. But Gemma still seemed to have her siren strength when she opened the bathroom door."

"She just healed up. Maybe the siren blood hasn't completely evaporated," Alex suggested.

Harper shook her head, like she wasn't convinced, then stepped away from Daniel and walked over to the railing. "What's going on? Is the curse broken?"

Gemma turned and smiled thinly up at her. "Yeah. It's over."

"But . . ." Harper trailed off, and Daniel stepped behind her and gently put his hand on her back. "You're still strong, and Thea is still here. I thought if the curse was broken, she'd turn to dust."

"That was one theory, but it's wrong," Gemma said.

"Then what's the correct theory?" Daniel asked, and Gemma glanced back to Thea, like she needed answers herself.

"That we'll just slowly become mortal again," Thea supplied. "The siren powers will slowly drain from our body over the next few days, then we'll be regular humans again. I'll live out a natural, human life."

"Then how do you know it's over?" Harper asked. "If nothing's changed, then how can you be sure?"

"We didn't say nothing's changed," Gemma corrected her. "I can feel it. Inside." She paused, and her cheeks darkened. "I'm not as hungry."

"So you're sure?" Harper asked again.

Gemma nodded. "Yes. I'm sure."

Thea said something to Gemma too quiet for Daniel or anyone

up in the loft to hear. Then Gemma nodded, Thea turned and walked away. Gemma hugged herself and watched as Thea departed.

"What happened?" Harper asked. "Where is she going?"

"She wanted to go see the mountains or the plains or a desert." Gemma shrugged. "Anywhere she hasn't been able to see in thousands of years."

"So what does that mean?" Harper asked. "Are we finally free of the sirens?"

"Yes." Gemma let out a deep breath. "We're finally free."

FIFTY-THREE

Depletion

"I swear, Dad, breakfast has never tasted this good," Harper said as she shoveled another forkful of scrambled eggs into her mouth.

Brian watched her eat with a mixture of amusement and surprise. "I've made you this same thing a hundred times before."

"Nope." She shook her head. "This is better. This is the *best*."

Last night, after they'd all finally finished dealing with the mess of dead bodies and crashed cars out on the cliff, Harper and Gemma had gotten home very, very late. And then they'd sat up for a long time explaining everything to their dad.

Harper had hardly eaten anything yesterday, but she'd been too sore, tired, and anxious to eat when they got home. But when she woke up today, she was absolutely ravenous.

Brian had been awake for a while, so he'd already eaten breakfast, but he insisted on making it for her. Maybe it was just because he was her dad, and he wanted to do something nice for her. Or maybe it was a little because of how terrible she still looked.

In the morning, she'd caught sight of her reflection in the mirror, and it wasn't pretty. She'd showered last night to get off all the blood and dirt, but that still left her with plenty of scratches and bruises. Daniel had wanted her to go to the hospital to see if she needed stitches in her arm, but she just wrapped it in gauze, and so far it seemed to be doing fine. She had a gash on her left cheek, and a nasty bruise on her neck, but the rest she'd be able to cover with long sleeves and jeans when she got back to school.

"Hey, sleepyhead," Brian said, as Gemma stumbled into the kitchen. "I thought you were never gonna wake up."

She didn't have a scratch on her since she'd healed up entirely last night. Her eyes looked a bit tired, and she clearly wasn't very awake. But otherwise, Gemma looked about the same as she always did.

"What are you all doing up so early?" Gemma yawned and collapsed into an empty chair at the table.

"It's noon," Harper said between bites of food. "It's not that early."

"Maybe not, but I'm still exhausted." Her hair was coming loose from the messy bun she had it up in, and she readjusted it.

"You look better than you did last night," Brian said, then he looked at Harper. "You, not so much."

"Thanks, Dad," Harper said dryly.

"I'm just saying that your sister's right. You probably should rest up," Brian told her.

"I'm fine. I'm better than fine," Harper insisted. Her elation seemed to ward off most of the pain, but she'd taken a couple Advil when she woke up to get rid of the rest of the soreness and body aches. "But Gemma did heal awfully fast."

"Yeah, I'd mostly healed last night when I transitioned back from the monster."

"So this is really over?" Brian rested his arms on the table and looked at Gemma. "You're sure that you're not a siren anymore?"

"Yes, it's over," Gemma said firmly. "I can already feel my siren powers waning. They'll be entirely gone in a few days. It's hard to explain it, but I just *know*."

Harper had finished all her food, so she pushed the plate aside and looked at her sister. "You're absolutely sure?"

"Come on, guys." Gemma laughed, but it sounded a tad uneasy. "I think I would know if I were still a siren. Okay?"

Harper studied her and shook her head. "I just can't tell anymore."

"What do you mean?" Gemma asked.

"I don't know if this is you-pretty or siren-pretty."

Gemma smirked. "I'll just take that as a compliment."

The doorbell rang, so Harper got up to get it. When she left the kitchen, Brian was trying to talk Gemma into eating some of the extra sausage he'd made, but she was declining.

"Wow," Alex said when Harper answered the door and found him standing on the doorstep. "Penn really did a number on you."

"Yeah, Penn was pissed. But she's dead now." Harper couldn't help but smile when she said it.

Penn had been torturing her and the people she loved for so

long, and now it was like a giant, monstrous weight had been lifted. She hadn't felt this happy in a very long time.

"You actually look perfectly fine," Harper told Alex. He had a bruise on his arm, but that was about all she could see, and he was wearing a T-shirt and shorts.

"I know. Most of the blood just washed off, and there wasn't much underneath," he said.

"Come on in." Harper opened the door wider. "Gemma's in the kitchen eating breakfast. I think there's some leftover sausage if you wanna join us."

"Sure." He shrugged and followed her into the kitchen.

When Gemma saw him, she smiled, and her whole face lit up. "Hey."

"Hey." Alex went over and kissed her, until Brian cleared his throat loudly. Then Alex straightened up and smiled politely at him. "Morning, Mr. Fisher."

"Morning, Alex," Brian said gruffly, making Harper laugh a little as she sat back down.

Alex pulled up a chair closer to Gemma. "How are you feeling?"

"Pretty good. Just sleepy." She yawned again, as if to emphasize it, and she reached over, holding Alex's hand under the table.

"So after breakfast, I was thinking I would go out to visit Marcy," Harper said. "You wanna join me?"

Gemma shook her head. "No. I think I'm gonna take a nap."

"You just woke up," Harper said, dubious.

"I'm tired," she insisted. "Losing my powers is exhausting."

"Okay." Harper shrugged and turned to Alex. "What about you, Alex?"

"If Gemma's just gonna be napping . . ." He trailed off and looked to Gemma to see if it was okay.

"You go ahead," Gemma told him. "Marcy's always liked you, and she could use some cheering up."

He looked perplexed. "I thought Marcy hated me."

"No, that's just her personality," Harper said.

"Do you guys mind if I go lie down?" Gemma let go of Alex's hand and pushed herself back from the table. "I think I woke up too early, actually."

"You sure you're okay?" Brian asked, concerned. "You didn't eat any breakfast."

"Yeah. I'm fine. I'll feel better if I sleep some more." Gemma stood up. "Tell Marcy that I'm sorry and thanks for everything."

"Will do," Harper said.

Alex stood, so Gemma leaned up and kissed him. She made sure to keep it short enough so her dad wouldn't have to clear his throat again, then she waved 'bye to everyone and headed to her room.

"She's acting strange, right?" Harper asked once she heard Gemma's feet on the stairs. "You all agree with me."

"Yeah, but after last night, can you really blame her?" Brian asked.

"And if she's losing all her siren powers, that has to feel really draining," Alex agreed, and sat back down. "Going from super-strong to, you know, mortal again has to feel strange."

Harper considered it, then nodded. Physically, going from an immortal creature back to a normal teenage girl had to be a crazy feeling. Not to mention all the stress and fighting last night.

"Yeah. That's probably it," Harper agreed.

"Alex," Brian said, making Alex sit up straighter. "I don't want you to think that since you helped save my daughters' lives that I'm gonna let you do what you want now. The old rules still apply. If I catch you in Gemma's bedroom, I will feel absolutely no guilt in cutting off whatever appendages you're touching her with."

Alex gulped. "That sounds fair, Mr. Fisher."

FIFTY-FOUR

Requiem

Marcy lived in a tiny apartment above a souvenir shop two blocks from the beach. All summer, she hated it because of the tourists, but in the winter, when no one was around, she loved it.

Harper and Alex stood on the landing outside her apartment door. Between the buildings, she could see Anthemusa Bay, and she could hear the sounds of people laughing and music playing.

"Hello." Lydia opened the door, smiling brightly.

"Hey, Lydia, I didn't know you were here," Harper said.

"Since Marcy lives alone, I thought I would come play nursemaid." And that explained Lydia's tiny white hat with a red cross on it.

"That's really nice of you," Harper said, and she gestured to Alex. "I'm not sure if you've been properly introduced, but this is Alex Lane. He's Gemma's boyfriend."

"No, we haven't met, but it's nice to meet you." She shook his hand. "I'm Lydia Panning."

"I've heard a lot about you," he said.

Lydia did a small curtsy in the fluffy pink skirt she was wearing. "I hope I live up to your expectations."

"How is she doing?" Harper asked, hoping to get an update before they went inside the apartment.

"Okay. She's spent most of the morning on the couch, cuddling with her ferret Bruce and watching old Scooby Doo episodes." Lydia lowered her voice. "She's been crying some, but I think that's more about Kirby than any physical pain."

Harper nodded. Marcy had always had a terrible time expressing normal emotions, even when she was grieving. When Lydia came inside, Marcy was sitting on her couch with her injured leg propped up on a beanbag chair.

On the wall behind her was a huge, framed, black-and-white photo that was supposedly of the Loch Ness Monster, but really it just looked like a stick to Harper.

"Hey." Harper smiled and sat down on the couch next to her. "How are you holding up, sweetie?"

"'Sweetie'?" Marcy gave her an odd look. "I messed up my leg. I didn't turn into an octogenarian with a penchant for kittens."

"We just came to see how you're doing," Alex said, and he leaned against the arm of the couch next to Harper, as if he were afraid of getting any closer to Marcy and disturbing her.

Marcy shrugged. "All right, considering."

"I was gonna make her some soup," Lydia said. "It's my grandma's special recipe. Do you guys want any?"

"You should totally try it," Marcy said.

"I'm okay. I just ate." Harper patted her belly.

"So did I, but I'll have a bowl," Alex said.

Lydia disappeared into the small, adjoining kitchen, and soon they heard pots and pans banging around. Scooby Doo was solving some kind of mystery involving an old groundskeeper on the television, and Marcy watched intently for a few minutes before turning it down.

"Have you talked to the police anymore?" Marcy asked, looking over at Harper.

"Not since last night."

With everything that had happened, they'd thought it was best to call the police. After they got rid of Penn's and Liv's bodies, of course. Harper had thought that Thea had left the area, but she'd really just gone down the hill to get Liv's body.

Once she came back with all of Liv's parts, she threw them over the cliff, and Gemma and Daniel did the same with Penn's body. Thea claimed that in the saltwater, the siren's body would dissolve over a couple hours, so there'd be nothing to find.

As for the sirens' house, they cleaned up as much of the blood as they could, then they locked it up and left it. Thea said that since Penn had scared everyone away, they could leave it empty for a long time before anyone noticed. So they'd decided to wait a week or two, then, just to be safe, they would burn it down, destroying any other evidence that was left behind.

The only thing they'd really told the police about was Kirby, and that had been simpler. They said that Marcy was driving up to the cliff to be alone with Kirby. Then a tree damaged in a bad

storm in August had fallen over, landing on the roof. She skidded out of the way, smashed into another tree, and Kirby had
gotten killed in the wreck.

It might have sounded unbelievable, but thanks to Gemma's
and Thea's residual siren charms, the cops seemed to believe it.
And besides, there wasn't another obvious reason for a fallen tree
or smashed-up car.

"You think they bought it all?" Marcy asked.

Harper nodded. "Gemma and Thea managed to convince
them."

"Here." Lydia came into the living room carrying a salt-and-
pepper ferret that was at least twice as fat as any ferret should be,
and she handed it to Marcy. "He keeps trying to get in the pot."

"Bruce loves his chicken." Marcy petted him as he tried to
nibble on her fingers. "It's 'cause he's a member of the weasel
family. They're super into birds."

"How are you doing with the whole Kirby thing?" Harper
asked, deciding that it might be a good time to bring it up since
Marcy was holding Bruce.

"I don't know. We weren't dating for very long but . . ." Tears
welled in her eyes, looking even larger through her thick glasses,
and she shook her head and sniffled. "What's done is done."

"Did you hear when his funeral is?" Alex asked.

"Not yet. I haven't talked to his parents or anything, and I
don't want to." She held her ferret closer to her, and he sniffed at
a lone tear that slid down her cheek. "So I'll probably just find
out when they post it in the obituary."

Harper reached over and rubbed her friend's back, and surprisingly, Marcy let her. Which meant that she actually had to be really upset about all of this.

Lydia came in a few minutes later carrying two bowls of soup. "Here you guys go." She handed one to Alex, then handed the other to Marcy, trading it for Bruce. "How is Gemma doing today?"

"Good. She's pretty tired, so she's at home sleeping," Harper said. "She wanted me to send you her best."

"I don't know what that means." Marcy shrugged. "So tell her that I send her my awesomest."

"So . . . is she human?" Lydia asked, trying to sound nonchalant. She stood off to the side of the room, petting the ferret.

"Yeah. Penn's dead," Harper said. "It was like Diana said. With her dead, the curse is broken."

"Well, actually, Diana said, 'If you tried to kill Penn, then you wouldn't need to break the curse.'" It was the overly casual way she said it that unnerved Harper, like she was trying too hard to make it sound like none of this mattered, but she really thought it did.

"Yeah, that's what I said," Harper said, nearly snapping at her.

"No, it's a little different." Lydia set Bruce down. "Because I was talking to Pine about the translations, and it doesn't sound like it matters if you kill Penn or any of the sirens, as long as they're replaced."

"The translation is wrong then," Harper told her harshly. "Because Gemma said the curse is broken. Tell her, Alex."

"It's over," Alex agreed, but he sounded confused, like he didn't completely understand the exchange between Harper and

Lydia. "I mean, I asked her directly, and so did Harper, and she says over. And why would she lie?"

"Maybe she doesn't know," Marcy suggested.

Lydia shook her head. "She would *know*."

"Exactly. And both she and Thea said they can feel that the curse is broken," Harper said firmly. "They could both feel their powers waning, and that's why Gemma is so tired and out of it today."

The room lapsed into an awkward silence, so Alex took a bite of soup, and very loudly said, "Mmm. This is really good soup, Lydia."

"Thanks." She smiled politely.

"My dad had the car towed into town," Marcy said. "She's pretty totaled, but I'm optimistic that they might be able to save her."

"The Gremlin?" Alex asked. "Wouldn't it be cheaper to buy a new car than fix her?"

"Lucinda's not just a car," Marcy corrected him. "You saw her. She's magic. And even if I have to work at the library for the next eighty years to pay to get her fixed, it'll be worth it. Oh, but that reminds me, I should probably call in for Tuesday."

"But today's only Sunday," Harper said.

Marcy shrugged and dug in her pocket for her cell phone. "My leg will probably still hurt."

FIFTY-FIVE

Favored

He'd taken a long, hot shower for the second time in the past twelve hours, and it finally felt like he was getting rid of the dirt and grime. Daniel hadn't been that injured fighting Penn, but he'd gotten plenty bloody cleaning things up. Not to mention how gross he'd felt during the minimakeout session/S&M scene he'd had with Penn before Harper had arrived.

He slipped on a T-shirt and a pair of pajama pants, deciding that today called for comfort above anything else. As he walked out of the bathroom, he was still rubbing a small towel through his short hair, and when he lowered it, he saw Gemma.

"Whoa." He put a hand to his heart since she'd scared the crap out of him. "What are you doing here?"

"I wanted to talk to you."

She stood barefoot just inside his doorway, and her sundress was dripping water onto the floor. In fact, all of her was dripping wet, even the golden brown waves of hair that fell down her back.

"How'd you get here?" Daniel asked suspiciously.

"I swam."

"Like . . . mermaid swam?"

She smiled, but it didn't look convincing. "Before all this, I used to be on the swim team, remember? I swam in the bay all the time. I can do that whether I'm mortal or not."

"You didn't answer my question, though. How did you swim here?"

"With my legs." She lifted one and wiggled it, as if to demonstrate.

"Okay." He relented and held out his towel to her. "So to what do I owe this pleasure?"

She ran the towel through her hair, squeezing out most of the excess water. When she'd finished, she handed him back the towel, and he set it aside on the kitchen counter.

"Thank you," she said. "I mean, not just for the towel. You did so much for me."

"I didn't really do that much." He shook his head. "I think it was mostly you in that fight last night."

"No, I'm not talking about just last night. You *gave* so much. You were willing to give up everything to protect me, even your life. I know that it was for Harper to protect her, but that still means a lot to me."

"It wasn't just for Harper." He looked fondly at her. "Yeah, part of it was, but even if she hadn't been in the picture, I would've done it for you."

"I think I knew that." She smiled, then laughed a little. "This is gonna sound weird, but I kinda think you're my best friend."

"It's not that weird. You're probably my best friend, too," he realized. "Outside of Harper, I think I talk to you more than anyone else. Except maybe Pearl."

"She does have amazing clam chowder," Gemma said, referring to the owner of the diner that served Daniel's favorite soup.

"She does," he admitted. "So maybe she's my best friend, and you're like my backup."

Gemma smiled at his joke, then went on. "I can't ever thank you enough for what you did, even if I had all the time in the world."

"Can't help but notice your use of the past tense for 'had' there. How much time do you have?"

"The rest of my life," she said, and she wouldn't look at him.

"Mmm." He leaned back against the counter. "Your being so evasive isn't really putting me at ease."

"I just came out here to tell you that I don't know how I can thank you."

"You don't need to thank me," he insisted. "Your being alive and safe is thanks enough."

"You were gonna die, Daniel!" Gemma reminded him. "That was huge. You can't just brush that off."

"I wasn't gonna *die*. I was gonna be a siren, and I don't know. That might not have been so bad." He smirked. "You and me, we would've taken on Penn and maybe ruled the world."

She rolled her eyes as she smiled. "Yeah, it would've been great. If you don't mind dining on human flesh."

"It's probably one of those things that you get used to."

All the humor in her expression disappeared, and she lowered her eyes. "I hope not."

"Yeah, me, too."

"And I know it sounds weird that I came out here to thank you, and now I'm going to ask you a favor." She bit her lip and looked up at him nervously.

He arched an eyebrow. "A favor?"

"I want you to promise me that no matter what happens, you'll be with my sister and take care of her."

He waited a beat before shaking his head. "I can't promise you that."

"But you love her!" Gemma insisted.

"That's why I can't promise you that. What holds us together needs to be love and mutual respect and desire. I can't be bound to her by guilt from you. That's not what's best for her."

Gemma sighed. "Daniel."

"I can promise that I will look out for her for as long as I'm alive, even if we're not together and even if she decides she hates me one day," he said. "But that's the best I'll do."

"Thank you."

"But why all this worry about your sister for the rest of eternity? Are you planning on not being around to protect her?" Daniel asked.

"No. I just . . ." She tried to play it off. "I can't be around her all the time, and I want to know she's safe."

"She's safe, but I have to be honest. It's you I'm worried about."

Standing in front of him, Gemma was at least a foot smaller

than he, and, dripping wet as she was, she looked even smaller. In an objective way, he knew that she was beautiful, but that's not what he saw when he looked at her.

Her golden eyes had grown harder over recent months, but they still had an innocence and optimism to them, and when she smiled, her expression still had that hint of little girl to it.

In her, he always saw a frightened child, trapped in a situation that they were fighting desperately to change. It was what he'd seen in her eyes that very first time he'd rescued her from the sirens, when she was still human, and Penn had cornered her on the dock next to his boat. And that was why he helped her then, and why he helped her still.

"I'm fine," Gemma said, and started backing toward the door. "But I should probably head back. Long swim."

"Gemma." He stopped her and stepped away from the counter, closer to her. "Did I ever tell you about when my brother died?"

"It was a boat accident, wasn't it?" she asked.

Daniel nodded. "He got drunk even though I had told him to stop drinking. He took a boat out when I asked him not to. And he crashed when I told him to slow down."

"I'm sorry," she said, sounding unsure of what else to say.

"I can forgive myself for that. He made all those choices to drink and drive a boat, and I've learned to accept his choices as best I can. He knew what he was doing, and I tried my hardest to talk him out of it. But he was five years older than me and wasn't about to let me tell him what to do.

"But the part I can't forgive myself for, the part that still haunts me, is that I didn't find him," he went on. "After the boat crashed, he was lost in the bay, and I went in after him, but I never found him." He'd walked up so he was right in front of her, and she stared up at him.

"Why?" she asked.

"Because I should've been able to save him, and it might not make sense, but I feel like I didn't do everything I could. Anything short of staying in that water until I died doesn't feel like enough."

"If he'd died, your dying wouldn't have brought him back," Gemma told him.

"I know. Logically, I know," he admitted. "But that's not how it feels at night when I'm lying awake."

"You can't blame yourself for his death."

"I've had plenty of therapy about John's death, and that's not why I brought it up."

"Then why did you?"

"Because I know that something's going on with you, and I don't know what it is," Daniel said. "But I don't want to find you dead and know that I didn't do everything I could to save you."

"Daniel, you won't find me dead, and you've done absolutely everything you can. You've done so much more than you ever needed to."

She stood on her tiptoes so she could lean in and kiss him on the cheek, then she put her arms around him. He hugged her back as she squeezed tighter, and he kissed the top of her head. Then she stepped back, and when she smiled up at him, there were tears in her eyes.

"I love you. I'm not in love with you, but I do care about you," Gemma said.

"I care about you, too. An awful lot."

"I should go, though." She stepped toward the door. "But please do me a favor and stop worrying so much. Everything is going to be fine, you'll see." She smiled and her brown eyes twinkled in a way that almost made him believe her.

Then Gemma turned and ran out the door, racing down the path to the bay. He considered going after her so he could see if she did really swim away using her legs, but he thought he already knew the answer.

FIFTY-SIX

Holiday

Since Brian didn't have work on Monday because of the holiday, he suggested that they spend the day together as a family. Not just because they'd all been through so much lately, but Harper had to go back to Sundham, and Gemma was set to begin her junior year the next day.

Gemma thought it sounded perfect. After her clandestine visit to Daniel's yesterday, she'd spent the rest of the afternoon with Alex. So it'd be great to spend the day with her family.

It was the last official day of the summer season, and most things were closing early. It also meant that the tourists were heading out. The At Summer's End Festival had made the past week the busiest of the year, and now, with the crowds dispersing, it made Capri feel almost like a ghost town. But that was definitely a nice thing.

Gemma, Harper, and their dad took a walk down to the beach,

grateful not to wade through kids or suntanning ladies or discarded beer cans. They tried skipping pebbles on the water, which didn't work at all, but at least it was fun to try.

For lunch, they went to Pearl's Diner, and they talked and laughed about old times. It wasn't until then—when they were laughing so hard that Harper couldn't breathe, and Brian's face was turning red—that Gemma realized how long it had been since she'd seen either of them so happy.

This summer had weighed on them so heavily, but even before that, her sister and her dad had gotten so caught up in trying to take care of everything that they'd almost forgotten to have fun and be happy.

When they went back home, Brian decided to teach them how to play poker, insisting it would be a useful skill for them in later life. Harper took to the game right away, and it didn't take long before she'd completely wiped both Gemma and Brian out of the pennies they'd been playing with.

By then, it was starting to get late, so Harper went up to pack her bag to return to college. Gemma was sitting in the living room with her dad, watching an old *Rocky* movie he'd seen a hundred times before, when something slid through the mail slot in the door.

"What the heck is that?" Brian asked. "We don't get mail on Labor Day."

"I'll get it." Gemma held up her hand, stopping him before he got out of his chair, and she went over to retrieve a single slip of paper on the floor.

At first, Gemma thought it was a postcard, except it looked so warped and worn. But as soon as she picked it up, she knew exactly what it was.

It was an old photograph of Gemma, Harper, and their mom, taken shortly before the accident when their mom still lived at home. It had been on her bedside table for years, but when Gemma ran away to join the sirens, she'd taken it with her, which was how it'd gotten so damaged. But she'd forgotten it at Sawyer's house when she escaped.

Gemma turned it over, and on the back in lovely handwriting, a message had been scrawled.

Found this in a junk drawer with Lexi's old stuff. Thought you might want it back. Thanks for setting me free.
—Thea

"What's that?" Harper asked as she came down the stairs behind her.

"Thea was just returning something I'd lost." Gemma held it up for Harper to see.

"Did you take that with you when you ran away?" Harper asked.

Gemma nodded as her sister handed the picture back. "I accidentally forgot it, and somehow Thea found it again."

"That was nice of her to give it back. But I would've thought she'd left town by now."

"Me, too," Gemma agreed.

"Where do you think she's going?"

Gemma shrugged. "Anywhere she wants."

"I should get going now." Harper turned toward the living room when she spoke, and Brian muted the TV and got out of his chair.

"Did you get any homework done?" he asked as he walked over to where she and Gemma stood by the front door.

"Some, but I have plenty left to do," Harper admitted bleakly. "Fortunately, it's still really early in the semester, so I have time to get my grades up."

"So you probably won't be able to visit for a while," Brian said.

"For a little bit, I probably shouldn't," Harper agreed. "But you know me; I can't stay away for too long."

She faced Gemma and embraced her tightly. They didn't hug that often, but this time, they were both slow to let go of each other.

"Thanks for coming home to save me," Gemma whispered.

"What are sisters for?" Harper asked with a small laugh.

"I love you."

"I love you, too," Harper said, and finally released her. She hugged her dad, and he gave her a quick kiss on the cheek. "'Bye, Dad."

He held the front door open for her. "Drive safely, and call me this week to let me know how things are going in school."

"Will do."

Harper went outside and walked across the lawn to her Sable, parked in the driveway. Gemma almost wanted to follow her out and wait on the steps and watch her go, like she did when she was little, and her mom dropped her off at day care.

But she didn't. She just let her sister go and closed the door.

FIFTY-SEVEN

Sentiment

The sun was setting as Harper crossed Anthemusa Bay, and the breeze felt wonderful blowing through her hair. As she got closer to Bernie's Island, she was surprised to see Daniel standing at the end of the dock, waiting for her with his hands shoved in the pockets of his jeans.

When Harper pulled the little speedboat up, he tied it off for her, then he took her hand and helped her out.

"You didn't have to wait for me," she said.

"I know, but I wanted to." Daniel took her book bag from her and slung it over his shoulder.

They went on the dirt path up to the cabin, the air smelling of the creeping charlie and pine. The tall trees kept out most of the sunset, so it was nearly dark as they walked.

"You're awfully quiet tonight," she commented, as they reached his house.

Elegy

"You texted and said you wanted to talk. So I thought I'd let you talk first."

Inside the house, he set her bag down by the door. He offered her something to drink, which she declined, then she sat down on the couch.

"Why don't you sit down?" Harper asked, patting the empty spot next to her.

"Okay." He seemed hesitant, but he did as she asked.

"Are you nervous?"

His hazel eyes settled uncertainly on her. "Should I be?"

"No. It's not bad. Honest."

"We'll see." Daniel leaned forward, resting his elbows on his knees, and he looked like a man who was waiting for a bomb to drop.

Harper took a deep breath and began what she wanted to say. "Since we've been together, everything has been so crazy and so intense."

"That is true," he agreed, but sounded reluctant to do so.

"And we've hardly even had a chance to just be together or do normal couple things, like argue over what to watch on TV. Then everything happened with Penn, and now I'm away at college."

He folded his hands together and stared down at the floor. "I know."

"And in everything we've been through, you've proven to be strong and loyal and patient and wonderful, and I've grown to love you so very much."

"You're doing that thing again." He inhaled sharply through

his teeth and rubbed the back of his neck. "You're saying something nice, but you make it sound so *bad*."

"I love you more than I've ever loved anyone," she continued pouring her heart out to him, mindless of his growing apprehension. "You aren't the man of my dreams because I could never have dreamed someone as amazing as you. I wouldn't have thought that anyone as wonderful and as perfect for me as you existed. But with all that, I've realized something."

He sighed. "And here it is."

"I don't know your middle name," she said finally.

He stared down for a second, then he cocked his head and looked at her. "What?"

"We skipped all the fun getting-to-know-you stuff, the first-date questions. Maybe because we were kinda friends first, or maybe it was because we both thought we could die at any moment. But we were almost instantly in a serious relationship."

He opened his mouth, then closed it. Shaking his head, he said, "My middle name is Grant."

"Mine's Lynn. My birthday's January 9, so I'm a Capricorn," she said. "I think that you're a Scorpio."

"Yeah, I am. But what is this we're doing here?" He motioned between the two of them. "What's going on?"

"I thought that if I love you, and want to spend the rest of my life with you, that I should get all the first-date stuff out of the way."

"Oh, you are tricky." He narrowed his eyes at her as a gradual smile spread out across his face. "You psyched me out on purpose."

"I did," she admitted with a laugh.

He shook his head, then he leaned over and kissed her. She put her arms around him, pulling him to her, but then he stopped her.

"Hey, wait." He stood up. "I wanna give you something."

"What? What for?"

"I just finished it yesterday." He held his hand out to her. "It's in my room."

Taking his hand, she let him lead her into his room. He flicked on the bedroom light, and in the middle of the floor at the end of his bed was a wooden chest. It reminded Harper of a smallish pirate's chest, made out of a smooth wood, but in the center was a very unique detail.

Older, faded wood had been carved out in the shape of a heart. Branches had been wrapped around it, outlining the heart, and in the center of it, "Harper" had been very delicately carved into it.

"You made that?" Harper asked, in awe.

"Yeah. I bought some of the wood, but most of it is reclaimed. Some of the wood around the front of the house was rotted, but the parts that were still good, I used for the heart."

Harper crouched in front of it, running her fingers along the top and carefully over the heart.

"The branches for the heart came from the rosebush." He pointed to it. "I know how much you love this island, and I know that you're gonna be gone at school for a long time. Doctors go to school for years and years. So I thought that if you could put your books and stuff in there, then, while you were away, you'd always have a little bit of here with you."

"Daniel." She smiled up at him with tears in her eyes. "That's so sweet."

"Thank you."

She stood up and looked up into his eyes. "You really are the perfect guy."

"It helps that I have a girl who I want to try to be perfect for."

When she kissed him, she remembered everything he'd done for her, everything he'd given, and all that she wanted to give him. She loved him more deeply than she had loved anything before, and now all she wanted to do was be with him.

She wrapped her arms around his neck, pulling him closer. His arm encircled her waist as she kissed him more forcefully, then he picked her up and carried her back toward the bed.

When he set her back down, gently, his mouth separated from hers long enough so he could pull off his shirt, and Harper took the chance to do the same. And within seconds he was on her again, his lips trailing down her neck so his stubble scraped against her skin.

She'd worn a front-clasp bra, and he unhooked it as his mouth encircled her breast. She wrapped her legs around him, pressing her thighs against his waist, and that seemed to be all the encouragement he needed.

His lips were on hers again, kissing her fervently as she undid his pants. He sat up, pulling them down and roughly kicking them off, while Harper removed her own jeans. And then he was back with her again.

He started out slow, easing himself inside her. She clung tightly to him, and when he kissed her, she moaned against his lips. Then they were moving together, faster and more deeply, as Harper felt a wonderful, almost serene heat spread through her.

Every moment before this one became worth it, every single thing that she had gone through suddenly made sense, because it all brought her to this, brought her here to Daniel's arms, exactly where she belonged.

FIFTY-EIGHT

Fragmentary

The picture lay on the top of her comforter next to her, and Gemma stared down at it. Her notebook was open, and she was supposed to be writing in it, but she kept staring at the picture of her, Harper, and their mom. In the warm light of her bedside lamp, that photo had become the most distracting thing in the world.

"What are you doing?" her dad asked, poking his head in her room.

Gemma was quick to flip the notebook shut, hiding anything she'd written, and she smiled up at him. "Just journaling."

"I didn't know you still did that." Brian walked over and stood next to her bed.

"I do." She shrugged. "Sometimes."

"I'm really glad that you're home and you're safe." He reached down, stroking her, then he bent down and kissed the top of her head. "I love you so much."

"I love you, too, Dad."

He turned to head back out. "Don't stay up too late. You have school in the morning."

"I won't," she said, then just before he left, she added, "I had a really great time today. Thanks for spending the day with me."

"Me, too." He smiled, then shut her door and went down the hall to his own room.

After he'd gone, Gemma let out a deep breath and flipped the notebook back open, looking over what she'd written. She went over it several more times, making sure it had everything that she wanted to say.

When she was sure it was perfect, she rewrote it in her most legible handwriting, then gave it one final read-through.

To Dad & Harper—

By the time you read this, I'll already be gone. I'm sorry that I didn't tell you what was happening, but I didn't want you to spend our last few days together being frantic and worried. I've tried everything I can think of to break the curse, so I thought it would be better if we could just enjoy the little time we had left. And I did. I enjoyed the last couple days we spent together more than you'll ever know. They were some of the best days of my entire life.

I'm sorry for everything I've put you both through. No other girl in the world is lucky enough to have a family as supportive and loving and amazing as you guys.

I want to you know that I'm not scared or upset. I made my peace with this. I'm only sad that I won't get to see you guys more. Wherever it is that sirens go after they die, I know that I'll be missing you.

I love you forever and always.

—Gemma

With the letter finished, she set it on her bed, next to the picture. She'd put on her pajamas so that her dad would think she was going to bed, but she changed out of them and put on her favorite dress. If she had to die, then she wanted to do it as much on her terms as she could.

Once her dad was asleep, she laid everything out on her bed the way she wanted him to find it. She almost put on shoes, but then realized that where she was going, she wouldn't need shoes or her cell phone. So she left them both beside her bed, and as quietly as she could, she crept down the stairs and out the front door, into the summer night.

FIFTY-NINE

Reprise

"Y ou can't say your favorite movie is *Phantom of the Opera*," Daniel insisted.

She lay in bed next to him, one of his arms around her and her head resting in the crook of his arm. He was still shirtless, but she'd slipped on his Led Zeppelin T-shirt, and she was already plotting a way to sneak it into her bag so she could take it with her to college.

"Why?" Harper laughed. "It's a really good movie."

"I don't know if it's good or not. I haven't seen it. But you can't say that's your favorite movie if you love *The Devil Wears Prada* more," he argued.

"I love that movie, but *Phantom* is a better film. And it sounds better when I say it."

"It doesn't matter what people think or what's better," he insisted. "It's about which one you love more."

She shook her head. "Nope. I stand by my decision."

"You know, it's a good thing we're having this conversation now and not when we first started dating, because then I would think you were a liar, and I don't date liars."

"You're still here, aren't you?" She looked up at him, smiling.

"I am. But only 'cause you tricked me into falling in love with you first. Now I'm stuck with you forever."

"Oh, rough life." She laughed, and he sat up a little so he could kiss her.

Her phone began ringing loudly in the pocket of her jeans, which were still discarded on the floor from when she'd removed them as she got in bed with Daniel. That was before they'd had sex, and before she decided to venture into more first-date questions and got into the argument about her favorite movie.

"You should not get that," Daniel said.

She sat up, glancing at his alarm clock. "It's late, so it's probably important." She pulled away from him, and he sighed and flopped back down in bed.

"Lame."

Harper crawled to the edge of the bed and leaned over so she could fish her phone out of her pocket. She managed to grab it and answer it a second before it went to voice mail. "Hello?"

"Hey, Harper, it's me, Professor Pine. I know it's kinda late. I hope I'm not bothering you."

"No, not at all." She ran her hand through her hair and grimaced. They were supposed to have a meeting to talk about the scroll tomorrow, but with everything having changed so fast, it had slipped her mind. "Now's a good time."

"Oh, you are such a liar," Daniel said from behind her, and she shot him a look.

"I just got back from Macedonia, and I was thinking about what you'd said."

"You mean about the ink?" she asked.

"It seems to repeat the same phrase a lot—'blood of a siren, blood of a mortal, blood of the sea' over and over," Pine explained. "I think that's what the ink is made out of. Blood and ocean water. It also mentions the phrase 'wash it away' once, right after the 'blood of a siren, blood of a mortal, blood of the sea.'"

"Maybe. But um, I should tell you that we kinda sorted everything out, and we don't need the translations anymore," Harper said sheepishly. "Sorry for bothering you so much."

"No, you didn't bother me at all, and I'm glad you got whatever sorted out that you needed to get sorted. But do you mind if I keep checking into this?" Pine asked. "It's still fascinating stuff to me."

"Yeah, of course, if you want to," she said, relieved that he wasn't upset. "I think my sister planned on giving Lydia the scroll, in case you want to see it."

"Thanks. Awesome. I think I will."

"And thank you again. I really appreciate it." And she did, even if they hadn't ended up using his help. He'd done a lot of work for them.

"No problem. And if you ever come across any other weird scrolls, don't hesitate to give me a call."

"Will do," Harper said, and ended the call.

"What was that about?" Daniel asked.

"It was Pine." She pulled her knees up to her chest and leaned on them as she twirled her phone in her hand. "He was calling me about the scroll."

"Did he find anything out?"

Harper shook her head. "Not really, I guess. He was just saying the curse talks about blood a lot. Which is interesting because the ink did react to blood, but it didn't do anything. Like the curse didn't break, the ink didn't wash away . . ."

"So why'd he call?"

She chewed her thumbnail, thinking. Then she furrowed her brow, suddenly remembering something her mother had said. "He said the scroll said something about 'wash it away.' You know what's strange? I went to visit my mom last week, and she kept saying that Bernie told her to 'wash it away.'"

"Wash what away?"

"I don't know." She looked over him. "Do you think she knew something?"

"How would she know?"

She shrugged. "She talked to Bernie a lot all those years ago, and she knew when Gemma was in trouble before, when she ran away. Mom's brain doesn't work like it should anymore, but she still seems to sense things."

"Like the way you and Gemma can sense each other?" Daniel asked.

Harper nodded. "Kinda."

"Do you wanna call your sister?" Daniel asked. "She should hear about this, even if the curse is broken."

She considered it, then shook her head. "I'll call her in the morning. I think she said she's going over to Alex's tonight, and I want to give them some alone time together, after everything they've been through."

"Are you sure?" Daniel asked, and there was something in his voice that made her look back at him. An uneasiness, and his hazel eyes were conflicted.

She turned around, sitting on her knees, so she faced him. "You're freaking me out a little."

"I'm not trying to. I just wonder if Gemma's telling us everything, about the curse being broken and all."

Harper considered it, then shook her head. "I think it's just hard for us to wrap our minds around the fact that it's all actually over—we have our lives back. And see the change in Gemma. She seems happier now, more at ease. I'm sure she'll keep changing a little bit every day as her siren powers drain away. But it's all over now, Daniel, and I want to learn to let go for once and not worry about everything."

Harper lay back down, but Daniel stayed sitting up for a few more seconds. When he did lie back, she curled up next to him, resting her head on his chest, and he put his arm around her. "Just make sure you call her tomorrow morning, even if what Pine said is nothing. You can never be too safe."

SIXTY

Mortality

For a while, she only sat on the roof outside Alex's window. The curtains were closed, but through a gap in the middle, she was able to see into his room just fine. He was in bed, but he was reading a book and didn't notice her right away.

In a way, Gemma hoped he never noticed her. She'd come here to say good-bye, but maybe this would be better. It would be much easier on both of them. No tears, no pleading, just slipping away.

And maybe that's what would've happened, but she couldn't bring herself to leave. Even with the full moon shining brightly above her, and the water calling to her, she couldn't make herself walk away from Alex.

Then he looked up from his book, and he saw her. She could've run away then, but she didn't. She just smiled at him as he walked over and opened the window.

"Shouldn't you be in bed?" Alex asked with an easy smile.

"Not tonight." She'd barely gotten the words out when the tears started falling.

Apprehension instantly darkened his expression. "What's wrong? Come inside."

"I can't."

"What do you mean you can't?"

Gemma took a deep breath and swallowed back her tears. "I have to tell you something, and I didn't plan on telling you, but now that I'm here, and all I want to do is be with you, I have to."

"What?"

"The curse isn't broken," she said, and her voice caught in her throat.

He didn't speak or even seem to breathe for a moment. "What are you talking about? You told me it was."

"I know, but . . . I lied. I didn't want to worry you, and I just wanted to enjoy the last few days without everyone's being all frantic and sad."

"If the curse isn't broken, then . . . what does that mean?" Alex asked.

"There have to be four sirens. When one dies, they have until the next full moon to replace them. Right now, there are only two sirens, and the moon is full."

He looked past her, staring up at the moon above them, fat and radiant and undeniably full, then he looked back down at Gemma. "But . . . you're still alive. It's wrong."

"I have until the end of the night, when the sun comes up."

"Gemma . . ." He shook his head. "No. Where's the scroll?"

"I threw it away. I told Lydia I'd give it to her, but I was trying to break it last night, and I just got frustrated, and I hate that damn thing, so I threw it in the garbage."

Last night, she'd barely slept. She stayed awake, going over the scroll again and again. Trying things she'd tried a hundred times before just to be sure there was nothing more she could do. But, finally, she'd given up and thrown it in the trash can behind her house.

"We're getting it. We'll break it," he insisted.

"Alex." She tried to stop him, but he closed the window and left his room.

She jumped down from the roof and met him on the lawn between their houses. He went straight to the garbage and dug through it until he found the scroll. And the next few hours became exactly what she didn't want to happen.

In his desperation to save her, he became fixated on the scroll. They went into the kitchen of her house as he tried everything that she'd already tried, that Harper and her dad had tried, but it was all to no avail.

Sometimes, he seemed to realize how futile it was, so he'd give up and just hold Gemma in his arms. She'd lay her head on his shoulder, relishing the way it felt when he enveloped her. That was exactly how she wanted to spend her last few hours on earth.

Those soft moments together only seemed to drive him on. After a few minutes of holding her, he'd go back to the scroll, determined to break the curse. But he never did.

As the night wore on, Gemma became increasingly weaker. A chill seemed to be growing inside her, a cold that spread outward from her stomach. When she began to shiver, Alex went into the laundry room to find something to cover her up with. He came back with the shawl that Harper had brought home from the sirens' house, freshly laundered, and he wrapped it around Gemma's shoulders before he went back to the scroll.

The watersong grew louder. It wasn't painful or obnoxious, like it had been when she went to Charleston, but instead, it sounded more like a soft lullaby, like the waves were singing her to sleep.

Her life was draining from her, and she could actually feel it ebbing away. It was like she was very slowly losing consciousness, and she knew she didn't have much time left.

She sat on the kitchen floor, her head resting against the wall, the wrap pulled tightly around her, and her voice came out in a tired whisper. "Alex. I need to go to the water."

He'd been standing over the sink, dousing the scroll in water, but he turned to look back at her. "What do you mean? Why?"

"I'm getting weak, and I need to be out in the water," she explained simply. "I just feel it."

Alex started to argue, but when he looked back at her, his words fell silent on his lips. She was fading away, and she looked like it. The normal tanned glow of her skin had become ashen. Her hair no longer glistened, and she was struggling to keep her eyes open.

He rolled up the scroll and shoved it in the waistband of his pajama pants, then he came over and helped her up. He offered to drive her down to the bay, but the sky was still dark enough.

They had time, and she'd rather enjoy the night and walk the several blocks down to the water.

That proved to be harder than she thought, and within a block, she no longer had the strength to walk. Alex scooped her up, holding her to him, and she rested her head against his chest as he carried her down to the bay.

He waded out into the waves, and when he made it deep enough that she could feel the seawater splashing on her, her skin began to flutter. She thought she'd be too weak for it, but it actually gave her a small burst of energy, and as her legs transformed into a tail, Alex let her go.

She floated nearby because she wasn't ready to leave him, but when the time came, she'd swim as far away from him as she could get. No one told her what it looked like when a siren died like this, but she didn't want him to have to see it.

The sky began to turn pink as the sun approached the horizon, and Alex reached out, pulling her to him. He held her in his arms and kissed her softly.

"I don't want to lose you," he said thickly.

"I should go."

"No. Not yet." He hung on to her tighter, and she let him, but only for a second, then she pushed away. "No. Stay. Just a few more minutes."

"Alex, I can't." She shook her head as her tears mixed with the saltwater.

"There has to be something." He pulled out the scroll, and in terrified rage, he gripped it and tried to rip it in half. But the paper didn't tear. It was like a thin sheet of metal, and sliced through his finger, leaving a nasty gash. "Shit!"

He let go of the scroll then, letting it float on the water, and Gemma swam over to him. She pressed her shawl against his cut. But instead of looking at his finger, her eyes went to the glowing paper beside him.

Whenever the ink was exposed to water, it would glow a little. But Alex's blood had dripped on it in large drops, and as the saltwater mixed with it, the ink began to blaze like Gemma had never seen before. The words were actually on fire.

"Oh, my god." Alex grabbed the scroll before it floated out to sea. "Is this it? Is the curse breaking?"

She shook her head. "No, the words are still there."

Alex shook his head, and she could see his mind racing, as he tried to put it together. "Blood of a siren, blood of a mortal, blood of the sea. That's how a siren is made."

"It doesn't work, Alex," she tried to tell him. "I already—"

"Please. Gemma. Just try it again. We have to try," Alex insisted with such a fierce desperation, and she didn't have the strength to argue with him.

So she bit into her finger, tearing out a chunk with sharp teeth, even though she had already tried this once before and it hadn't worked. But as her blood dripped down, mixing with Alex's and the saltwater, Gemma found herself hoping that this time it would be different.

Right before their eyes, the words burned up and disappeared. Anywhere the mixture touched, the ink vanished, and then quickly, even where Alex hadn't spilled his blood, all the words were gone.

The scroll was blank. And Gemma held her breath, waiting for more changes to come. But they didn't.

"It's working." Alex gave her a relieved smile. "The curse is breaking."

"I don't think so, Alex." Her tail steadied her as she put her arms around him. Nothing had changed. She didn't feel different, and her scales were pressed up against him. "Maybe it's just too late."

"No. It can't be too late. No, Gemma." Tears were in his eyes. "I love you."

"I love you, Alex."

He stared into her eyes, brushing her wet hair back from her forehead, then he kissed her, desperately, as though if he could just love her enough, then it would save her. He held her tightly, one arm pressed against the smooth scales of the tail that rose up the small of her back, and she could taste their tears with the saltwater.

The sun rose behind them, and as she felt the first rays hitting her, she closed her eyes and clung to Alex.

SIXTY-ONE

Vestige

She hadn't seen as much of the world as she'd wanted to. In fact, she'd hardly seen any of it. Thea had spent thousands of years roaming the planet, but she had hardly gone anywhere since so much of it was too far inland.

That, and Penn always dictated where they went. Penn couldn't stand the call of the watersong, so she refused to go anywhere that caused her the slightest bit of pain. Thea had thought that with Penn gone, she'd finally be able to explore all the places that had been blocked off to her.

But as it turned out, Thea didn't do so well against the watersong, either. She didn't go very far, and she always seemed to end up back in the ocean.

Still, the last two days of her life couldn't be called bad. In fact, they were some of the very best she'd had in a very long time. Without all of Penn's demands and threats and constant tantrums, everything had felt so much nicer.

Though Thea wished that Aggie had been there to share it with her, and even Ligea. She had loved them, and she still missed them. Penn had all but forbidden her to talk about them anymore, and Thea wondered once again why she'd listened.

It wasn't that she was scared of Penn, but Thea felt intrinsically that she'd failed her. Since the day Penn was born, she had felt unloved and abandoned, and she had been by her parents. Thea had always tried to make up for that, but all she'd ever done was make things worse.

The horrible truth was that the curse was her fault. If she'd yelled at Penn that day, the day they'd left Persephone alone, or if Thea had simply let Penn go off without her, then none of this would have happened. So she'd spent nearly her entire existence trying to make it up to Penn for allowing her to be cursed in the first place.

The real kicker at the end of all of this is that Demeter's curse centered around their love of swimming, but Penn had never even cared for it that much. She'd been smitten with Poseidon, that was all. It had been Thea who loved the water, and, somehow, she loved it still today.

She waded out into the water, relishing the way her legs fluttered for the last time as they turned into a tail. The sky was lightening above her, so she swam out on her back, floating out farther into the ocean.

Her thoughts went back to her sisters, and all the fun they'd had when they were young, before all this madness with Demeter. Penn had claimed that everything had been a horrible struggle. Things were hard, but what Thea remembered most was how much she had loved them all.

She missed them terribly, and though she hoped she would see them again, she doubted she would. With everything she'd seen, Thea wasn't completely sure she believed that there was a heaven, but even if there was, she most certainly wouldn't be going there.

As she felt the rays of the sun warming her skin through the water, Thea closed her eyes. The tingling started first in her fingers, and she was relieved that it didn't hurt. It actually felt good, like a whole new transformation, as her body slowly dissolved into ash.

Soon, there was nothing. The dust was lost in the sea. And Thea was gone.

SIXTY-TWO

Severed

The panic was so intense, Harper sat up straight in bed. She was covered in a cold sweat, and she put a hand to her heart. Something inside her had been severed.

"No," she whispered.

Daniel, still groggy with sleep, sat up slowly. "What? What's going on?"

"Something's wrong. Something's happened to Gemma."

"What are you talking about?" he asked.

She pressed her hand more firmly to her chest, as if that would make the feeling change. "I can feel it. Something's wrong."

"Call her," Daniel suggested.

She reached over and grabbed the phone, but Gemma never answered. That was about what she'd expected, though.

Harper dove out of bed and grabbed her jeans off the floor. "I have to go."

"Go where?" He got out of bed much more slowly than she

did, though it was clear he was trying to move fast. "Harper. Wait."

She folded her arms across her chest, hugging herself as Daniel hurried to put on his jeans and a T-shirt.

"I can't feel her," Harper told him plaintively.

"What?"

"It's like she's not there anymore."

Daniel pursed his lips, but he didn't say anything. Something about that frightened her, that he didn't try to comfort her or convince her that everything would be okay. Instead, he just picked up the pace, and when they went down the path to his boat, they were both running.

His boat took a minute to start, but this seemed to aggravate Daniel as much as it did Harper. He kicked it and cursed under his breath, then *The Dirty Gull* finally chugged into life.

The ride across the bay had never seemed to take so long. The early-morning sun was blinding as it reflected off the water, but Harper kept her eyes fixed on the shore.

When Daniel docked the boat, she jumped off. She started to run toward the parking lot for her car, but then she stopped and changed her mind.

"This way." She pointed toward the beach just as Daniel reached her.

"What? Why?"

"We need to go this way," she insisted, and started jogging down the path to the beach.

"How do you know if you can't feel her?" Daniel asked as he ran after her.

"There's something, but it's not the same."

On the beach, her feet slipped in the sand, but she didn't let that slow her down. She could see a lone figure, sitting in the sand far away from them. As she got closer, she started to realize that the figure was Alex, and that he was totally alone, staring out at the waves.

"Alex!" Harper shouted, and by the time she reached him, she was screaming. *"Alex!* Where's Gemma?" He got to his feet, looking confused, and she grabbed him by his T-shirt. "Where is she?"

"There!" Alex pointed out to the bay, sounding totally baffled by her intensity.

"Where?" Harper asked, but all she needed to do was turn her head.

Gemma was several yards away, in the water. "I'm right here."

"Oh, my god, Gemma." Harper ran into the water, not caring if she soaked her clothes, and hugged Gemma, crushing her to her. "I thought you were dead."

"I'm not dead," Gemma said, laughing and hugging her back. "I'm just not a siren anymore."

Harper pulled back to look at her, but she kept her hands on Gemma's shoulders, as if she would disappear if she let go. "You already weren't."

"No, I was before. I lied. But now I'm really not."

"How do you know?" Harper narrowed her eyes.

"I'm in the ocean, and I have legs."

The water came up to Gemma's hips, and she pulled up her dress, revealing her normal legs. No fins, no scales. And then

Harper really looked at her and realized that Gemma looked different. Her eyes were still the color of burned honey, but they were less sparkly. She was still beautiful, but she appeared younger—less like a model on a magazine cover and more like a normal, teenage girl.

That explained the feeling of being severed from her sister. There'd always been a strange bond, but when Gemma had become a siren, it grew more intense, which was how she'd been able to find her in Sawyer's house when she ran off.

But now, without the paranormal element amplifying it, the bond had returned to its normal state, and she could barely feel it.

"How?" Harper asked in disbelief. "What'd you do?"

"We were so close, Harper," Gemma said with a wide grin. "The blood of the siren, the blood of the mortal, the blood of the sea—that's how to wash away the curse, and how I became a siren. But we were missing one thing." She pointed back to where Alex stood on the beach, and Harper noticed the golden shawl shimmering in the sand next to him.

"That's the golden shawl we found you wrapped in the night after you became a siren," Harper remembered, then looked back at Gemma as the shawl's importance dawned on her. "That was the golden fleece that Pine was talking about."

"What?" Gemma asked, staring at her quizzically.

"The golden fleece," Harper repeated. "Pine told me that he translated something in the scroll about it, but he thought it had to do with Jason and Argonauts."

"It was Persephone's shawl," Gemma explained. "The sirens had told me that before, and Demeter told us that Persephone had been found in it after she died, wrapped up much the same way I was when you found me on the shore after I became a siren."

"The whole curse is about Persephone, so Demeter made her a part of the curse as much as she could," Harper realized. "She made the sirens use Persephone's golden shawl."

"Right. To become a siren, I had to drink the blood of the sirens, the mortal, and the sea, and I had to be wrapped in the shawl and tossed in the ocean," Gemma said. "So to break the curse, I had to reverse it, using the mixture of blood, and I had to be wearing the shawl in the ocean. Do everything like I did before, but just undo it, using the blood to erase the ink on the scroll."

Harper smiled at her sister. "What are you doing in the water now?"

"I wanted to see what it was like to swim with legs again, and it's better than I remembered."

"So now you're completely sure it's all over?"

Gemma laughed. "I'm positive." And just because she could, Harper hugged her sister again.

"You scared the crap out of me, Gemma," Daniel said as he slogged through the waves to reach them. He put one arm around Harper and the other around Gemma, embracing both of them tightly.

When Alex waded out to join them, Gemma separated from the other two, ran to him, and jumped into his arms. Her legs wrapped around his waist, and he held her as she laughed.

Harper turned and looked up at Daniel. "You know, for the

first time I really *feel* like this is over. I thought it was over before, but now I know in a way I didn't, and it's like a huge weight has been lifted."

"It's really over." He put his arms around her, pulling her to him. "Now just as long as you don't get tangled up with a pack of vampires or deranged witches while you're at college, everything will be wonderful."

Harper smiled. "So I just have to avoid those things, and everything will be perfect?"

"No, I'm pretty sure that as long as we're together, we've got it made."

As the waves splashed around them, and her sister laughed in the distance, Daniel bent down and kissed her, and Harper knew that he was absolutely right.

April 11

Harper stood on the stepladder, stretching out as she taped up the end of the streamer on the exposed beams of the cabin. Then she climbed down and put her hands on her back, admiring her handiwork.

"The streamers and balloons might be a bit much," Daniel said from behind her, and she glanced back to see him putting out paper plates and plastic cups on the dining-room table.

She turned back to the room, tilting her head to get a new perspective on the streamers and balloons she had taped up all over Daniel's cabin. "You think?

"Well, Gemma is turning *seventeen,* not seven," he said.

"Whatever." Harper shrugged. "She'll like it, and I do what I want."

"Ooh. You've gotten such an attitude since you've been home from college," Daniel teased as he walked over to her.

"Where are they?" She ignored him and glanced over at the clock hanging above the fireplace. "They should've been here by now."

"Well, Alex just got home for the weekend," Daniel said as he slid his arm around her waist, pulling her closer to him.

"I know. We shared a ride back from Sundham," she reminded him.

"Yeah, but you know, he and Gemma are probably spending quality time together."

Harper wrinkled her nose. "Gross."

"Hey, you didn't think it was gross when we were spending quality time together this morning."

His other arm encircled her, pulling her close to him, and Harper didn't resist. She loved it when he held her like that, crushing her to him, as his mouth pressed against hers. A familiar heat radiated through her, and she wrapped her arms around his neck.

Even after all this time, and all the kisses they'd shared, some of them in bed earlier this morning, each time he kissed her, there was still that hint of urgency and desperation, like they'd never really be able to get enough of each other.

Harper would've gladly stayed in his arms, kissing him all afternoon, but she heard their guests coming up the walkway on the island.

"They're here," she said, and since he looked so thoroughly disappointed at having to let her go, she gave him one more quick kiss on the lips before separating from him.

She was readjusting her shirt when Marcy opened the door to the cabin, carrying a birthday gift. Alex and Gemma came after her, hand in hand.

"Where do you want the gifts?" Marcy asked, but she was already setting hers down on the kitchen counter.

"There is fine," Daniel said, pointing to where she'd put it.

"So are we having cake or what?" Marcy asked, interrupting them.

"There is a cake," Harper assured her, and went over to the fridge to pull it out. "I thought we could let people sit down for a minute first."

"There should never be a holdup on cake," Marcy insisted.

"Why are you in such a hurry?" Alex asked her. He stood off to the side of the kitchen, leaning against the counter with one arm around Gemma. "Got a hot date tonight?"

Gemma groaned. "No, Alex, don't even ask."

"What? Why?" He looked down at her in surprise.

"She's dating a ghost," Gemma supplied.

"I am not *dating* anyone," Marcy said defensively. "I've just been talking to Kirby a lot. We're friends."

"So do you guys make a lot of pottery together?" Daniel smirked. "You know, like *Ghost*?"

Gemma shot him a look. "Don't encourage her, Daniel."

"Shouldn't Lydia be telling you that this is all dangerous?" Harper was putting seventeen candles in the cake, and she looked across the table at Marcy. "You shouldn't be messing around with this kind of thing, right?"

Marcy shrugged. "As long as I'm not holding Kirby back from crossing over, Lydia thinks it all seems fine."

Harper turned back to Gemma and decided to change the subject. With the sirens out of the picture, she wanted to avoid talking about the supernatural as much as possible, and that included Ghost Kirby.

"Speaking of dates, how is Dad doing?" Harper asked.

"Good. He's seen Sarah twice, and it all seems to be going well," Gemma said. "I haven't met her yet, but I told him that he better introduce her soon."

"Me, too," Harper said, and hoped that she didn't sound quite as needy as she felt.

Overall, she'd enjoyed the past eight months being at Sundham University. Now that everything with the monsters was over, and she was able to actually concentrate on school, it was going well, and sometimes, she even had fun.

With Alex's arrival at Sundham for the spring semester, it had been even nicer. They had two classes together, which helped when it came time to study, and it was great being able to carpool back and forth from Capri. But honestly, Harper was happy to have a friend around, especially one who understood everything that had gone on this past year, and it helped make her slightly less homesick.

Thankfully, Alex and Gemma seemed to be handling their time apart fairly well, and Alex made frequent trips home to see her. Gemma came up to Sundham as often as she could, but since she'd taken up Harper's old job at the library, it wasn't as often as she would've liked.

Gemma and Alex tried to make the most of their time. Right now, she was sitting on the counter, and Alex was standing next to her with his arm wrapped around her waist. Every time they thought people weren't looking, Harper would catch them out of the corner of her eye, kissing or whispering in each other's ear.

They reminded Harper of magnets, drawn to each other so fiercely that nothing could ever really tear them apart. While Harper had had some reservations about Gemma and Alex when they first started dating, it was now clear to her that they were deeply and hopelessly in love.

Maybe she understood that better now because she felt the same way about Daniel. She looked over at him, getting soda out of the fridge, and she couldn't help but smile. Being away from him at college was hard, but both she and Daniel knew it was the right thing to do.

Now, with their dad dating again, being away from him and Gemma felt even stranger. She called her dad and Skyped with him, but, Harper was still afraid she might miss something.

Brian had met Sarah at Pearl's a couple of weeks ago. When she talked to her dad on the phone, he'd sounded so much happier lately, and Harper was pleased to see him finally moving on. Honestly, with Gemma talking about going to Sundham after high school, Harper had begun to worry about their dad being alone in that house, but now it sounded like he was finding happiness for himself outside his daughters.

Gemma was doing a fairly good job of keeping Harper

apprised of their relationship. But she was chomping at the bit to meet the new woman in her dad's life.

"Parents dating is so gross," Marcy said. She reached over and tried to put her finger in the frosting, but Harper slapped it away just in time.

"People putting their hands in food is even grosser," Harper said, and Marcy stuck her tongue out.

"If our mom could date, she'd definitely be pining for some Cody guy," said Gemma.

"Cody who?" Marcy asked.

Gemma shook her head. "I don't know, but she took down all the Justin Bieber posters and replaced them."

"Personally, I don't care who she's into," Harper said as she started lighting the candles on Gemma's cake. "Just as long as she keeps doing better like she has been lately."

Gemma had finally confessed to using the siren song on Nathalie, which is why she'd started acting strangely at the end of summer. The exact words Gemma had used had been *I want you to remember all the things you forgot. Everything about Harper and Dad and me. I want you to come back.*

Nathalie had tried, and she had shown some improvement, but she'd never be able to come all the way back. Her brain had been damaged, and the siren song was powerful and seemed to encourage her synapses to fire, but it couldn't make destroyed tissue grow back again.

But she had more moments of clarity than she'd had in the years since her accident. She remembered more things, and when

Harper and Gemma made their Saturday visits with their mom, she seemed more contented within her condition. Gemma had also used the siren song, saying *You'll never feel a headache again*, so Nathalie's frequent migraines never came back either, and that certainly helped.

Thea had told Gemma that, eventually, the effects of the siren song might fade, but so far, they'd held strong. Not just with Nathalie, but with Mayor Crawford and the police as well. Penn had used the song to convince the mayor not to look for his missing son Aiden. For a long time afterward, Daniel had struggled with confessing his role in getting rid of the body, just so the mayor could have some closure.

Eventually, he submitted an anonymous tip, telling the mayor where to look for his son's body. But Mayor Crawford wouldn't hear of it. He insisted publicly that his son was living on an island, happy, and if anyone tried to contradict him or suggest they conduct a search, he wouldn't hear of it.

Daniel suspected that the mayor's own denial might be feeding into that. It was much easier to live believing that his son was alive and happy than that he was dead.

For a while after the curse had been broken, Gemma had Lydia looking for Thea. She'd been hoping that Thea might still be alive, that the curse had only made her mortal again, but eventually she'd come to accept that Thea was gone. It was just as she'd said, and when the curse was broken, Thea had turned to dust. Only her memory remained, and Gemma and Harper would carry it with them for the rest of their lives.

"Okay," Harper said as she lit the last candle on the cake

and smiled at her sister. "Blow out all the candles and make a wish."

The birthday party went on the rest of the afternoon, with them laughing and talking. When the sun began to set, people started saying their good-byes. Harper stayed behind to help clean up. Still, she walked out to the end of the dock, watching Gemma and their friends float back to the mainland in Bernie's old boat.

When she came back to the house, Daniel was already pulling down some of the streamers. She grabbed a stepladder to help him, but he stopped her.

"That can wait," he said, taking her hand.

"Why?" Harper asked, giving him an odd look. "You were already cleaning up."

"I was just getting a jump-start while you were busy. But it'll still be here when we come back in." Still holding her hand, Daniel took a step back, pulling her toward the door.

"Where are we going?" she asked with a laugh.

"Just out back."

The small island was covered in tall cypress and loblolly pines, so the setting sun left slivers of orange all over the ground. Wind rustled lightly through the trees, causing the branches to sway and dance, and other than the trees, the only sound was that of the ocean waves lapping against the shore.

It felt so quiet and secluded, and almost magical. When she was a kid, and Bernie McAllister had babysat her, he'd told her stories about fairies, and even as logical as Harper had been, she'd secretly believed some of his fantastical tales. The island made it so easy to imagine.

The pathway around the cabin was partially covered in Creeping Charlie, and as she stepped, it crunched beneath her feet, filling the air with the minty scent. But, very quickly, it was overpowered by the large roses behind the cabin. The sweet perfume of the flowers overpowered nearly everything on the island, and even though it was early April, they were already in full bloom.

Bernie's late wife, Thalia, had planted the bush, and after meeting with Diana/Demeter last summer, Harper had come to believe that the rosebush was supernatural.

The roses were the most vibrant shade of purple Harper had ever seen. It was so early in the season, and they were already the size of her fist, but soon they'd be even twice that.

Daniel had made a bench, and it was posed right behind the cabin, facing the rosebush, which loomed over the rest of the garden. He motioned for Harper to sit down first, and once he joined her, she curled up next to him, resting her head on his shoulder.

"Thank you," Harper said as the last rays of sunlight broke through the trees, dancing on the bright flowers of the bush, and the sky darkened above them.

"For what?" Daniel asked.

"For suggesting we come out here. It's really beautiful."

He turned his head slightly, so he could look down at her. "You're really beautiful."

Harper laughed. "Stop."

"No, I mean it." He pulled away from her so he could turn to face her, and his lips twitched into an anxious smile as he took her hands in his. His hazel eyes met hers, but there was something in them she couldn't read. "You're so beautiful, and I love you so much."

"I love you, too," Harper said hesitantly, afraid of what he might be getting at, and she sat up straighter.

He lowered his eyes and swallowed. "This last year, we went through so much, and there were some really terrible things that happened. But it's honestly been the best year in my life because I've been with you." He cleared his throat. "I can't really envision the rest of my life without you."

"Daniel, what's going on? Is something wrong?"

"No, nothing's wrong." He smiled at her, but it looked forced. "I guess what I'm trying to say is that I don't want to imagine my life without you."

When he let go of her hands, he laughed nervously and dug in his pocket. Then he dropped to his knee, and Harper realized what was happening. Her hands started trembling, and her jaw dropped as he produced a small ring box and opened it for her.

She couldn't even see the ring, though. Tears were blurring her vision as she stared down at him, and her heart raced in her chest.

"What I'm saying is . . ." He paused, swallowing uneasily. "Harper Fisher, will you marry me?"

She took a deep breath, terrified she might sob or scream, and when she finally spoke, her answer came out weak and shaky. "Yes."

"I mean, we don't have to get married right away," Daniel hurried on, apparently not having heard her whisper of a reply. "We can wait until you're done with college or whenever you want. But I wanted to make it official—"

"*Yes,*" Harper said, louder this time, and she smiled down at him. "Yes, of course I'll marry you."

"Really?" He laughed in relief, and with his own slightly tremulous hands, he slid a small diamond ring on her finger. "I was so afraid you'd say no."

"How could I say no?" she asked. "I can't imagine my life without you, either."

He stood so he could kiss her, and she wrapped her arms around his neck. Under the starlit twilight, Harper kissed him deeply, knowing that she'd never love anyone as much as him, and when he held her in his arms, she breathed in deeply, savoring the magic that was all around them.